06/29/2022
Sumter, SC

SWEET DADDY CREEK CLUB
The Happy Place

TOM WINSTEAD

Library of Congress Registration Identification #1-9880623111

Library of Congress Registration Number TXu2-277-263

ISBN: 978-1-66780-434-7 (printed)

ISBN: 978-1-66780-435-4 (eBook)

SWEET DADDY CREEK CLUB

PRINCIPAL CHARACTERS

Chip Storrington	Main Character
Sam Dillinger	Partner and Friend
Dawn Summers	Clerk of Court Assistant
Jimbo (James T. Ferguson)	Friend
Richard Werdna	Grand Daughter's Husband
Ronnie	7 year old Great Grandson
The Judge	Former Narc Agent
Uncle Sam (Samson)	Jimbo's Uncle
Drueboy & Leutisha	Drug dealers & killers
Gary Rollins	Police
Verne	Sweet Daddy Club designer
Truong Nguyen	South Vietnamese Businessman
Vince Barredo	Philippine Banker
Robert E. Grant	Car & Drug dealer
JC Byrdam	Sheriff
Ed Winters	FBI Atlanta Bureau Chief
Jeff	Chip's Dealer Friend

CHAPTER ONE

I FEEL LIKE SNOOPY in the Peanuts comic strip as he begins a new novel. I'm asking myself "What the hell am I doing in the middle of this God forsaken swamp; in a little Jon boat at that; a too-small, whiney, troll motor, not making much noise, but very little progress either. Rain is beating down on my face---it's cold. My fingers are numb and my nose is runny. But, as Snoopy says, "It was a dark and stormy night." It is just that; too damn dark and stormy and definitely too late for a man my age to be out.

The small, under-powered motor was humming from the strain of the weight it was towing. The motor isn't the real problem; it was dragging dead weight in the water behind us! Less than eight hours ago it had been a living weight; a walking, talking, breathing weight. His name is, at least was, Richard Werdna. A real bully of a bastard; he stood about five six, stocky, a muscular built young man, from a German family background; probably a Nazi in the family somewhere. He was particularly brave and macho around women, children and old men. He was mean! He was also stupid. I guess he never tuned-in when I'm sure someone told him, "You never screw around with an old man. He won't fight you. He'll just kill you!"

My name is Chip Storrington; I'm an investigator, not private, not public. I go where the need and the money are. At times I have been called a mercenary, because I'll go out of country if the price is right. At sixty-five I still like a little adventure. I'm not your typical 'mow the lawn and tend the flowers' type sixty-five; maybe in a few years, but not yet. I've trained and served with the Green Berets, Ranger groups and Commando Units; I've pulled special ops with the Delta Forces, too.

Doctors tell me I'm in unusually good health and physical condition for a man my age. At five-ten and a hundred-fifty pounds, most people don't believe my age. Being small works to my advantage, I'm fast. It's one of the benefits of spending twenty years in the military; the last five serving as a member of an elite, and secret, ranger force, the Philippine Mercenary Team (PMT). A group you wanted as a friend. We were based, "officially," in the comfort of Clark Air Base in the Philippines, but in reality we 'lived' in the 'boondocks', jungles and swamps of Vietnam, Thailand and Laos. Much of our training was in the jungle among the Moro-Moro tribe; a group of head hunters in the Northern Philippines. My troops called me 'hard-ass', among other things; provided I wasn't in hearing distance! I insisted on doing the job right, the first time, even if it was the hard way. You 'toed-the-line' or you're dead! You don't get a do-over in this business.

Through my "retirement" years, when I wasn't working, much of my time was spent working out in the gym and running five miles a day. I stay proficient in karate, judo and old fashioned street fighting. I can hold my own with most men half my age. Even when they think I'm just some old fart who doesn't know what's going on.

Snapping back to reality I'm thinking to myself, what am I doing out here? Cruising down a narrow section of the Black River, about as far East as it went. I'm looking carefully for a small slough that will hopefully lead me to the south end of Myrtle Beach, the playground of South Carolina and the East Coast. This small slough, if all the maps and Google Earth are correct, is supposed to lead me deep into the back side of Huntington State Park, to a brackish yet freshwater lagoon that is the feeding ground of a hundred or more, always hungry, gators, big gators! I would have to be extra careful not to tip this small boat and wind up being breakfast. I had assigned that little task to Richard, the butthole. It would be his last assignment. In a matter of a few minutes these hungry reptiles would strip the meat from his bones. The 'gators wouldn't have to worry about the clothes getting in their way. I had stripped him, burned his clothes and buried the ashes. No need to leave the slightest chance of any evidence. What's left of the bones will sink into the filth and muck on the bottom, never to be seen again.

Actually, his predicament was not my fault. I had personally warned him not to screw around with my granddaughter, his ex-wife, and mother of my great-grandson. Do it, "…. and you'll pay the price!" I had explained to him. Some people never pay attention.

It began when Richard and my granddaughter split, got into a fight and he kicked her. To make it worse, little Ronnie was watching. It left a lasting impression; it gave him nightmares for several months. I had carefully explained "If you want to talk with them, you call me and I'll be the go-between. No arguments, no more fighting. It's going to be peaceful contacts or I will get involved. You don't want me involved!"

That only lasted a few months.

He didn't listen, didn't learn. The calls and harassment began again; calling them several times a day trying to create friction between Ronnie and his mother. I finally just got tired of hearing about him, his 'bad-assing', and whatever else he was doing. So I got 'involved'!

It was a Saturday morning and T-ball time and Ronnie's dad usually showed up for the game. I thought it would be a great time to put an end to this bullshit once and for all. I would show up also and talk with Richard, and if he wasn't in a talking mood, I would put him in one by breaking his damn neck. I had had enough of his crap. Sure enough, he came up to little Ronnie and began talking trash about how his mommy had walked out on them, she didn't love Ronnie any more, and all kinds of crap. Little Ronnie ran off crying to his mommy. I walked up to Richard and, in a friendly way, laid my left hand on his right shoulder, blocking his right arm, just in case he didn't want to 'talk'. He had the bad habit of acting before thinking. My right hand was cocked to grab him by the throat and crush his windpipe.

Not a hard thing to do. Besides, it really wouldn't be my fault. An 'old man' like me? It would be an accident; I just accidently hit him while trying to defend myself. Besides, he needed to get the message, "don't screw around with an old man…he really **will** kill you!"

He was smarter than I thought; he looked at me, eye-ball to eye-ball; his expression changed. A surprised look came over his face; He quickly turned and walked meekly away. Maybe I don't hide my feelings as well as I used to.

There's that thought again, "What am I doing so deep in this damn swamp?" Why would I go to this length to dump this guy? Who would care? I doubt his momma would even miss him! I could have just dumped the body at the head of the swamp and be done with it. But I needed to be careful. I had no reason to be connected to Richard. That ended several years ago … but I never forgot! Evidently he did. He started the harassment again. The Black River Swamp reminded me of the swamps of Vietnam; I keep getting flashbacks to the jungles and nasty swamps of Vietnam.

It was the middle of May 1966; I was on an Air Force C-130 Hercules cargo/troop carrier aircraft, we were approaching a narrow dirt air-strip in the middle of the jungle, deep in the Mekong Delta. The Aircraft Commander told me to have my squad ready to jump and roll when we hit the ground; the Viet Cong loved to lob mortars and RPGs, rocket pro-pelled grenades, at incoming aircraft as they landed. The AC said when we reached the end of the strip he would pop open the cargo ramp as he made the turn. He would not stop. We were on our own. We were to jump out and run like hell for cover. He said maybe we would draw the VC fire while he took off. Nice guy.

Incidentally, this is where I picked up my only "battlefield wound"! As we began our descent into the VC dominated jungle, small arms fire hit the plane from several directions; an explosion near the aircraft shook the plane violently, we thought we had been hit by an RPG or surface-to-air missile. I suddenly felt a sharp pain curse through one of my fingers and blood began to flow --- SHRAPNAL! Jim Carter, the aircraft commander saw the blood and made an entry on the flight log; he turned toward me and told me, *"That just earned you a Purple Heart!"* No way I yelled back; "He said you draw blood in a combat zone you get the medal!"

I yelled back, against the noise of the engine, "Take my name off that damn, log; no way in hell will I tell my grandkids I got the purple heart for cutting my finger on a can of beanie-weenies!" I finally succeeded in getting stricken from the PH list. Besides, I won the battle --- I ate the entire can before we hit the ground.

The AC dropped the C-130 into a steep decline and put it down on the very short, clay, makeshift, runway. I yelled above the engine noise for my squad to get ready to move out fast and don't stop until you reach the jungle. As the engines reversed to slow the plane quickly, we moved to the rear onto the cargo ramp. As we approached the end of the runway the ramp began to slowly lower. I thought, "Christ, I hope they don't pop a mortar round inside. At least until we're out of the aircraft. Then, even before completing the turn, the engines began roaring loud enough to blot out the sound that any exploding mortar might make; the AC began pouring power to the engines, and kicked it into high gear for a quick take-off. We jumped and ran like hell to keep the plane between us and the jungle where the VC was hiding. There was no mistaking that they were there. They made their presence known by the never ending small arms fire at the C-130; and us!

Just as we hit the ground and started running, a shell landed just short of the aircraft and threw up dirt and mud but missed the plane. 'Stuntman' Jim Carter, the AC, kicked it full throttle and was out of there and climbing as steep as the one-thirty would climb without stalling. He wouldn't be back. He was based back at Clark Air Base in the Philippines; my home-base; civilization. When and if we made it out of this Viet Cong, snake infested, stinking, jungle and swamp-hole, we would have to do it ourselves. But that's another story.

Something churned in the water and snapped me back to reality; back to the here and now, and the swamp. I looked around and saw a large gator trailing us. We must be nearing the slew because I could hear more sounds. Maybe the one trailing me had sent out invitations. Come to the big feast, we're having human tartar!

I made the turn into the slew that fed into the lagoon and I immediately knew this was gator territory, and I don't mean the Florida Gators football team either. I think they were already getting a whiff of fresh meat and were coming closer. The big one that had been trailing the boat darted in and took a bite and started pulling it away. The boat slowed and the tail started dropping lower in the water as the gator pulled. I knew I had to cut the line before he pulled it over and I would be joining Richard for breakfast. We would be the main course. I pulled my jungle knife that I carried for special occasions; I had brought it from Vietnam, I wouldn't leave home without it.

I cut the line just in time to see two really large gators cruise in and hit the body on the other end of the line. I let it go and watched it slide under the quiet water. Except for the churning of the water, stirred up by the gators, it was awfully quiet. I carefully turned the boat and kicked that little trolling motor on as high as it would go. I wanted to get the hell out of there. Just as fast as I could!

I made my way back out to Black River and headed up-stream near where I began. I pulled over to the bank and got out, being very careful not to disturb or step on any 'cotton-mouths' that might be laying around in the sun. It was just past noon. It had been a very busy morning. I took the trolling motor off the transom, double checked to be sure nothing was left inside or on the boat, knocked a couple of holes in the bottom and gave it a shove that took it to the middle of the river. I stood and watched it sink. I picked up the motor and walked back up river for about a hundred yards or so, then slung the motor as far into the river as I could throw it. It sank immediately. I started for the clearing where I had left my car, about a mile away.

CHAPTER TWO

BACK IN THE WARMTH of my den, fireplace glowing, I lay back in my recliner, reading the newspaper; now this was the life. Everything is quiet and peaceful. Except . . . I keep hearing a noise in the backyard; probably dogs or cats playing around. A lot seems to go on in this old neighborhood. It used to be called 'upper middle class'. Now it has no class. It's just the 'hood!'

Most neighbors are good upstanding citizens that look-out for each other. It's just the drug dealers and users that decide to take a stroll through our 'hood' that bothers me. There's that damn noise again. I better get out of the comfort of my recliner and check on it. I reach down to the side of the recliner, to a special pocket I had custom made and installed. I pulled out my old, WWII military issue, Colt .45, M1911A1 pistol. I had held on to it when I left Vietnam. Just as I turned to face the door it blew-open; some big, ugly, scarface looking dude with about a size 13 foot had kicked the door right out of the frame. He got about two feet inside, pointing a small 9mm Rutgers handgun at me when I blew his big ugly face off. The police would have to use fingerprints to ID this dude. There wasn't enough dental or mouth left to work with. I picked up the phone and dialed 9-1-1, then lay my .45 on the table, picked up my newspaper again and began reading.

Sirens screaming, blue lights flashing, about half a dozen black and whites scramble into the driveway. Doors burst open, cops spill out with weapons at the ready and come running into the house. Just as a young, shave-tail patrolman was cuffing me, while I was trying to tell him that my weapon was on the table and explain what happened, a detective friend whom I had known, partnered with, and become close friends with in Vietnam came in.

"What the hell are you doing," he asked the patrolman, "take those cuffs off, now!"

"He shot this man, and I just. . ." said the patrolman.

"Just my ass," said Sam, "take them off right now. I'll take responsibility for this guy."

Police Lieutenant Sam Dillinger, no relation to the famous John Dillinger, was bigger and meaner than the original John, I'm sure. Sam and I were together on several really tough special assignments in Vietnam. He had saved my ass on more than one occasion, and I had saved his, too. He liked to throw his six-four, two-hundred fifty pounds of hard muscle around; especially in the bars. Sam had been a hard-drinking, hard-fighting, close friend that was good to have around when there was trouble.

"OK Chip, what's the deal?" he began. "Tell me something good. I'm glad when you shot him he fell inside the house and wasn't knocked back out the door," Sam said. "That makes it a little easier."

I explained, "I was sitting here having a beer, watching television and reading my newspaper, when the door just exploded, right off the hinges. Well, the rest is history. And so is that son-of-a-bitch! I put my .45 down, picked up the phone and called you guys. I believe that's your job; clean-up the mess and haul that piece of shit out of here."

Sam said, "Don't worry, as soon as the medical examiner is done, we're out of here and you can go back to your beer."

CHAPTER THREE

THE NEIGHBORHOOD WHERE I live alone, and had for the past ten years, had changed. The kids had grown-up and left town; my wife had had enough of the "hood," so she moved to Southern California to begin a "new" life. When we, wife, kids and I, first moved in forty years ago, it was known as a good, family neighborhood; a good place to raise kids. This was not so any longer. The druggies and muggers had moved in a few blocks down the street. Somebody was getting shot almost every week. Drive-by shootings were becoming common place. You could be sitting in your house and get shot. A few weeks ago it happened again. A two-year old child was sitting in her living room with her parents when two shots ripped through the front door. One struck the child killing her where she sat.

What I don't understand is how the criminal element seemingly operates openly without ever getting caught. The ones that are picked up are just the little guys who are caught up in the system and circumstances. It's the only way they know to make a little money to feed their own kids, and habit. Any others that are arrested and brought to trial only receive a slap on the wrist and then go on their merry way, ready for his next deal. It looks as if someone is looking the other way.

The citizens are always complaining about the high crime rate in the city and especially in this neighborhood. What's that you hear when people don't like what's happening? 'Somebody needs to do something'! It's kind of like the weather and taxes, everybody complains but nobody does anything about it. The mayor, the police chief, the sheriff could do something. If you talk with them, they'll tell you, "When we arrest the sorry bastards, the judge just tells them they are bad boys, slaps them on the wrist, and either lets them off or maybe gives them thirty days in the lock-up. They get out and laugh at us!"

Well, maybe if they won't do anything about it, it's time I did something about it! This is my home, my neighborhood. I'm not going to sit by and let a bunch of damn druggies make me move!

I guess the first step is to notify the assholes that they have to move. That their bullshit is not going to be tolerated any longer. I believe in treating everyone fair. I sat down at my computer and composed a poster:

ATTENTION DRUGGIES & DEALERS

The end is here!

Drug pushers and dealers will no longer be allowed to operate in this neighborhood!

Make it easy on yourself and MOVE! NOW!

You will be allowed thirty-days to re-locate to another neighborhood where

No-one cares. THIS NEIGHBORHOOD CARES! We are cleaning house

And you are not wanted here.

After thirty-days any known pusher or dealer, or anyone caught doing so

WILL BE ELIMINATED!

PERMANENTLY!

I put on a pair of latex gloves, printed and placed a hundred of these in every possible place in the neighborhood where they would be seen. Telephone poles, doors of empty houses, any place where druggies like to hang out. The gloves were a safe-guard. As soon as the police got wind of the poster, or saw one, they would try to find out who was responsible. They would look for finger prints on the poster. I knew I had bitten off a lot to chew on. I had cut out a major job for myself. Especially the dealers and pushers would try to see if it was for real. If anything would really happen, or if some mother or other parent had put the posters up to try to scare them off. And that would never happen. They would put up a fight and protect their territory.

CHAPTER FOUR

DAYS BEGIN TO GET shorter and dark comes a little earlier in October and the night people – the night creatures - come out to prey on their targets. Alcolu, South Carolina is no exception. Alcolu is a small southern town, located just off I-95 in the middle of the state. And has a big crime rate that goes up year after year. If you believe the police chief and the sheriff when they're running for reelection, the crime rate is down. With a population a little over twenty-nine thousand, it's a unique place. It started as a small, logging town, located in the middle of tobacco farming country. At the beginning of WWII the military had established an air base about twenty miles outside of town, that kind of jump started the population growth. A few years ago, the city had the highest murder rate per capita in the U.S., including Chicago and New York.

Well, my thirty day notice was up! Time for me to let the hard-core dealers and pushers know that I mean business. It's time for me to go to work. I climbed the stairs to my attic and went to the back corner. I pulled a box from underneath stacks of other boxes that had collected thirty years of dust. I pried open the lid and took everything out and laid it on the attic floor. I then pried open the false bottom and removed a high-powered Russian 9x18mm Makarov (MK-9) handgun that held a twelve round magazine. It wasn't made to wound. It was made to kill! Let my friends at the police department try to match this up with anything known in the US. I had taken it off a dead Viet Cong in Vietnam when he wanted to go face-to-face with my Colt .45. I grabbed two other magazines and a silencer, then I resealed the false bottom so it couldn't be noticed and put this special box back underneath all the other storage items and boxes.

It was ten o'clock on a very dark and actually, calm night. I was dressed in all black, including gloves. Light-weight sweat pants that I had 'special' made so that I could carry 'special items' in the pockets and nobody would ever notice. The right front pocket was large enough to conceal the MK-9 and the specially made swivel-holster that I could level at anyone, and blow them away without ever removing the weapon from my pants. They would never see it coming and never know what hit them. On the right pants leg, in front of the pocket, at barrel-level of the MK-9, was a hidden-slit so when I fired from the swivel holster it wouldn't leave a burn hole in my pants. A black, light-weight, "hoodie" and black athletic shoes completed my outfit. No one would or could see me, even if they tried.

I stepped out of the back door, in case anyone was looking in my direction. I moved silently down the street. I had about three blocks to go where I knew the pushers, dealers, and other shit-heads made their contacts and sales.

I didn't have to wait long. I spotted two guys lounging around the street corner, as if they were waiting for someone. It wasn't hard to figure out what, or who they were waiting for. One of them was a large black dude; probably about two-fifty and six foot-three or four. He was looking at one of the posters on the telephone pole next to him. He pulled it down, balled it up and threw it on the ground and stepped on it. *"You probably shouldn't do that,"* I thought.

The other guy was a smaller, white, young, man who might tip the scales at 200 or so, and stood somewhere around six feet. He acted like he was afraid he was going to piss off the big dude. Pretty soon a new looking, black Volvo SUV comes down the street moving rather slowly, the driver nervously looking all around; looking for his contact, his dealer. The Volvo pulls up to the two and stops. The two guys walk up to the driver's side window and a conversation begins. Negotiating I guess. I stand in the shadows and watch the transaction take place. The driver opens the door, picks up a small briefcase and opens it. From the interior light of the car I can see it is money; a lot of money.

The big, black dude looks in the case and checks the bills. He turns to his smaller "side-kick" who hands him a large package. He then turns and hands the package to the driver of the Volvo, who reaches for the package. Just as his hands grasped the package his forehead exploded! While they were dickering around, I had taken my MK9 from its holster, screwed a silencer on it and leveled it at the driver; right between his eyes!

The two dealers, with panic in their eyes, turned in the direction of the little puff sound since I was so close. At the same time I saw that the big dude had a pistol in his hand and was raising it. He never got it as high as his waist when he caught my second shot, between the eyes. The smaller dude was screaming and yelling. He still couldn't see me standing in the darkness of a vacant house. He was so scared he fainted. Not only that but he shit in his pants.

I hurriedly walked over to the car and saw the driver was holding a revolver in his left hand. Self-protection, I guess, or he wasn't going to let them keep the money. I quickly removed the pistol, squeezed off a couple of rounds then placed it in the hand of the still living, but out-cold, young man. Let the cops work on that and see what they come up with.

Then I got the hell out of there and headed home!

Midnight; 'Breaking News' on the television: "Drug gang shoot-out in Alcolu!" I guess someone must have found the bodies and called the cops.

The lady reporter went on to explain that, "According to police reports there has been a shoot-out among drug gangs in Alcolu earlier this evening; likely a deal gone bad between the two rival gangs. Two people are dead and one person arrested by the police, who found the shooter trying to get away while still holding the revolver that police said is apparently one of the weapons involved in the shoot-out. One of the dead men still had his pistol in his hand."

She went on to report that, "Police recovered a large package containing pure cocaine in the vehicle where one of the dead men still lay. They also found ten-thousand dollars in a briefcase next to the other dead person who lay on the ground where he was shot."

Newspapers and television reporters were having a field-day for the next week, trying to explain what had happened. They interviewed the entire neighborhood and even showed one of the posters on TV and "wondered out-loud" if there was a connection.

Pete, the young, white, dude was charged with murder of the other two, and sale and distribution of cocaine. He'll probably come up for trial in a year or two under our 'speedy' justice system. The cops didn't try to explain the ballistics involved in the shootings. It would be too complicated. How do you explain a Russian weapon shooting someone when it doesn't even exist? Not in the US anyway.

Nothing more was said about the money, but word on the street was, it wasn't just ten thousand dollars. According to word floating around the jail-house, Pete was saying it was supposed to be one-hundred thousand dollars in that briefcase. Only ten thousand made it to the evidence room. From just asking around, the scuttlebutt is that this is nothing unusual. A lot of the cash that's supposed to go to the evidence room never makes it there.

If that's the case, I wonder where it goes. This may take some looking into. Then again, a lot of the drugs that are recovered on traffic stops and individual investigations, never make it to the evidence room either. Somebody is probably getting real wealthy from this. I decided I would take a look into this later, when I had more time.

CHAPTER FIVE

AS I DROVE AROUND the 'hood' I noticed that many of the posters that I had placed in conspicuous places had been torn down or now contained comments like, 'Fuck You'! or 'YOU Move Asshole'.I really thought, *"That isn't very nice of these shitheads!"* They evidently didn't get the message. Maybe I should 'discuss' it with them once more. Just so there won't be any misunderstanding.

I decided to play a little psychology game with them. I printed more posters. This time it read:

ATTENTION DRUGGIES & DEALERS

Don't write or draw on my posters!

Drug pushers and dealers will no longer be allowed to operate in this neighborhood!

Make it easy on yourself and MOVE! NOW!

You no longer have thirty-days to re-locate.

Neighborhood cleaning has begun.

THE FIRST ONES HAVE BEEN ELIMINATED!

ARE YOU NEXT?

Don't Take A Chance!

It was another one of those 'dark and lonely' nights when I decided to venture out into the 'hood' again. It didn't take long for one of the neighborhood pushers to show up. He was alone. That was kind of unusual for this crew. I waited until he was in a dark spot, near one of the posters. Very quietly I sneaked up behind him and placed the barrel of my MK9 against the back of his head. He started to jerk away but I held him and told him, "You really don't want to move do you?"

He started to jerk away again and said, "You mothua…!" That's as far as he got when I hit him in the back of the head, as hard as I could, with the barrel of my gun. He just crumpled to the ground, unconscious.

"OK, asshole; you shouldn't have moved!" I said. I grabbed him by the collar and drug him underneath the street light and propped him up against the pole. I checked his pockets and backpack. He must have had a full kilo of 'coke' and I counted a dozen hits of 'crack'. I took one of the posters off the pole and placed it on his chest. I left the drugs stashed in his lap. Let the gang, and the police, if they found out about it, mull that over for a while.

The next few days there was a lot of chatter going on, seems someone was going around shooting and beating up on the druggies. Even heard some cops talking about it over coffee in the Cut-Rate Drug Store one morning. The lunch counter was the local watering hole for coffee and B-S every morning. This is where you came to tell your biggest fish tale or about the trophy buck you shot over the weekend. If you got enough interest in your tale, you could come back for lunch.

Even though he was big and tough as nails, Sam was a friendly guy. He turned, looked at me, with a certain look in his eye, and asked, "Chip, you heard any rumblings around your beat about guys getting beat-up or shot?"

After we left Vietnam, Sam went on to serve, and eventually retired, as an Army CIA agent. He spent twenty-plus years investigating every type of military crime from Washington, DC to Vietnam. He had even assisted in the My Lai massacre investigation back in 1968. I never really agreed with the outcome. In wartime you don't wait to see if the enemy is going to blow you up first and you ask questions later. In those days, when the VC was using women and children with explosive vests and belts on, you didn't take a chance. You shoot first and then think about what questions you might ask. You can't fight a war from Washington!

"Sam," I said, "I don't give a 'rat's ass' if those druggies and pushers kill each other. And, the sooner, the better off this town will be. I just go on minding my own business."

"Yeah, right," Sam said.

Sam continued, "I know you, Chip, you don't just sit around on your butt if you know something's going down. With all the thugs and drugs passing through our area, I wouldn't doubt but that you were up to your ass in finding out who's doing what."

"Speaking about who is doing what, what do you guys do with all the shit you confiscate; all those big hauls of cash I keep hearing and reading about. I'll bet the "Narcs" get a cut from what they bring in," I said.

"Not after they bring it in," Sam said, kind of hesitantly.

Sam quickly tried to change the subject, but I pressed a little further. He looked around as if to see if anyone was listening, then whispered, "I believe those damn Narcs are skimming a lot of the cash off before it's ever counted and brought in. Some are living too 'high-on-the-hog' for the salary they make." He thought a minute and said, "… can't say as I blame them too damn much, for the little pittance they pay us. I can't say that I wouldn't do it too if I had the opportunity."

CHAPTER SIX

IT WAS LATE ON a Friday afternoon when Sam and I went to the backside of Pocotaligo Swamp, to one of our 'secret' fishing spots; thought we might pick up a few bream or crappie for a little fish fry and have some friends for a get together over at Sam's house. He didn't live in the hood like I did; he had a more modern place. Besides, I wanted to discuss the 'narc scene' in a little more depth with him.

This side of Pocotaligo was more or less deserted; very few fishers or hunters cared much about coming in this area. There had been a lot of rumors in the past about some strange creatures wandering around back here. I never recall seeing anything really weird except maybe the extralarge wild boar. A few others who had seen it estimated it weighing at least fifteen hundred plus pounds; I agree that it probably weighed that much or more. I had seen plenty of deer, gators and many other species; some say they had seen bear in the swamp.

I think the biggest scare came from the finding of three or four bodies at different times. Some shot, some knifed, but all looked as if they had been dragged in through the swamp. The bodies were in different, grotesque condition when found; gators had bitten off pieces as had other types of animals. You can never tell what happens in the dense, dark depths of a place like this.

I realized that Sam hadn't spoken since we got out of my truck and started walking. I turned to him and asked, "Why are you so quiet, you uptight about something?"

"Hell no," he answered; "I'm just keeping my eyes and ears open in case something or somebody comes charging out of the bushes. You know me better than that Chip; I aint taking no chances."

I noticed that Sam was carrying his fishing gear in one hand and had his .38 caliber police revolver in the other. I laughed, but also knew that was the smart thing to do; I doubled checked my back waist band where I kept my weapon.

We got to our hidden fishing spot and got settled down; didn't see any bear, boar or even a rabbit running around. We found a dry spot and had been sitting there for about an hour when we heard noise, something or someone crashing and sloshing through the water behind us. Not that it frightened us, but in less than an instant both Sam and I had turned, with weapons out, to face the 'creature' that was quickly approaching.

Laughter! Me and Sam looked at each other; what we were hearing was laughter and it was getting closer, splashing through the swampy, muddy water through the bushes and trees. Suddenly two raggedly dressed, homeless looking men came into the opening behind us; they were laughing wildly, jumping and dancing, looking excited. When they saw me and Sam they stopped dead-still in their tracks; they were as shocked as we were; even more so when they saw our weapons in our hands; they dropped to their knees. Probably crapped in their pants; they didn't smell too good either.

One cried out, "Please mister, don't shoot us, we're just trying to find our way out of this place; please."

The other one cried out also, "We didn't know; it was an accident we just found it, please don't shoot us; we won't tell anybody. We just want out of this swamp."

Sam told them, "Both of you get out of here, jump in the water and get a bath, you stink." They jumped up and ran down the road leading out of the swamp.

I chuckled and remarked, "Sure scared the hell out of them when they came through the bushes and saw us sitting here; they probably won't stop running until they get back to town."

"I don't know about you Chip, but I think our fishing day just ended, I'm for heading back to town myself; what about you?" Sam said.

"I'm with you; since we began this little venture to catch fish, why don't we go to Big Jim's and get a big seafood dinner?" I asked.

"Well . . . "

"I'm buying, this ones on me," I said.

"Thought you would never offer," Sam responded.

Freshly showered and dressed I walk into Big Jim's at eight o'clock, spotted Sam in a booth near the back of the dining room and sat across from him. Our waiter came to take drink orders; we both ordered beer. While waiting we chatted and laughed about our fishing afternoon in the old Pocotaligo; laughing at ourselves after admitting that we were a little scared when we first heard the noise.

Sam, still grinning said, "I'm not saying that I was really afraid, but I sure as hell beat you on the draw."

"I'm not too sure about that," I replied chuckling more; "Just because I peed in my pants doesn't mean that I was scared or anything, besides I still think I beat you on the draw." We hooted so hard people turned to look at us.

"Speaking of scared, those two nasty looking guys who came out of the swamp were so frightened that I actually believe one or both shit in their pants; sure smelled like it too," Sam stated.

We weren't the only noisy diners in Big Jim's that night. We heard loud laughter and a little yelling from across the dining room. I was sitting where I could look directly at the table where the noise was coming from. Two well-dressed men were having the time of their life; there was a bottle of champagne cooling at their tableside while they were cutting and eating the largest filet mignon that Jim served. These guys were in a celebrating mood and evidently money was no object.

Sam turned to take a look; he watched for several minutes then turned back to me and asked, "Chip, did you take a close look at those two?"

"I looked and saw two happy men celebrating something, nothing wrong in that," I replied.

"Then put on your 'investigative' eyes and thoughts and take another look, a closer look," Sam said.

I did, and took a hard look; suddenly realization struck me, I glanced back at Sam and said, "Sam they look like . . . "

Sam cut me off and said, "You're right; that's the two homeless, lost souls we saw in the swamp a few hours ago."

"Yeah," I answered. "They must have taken your advice and jumped in the water and took a bath; but I don't believe they stock clothing that looks like that; at least not in my old Pocotaligo."

"Let's go chat with them for a couple of minutes," Sam remarked as he got up from our booth. As he stood he placed his badge on his belt where it would be easily seen. As we approached the table the two looked up at us.

Sam spoke to them, "Good evening gentlemen."

The man closest to Sam looked up and you could see panic settle in his eyes and fear sweep over his entire face. The other looked at me then at Sam, fear struck; he dropped his full glass of champagne spilling it in his lap. They both looked at the badge on Sam's belt.

Sam asked, "Mind if we sit down for a moment?" Sam and I didn't wait for an answer, the men nodded in agreement. Sam continued, "I see you took my advice and got yourself cleaned up --- and even got new clothes – very nice." Sam reached over and felt the material on the lapel of the sports coat one was wearing. "Very nice; cost more than any of mine, at least on a policeman's salary anyway.

"This afternoon you told us that you were poor homeless men. Now look at you. You guys have done well for yourselves, in a very short period of time, I might add. Tell me how you did it, I need to know, I could certainly use some fast cash," Sam continued. "Or maybe you robbed a Seven-Eleven Store or a country grocery store; or hey, maybe even a bank; that would bring the most cash."

"No sir; no sir," said the larger man sitting next to Sam. "We didn't rob nobody, we didn't steal anything. We found some money in a bag . . ."

"Hold on," Sam said; "let's take a stroll outside for a few minutes; we don't want to tell the whole town that you probably robbed somebody."

Sam called the waiter over and explained that we were going outside for a few minutes, to leave the men's food and drink at the table. He also told him to put our order on hold until we came back inside. The four of us walked out to Sam's Police Cruiser; the two men were about to crap in their newly purchased pants; scared is not the word for their expressions.

Before Sam could begin asking them anything, they began talking a mile-a-minute. They said that they had spent the night in a barn just on the other side of a fence on the edge of the swamp, sleeping on some hay. The larger one said that they had awakened right at daybreak, before the sun came up; they didn't want to be caught on somebody's property. The other one, the smaller of the two, chimed in adding that they had found a large, black trash bag that didn't have much of anything in it, just a little trash in the bottom, they didn't look to see what it was; they threw a few sweet potatoes and ears of corn in on top of it and got out of there before the owner got up and came to the barn. They went back into the swamp and stopped to look in the bag and found money, a lot of it.

The larger man said, "Since it was in a trash bag we thought that it had gotten lost or somebody had stolen it, so we decided to keep it. We buried it in a dry spot in the swamp where we sometime have to spend the night. When we saw you folks this afternoon we thought you were after us; but you let us go. When y'all left, we went back and got the money and decided to come get ourselves something to eat; we haven't eaten nothing but scraps for days now."

I asked, "How much cash did you find in that trash bag?"

The two men looked at each other and the smaller one stuttered, "You won't ever believe this, but there was eleven thousand dollars in that bag; we have never seen that much at one time."

The larger guy added, "We haven't spent much of it; we got a hotel room, bought these new clothes and came here to eat a meal. Please don't arrest us, we will be three-time losers; take the money back and we won't cause no more problem; we just need to go pay for our meal and we're out of here; please."

Sam nodded to me and we walked a few feet away and discussed briefly what I had mentioned to Sam earlier about narc officers skimming money from what they confiscated. Sam and I agreed on a major point and went back to the two men.

Sam told them, "I'm not only not going to arrest you; I'm going to do you one better than that, you go back inside and finish your meal and leave, leave Alcolu, go to some other town, maybe Orangeburg or somewhere and start over, start living a decent life for a change. Can you do that?"

"Oh, yes sir; yes sir; you're not going to arrest us, you're letting us go free? How do we get the money to you, where do we take it?"

"That's another thing," Sam told them, "you two keep it and use it to start over and don't ever tell anybody where you got it; if you do, you know what will happen, you will spend a long time in prison, a very long time."

With that said and done we all went back into Big Jim's and had dinner. Me and Sam had a lot to talk about. Keeping our voices low we discussed several possibilities; we kept coming back to the same scenario; the money had been part of a drug bust and was skimmed from the take before turning it in.

Sam looked at me and asked, "You know who owns that property on the other side of that fence?"

"Yeah," I replied, "I know; the judge for this district. He bought all that property before he became a judge, while he was still a narc agent." I now knew where the money had come from! Before becoming a judge he was a police captain who had worked several years as an undercover 'Narc Agent;' a typical cop; with the shaved, bald, 'skinhead' look. He was a nice enough guy, if you were friends with him; complete asshole if not. He could smile to your face while sticking it in you from the rear. He headed up the Narcotics Division of the local police department. Everything that went on had to go through him for approval. Before he was promoted and "hand-picked" to head-up the Division he played the part of a dirty, grungy looking, homeless type; a druggie who you didn't want to be around. He had played the part for several years. He played the part well and he trained his cohorts well also. They didn't fart without asking him first.

When they made a drug bust, everything that was confiscated was brought to him; he distributed some among his "followers and friends," and put some in the Evidence Room. It looked good – on paper. He was happy and his underlings were kept happy and all were living very well on a small patrolman's salary. His superiors were happy also; the numbers looked impressive. No complaints from there.

I have a minor problem with 'The Judge'. He is a retired police captain. He doesn't make much in the way of retired pay. Before retiring his pay was only about $35,000 a year, much less in retirement. He owns a large farm or ranch as he calls it. There are several hundred acres of it. I guess it really is a ranch since he has several prize horses, some cattle including a couple of Texas longhorns in the 'herd.' He has some small 'ranch' machinery too, like 4x4's, a tractor, and jeeps that he likes to run about the ranch in. He not only has his-own private shooting range, but a small, dirt landing strip for his twin-engine Cessna airplane, too.

You probably want to be real careful if you decide to go wandering around the 'ranch' some dark night. Maybe even in the daylight if he wasn't expecting you.

So what's my problem with 'The Judge?'

He is now the District Judge – elected 'by the people'!

CHAPTER SEVEN

I NEED SOME PRIVATE thinking time if I'm going to unravel some of these latest revelations. It's time for me to take a few days and head off into the woods to my private 'retreat' my 'hide-away', deep in some shadowy woods. I call it the *"Sweet Daddy Creek Club."* This is where I go when I need time to myself, to be alone, drop a line in the creek (where there are no fish), and just sit back and think. The Sweet Daddy Creek Club --- is my *'happy place'*.

The Sweet Daddy Creek Club used to be an old "Negro Saturday Night juke joint type place." It was built as a shack deep in the woods back in the late twenties or early thirties. A place where the old time black folks could go on a Saturday night, after picking cotton all week, and "let their hair down!" Music from the old jukebox would be loud enough to hear across three counties, except it was far enough back in the woods that the trees muffled the sound. There would be a whole lot of dancing, jukein' and 'jivein' going on. You can bet there was a lot of moonshine making the rounds too. The club was kind of in the heart of 'moonshine country' in the middle of South Carolina.

"It was the kind of place," Jimbo said …"where if a white man could be black on a 'Sadday' night, he never would want to be white no more, ha, ha, ha."

I found it by chance when I used to drive old highway 521, one of the narrow, two-lane, back roads between Alcolu and the North Carolina state line. I would always notice this old sign propped up against a tree, near a small path that looked like it led deep into the woods. It was just an old, faded out, hand-painted, wooden sign. But it would catch my eye every time I saw it – *"Sweet Daddy Creek Club."* That's all it said.

About fifteen years ago that sign got the best of me. I stopped one day on my way back from Charlotte, parked on the side on the road and walked a little ways down the path. I never did see anything or anybody. Once back on the road, I drove to the nearest house I could find to ask about the old club. I soon located an old black man, must have been in his late seventies or early eighties, and he remembered the old Sweet Daddy Creek Club. He used to go there on Saturday nights when he was in his late teens. His name was James T. Ferguson. "But just call me "Jimbo!" he said.

This was the first of many visits with Jimbo; we became close and good friends. We would sit and talk for hours and drink a beer or two. He told of some of the wild Saturday nights at the Club and the fun they had. He said, "My daddy and my granddaddy were big in the 'shine' business. They had the biggest and best still anywhere 'round here." He added, "I used to haul that shine 'round three counties. That's how we survived in poor times."

"You weren't afraid of getting caught," I asked?

"Nah," he said laughing, "The police were more crooked than we were. They never did find the still, but they did stop me one night on a run. My granddaddy was with me. He got out of the car and went 'round to the back with the policeman and they talked. I saw my granddaddy hand him some money, then reach in the trunk of the car and hand him a jar of that 'shine,' and that was the end of it. We went on our way."

On my next visit I asked Jimbo who owned the old club and the property it sat on. He told me that one of his uncles owned it and used to farm it until he got too old and crippled. Now it just sat there unused.

"Think he might want to sell it," I asked?

"Might be," said Jimbo, "He's got a lot of hospital bills and other things. I believe he could use the money," he said. "He's too old to run his still anymore, besides, not much money in shine these days."

I made arrangements to meet up with Jimbo's Uncle Samson (like in the bible) and found that he owned about a hundred twenty-five acres. All the way from the road back across into the edge of the next county. The Sweet Daddy Creek Club sat near the front side of the property with about ten acres or more between it and the road. It was completely surrounded by a pine forest that had not been timbered or plowed since the early days of the Club; probably on purpose. It would be hard to see or find unless you knew just where it was.

It was perfect for just the type of retreat and private place I had been thinking about for years. Samson and I talked a couple of times and he agreed to sell me the place for five hundred dollars an acre. I bought a hundred acres on the front side. That gave me the right of way and ownership of the path that led to the Club. Now I would have to find the old clubhouse.

I met up with Jimbo and 'Uncle Sam' the next Saturday afternoon and we went tramping off down the path into the woods to see my new 'home-away-from-home,' the "Sweet Daddy Creek Club." After walking along the path for almost a mile, we came to it. It was about what I expected. An old, wood frame, barn type building, the wood mostly rotted, but not exactly falling down yet. You could tell that the possums, raccoons, snakes, and no telling what other kind of varmints had made it their home. They would just have to find another lodging place, this was now my kingdom. It was going to take some fixing-up. A lot of fixing-up!

Since I already had an idea in my mind of what I wanted, and what I wanted it to look like, I thought I might as well get started. So I took out my phone and pulled up the contact list and found the perfect match, Charlie Neilson a 'handy-man' type 'fixer-upper,' who used to have his own contracting business building houses and small office buildings; until old man alcohol and drugs got to him. I wanted somebody who could do the job I wanted, but would never remember just where he did it, or when. Charlie was my man.

Jimbo, Uncle Sam and I went back out to where the car was parked. We got in and drove about five miles to a crossroads, where one of their friends had opened an old fashioned, southern bar-b-que place. You could eat-in or take-out. It was an old barn type place that you probably would expect to get 'toe-main' poison, hepatitis or some other kind of disease, so we sat down and ate-in and washed it down with a couple bottles of beer.

I asked Jimbo and Uncle Sam if this was going to turn into one of those Saturday night juke joints that would start 'rockin' pretty soon. No such luck. It's just a BBQ restaurant where most folks in the surrounding county came to eat. It was easy to figure out why, too. It was the best BBQ you ever tasted and was served with baked beans, coleslaw, and hush puppies. Washed down with another couple of bottles of good old American beer and, as the Budweiser folks say, "It doesn't get any better than this!"

After eating, Jimbo, Uncle Sam, and I sat back, propped our feet up on a chair in front of us, ordered more beer, leaned our chairs back on the two back legs, and just talked about the "old" days. About the heyday of the Sweet Daddy Creek Club when it was 'the' place to go on a 'Sadday' night, and we talked about some of the other juke joints that used to be nearby.

"It was sort of like a tradition. You got dressed up in your finest duds and hat and go to the club," Jimbo said.

"Ain't that way no more," Uncle Sam said, looking kind of wistfully. He added, "Life got too complicated, used to be simple. People helped people without being asked. They helped each other raise their children, too. A neighbor child over at your place misbehave, you whooped 'em, and they momma or daddy would thank you for doing it. Now, you do it and they want to shoot you."

I don't know if it was the beer, the food, or the reminiscing that was responsible for the down-turn in moods, but it was getting late and time to go. I had a lot to get started on tomorrow, even though it was Sunday. I had to get to Charlie and get him sober, and dried out.

Getting together with Jimbo and Uncle Sam kind of became a tradition; we started getting together at least once a month for the bar-b-que, beer and just talk.

CHAPTER EIGHT

BACK IN MY 'LITTLE house in the hood', sitting at my drafting table in the den, I was sketching the plans for the brand new "Sweet Daddy Creek Club" when the news came across that there had been another shooting in Alcolu. This time it seems that one of the big druggies by the name of 'Drueboy' had been skimming off the top of the 'the judge's' take and was in hiding with his girlfriend, Latisha. They had rented a house in a nice, legitimate, residential area of town; across the street from the local cemetery. How convenient.

It was Halloween night; Drueboy and Latisha were in bed about to get serious when there was a knock at the door. Drueboy, so scared he was petrified , yelled at Latisha to grab the money and get out the back door. He grabbed up his AK47, a full clip and sprayed through the front door. He turned and ran for the back door not knowing that police were already in the area on patrol. It was Halloween night!

The knock on the front door had been a nine-year old boy. "Trick-or-Treat" were the last words the young boy ever spoke. His father and five-year old brother were standing out in the yard; they were hit by the flying bullets also.

When the police patrol first heard shots they were almost in front of the house. One officer called for back-up while the other headed around the back of the house just in time to see Drueboy coming out of the house holding the AK47 in one hand, trying to hold his pants up with the other, and running for the fence like his pants were on fire.

"Drop it and get on the ground," shouted Gary Rollins, a veteran of fifteen years on the force. "You make one move, no matter how small, and I'll blow your ass to kingdom-come," Gary hollered.

Shocked that the cops were already there, Drueboy spun around and squeezed off a burst from his AK47 towards the voice. Gary responded with his police revolver hitting Drueboy in the chest and legs. Screaming like a stuck pig Drueboy threw the AK47 down as he fell to the ground spurting blood from the wounds, screaming as he fell. "Where's the money bag," demanded Gary, "We know you had it hidden here we've been watching your ass!"

"I don't know what you talking about, man," Drueboy cried out, shrieking. "I'm just minding my own business, when somebody tried to break down my door. What I'm supposed to do? Let them in and shoot me? I'm bleeding; I'm dying, help me, don't let me die," he yelled.

"You thought your 'friends' had found you after you skipped out with their two- hundred-grand, didn't you?" Gary snarled. Part of that two-hundred-grand is going to be mine, he thought to himself.

Gary cuffed him and dragged him to the front of the house where they saw Latisha already in cuffs and in the back of a patrol car. Sitting on the hood of the patrol car was a black bag. Gary knew what was inside the bag. He opened the bag looked inside and saw a bag full of cash, piles of it, separated with rubber bands. "Anybody get a count on this?" he asked.

"Not yet," replied one of the patrolmen, "We were waiting on you; R.H.I.P you know. Rank has its privileges!"

Gary was glad to hear that. He would take his 'cut', give a 'bonus' to each of the others, and turn the rest of the money in for evidence.

The EMS Ambulance arrived to haul Drueboy to the emergency room; Garry sent two of his officers to accompany them and to arrest Drueboy - if he survived.

I couldn't help but wonder just how much of the 'bust money' would actually make it to the evidence lock-up room. I also knew that I needed to get my act together as quickly as possible if I wanted to find out just who was paying off who in this town. I need a place to work from, a headquarters. A place only I know about; except maybe a couple of my "closest" and trusted friends and companions. I would have to be very selective who I take there.

CHAPTER NINE

WATCHING THE LATEST NEWS on television, I suddenly realized that the shootings and muggings in 'my hood' had certainly taken a down-turn after the last couple of times I had gone out, and blown the balls off a couple of druggies and dealers.

In fact, I thought, 'my hood' is coming together like it used to be. It's almost a neighborhood again. Things were beginning to look up. Now, if only I could find out whom some of the power brokers behind the local trade were, maybe I could get a few things cleared and cleaned up.

But for now, it's back to the drawing board. I need to get my operational headquarters set up as soon as I can if I'm to solve all of the local problems; fat chance of doing that.

I knew exactly what I wanted, but I didn't have the plans, except what was in my head. I knew I could call my friend Verne, tell him what I wanted and what I wanted it to look like, and he could knock out the plans while others were still thinking about it! And, he wouldn't ask questions.

I want a large mountain cabin; even though I don't have a mountain to build it on. It has to be rustic; like an old, huge barn or log cabin, built from old timber and logs. It has to look old; not new; but still must have all the modern touches. I want the outside to be from old lumber; to make it look mostly like an old, run-down, deserted building. It's to have a huge double-size fireplace; a big great room that can handle a small crowd; if I ever decided to invite people over. I would also like to have a mountain stream running across the back of the property, instead of the swamp that was there. Still don't have a mountain to put it on, though.

Well, it's time to get my thoughts to Verne so he can get started. Time is not on my side.

I took my sketch to Verne and described what I wanted. I also told him I didn't want any questions.

He said, "Whew, that's gonna cost you some big bucks. Everything will most likely have to be custom made." You ready for that?" he added.

"Just keep it under two-hundred fifty grand," I replied. "We're going to do this on a 'cash' basis," I told him. "Materials, labor, whatever, and it's all going to be completed in cash," I added.

"I hope you got a lot of it stashed away somewhere handy," Verne said.

I didn't tell Verne, and he didn't need to know, but Uncle Sam and 'Uncle Vietnam' were paying for this one.

CHAPTER TEN

IT STILL PISSES ME off when I think about where the money came from. It was February 1967 in Saigon, South Vietnam; I was having dinner with a group of rather wealthy South Vietnamese business 'tycoons', members of the South Vietnam Jaycees. I was there to speak to the group of 'older' Jaycees, a group which is called 'The Senate'. I had spoken to them about the eternal values of the Jaycee Creed. You know; good stuff like, people are generally nice, honest and really want to help each other; something from the Jaycee Creed about "People Helping People." And how the international community should come together and help each other, and help the people of their native land live better and prosper. It sounded really good, one of my best speeches. Too bad it doesn't work when you get people involved.

Anyway, the gentleman to my right, Mr. Truong Nguyen, a very friendly and all around nice guy, and I had been making small talk and just visiting, being socially conversational and getting to know one another. Suddenly he asked, "Chip, do you know of anyone who has copper connections in the States?"

"Copper connections?" I asked.

"Yes," Truong replied. "I am currently in textile manufacturing, but I would like to divest and go into some other ventures."

Currently in textile manufacturing my ass; he personally owned the largest textile manufacturing business in all of Vietnam, plus several other businesses.

Then he continued, "I receive $250,000 US dollars each year from the U.S. Government, and I have no place to put it or to invest it. I can't just return it; I need to do something with it. There is a big shortage of copper in Vietnam and I would like to make contact with someone who could help supply it for me."

$250,000! No strings attached! That's what really pissed me off. My government; the same government for which I worked for a pittance a year; and what these wealthy bastards earned every month. Maybe every week for all I know.

I thought for a few moments then looked him straight in the eye and calmly and thoughtfully said, "Actually, I do know of someone. I have some friends who are in the copper business and I am sure they would like to expand their operations. But it would take some time to get together with them, but they would want substantial cash up front; we're talking international business and that will take time to set up and get started. Dealing in copper is a little touchy right now, if you understand what I mean."

"Of course," Mr. Truong replied. "I understand, it is the same here in Vietnam; that would not be a problem. But it must be done without anyone else involved or knowing about it. If your Government became aware, they would surely stop sending the money to me."

"This would all have to be done, as we say, 'under the table', if you get what I mean," I said; "I think it best if no one else knows or, even hears about it, if we can work out an agreement." I told him.

"I fully understand, and the same applies here, to me, no one must ever know of our agreement. It could cause major problems between me and both governments. How can you get the funds back through customs, will that present too much of a problem for you?" He asked.

"Flying by military aircraft in and out of the war zone doesn't involve customs," I answered.

We agreed to meet the next afternoon at the same expensive, upscale restaurant. He would bring the cash in a briefcase like the ones all the other customers seem to carry. I would be leaving Saigon two days later, a quarter million dollars richer, going back to Clark Air Base in the Philippines. Oh,

I would set up the operation and make arrangements to begin sending him some copper of course, and get a few more of his, or my, tax dollars before this deal was finished.

The next afternoon was Friday; a hot and 'sticky' day in downtown Saigon. I arrived at the restaurant around four o'clock so I could take a look around. Wanted to make sure everything looked normal and nothing 'unusual' was expected to happen. Finally, satisfied that everything was alright, I sat at the bar, had a cold beer and waited. Shortly before five, our agreed meeting time, Truong came through the door, carrying a briefcase.

He joined me at the bar, ordered a drink and made small talk. Then he motioned toward a table, off in a quiet corner of the room, so we could have some privacy. After more greetings and salutations, he picked-up the briefcase and held it on his lap, kind of under the table. He opened it and I saw bundles of $100 bills, a lot of bundles; 'made in America' type, neatly bundled with wrappers that stated, "National Bank of South Vietnam."

I reached in and touched a stack; I flipped through the stack as if I was checking to see if the stack was complete; and not counterfeit. As if I knew what I was doing. I looked up at Truong, nodded, and he closed the briefcase and sat it down on the floor between us. A quick estimate of the bundles and I knew there was more than a quarter million in that case.

I reminded Truong, and assured him that it would take some time; that this would not be an overnight transaction. He smiled, and said that as partners he trusted me and that time was no problem.

He also said, "You will find an extra $100,000 in the briefcase; that is a gift, or fee for being a partner and helping me get started in this new business venture." He hesitated a moment then added, "Also, there are additional funds in there that I need to get out of the country with someone I trust."

"Damn!" He was making it awful hard to rip him off, even though it was already partly mine. It was some of my own tax money that good old Uncle Sam was giving away.

Back in the Philippines I gave my friend, Vince Barredo, in Manila a call. Vince is the President and Chairman of the Board of the Philippine National Bank in Quezon City, the Wall Street of the Philippines. He was also the president of the Philippine Jaycees, my connection to international banking; only he didn't know it yet.

After a few minutes of pleasantries, Vince said, "Chip, I know you're not calling to talk about this damn, sultry, hot, weather we always have. What's on your mind?"

"Vince, I need some advice and probably some help from an expert in finances and money handling. I think you're just the person and just the friend I need."

I explained in detail exactly what I needed. Since it bordered on being illegal, hell it was illegal; I thought I should tell him the whole story. I knew I could trust Vince.

"Leave that to me Chip. Don't worry that thick skull of yours. I'll have it all set up by tomorrow evening and I'll give you a call with the details."

"How much is that going to cost me?" I asked.

"You know me better than that. I don't charge my friends for doing a little favor. Besides, somewhere down the line I'll get paid," Vince laughed.

Three days later I get a call from Vince, "Congratulations Mister Very Rich American. You're all set. You now have an account with the Philippines National Bank of New York, USA. You also have a balance of $1,650,000 US Dollars. It has been set up as an older account that has accumulated over time; it is available whenever you want it. However, I recommend not withdrawing it in really large sums each time. You don't want to draw attention to the account." He added, "You can make, or have deposits made to it automatically like any other account, anytime."

CHAPTER ELEVEN

BIG NEWS HIT THE headlines on Monday; "Sheriff Arrests Prominent Car Dealer in Big Drug Bust!" The story went on to say that car dealer Robert E. (Bobby) Grant had attempted to fly a load of cocaine from Mexico into Alcolu in his private plane. The sheriff and his deputies were waiting when Grant landed his plane on his personal landing strip on his farm about five miles out of town.

When Sheriff J. C. Byrdam went to put the cuffs on, Robert was heard to mumble, "You son-of-a-bitch. You set me up!"

Sheriff Byrdam was a typical, mild-mannered, small town, Southern sheriff with a large gut that hung over his belt. He had been sheriff so long that he had ownership of the job, even though he had to 'run' for re-election every four years. People knew better than to run against him. But, if you knew JC and he liked you, you could pretty much have your own way. He took care of his friends.

Rumor has it that periodically neighbors of JC would complain that sometimes they would hear a plane flying so low over their houses and out-buildings, they would think it was going to crash. It would scare the livestock and animals. Sometimes some of the neighbors would say that they thought they saw large bundles drop from the plane out on the back of JC's property.

JC would tell them that he would check it out. That would be the last anyone ever heard about it--- until the next time.

Robert E. Grant went to trial; was convicted of 'minor' drug dealing and, according to the judge, 'due to a technicality,' was sentenced to one year in the Federal penitentiary in Atlanta.

Six months later 'Bobby' was released on good behavior. He and his wife moved to Florida where he managed a large dealership with Katrina, his wife, as the bookkeeper. The following year he was arrested for embezzling two hundred grand. According to the scuttlebutt, Katrina took the fall and went to prison for a year. Bobby came back to Alcolu and bought another dealership.

Being the gentleman that he was, Bobby began courting his new bookkeeper, divorced Katrina while she was still in prison and married Beth, his new bookkeeper. She was a shapely, large buxom, blonde gal; she was, as the old saying goes, "built like a brick outhouse!"

CHAPTER TWELVE

AFTER MANY BACK AND forth trips to the Sweet Daddy Creek Club to check on the progress, it all finally came together. It had only taken six months from start to finish. It was just what I was looking for and hoping it would turn in to.

Driving down highway 521, from either direction, you would never know, or see, the path that led into the property. It was hidden from the highway by large grown-up brush and trees. You had to know exactly where to turn-in; it angled off behind several large bushes and trees that led you to a horizontal path, only a little wider than the first, that led you deeper into the woods and out of sight from the highway, the paths, or anything else, for that matter. It was the ideal location!

Driving down the winding path through the woods you still couldn't see the cabin until you suddenly broke-out into a clearing, and there it stood in all its splendor – the *Sweet Daddy Creek Club!*

It looked like, and once had been, an old, dilapidated, practically falling down, barn that had seen its better days in the last century. It had never seen a coat of paint and one would wonder what was holding it up. It looked great! I couldn't wait to get inside.

I pulled up near the front, parked and got out of the car. I'll have to get me a jeep if I'm going to keep coming here; especially in the rainy times. Those paths would get pretty muddy.

Hidden behind what looked like one of the loose boards was a key-pad that held the combination for entering the building. I punched in the code, heard the double bolt locks slide out of their locked position, opened the door and walked in. Unbelievable! Verne and Charlie had done themselves proud. I could easily tell that they had put their heart into this project. I stepped into the 'foyer.' I wasn't aware there was to be a 'foyer.' The walls looked as if they would cave in at any moment. The old, probably century old, planking was just like the outside, deteriorated, rotten, never seen paint or a paint brush. The floor boards were just as bad. I was afraid that I would fall through. However, they actually felt pretty solid and sturdy. I stomped my feet and they didn't give any at all. They had been laid over a solid foundation. There was another door with a keypad to punch in the combination to get into the next room. I punched in the code and swung open the door.

I stepped into the 'barn'! A beautiful, 50 x 50 foot, great room with a huge fireplace on one side; I could easily put thirty or forty people in here. The walls were of polished, log-hewn boards with matching floor and twelve-foot ceiling. They had installed four large ceiling fans with lights as well, and around the wall, subdued lighting that could be turned brighter or dimmer as desired.

Across the back of the huge room was almost floor to ceiling windows with automatic, powered drapes that open and close at the push of a button. The windows looked out over my "mountain stream;" only I still didn't have a mountain or a stream, it was a swamp! Pure, unadulterated, swampland! The view, however, was still very nice; a large, cleared area and the thick woods behind that. It provided the privacy that I wanted and would need. As I looked out I saw a large buck and two doe roaming across the yard. Perfect!

I crossed the room and entered the kitchen and dining area. They were oversized also and came complete with the latest appliances. Good for entertaining. But who would be entertaining out here? Continuing the tour I inspected the two large bathrooms and a large, master bedroom with its own bathroom.

Next was the 'Master Craftsman' room! My special work 'space'--- all of the latest IT equipment and electronic devices that I could ever possibly need as a special agent was in this room! This room had special access codes that required palm and facial recognition to enter! The walls were also reinforced with special materials.

The second floor was just as elegant and rustic as the first; three large bedrooms with baths for overnight visitors; not sure who that could possibly be. After completing my inspection I was happy with the results, Charlie and Verne had taken care of everything and the price tag had come to only $350 grand.

Good thing I had shipped more copper tubing to Mr. Truong before things got tough in South Vietnam and the Viet Cong took over. He had placed another six hundred thousand into my account, plus one million that I was to keep for him in case he could make it out of Vietnam and into the U.S. He was killed by the VC when they took over Saigon. I'm gonna miss old Truong. He was good people! He would have done a lot of good for his country.

Good old Vince, he kept the money invested for me and we watched it grow and Vince got his commissions and we were both happy; but sorry about Truong.

CHAPTER THIRTEEN

BACK AT HOME, IN my old neighborhood, I sat down to catch-up on the news and read where there were two more shootings and a drug bust just outside my "hood." I'm still curious about all the drug dealing that's going on. Something's still not quite right; especially with all the drug busts and arrests that's being made. Reading the local paper, it seems that pretty much the same hoods are being busted over and over. They are sent to jail and are back on the street before the arresting cops complete the arrest report. Things are going backwards. Somebody's got to be behind this. Somebody big!

Now that I have a place to work, maybe I can get a handle on what's going on.

My police scanner 'burps' and crackles and I hear the dispatcher say, " All units in the area of Loringwood Drive and Robney; report of a shooting at 506 Robney; a young kid is down; neighbors report a drive-by shooting just minutes ago. Be on the lookout for a black, '98 Chevy Impala with two suspects; use caution, they are armed and dangerous."

That's just four blocks from my 'hood'. They are getting closer again. I've got to get to the bottom of this. I've got to get to the root to this problem and cut it off. I guess I need to talk to some of the hoods who are pushing and dealing. It's time to venture out into the "hood" and talk with some folks who don't like to talk; might put up a little argument.

I put on a running outfit; this includes my 'back-pack., my Glock 9mm tucked into the back of my waist band. I head out for a jog around my neighborhood; it's about eleven o'clock; I want to see who may be out "pushing" and dealing. It didn't take long to spot a couple of guys on the corner. I knew one of them and knew that he had been arrested a few times for dealing, and sent to the local lockup; doesn't take him long to get back out on the street. He would be a good one to begin my discussion with.

"Hey Jeff, what are you up to man?" Jeff Ferguson was a small to medium type dealer, nothing big that put him away for long stretches at a time; just arrest, thirty to sixty days in lock-up then back on the street again.

Jeff turned, startled when he saw me. I think he almost shit in his pants. "I ain't doin' nothin', man. I'm just talking with some friends and minding my own business," he stammered. "What you doing out this time of night," he said, trying to calm his insides down. "Man, you ain't jogging this time of night; what you up too?"

"No, man, I'm just trying to get a little exercise to stay in shape," I said. "I haven't seen you around lately, where you been, off on a cruise or something?'

"Hell no Chip, I been on vacation, at the county's expense. You know they don't let me stay too long, they think I'm too valuable to keep locked up for long."

"How long did they keep you this time?" I asked.

"Two weeks and they told me to get back on "the job" or next time they would keep me and throw away the key." He laughed and said, "I know better than that. I make them too damn much money."

"By the way, I've been meaning to ask you something. You got time for a cup of coffee, I'm buying?" I said.

"Where we going to get coffee this time of night/"

"The Waffle House is open 24/7. I'll even buy late breakfast," I said.

"Sure" he said, "I'm always open for a freebie, even if it is only break-fast," he laughed.

"Let me jog back to the house and get my car and I'll be right back. No more than five minutes," I said.

We sat in a booth in the back of the Waffle House where we could have some privacy and quiet conversation; I ordered coffee; Jeff ordered two waffles, two eggs over easy, bacon, toast, orange juice and coffee.

"Looks like this little chat is going to cost me big-time, tonight," I said.

Jeff grinned, looked at me and said, "Hell, man, with all your money, we coulda' gone to the Waldorf and you woulda' never missed it."

He laughed, kind of nervously. He knew I was looking information for some reason. He just didn't know what kind of information, and about what, or worse yet, who!

"Relax, Jeff. We're just two old friends having breakfast together and talking; that's all," I said.

"Yeah right," he replied; still not looking all that comfortable.

"Seriously Jeff," I began, "This is strictly off the record; just conversation between you and me, nothing more. I just don't understand some things that are happening, and I would like to get to the bottom of what's going on in our 'hood.'

"We live in the same neighborhood. You don't want your kids growing up in an old, rundown, drug invested neighborhood, with a bunch of shootings and killings taking place every other night. Always afraid that somebody is going to shoot into your house, maybe kill one of your kids, or your wife. Or you," I told him.

Jeff just looked at me and said, "Who's going to stop it? Not the cops. Not the court. Not the Judge. They're the ones running the show. Ain't a damn thing me or you can do about it."

He looked away with a sad expression on his face.

"There are too many 'big-shots' involved and they making too much dough to give it up. They'll kill anybody they have to; anybody that gets in their way – me – you, don't make a damn to them," he said.

"That's what I wanted to talk with you about," I said.

"You and me; we can do something about it. We can create enough of an uproar, and kick enough ass to put a big-time scare into them. It might end some of your 'free vacations' at the county's expense though," I told him.

He chuckled , "Maybe that won't be too bad. I might even go straight; get a job; spend time with my wife and kids; I might even become a 'respectable' citizen again," he added thoughtfully, "If that's possible."

"It's possible," I said; "You may even become the local hero."

Jeff had already 'scarfed' up his two waffles and was finishing up the eggs, bacon, grits and coffee. He looked around to see who was in the restaurant.

It was now two a.m. way past my bedtime. You don't find many people in a restaurant at two in the morning.

Not seeing any other weird diners in the place, he turned back to me.

"You remember, a few years back, when that cop shot that dude in the back out on the highway, said he was running away when he tried to arrest him for drug dealing," Jeff said. "Story on the street, back then and still is, the dude wasn't running at all. He was standing still and was told to turn around and get in the patrol car. When he turned the cop 'popped' him in the back. He was dead before he hit the ground."

"Yeah I remember that. The cop was cleared and the papers said it was in the line of duty," I replied.

"Line of duty my ass! That cop is now the judge," Jeff said.

Something clicked in my mind! He was right. A couple of years after that incident, the cop had run for election for judge in the county. There was even some talk about how many other cops were out politicking for him; to the point that if a suspect, caught in an *infraction of the law*, promised to vote the 'right way', they would only receive a verbal warning. But if things didn't turn out the way the cops wanted, well the next time – and there would be a 'next' time.

The "Judge" was elected and held court, mostly for stuff like drug dealing, drug busts, traffic violations, etc. It began to make a little more sense to me now. My thoughts swiftly turned back to the trash bags in the barn!Although I had pretty much known all along the "where" the money had come from, I now knew at least one of the 'who's'.

CHAPTER FOURTEEN

THE NEXT MORNING I called my friend, Sam and told him I wanted to buy breakfast. He laughed, "Buy me breakfast? Hell Chip, just come right out and say it, 'you want something,' right?"

"Well, I did want to ask you a couple of questions," I answered.

"Yeah, questions like what?" Sam said.

"Tell you when I see you," I replied.

"Where," Sam asked?

"I'll see you at the Cut-Rate at 7:30 in the morning," I told him.

The Cut-Rate was an 'old-time' drug store that had an 'old-time' lunch counter and served the best, 'old time' breakfast and lunch you'll find anywhere. A few years ago they had even 'modernized'; they added a few booths. I knew we could have a conversation almost in private there. Most of the 'down-town' working people came here for breakfast or coffee every morning. Doctors, lawyers, the local cops and deputies and business people from all walks of life. Some of the biggest fish and hunting 'stories' you ever heard were told here. Clyde McMurphy owned and operated the Cut-Rate. He had inherited it from his father. In addition to everything else that needed to be done in a business, Clyde was also the Pharmacist. He had been known to 'prescribe' a medication for a friend when in need.

I got to the Cut-Rate about 7:15, went in and visited with the morning crowd for a few minutes and then took a booth in the back. Sam arrived right at 7:30 and after speaking to the regulars around the counter, he joined me.

"What's up Chip," he asked.

"Just the same old day-to-day stuff," I lied.

"What you want to talk about, Chip? You sounded like you had been doing some serious thinking. What's going on in that head of yours?

"I've been doing some serious thinking – and I want to do some serious talking with you," I said. "But, I need to know that you will not repeat anything we talk about or any idea we discuss," I added.

"Man, Chip. You know me. I don't tell anybody shit," He said.

"We've been through a lot of shit together, Sam. Some stuff that most anybody else wouldn't have survived and lived to tell about it.

"We've saved each other's lives more than once. You have always been a straight shooter with me, whether it was something I would like or not; and I've done the same with you. We don't pull our punches, we tell each other like it is," I continued.

"You really are getting deep, Chip. You're about to scare my butt," he said. But went on and said, "Just what have you got going that's not legal? Just because I'm a cop don't mean that I can get you out of trouble, or get you off if you get in trouble."

"I just need to know that if you don't agree with what I'm about to tell you, and ask of you, that you will just forget we ever talked," I told him.

"You know me well enough, we've been through enough together, and we've been friends and confidants long enough to know that if you shoot some asshole, I wouldn't say anything about it. Hell, I would probably shoot them for you," he said.

I knew he was telling the truth. I knew I could trust Sam with my life; in fact I already had, several times in Vietnam.

I began by telling him about my conversation with Jeff, our 'mutual friend." Only I didn't tell him Jeff's name. He knew Jeff, albeit it on a professional basis; he had arrested Jeff a couple of times for dealing.

I explained a little about the kick-backs from drug money; evidence that never made it to the station and the Evidence Locker. I told him about the judge and his power over the dealers and the cops.

Sam looked a little perplexed but not shocked.

Sam said, "Chip, you can get your ass shot off if anybody hears you talking, or even thinking like you're thinking. You and I talked a little about some of that crap going on before, and I know about some of it. I've even heard that there was some judge involved, but I don't know who he is. I'm not sure I want to know. I don't know who I can trust in the whole damn department anymore. Hell, I will probably get my ass shot off just for being seen with you."

"That's okay Sam," I said, "But somebody has to do something about the situation or this whole damn town is going down the tube.

"And, right now, I don't see anyone else giving a rat's ass about this town or anybody in it. They're all about getting rich off the dealers and users. They couldn't give a damn about the number of lives that are ruined and destroyed," I said.

The waitress finally came over and asked what we were having. We both ordered a big, country breakfast: country ham with 'red-eye' gravy, grits, a couple of eggs, coffee and toast. She wrote down our order and left us. She returned a minute later with our coffee.

We sat and sipped our coffee in silence; I could tell Sam was deep in thought. After about five minutes the waitress brought our breakfast.

We ate in silence.

We finished eating; the waitress took away the dirty dishes and filled our cups for the third time.

Sam broke the silence, "What do you want us to do, Chip?"

CHAPTER FIFTEEN

"WELL FOR STARTERS," I said, "We should probably do some careful planning. I want you to meet this friend I told you about; he is on the 'inside' of the dealing business; he wants out. He has begun to think of his family, his wife and two kids. He is afraid that some dark night he will be getting shots through his windows and doors, and his family will be killed or hurt. You know, 'drive-by random' shootings.

"We need somebody on the inside," I added. "It would be very valuable and probably necessary in order to accomplish what we set out to do."

"I suppose that's where I come in also," said Sam, "I'm on the inside of the police department and we're in constant contact with the sheriff's group too."

I briefed Sam on what I knew, and who the judge appeared to be.

"Too bad we don't have somebody in the courthouse also," I added.

"Hmm," said Sam, "let me work on that. I may know someone we can trust. There's a young lady who has made remarks about all the drug mess going on and nobody doing anything about it. When she talks about it you can tell she gets really pissed. She could be our 'inside' in the courthouse and the judge."

"We have to be careful, Sam, we don't want too many people involved in this. Never know when someone may slip up and say something they didn't mean to say," I said.

"She works for the Clerk of Court and handles all of the cases that come in; they also handle the confiscations – money and material. We might get a handle on how much is being skimmed off some of the busts that are being made. At least we'll have some idea of the amount.

"Next time she brings it up, and she does that real often, I'll let her talk about her latest case and feel her out about the amount turned in for the record. I usually have the scuttlebutt about what really went down and any money that was seized," Sam said.

"Does she know the judge," I asked?

"She knows him. He is always hitting on her. She doesn't like it and tells him to go hit on his wife for a change. He laughs and comes on stronger than before. She looks at him as if she could cut his throat and enjoy it.

You need to meet her," said Sam.

Dawn Summers was a beautiful, twenty-nine year old, natural blonde. At five-seven, 'and a half,' as she would describe herself, and 110 pounds, she filled out her form extremely well. She was friendly and very sexy looking. No wonder the lawyers hung out at the county Clerk's office all the time. They all were hitting on her. She probably had more free lunches and dinners than anyone else in the county. She was also single and had never been married.

"The 'right' man has never come around," she would say. "But I'm still looking, not in a hurry," she would add.

I met Sam outside the courthouse just before noon on Friday morning. He wanted me to meet Dawn. We walked into the Clerk of Court's office and this "blonde dream" walked up to us. Such beauty I had never seen.

Sam said, "Chip Storrington, meet Dawn Summers."

I must have been awestruck, because Sam said, "Chip, this is the young lady I was telling you about.

"Chip," he repeated, "Are you with us?"

Dawn laughed.

I said, in a kind of daze, "Aaah … I'm not sure. I may be in dream-land."

Sam laughed and said, "While we're waiting for you to wake up, why don't we go down to the Cut-Rate and grab lunch?"

"That sounds good to me," purred Dawn.

I didn't say anything, I just followed.

Dawn sat down in the booth and I sat beside her while Sam sat on the other side where he could face us as we talked.

Dawn turned in my direction and said, "This is one of my favorite quick lunch places. You can get a good meal or sandwich and still get back to work in short order."

When she turned, her knee brushed mine under the table. It was like I had been struck by a quick jolt of lightening that shot through my entire body. Was that on purpose, I thought? I must have blushed, because as I looked at her she smiled.

Sam grinned and said, "Chip if you think you can get it together, we can order now."

The waitress was standing there ready to take our order. All three of us ordered cheeseburgers and fries. Sam and Dawn ordered sweet tea; I ordered strong coffee. I needed to get my mind back on the purpose for our meeting.

Sam started the conversation by saying he had discussed with Dawn, some of what he and I had talked about earlier. And about some of the characters that I thought were involved.

Dawn said, "Yeah, I know one of the characters well enough. Unfortunately, I have to work with him all too often. He may be a judge, but he is also a 'butt-hole'! I dread to see him walk in. He heads straight to my desk and props his butt on the corner, leans over and tries to smell my cologne. Then he always has some cute-ass remark to make. I'd like to take that black robe he roams through the courthouse in and shove it down his throat!"

I laughed and asked, "You two been friends very long?"

Sam and I laughed while Dawn turned a deep shade of blush. She said, "I'm sorry, but he gets on my nerves and aggravates the hell out of me. He thinks he is God's gift to the female population; he is no kind of gift to anybody. I've heard a lot about his background; he has broken up the homes of three families."

"What do you know or have heard about his career and activities as a police officer and judge," I asked her?

Dawn replied, "There are a lot of stories and tales about how he handles a lot of his cases; he, the sheriff, and many of the guys on the police force are exceptionally close; unusual for a judge and mere patrolmen."

Sam spoke up, "I've heard a lot of the stories also. Back when he was just an undercover narc agent, he seemed to kind of 'run' the division; I guess he was a leader and got his superiors to follow his lead. After he got promoted to Lieutenant and officially headed up the group, I've seen him at work. The average cop was scared of him and did what he told them; although I don't personally know it for sure, but most of the guys seemed to start living a little better; I guess he started sharing some of the 'unofficial income' with them. They seemed happy anyway!"

Sam thought for a moment and added, "Knowing all this and proving it, is two different balls of wax!"

I said, "You are absolutely correct there, Sam. I don't have any idea right now, but we're going to figure a way. There is too much corruption going on in this city and somebody has to get to the bottom of it, and bring it out."

Dawn sat thinking over the entire conversation and responded, "If we're going to take this on and do something, we better put together a really good plan of action; and we better find us some help! The three of us will be found dead somewhere if we attempt it by ourselves." Then she added, nervously, "I'm not through living yet!"

With that we finished our cheeseburgers and headed back to the courthouse so Dawn could get back to work; Sam was going back to Police Headquarters, and I had a lot of thinking and planning to get done.

CHAPTER SIXTEEN

ME AND SAM WERE sitting in my old, 2004 Buick Rendezvous that had well over two hundred thousand miles showing on the speedometer; it was dark in the empty parking lot of an 'out-of-business' K-Mart Store on Broad Street. We were sipping on the cold remains of once hot coffee; waiting for my friend Jeff to show up; he had finally agreed to meet Sam and talk with us about some of the stuff he knew that went on in the city. We were parked close to the building, near the end where it was the darkest. We had been waiting for a half hour.

"Do you think he will show," Sam asked? "He probably doesn't care a helluva lot for cops, I'm sure he doesn't trust any of us."

I replied, "He'll show, Sam; the look on his face when he talked about his wife and kids, his family, told me a lot about Jeff; he's tired of the life, he's getting older and sorta wants to settle into a normal type life. I believe he'll show."

After another fifteen minutes I glanced in the rearview mirror and saw a figure hugging the wall of the old store, slipping around the side; it was Jeff! He quickly ran from the dark of the wall to the car and tapped on the door. I had already unlocked the back door; he jumped in to the back seat.

"Where's your car," I asked?

"Hell, man; I ain't bringing my car out here; somebody see me, I'm dead before tomorrow!" Jeff said.

I could believe that! He was right too; I knew it and Sam knew it also.

I turned in my seat where I could see Jeff better and Sam at the same time; "Jeff, I want you to meet Sam Dillinger, another friend of mine, he is a detective in the police department, been there a long time. He and I have been good friends for a lot of years; we were in Vietnam together and he saved my ass several times!"

"No more then you saved mine," Sam said

Sam and Jeff shook hands and Jeff said, "I've heard of you from some of my contacts and friends; they say you're the only cop they trust; that you are always square with them and treat them with some respect, whether they deserve it or not. You got a good reputation, man!"

"Thanks Jeff, I just try to do my best; everybody has the same rights," Sam replied.

Jeff looked over at me and said, "OK Chip, you said we could clean up this mess, how you propose we do it? How and where do we start," Jeff asked?

"That is the million dollar question," Sam chuckled.

Jeff said, "I can't just start telling you about things I know that are going down; they would figure out who was talking in a matter of minutes, and I would be dead in a matter of seconds!"

They both looked at me, Sam said, "You know Jeff can't be making a sudden change in his habits or the way he operates; he would be spotted right off. Any change has to be gradual and slow."

"You're right," I said. "Let's not make any changes in the way you work Jeff; you keep on doing what you've always been doing."

"What," Jeff exclaimed? "You want me to keep on dealing?" He looked at Sam and asked, "Y'all going to keep on arresting me and putting me in jail; even though you're sitting here telling me to keep on? Man that don't make much sense!"

"I think I'm following you, Chip" Sam said. "Jeff keeps up his usual routine; when he gets something he thinks we should know he commits something minor, we bust him, put him in the lock-up and we can interview him!"

"You got it!" I said. "It's legitimate, it's real and nobody knows any difference!"

Jeff thought about it for a few minutes and agreed, "I think that might work OK," he said. Then added, "I'm not going to tell you about the nickel and dime stuff; the little guys who do the small stuff to feed their family, their wife and kids; that's all they got, mostly good folks."

Sam and I agreed; we're not looking for the little dealers we want the big dealers, the bad cops and judges who are using their position and power to get rich off the backs of the little ones.

"Well," Sam said, "Since we've got an idea where we are headed with this, and somewhat of a plan, I have to get back to work; at my regular job before I get fired. In the meantime, we better figure out a tighter plan so we will know just what the hell we're doing."

I asked Sam, "Your regular job; what kind of 'regular' job are you working on these days?"

"I can never tell from one day to the next just what kind of case I'll be on," Sam replied. "Right now I'm checking on a neighborhood situation; not too far from your place, Chip. It seems that there are some illegal immigrants, Latinos, living in an old, run-down housing development over on Robney Street; it's owned by a former mayor, by the way; anyway the story is that they are afraid to complain to the police about being abused and robbed.

"They are hardworking people and don't cause any trouble to other folks; they just want to be left alone and not bothered. It sounds like there are a bunch of 'free-loaders' living across the street from them; ones who don't work at anything, just lay around drawing food stamps and unemployment and anything else they can get for free. The word on the street, and among the Latinos, is that those sorry bastards know when the Latinos get paid; so they rob them knowing the Latinos won't call the cops, because they are here illegally; they're afraid of being arrested and deported!

"It's really a sad situation; many of the duplexes they live in are in terrible shape. I understand some of the toilets don't work, the plumbing is all screwed up and when they complain to the rental agency all they get is the run-around. Again, they are too afraid to complain to the police or anyone else for fear of being deported. These are families we're talking about, women and children trying to make a life for themselves! They sneak into the good old USA, and get screwed!"

"You sound pretty uptight about that situation, Sam; what are you going to do about it; and how do you fix such a screwed up state of affairs," I asked?

Jeff said, "I've heard of that Sam! It's a pretty nasty set of circumstances. I feel sorry for those poor families; they are in a helpless situation – caught between the 'devil and the deep blue sea' and don't know how to get out!"

With that Jeff got out and left the same way he came in, sneaking along the dark side of the building. Sam and I waited another fifteen minutes to give Jeff plenty of time to be gone and clear, and then we left. I dropped Sam off back at headquarters to pick up his car and go home for the evening.

CHAPTER SEVENTEEN

I GOT BACK TO my house about midnight and decided it was time to take a stroll through my 'hood' since I had had a lot of other things on my mind lately. I dressed in my black outfit, got my MK-9 Makarov put the silencer on it and went out the back door in the direction of Robney Street. I saw several of my warning posters still where I had left them as I walked. But several blocks before Robney, I spotted a guy standing in front of one of my posters, it was on a telephone pole; he had a red magic marker in his hand and was writing obscene words on it. I couldn't say that I blame him, especially if I was a dealer.

I pulled out my MK-9, with the silencer, and took aim, just over his right shoulder, to the poster; I squeezed the trigger and the round went beside his right ear hitting the poster and showering splinters from the pole into his face. The red magic marker fell from his hand and he dropped straight down, to the ground; he was out cold! He must have thought that he was shot! I walked over to where he lay; his pants were wet and there was a puddle under him; he had peed in his pants!

I picked up the red magic marker and wrote on his white tee shirt, "Don't mess with my posters!"

I walked on toward Robney, it was pretty dark, most folks had gone to bed and quietened for the evening so I decided to give it up and go home myself.

At seven a.m. I'm sitting at the counter having coffee in the Cut Rate when Sam sits down beside me, he orders coffee also. "You're out bright and early," he said. "Did you hear about the big bust out on I-95 last night?" he asked.

"No," I replied, "I haven't seen the news or read the papers yet. What happened? Was it a big one?"

Sam said, "Probably the biggest ever in this area; scuttlebutt around the station this morning said it was a quarter-million, maybe more. The city cops are a little jealous since it was the county deputies that caught it. That means they won't get a cut, or at least not much."

"How much do you think will go to the evidence room?" I asked.

"Don't know," Sam replied; "But I can guarantee it won't be the full amount. That gang isn't about to let that much get away from them!"

I asked, "Half; you think half will be turned in?"

"I doubt it," he said. "More like . . . maybe fifty grand might go to evidence!"

"Damn," I said! A person could get pretty rich with that kind of payday!"

"Some have," said Sam!

"Bet I can name one," I added.

Sam's phone buzzed and he picked up, "Sam," he answered. "You're in luck, he is sitting right here with me, we're just having morning coffee, come on down and join us; you want to speak to him? Lunch? I'm sure that's okay with Chip, hold on; Chip you up for lunch with Dawn?"

"Of course; I'm always up for lunch, dinner or anything else with Dawn," I replied!

Sam laughed, "You heard the answer; we'll see you here at one."

Sam finished his coffee and said, "Well, it's back to work for me; I don't have the luxury of just loafing around all day."

I thought, "If he only knew half of what was going around in my head." I need to get back out to the Sweet Daddy Creek Club where I can concentrate and come up with a plan of some sort. After lunch I'll do just that, maybe spend the night there. Too bad I can't invite Dawn to join me; maybe later.

One o'clock lunch time with Dawn! The door opens, I look up and there she comes . . . not really walking, more like 'floating' towards me! But then the big ugly face of my best friend, Sam, follows her in. As we say here in Alcolu, 'DANG'! That's southern for DAMN!"Wipe that big smile off your face Chip, I'm having lunch with y'all," Sam laughed.

Dawn just smiled at us and sat down, next to me.

Sam laughed out loud and Dawn chuckled while they both looked at me.

"What? What's going on with you two? Y'all plan to pull something over on me?" I asked. "You don't get up early enough," I laughed.

The waitress came to the booth to take our order; Dawn and Sam ordered their usual cheeseburgers, fries, slaw and tea. I was hungry so I ordered the chicken and dumplings, sweet potato, collards, cornbread and sweet tea; with apple pie for dessert.

Dawn and Sam looked at each other, then at me. Sam said, "You must not have eaten for a week. You're probably planning on taking the rest of the day off and taking a nap."

I replied, "You know Sam, I've had those same thoughts, all morning. I'm glad you suggested it."

Dawn laughed and said, "You two are just nuts."

Dawn lowered her voice, looked around the Cut Rate and said, "The Judge came to see me this morning, along with two of his 'associates' from the sheriff's department. They were carrying this large bag filled with cash; $50,000 worth of cash! He said it was from a big drug operation they had set-up out on I-95 this weekend, where they made the bust. I-95 is the main corridor for transporting between Miami and New York."

I interrupted, "Were the two deputies the ones who made the stop and arrest?"

"They were part of the operations team," Dawn continued, "After the cash and drugs were confiscated, the two deputies were told to take it to the Judge to hold for the weekend, until they could bring it to the Clerk of Court's office this morning. After the drugs were inventoried and the cash counted and entered, they left. As they were leaving the deputies looked at the Judge, kind of laughed and one said, 'Fifty thousand bucks, not bad; I guess we all had a pretty good weekend!' the Judge motioned for him to be quiet."

"Rumor on the street last night and early this morning," Sam was speaking very low, "is that it was well over three hundred grand! Somebody made one huge haul off this; fifty grand turned in and no telling how much merchandise was picked up."

The waitress brought our food and we ate, mostly in silence, just some chit-chat about how the town was looking better and improving its image. Sam looked at me and said, "Chip I don't think I ever told you all about Dawn; maybe she has told you herself, about her background and training and wanting to be a cop and all that."

Dawn said, "We've not had the opportunity to just sit down and talk; heck, I don't know anything about Chip either, and how he got involved in all this stuff that's going on. Are you an undercover cop or special agent of some kind; something I've never heard of?" She asked.

We laughed and I told her, "No, nothing of the sort, just an interested citizen. But what about this special background of yours; I want to know more about that!"

We finished eating and ordered coffee and sat back and relaxed.

Sam said, "Dawn wanted to be a cop but she is too smart; the chief wants her to be a detective so he got her into the FBI Academy, up in Quantico. She finished number one in her class and they wanted to keep her. She even qualified for the FBI SWAT team. Dawn, you tell Chip your story, I've got to go back to work. I'll talk with y'all later."

Sam left us and I'm sitting there looking at Dawn, somewhat stunned.

"What, you don't think I could be a detective or an FBI agent?" Dawn asked.

"No, no; of course you could; you can be anything you want to be; you've certainly got the brains. Number one in the FBI Academy, SWAT team; Wow, that's really something! Congratulations!" I said. "I would like to hear more about your background and this desire to be a 'big time' cop.

Dawn smiled and made a move to leave and said, "Well, I would love to tell you, but it would have to be another time, I've got to get back to the job I'm paid to do. Otherwise, I won't have a job to get back to!"

I jumped at the opening, "When would be a good 'another' time for you?" I asked. "Like maybe a dinner, you know so we wouldn't be rushed for time and could talk?"

She stopped, thought for a moment, then said, "I really have a pretty busy week, but maybe Friday evening."

"Friday evening it is!" I said; "How about seven-thirty?"

As she was leaving she said, "Seven-thirty is fine. But we'll probably be talking before then anyway; see you later."

I got up and left with her; time to go to the Sweet Daddy Club.

CHAPTER EIGHTEEN

I TURNED OFF OLD highway 521 onto a narrow, partially muddy path, between a large 'clump' of bushes; after about twenty yards I made another sharp turn to the right, onto an even more narrow path, that headed into the heavily wooded area. The path was so winding that at times it seemed as if you were heading in the opposite direction. But after about a quarter of a mile or so I broke out into a small opening; there it was; my huge, old, run-down, falling apart, barn! It looked as if a pretty good wind would knock it over.

I stopped next to what remained of an old, rotted-out tree that some storm had taken the top half off years before. I pressed a button on my key fob and a small section of tree bark popped opened revealing a key pad; I punched in the special outside code; I didn't want any of the alarms in the 'barn' activated and setting off the total security system. I had designed my security in different phases; if someone came onto the property, it set-off the inside silent systems letting me know. I could check the cameras that covered the entire area. I drove on in and parked in the garage underneath the rear of the 'barn', next to my white FORD 150 pick-up that I used mostly on special assignments, when I didn't want to be identified; I went inside. My masterpiece!

I sat down in the great room; I had a lot of thinking and planning to get done. Let me see now: First, I've got a judge who is on the take, or he is running the whole show; Second, we have several regular uniform cops, maybe more, who seem to be following orders from the judge and possibly someone else; Third, I'm trying to clean-up my 'hood', and that involves not only the dealers, but a battle between Hispanics and their black neighbors who are robbing them when they get paid.

I guess cleaning up the 'hood' will have to take a lower priority; the judge comes first; but, that may help with all the other crap going on also. I sat back in my recliner, leaned it back and the day ended.

My phone woke me about ten-thirty; that's ten-thirty PM; like night time, dark outside! It was an old friend, Jerry Buckner, the Governor of Virginia.

"Sorry to call you so late, Chip," he began, "But I need some advice and your help."

"I was still awake Jerry," I lied, "What's going on in the 'love state'?"

"People have gone completely out of their minds," he said. "Have you been watching any news down there, about the riots and pulling down statues, destroying businesses and looting? I tell you Chip I believe our country is being taken over by mob rule!

"But I'll also tell you another thing, they may get away with it in Seattle, Portland and other places; but I'll be damned if I'm going to let them do that here in Richmond! That's where I need 'some' special help. Are you still doing special assignment operations, in country, like before?"

I replied, "You know me Jerry, I go where I'm needed, and of course where the money is."

Jerry said, "I don't know how you, or anyone else for that matter, can actually stop it; but somebody has to get to the leaders of these gangs and have a serious talk with them; we don't need any more of this violence, it's tearing the country apart. These gang members, you know they are part of this state and this country as well; at least most of them. But as you and I know, they have been infiltrated by Antifa and other foreign elements; which I think is a bunch of foreign special agents at that. If you recall, when Iran changed their caliphate, one of the first things they did was to blow up most of the country's monuments and statues, especially the religious ones! That's what this group is beginning here in our own country. I tell you Chip, this is only the beginning!

"I believe if someone who can speak the language of the regular, peaceful protesters, can get to them and get their attention for a few moments, they will stop this rioting and tearing the city down.

Do you think you or some of your contacts can talk with them?" he added.

I told Jerry, "I don't know if they will listen to anybody at this point. I think it goes much deeper than that!"

What I didn't tell Jerry was that I had been thinking about the mess for several days; I can speak their language and plan to do just that.

Jerry spoke again, "Chip you're familiar with Monument Avenue that's lined with statues of famous Confederate, and national heroes from the Civil War and beyond, well I've received information that the rioters and gangs are planning a protest there this weekend. They are planning to pull down as many statues and do as much damage as they can. I've got to find a way to stop them; and fast!"

"Let me think about it, Jerry; you know we have the same problem down here, just not as bad as Richmond and DC and the others. I'll get back to you before the weekend," I told him.

"Thanks Chip; the sooner the better."

I sat back in my large recliner in front of the huge fireplace with no fire, too hot outside, but very nice and comfortable here inside the Sweet Daddy Creek Club; I just sat and relaxed and did some thinking and strategic planning. I will probably need some help and the only person that I know who might even consider such a volatile action scenario is Sam. He's actually the only one that I would trust.

I looked at the clock, eleven-fifteen; not too late to call Sam. I punched in his number and let it ring several times. Finally a tired, sleepy voice answered, "Hello."

"I didn't wake you up did I Sam, it's not even midnight yet," I asked?

"Chip don't you ever sleep? What's so important that it couldn't wait 'til morning," he said?

I gave him a quick rundown of my conversation with Jerry and asked his thoughts on the situation and suggestions on how we could handle the matter. After about fifteen minutes we agreed to get together in the morning to discuss it further. Not ready for sleep I went down to the lower level where the garage is located and to my weapons room off to the side, behind a hidden door. This is where I keep my weapons secure.

I went to a large cabinet with doors and three large drawers underneath. I opened the bottom drawer and picked up one of the two cases containing a special weapon; a sniper rifle with a telescopic scope powerful enough to bring a target into focus from over 850 yards with unbelievable accuracy; each rifle also had a suppressor to keep the noise level down. The cases contained a fully equipped Sako TRG M10 designed especially for precision sniper operations. I keep both locked and loaded with two magazines of eleven rounds each of 7.62x51mm, or I can switch to the Winchester .300 Magnum magazines.

Sam and I both had used such a weapon in Vietnam on several occasions. They got the job done! He would probably crap in his pant when I told him what the plans I had in mind were. I checked both cases, rifles and the supply of ammunition; satisfied I went back upstairs and to bed.

I walked into the Cut Rate at seven-thirty and there sat Sam, he already had a cup of coffee in front of him.

"You're out early this morning," I said.

Sam replied, "When somebody calls you at midnight and lays a major problem on you, you just might find it hard to go back to sleep too! You kept me awake all night, my friend!"

"Sorry about that Sam, but I had to talk with somebody and you're the only one I could call at that time of night," I said.

"You could have called me," said a voice from behind.

We both turned and saw the smiling face of Dawn.

"What are you doing out so early," Sam asked her?

"I had a lot on my mind also," she replied; "and I've got a lot of work to get done so I thought I may as well get up and come on in. Besides, I figured you two would already be here to buy my coffee," she smiled.

I told her, "Dawn, we'll even buy you a full breakfast; lunch; dinner; you just name it!"

"Now that's pretty generous," she said, "especially since you're supposed to be buying my dinner Friday evening anyway."

"Oh no, I haven't forgotten, but there may have to be a change of plans," I said. "Sam and I were just beginning to discuss a situation that came up last night, and we may have to be out of town for most of the weekend."

"Out of town, what are you two up to; is this some sort of special ops thing you have going, and not letting me in on it," she asked?

"Beats the heck out of me, Dawn," Sam said, "Chip and me talked about something last night, but I haven't heard anything about 'out of town'!"

"I started coming up with a plan after we talked last evening," I told Sam.

"And, this doesn't involve our operation concerning the judge and law enforcement people," I said, looking at Dawn.

Dawn, looking kind of disappointed asked, "Does this mean that I only get to work in just this one area? I have been pretty excited about the three of us working as a team, on different projects; maybe even special ops missions!"

I was somewhat shocked, and it showed as I stammered, "What special ops missions; what kind of team did you have in mind; and what would we be doing . . . as a team . . . that is?"

Sam was equally shocked! He asked Dawn, "What is it that you think we do? We've done some special assignments on occasions; pretty dangerous ones I might add, but that doesn't mean we are into something every day or every week. Chip and I have just taken on worthwhile projects as they come up and people ask for our help, that's all!"

"I get all that," said Dawn. "I figured that out awhile back, just watching and listening to the two of you talk and how you act. Y'all aren't as smart and secretive as you may think! I want to work with you! That's why I went to the FBI Academy; I wanted to be a special agent and have a little excitement in my life. I'm not ready to settle down just yet!"

They both turned and looked at me; I'm just sitting dumb-founded at all that I'm hearing; almost in a state of shock myself. I just kept sitting there in silence, not really knowing what to say to either. Both kept looking at me and waiting for me to speak. I sat and sipped my coffee; they kept looking back and forth between each other with a quizzical expression on their face.

I took another sip of coffee, slowly got up and walked to the restroom. After about five minutes I returned to the table. As I approached, I said, "Good morning; how the hell are you two this fine morning?" I sat down and took a sip of coffee.

Dawn and Sam looked totally bewildered at each other and back again at me, neither spoke.

Maxine, our waitress, the same one who normally waited on us, came up and said, "Are y'all going to order breakfast, or are you just going to sit there in a daze all day?"

Dawn 'snapped' to first and told her, "I'll have the small stack of pancakes with bacon, and more coffee."

Sam ordered, "Sausage, grits and eggs over easy with a side of toast for me."

Maxine looked at me and said, "Well Mr. Chip, are you finally awake enough to order your own, or maybe you would like for Dawn to fix your breakfast?"

Sam's laugh shook the table almost spilling the coffee pot that Maxine had sat down on the edge!

Dawn laughed also, choking on a mouthful of coffee she had just taken.

"I believe I'm surrounded by a bunch of smart asses this morning," I said! "If I'm going to have to put up with these two today, you better bring me something with plenty of energy. Bring me the country ham and grits with red-eye gravy, two eggs over easy, toast, jelly and more coffee!"

"Huh," Maxine said, "That won't give you more energy, more'n likely it'll give you a heart attack; just don't have it here," she said as she started back to the kitchen.

Sam said, "Well, welcome back to the real world, Chip; I'm glad you could join us."

I looked at Dawn and asked her, "Are you serious about wanting to be part of a team; a group of guys who never know for sure where they're going or if they will ever get back . . . alive, that is?"

"I'm as serious as that heart attack Maxine mentioned; that's why I went to the Academy," she replied. "I told you I want some excitement in my life before I die!"

"If you do, you just may well die before you get old," I told her!

"He is telling you the truth, Dawn," Sam said. "This is something you better think about a long time before you jump into something of this nature."

Dawn, looking very serious said, "I have been, I've been thinking about something like this since before I went to the FBI School; I know what I'm doing, if you two will let me work with you, you won't be sorry."

Sam and I looked at each other, then we looked down at the table and just sat there for a few moments. Our concentration was broken when Maxine brought our breakfast and said rather loudly, "All right my friends eat heartily and enjoy!"

We ate our meal in complete silence, neither of us speaking. I was deep in thought about the Sweet Daddy Creek Club; it was my private, quiet, get away from it all, place; my happy place; it was also my headquarters. Even Sam wasn't aware that I had it, in fact no one else did; I had never mentioned it to anyone else.

My thoughts were running along the lines of: *'if we're going to operate as a special ops team, we have to have a team headquarters, I guess this is probably the time to bring the team on board. I never had any doubts about the loyalty and confidence of either Sam or Dawn. Sam and I had been in plenty of battles and scrapes together and knew we could count on the other. Dawn was new to this style of life, how would she react under fire, would she be one we could rely upon when the chips were down?'*

I looked up and locked eyes with both Sam and Dawn and asked, "Could you two meet with me about six-thirty this evening?"

Dawn spoke first, "Sure, where?"

"Me too," Sam said.

"How about in the back parking lot of Logan's Steakhouse," I asked?

They both agreed and we finished our breakfast and left.

CHAPTER NINETEEN

ONLY A FEW CARS sat in the parking lot of Logan's when I pulled in at six-fifteen. I came early to sit and think for a few minutes and to observe others as they came and went. I guess it was more to reassure myself that I was making the right decision to let Sam and Dawn in on my operations. With Sam I was never in doubt, but I had not known Dawn for very long. I wanted to be sure that it wasn't just because she was so damn beautiful! Although I had already checked her out; qualifications, background, the FBI Academy, college, high school and any place else that might have or ever had a contact with her, she was clean! I was really happy about that too.

I saw Dawn's car as she pulled in and parked beside me, then Sam's pick-up came in and pulled into the space on the opposite side of Dawn. As they arrived each got out and got into my large, black Buick Enclave.

"OK, we're all here," said Sam; "Now where?"

"For starters, we're going out to my place, where we can sit quietly and talk about what we do; individually and as a team. You're both in for a huge surprise tonight and I almost feel like I should ask y'all to take an oath of silence or allegiance, or something; maybe a pledge of loyalty to the team as we form, maybe I should say IF we form as a team," I announced!

"Man, you're creepy as hell, Chip; what are you talking about? You say we're going out to your place, you mean you're taking us to your hood; you know we can't talk there, we're apt to get shot just for being there!"

Dawn said excitedly, "Creepy maybe, but still exciting; lead on Chip!"

I started the engine and drove out of the parking lot and took a left in the direction of 'my hood'. At the intersection of Broad Street and the Camden highway I turned toward Camden.

Sam said, "You're not taking us to the hood are you Chip?"

"Nope," I replied, "relax and settle back for the ride; it'll only take us about thirty minutes to get to where we're going. I told you, y'all are in for a big surprise."

Dawn laughed and said, "You're right Sam, he is a little creepy tonight."

I laughed it off and responded, "We'll see who is the creepiest when we get to our new headquarters."

In unison both Dawn and Sam almost yelled, "Headquarters?"

Sam kept talking, "What are you talking about Chip; what kind of headquarters; headquarters for what?"

"If we are going to work as a team," I began explaining the set-up; "Especially a special ops type team, with missions in different locations, we need a quiet, secure place to get ourselves and plans organized. It's not something that I was keeping from you Sam, it began as my special retreat; a place I could go, lay back and just plain relax and put everything else behind me, no worries. But the more I thought about it, and the more I planned it, it kind of grew into a combination of a retreat, a hideout, and then my headquarters. No one else knows about this, until now. You two will be the first besides me to ever see it.

"As of right now it is our headquarters! I wasn't exactly joking when I mentioned that I should ask each of you to take a loyalty oath about this; I was including myself in the oath also, for your protection, too! Sam, you and I have known each other long enough and been through some tough battles; I always knew you had my back, and I think you know the same as far as I'm concerned.

"Dawn, I haven't known you for very long but Sam recommended you very highly and has a lot of confidence in you; that's good enough for me. Besides, as I said, I have checked you out thoroughly and I think you're a good fit for whatever may come our way.

"Now, with all that said, if either of you don't want to be a part of this; because it can, and at times will get dangerous; now is the time to say so and you can pull out with no B-S or hard feelings We can turn around right now and go back, have a nice dinner and go home for a comfortable evening."

"You are absolutely crazy Chip" Dawn exclaimed! You've just described exactly what I told you that I have been looking for; no way am I pulling back! You want an oath; I'll give you an oath!"

Sam just remarked, "Chip, you are so full of shit; if you think your little speech could ever make it cross my mind not to be included, you're more full of it than I thought! I'm like Dawn; you want an oath, how many copies?"

I laughed, "Alright, I get the picture; you're both going to think about it! I was pretty certain that you guys would be in for it, or I would never have considered mentioning it. But I had to be certain that you both understood what you were getting in to and the dangers involved. Sam I know you already know the ins and outs of special operations, but we just need to be sure that Dawn understands and can react instantaneously in situations that call for it."

Dawn spoke up after being quiet for most of the ride so far, "Hey guys, I already know that I'm a female in what used to be an all-male outfit, but that doesn't cut it; neither of you ever put yourself in danger to try to save me from anything. I'll hold my own or I won't be worth a nickel to you when the going gets real tough. You've told me "we'll have each other's back" well that goes both ways, you can count on me to have your backs, too!"

We had already passed through Rembert and heading North on highway 521 when I started slowing down; it's very dark out with no moon to guide us, I spot a certain bush, my landmark, and turn in off the road onto a small, pitch-dark path and took another right behind several large 'clumps' of tall bushes and towering pine trees..

Sam asked, "You taking us to the woods? Do you really know where you're going Chip? Dawn, we better watch ourselves, we are in uncharted territory; I have no idea where in hell we are!"

Dawn laughed out loud, "Are you scared, Sam? Don't worry, like I said, I've got your back!"

We all laughed as we pulled into the small opening where the Sweet Daddy Creek Club was located. I had not told them the name yet. It was so dark you could only see a form toward the back of the clearing, couldn't tell what it was though. I stopped next to the old tree and reached out, I pushed the button on my key fob and the little door popped open.

I heard Sam say, "Damn!"

I punched in the code to turn off the inside alarm system then I punched another code and small lights came on illuminating the small path leading to the 'barn'. Based on a time delay code I had entered at the tree panel, several flood lights came on as we got closer, they lit up the barn and the entire area.

I heard Dawn draw in a deep breath and slowly said, "Wow . . . that looks like a . . . "

"Barn!" exclaimed Sam. "Chip are you taking us to a barn, in the middle of nowhere; it looks like it's about to fall over!"

I laughed and replied, "That barn is my Sweet Daddy Creek Club! You're going to like it!"

I decided to take them in the front door and watch their reaction when they first saw everything, including just getting in through the security system. We walked to the steps, which looked as if they wouldn't hold either of us. Dawn and Sam just stood there and watched. I pulled back an old wood board to reveal the security pad buttons and punched in the code and opened the outer door; Dawn and Sam followed.

Sam remarked, "That didn't feel like a wood floor or that it was about to fall in when I stepped on it; it felt more like concrete."

"It is," I said as I stepped to the second door and opened a second, hidden security panel; I punched in a different code and opened the door into the first floor main entrance and directly into the great room. I stopped and turned to look at Sam and Dawn; they were standing wide-eyed, just staring at everything they could take in; really in disbelief.

"Well, what do y'all think; think this will make a good headquarters to operate from," I asked?

There was no answer as they stood there in complete silence, just looking around and turning again to reassure themselves they weren't dreaming.

Dawn regained her voice first and said, "WOW, this is some barn! Wow, I've never seen anything like this."

Sam spoke up, "Tell me when I wake up, and explain to me what it was that I saw in my dream!"

I laughed and told them, "We'll take the twenty-five cent tour a little later; right now take your time and just kind of wander through the whole place then we can sit down and talk; I'll let you in on the entire story of how this came to be; and why I call it the Sweet Daddy Creek Club."

After about fifteen minutes or so, Dawn and Sam came back into the great room, sat down and Sam said, "Chip this is some kind of place; I've never seen anyplace like it, in all of my travels; it's beautiful!"

Dawn looked flabbergasted and said, "This is a dream kind of place; it is unbelievable! But why out here in the middle of some dark woods where nobody will see it? And why make it look like a run-down barn; one that's about to fall over if a wind was to hit it? I don't understand that at all," she exclaimed!

"Well, let me explain," I said. "The Sweet Daddy Creek Club used to be an old 'Negro Saturday Night juke joint type place' built back in the late twenties or early thirties. It was a place where the old time black folks could go on a Saturday night, after picking cotton all week, and "let their hair down!" Loud music from the old jukebox could be heard across three counties. There would be a lot of dancing and 'jivein' going on. You can bet there was a lot of moonshine making the rounds too. The club was kind of in the heart of 'moonshine country' in the middle of South Carolina.

"I found it by chance when I used to drive old state road number 521, one of the narrow, two-lane, back roads between Alcolu and the North Carolina state line. I would always notice this old sign propped up against a tree, near a small path that looked like it led deep into the woods. It was just an old, faded out, hand-painted, wooden sign. But it would catch my eye every time I saw it – "Sweet Daddy Creek Club." That's all it said.

"About fifteen years ago that sign got the best of me. I stopped one day and parked on the side of the road and walked down a little path. I never did see anything or anybody. Once back on the road, I drove to the nearest house I could find to ask about the old club. I soon found an old black man, must have been in his eighties, and he remembered the old Sweet Daddy Creek Club. He used to go there on Saturday nights when he was in his late teens. His name was James T. Ferguson. "But just call me "Jimbo!" he said.

"This was the first of many visits with Jimbo; we became close friends. I haven't seen him in a while though; I've got to check on him. We would sit and talk for hours and drink a beer or two. He told me that his daddy and granddaddy were big in the 'shine' business. They had the biggest and best still anywhere 'round here." He would laugh and tell me how he used to haul that shine 'round three counties.' That's how they survived in poor times.

"I asked him if he was afraid of getting caught, Nah, he would say, the police were more crooked than we were. He said he was stopped one night when his granddaddy was with him, when the policeman came up, his granddaddy went to the back of the car with the officer; he saw him hand the officer some money, then reach in the trunk of the car and hand him a jar of that 'shine,' and that was the end of it. He said they went on their way."

Dawn spoke up and said, "That's a lot of reminiscing Chip, it's a great, wonderful story and I can even feel some of what I think you're feeling about this place; it's very special. I can even think back in time, like you were describing, with Jimbo, and bring tears to my eyes.

"Hell, me too," Sam blurted out with a sad look on his face. "But this must have cost two fortunes Chip. I knew you had plenty of money, but didn't know you could afford something like this; this is your private mansion, or castle, or whatever you want it to be."

"As I told you earlier, if we are going to operate as a team it's important that we have a central operating point for planning and carrying out missions and special ops. This may be a little inconvenient, out here in the woods, away from everything, but it is private and it is secure!"

"Yeah," exclaimed Sam, "I noticed that; first when you stopped by that old tree and the side of it opened and there was that security panel; then only after we reached a certain point did the outer lights come on."

Dawn said, "When they came on I saw two deer run off into the woods."

"Deer and several other kinds of animals wander around out there at night," I said.

Sam continued, "Then when we went up those 'rickety' steps, I thought I was going to fall through, but they didn't budge at all; I knew something was going on, but when you popped open the old piece of board siding and I saw up close the security panel, I realized then you had something very special sitting here."

"After seeing the inside, I don't believe there is any danger of a storm blowing this over," Dawn said.

Sam said slowly, "I'm beginning to get the picture Chip. Your old Vietnam connection helped finance this; the one you told me about years ago; I'll be damned! That is great! I agree with you wholeheartedly about a headquarters; this is perfect! I love it!"

"I agree also about needing a headquarters, and I'm with Sam, this is absolutely perfect; but one question, this is your private place, your retreat; are you saying that you are giving us full access to come here, anytime we need to?" Dawn asked.

I replied, "That's what it sounds like doesn't it? Of course, this is now the headquarters of the 'Sweet Daddy Creek Team'; code name: 'SDCT'! Now isn't that wild!

"But it will still be my 'Happy Place'; the place where I can get away from the rest of the world; my private spot to come to and do nothing, just relax sit back and think."

We spent the next three hours going through the entire barn from room-to-room and top-to-bottom, including the garage spaces in the back and the weapons room. Sam suggested we might need to add additional armament items to the room from time to time.

I gave both a slip of paper that had the codes and told them, "Remember these codes; you'll need them to get on the property and to get inside the barn. Do not, under any circumstances, lose the codes or let anyone else see them; my suggestion is to memorize them and eat the slip of paper," I said, only half-jokingly.

Sam said, "I know you're joking, but I also know you're serious; we're going to have to be very careful about what we talk about and aware of who may be in listening distance. Now Chip, about this project you have in mind for this weekend; you realize it is already Tuesday evening and we haven't even begun to discuss it. Will it involve all three of us or just you and me?"

"Alright, here's the deal," I began. "First, when I tell you what the mission is, you may not want to participate, and that is okay, it's your choice. Secondly, I'm not sure how you will fit in on this Dawn, this came up before you got involved."

Dawn interrupted, "If I'm part of the SDCT, then I am already involved and I will do my part, whatever it is!"

I looked at Sam and said, "You and I know that some of the 'projects' we're called on to accomplish, aren't exactly legal; in fact they can be criminal; I don't think we talked to Dawn about that side of it, and I haven't told her yet either."

"Well, when we talked about the team, I didn't give it a thought, I just assumed that Dawn would, automatically understand that the nature of this life would sometimes call for doing some things that were not exactly 'legal,'" Sam replied.

Dawn spoke up kind of exasperated, "Look you two, I've read enough mysteries and covert ops books and seen enough movies, that it has already crossed my mind; I know it's a dangerous business, so forget trying to figure what's best for me. I sincerely appreciate it, but I will hold my own or I don't belong here. The gamble, from the way I see it, is yours!"

With that settled, I said, "Alright then, let's get down to business. This will be the very first 'co-op' mission for the team. A close friend of mine happens to be the governor of Virginia and all these protestors are giving him hell; I'm sure you've seen it on the news or read about it. These paid anarchists, or Antifa, or whatever they call themselves, are planning to pull down a bunch of historical statues this weekend. I don't know if either of you are familiar with Richmond and its Monument Avenue or not; but the street has huge statues down both sides of the street, and in the median; statues of Confederate, Union, and other heroes of the Civil War and beyond.

"Our mission is to prevent it from occurring and or stop it if it gets started! Not only that, but right here in South Carolina, in Columbia, there are plans to do the same thing this weekend. I think it is a coordinated effort but it may just be happenstance. We get paid for the one in Richmond; if we do the same here in South Carolina it will be gratuitous, but I believe it will be a big help to us, and the country in the long run."

Sam said, "There may be a hundred or more protestors in each these; what do you propose, what type of plan have you come up with? The three of us could never hold back a determined crowd as large as that, a hundred police can't do it!"

"I know that," I said. "Here's where the criminal element comes in. Sam, you and I have talked, maybe not seriously, about the way to stop something like this, but it may be the only way at the moment. What these Antifa folks do, in order to pull over a statue of this size, is to send one person up to the top of the statue and loop or tie a large rope or chain around the neck of the statue; then with enough manpower, or a pick-up backed up to it, they can topple it. Remember, these protest leaders and Antifa people are highly paid to do their dirty work and stir up trouble among the citizens. It's destroying our country!

"My thought at this point is we take out the person who gets to the top; I'm talking about a sniper shot from a distance; using a noise suppressor so no one will hear the shot. When that person hits the ground I believe the protestors will back away, especially if they see a large bullet hole in his head! I repeat; these protest leaders and Antifa people are highly paid to stir up trouble among the citizens; they're very good at it, they have been well trained. It's destroying our country!

"Whoever takes the shot will have plenty of time to slowly leave the area."

There was dead silence, no pun intended. Several minutes passed before anyone spoke.

Dawn asked, "Chip you also mentioned Columbia, that this Antifa has plans to destroy monuments or statues there; what do you have in mind for Columbia?"

"This is where it gets kind of 'hairy' and a little complicated," I replied. "If we're going to take someone out, permanently, it needs to make a statement to all of these groups, where ever they may be. So, my initial thought is to take another of these leaders out . . . at the exact same time!"

Sam asked, "How in hell do you propose to do that, Chip, at the exact same time?"

"That's where the 'hairy' and complicated comes in," I said. "I take the one in Richmond and you and Dawn take the one in Columbia. We synchronize our watches, we get in place and set-up early enough and keep a close eye on the protestors. We will be in radio or phone contact at all times so we can time our shots, assuming of course that is their plans. I'm thinking that this Antifa group is trying to make a dramatic impact by timing it close. Either way, if that doesn't work, we each take our shots and get the hell out. In the meantime, we will need to locate a vacant building, apartment or hotel room with windows that will open, that may be a little touchy and hard to find. That's why we have to run all of this down prior to the weekend. If there is the slightest hitch in getting set-up, or in accomplishing the assignment, we abort! We will not take any chances under any circumstances; understood?"

Dawn asked, "What will I be doing; how will I be helping?"

"This will be your assessment run, Dawn; you will receive first-hand experience of being on the scene and observing all the action as it goes down," I told her. "I'm flying to Richmond tomorrow morning to locate a place near where the statues of Robert E. Lee and George Washington are situated. Maybe some others also; this maniac group has mentioned several others. I really don't think it matters who it is, they only want to create chaos; we're going to stop it, one way or another!"

Sam worriedly said, "I have heard someone mention that the statue of Washington, at the foot of the steps to the State Capital was coming down this weekend; that's got to be it. That's where they will hit in Columbia."

"I'm off tomorrow," Dawn spoke up, "Sam if you can get away, we can go check it out and find a secure spot to set-up and work from."

"Sounds like a plan to me," Sam said.

"Me to," I added, "We will meet back here tomorrow night, finalize a plan of action and get the equipment that we'll need together."

"Whoa up," Sam said; "We better meet at the Cut Rate or someplace where I, and Dawn, know how to get to. At least for me, I would never find this barn again in a hundred years."

"Me either," said Dawn laughing. "I'm going to have enough trouble memorizing the codes you gave us."

"All right, make it the Cut Rate, how about six, in the back parking lot; you can leave your cars there or follow me in yours," I told them.

CHAPTER TWENTY

I PULLED IN BEHIND the Cut Rate Drug Store at six-o-five and saw Sam's and Dawn's cars waiting. I parked in between the two; they had just arrived they said, as they got into my car.

"Did you decide to follow or ride with me to the barn," I asked?

"Both," Sam said. I'm going to follow, so at least one other person will know how to get there," he hesitated then added, "maybe; I'm not sure I'll remember which bushes to drive in to, even later. Dawn will go with you; you should also have her follow you in daylight; that place is not easy to locate."

Sam got back in his car and Dawn climbed in beside me. We drove out and turned right onto Broad Street until we veered right onto Highway 521, through Rembert. After about twenty-five minutes it was getting pretty dark. I began slowing down and watching for a small reflector I had placed about twenty yards before my entrance, to give me time to spot it and make the turn; I pointed it out to Dawn also. On the drive Dawn and I just chit-chated but I did emphasize our Friday night dinner date, even if we had to postpone it because of the mission. I was taking a 'liking' to this girl!

We made the turn and saw Sam's headlights in the rearview mirror as he made the turn also; we passed through all the security check-points, the outer lights came on and we parked in the garage at the back. Inside, we went into the great room dropped our jackets, briefcase, folders or whatever we were carrying and went into the kitchen area.

Sam said, "I hope you've got some food in here, I didn't eat lunch and haven't had time to catch anything else either."

"I ate lunch," Dawn said, "But it's supper time now; let's see what Chip keeps on hand for guests."

"You're going to have to help yourself," I responded, "There is stuff in the fridge and there is the pantry and it has can soups and stuff; you have to fix your own though. There is a variety of drinks also."

After snacking we gathered in the 'work' room as I call it, it's actually a small conference room with a small size conference table and chairs where a group of six or eight could work.

"Let's get down to work," I said; "we've got some strategic planning to do. Now, here's what I came up with in Richmond; the statue this group is panning on taking down is the Robert E. Lee on Horseback statue in the center of Robert E. Lee Memorial Circle on Monument Avenue; that would make the largest impact on the public. There is a mid-range, five story hotel located a little less than two blocks away. I have booked a room facing the Memorial Circle on the fifth floor for Friday and Saturday night.

"Barring any slip-ups, whoever climbs up the statue with a rope or chain in their hands, will come down much faster than going up. One shot, through the head, clean; and I'm out of there; they'll probably first think that the person slipped and fell, they won't hear the shot! Since I will have weapons and ammo with me, I'll have to drive to Richmond. I don't think the airlines would appreciate me hauling a sniper rifle on one of their flights. Now let's see what you have for Columbia."

Dawn looking a little perplexed said, "You said the hotel was almost two blocks away from the target, that will have to be some shot to be that accurate and with a special weapon, too."

Sam grinned, "That's what I was talking about Dawn, it will be a sniper shot, with a special weapon; and I'm sure Chip already has the necessary equipment for the occasion."

"We will take a look at what we need in a few minutes," I said.

Sam continued, "Dawn and I scoped out the area around the statehouse and the best point, we believe, is the old Columbia Hotel, it's a block away and with all the noise these buttholes make, no one will be able to hear the shot. Like you said, the first one to the top is the first one down, then, we're out of there."

"It sounds as if we're all on the same page," I remarked; "So I assume you both are still in; but understand, it's not too late to back out if you're uncomfortable with what we have to do. We will have other assignments along the way that may not be as blatantly criminal as this one. I will certainly understand if you want out."

"You're not talking me out of this," Dawn said quickly!

Sam laughed and said, "Let's go show Dawn the weapons we'll be using."

We went down to the garage underneath the back of the barn and to the special weapons room with its own security set-up.

Sam whistled and said, "Damn Chip; I have never in all my 'born days' seen anything like you have established here. I believe you've got the Pentagon beat. You've got more security than the White House!"

I unlocked the door and we went into the weapons room and I heard Dawn draw a deep breath, "Wow," she said; "Who would ever believe a place like this out in the middle of nowhere! This is probably the most secure and most unlikely place in the entire country," she exclaimed!

They both stood looking at the wall before them that held all kinds of weapons that I had collected over the years; AK47 assault rifles, AR15s, several shotguns, handguns, a Browning automatic rifle, plus numerous handguns of various caliber and makes from several different countries. I punched in another code and a hidden drawer came sliding out from under the wall of weapons revealing several other weapons: two RPGs, a couple of portable mortar launchers and several sniper rifles, all with telescopic scopes and noise suppressors. The entire room looked like an assassin's home.

I picked up two of the sniper rifles and handed one to each.

I said, "Sam I know you've used one of these before, but Dawn have you ever had the opportunity to fire one, maybe at the Academy?"

"No, but I'm sure you two will teach me, besides, I'm a fast learner," she remarked. "But," she added, "Where would you teach me? You certainly can't be firing weapons around here without someone noticing and reporting it."

Sam asked Dawn, "Didn't you notice the swamp out back? You'll be able to see it in the daylight, hard to tell what it is at night; but if you look across the swamp, you'll see a large embankment, a 'berm' of dirt, packed probably fifteen feet high; that is Chip's firing range. With the noise suppressors no one will hear anything beyond a few yards. Not only that; with the snakes, a gator or two, and no telling what else, nobody is going to want to go traipsing through that swamp!"

We reclosed the weapons room and went back upstairs to the great room. I went to the massive window overlooking the swamp, I pressed the button for the drapes and they opened and I flipped on the flood lights on the swamp; there were three large deer standing at the edge, they looked up to see where the light was coming from; they stayed put for several minutes and when nothing happened, they slowly ambled off into the woods.

Dawn and Sam both drew in an audible deep breath.

Sam said, "I think I'm going to like this place, a lot!"

"Me to," echoed Dawn.

"Like I said earlier, this is my happy place."

"I believe we're all set then. Let's meet back here early Friday morning, I've got a good day's drive to Richmond; we can get the equipment and ammo we need for the weekend fun-fest! Then let's come back, say on Monday evening, we can evaluate and analyze how we made out," I said.

Dawn asked, "Can we make it on Sunday evening, after you get back? We can sit and watch the news to see what effect it is having."

I looked at Sam and he said, "Suits me, Sunday evening it is."

"In the meantime, I'll see both of you early Friday morning," I said as we left together.

CHAPTER TWENTY ONE

SUNDAY AFTERNOON, FIVE O'CLOCK, I'm sitting in the great room watching the "Breaking News" on the big screen when a small screen popped up in a corner of the bigger one; it showed a car entering the property, it was Sam coming in; the cameras had picked up the motion of his vehicle as it approached the panel in the old tree. Sam popped open the hidden panel, entered the code and drove on in. He parked in the back by the garage, got his equipment out and put it by the weapons room door and came on up to where I was waiting. He grabbed a beer from the fridge in the kitchen and came in and sat down.

"What a weekend!" he exclaimed. "I haven't had time to check the news; I guess that's about all that's on right now."

I replied, "I have just turned it on. When I got back earlier I just lay back in this recliner and I have been taking a nap. We'll see in a few minutes as soon as the evening news programs begin."

I got up went to the fridge and got myself a beer, too. The small screen popped up again in the corner of the big screen, it showed Dawn approaching; she punched in the code and drove in and parked next to Sam's car and came on up to where we were waiting. She went straight to the fridge and pulled out a beer, without speaking she popped the top and toke a large swallow, and then turned to face Sam and I.

"Happy fourth of July," she said sarcastically! "I can't believe all of the crap happening this weekend. I used to think there was some "good" in everybody, but now I'm really not sure!"

"Calm down Dawn," I told her, you and Sam did your part, I did mine and everything went as planned and we got the job done; and by the way, Sam tells me you handled yourself very well and professional. You can't let the stuff we do get to you personally. We were just getting to see how the news media, and the police, treat the story."

Sam said, "Don't worry Chip; Dawn can handle herself, she will make a great partner."

I asked, "Did y'all have any problems getting set up or too many people near that could create suspicion?"

"Not at all," Sam said. "Everything went pretty smoothly; Dawn and I had gone over and checked it out; we were able to get a suite at the old Columbia Hotel in the next block, it gave us a straight shot to the statue. We kept our phones and headsets on listening for your signal or call to try to time our shots as close as possible."

Dawn said, "You should have seen Sam, Chip. He calmly opened the case removed the rifle, added the scope and silencer, got into position, so I raised the window for him; as soon as that butthole protestor, Antifa, or whatever he was, got to the top of "old George Washington", Sam squeezed the trigger, there was a small "puff" and that was it! Sam disassembled the rifle, replaced it into the case and we were out of there! How did Richmond go?"

I replied, "Pretty much the same. I set up in that old hotel I told y'all about, and like you said, a quick little "puff" and I packed up and left. I drove down I-95 to Wilson, in North Carolina and spent the night; I got back here late this afternoon."

The 'big screen', tuned to the local Columbia station, came on blaring loudly, "Breaking News!"

Then the host of the "Evening News at Six" program came on and made the announcement that one of the 'peaceful' protestors had fallen from the top of the monument that was located at the foot of the steps to the State Capital building! He then turned the story over to the on scene reporter.

The reporter said, "It looks as if the young protestor was trying to tie a large rope around the neck of the statue of George Washington, when he slipped and fell to his death among the crowd of other protestors at the foot of the statue. The group leaders had planned to pull the statue over using the power of the large crowd of protestors. Needless to say, their efforts tragically failed when the person fell to his death. There was not a second attempt to get to the top of the statue. However, one of the leaders remarked that they would try again another day. Back to you guys in the station."

"There is more "Breaking News" tonight," the host reported! "We have just received a report of a similar event in the Richmond, Virginia area. One of a rather large crowd of peaceful protestors was attempting to bring down probably the most famous statue of Robert E. Lee, the one on horseback; it is a huge statue located on Richmond's Monument Avenue, a street that is lined from one end to the other with statues of Civil War heroes and from other events.

"The story is very similar to the one here in Columbia; a young protestor had climbed to the top of the statue with a chain, instead of a rope in this case, and was attempting to loop it around the top of the statue when he lost his balance and fell to the concrete base on which the statue sat. This is a tragic ending for a group of citizens trying to express their beliefs and feelings concerning how their government is handling the country."

Dawn said, "Do you think they will realize it was a bullet that caused them to "slip"?

"If they do an autopsy they will," Sam replied. "A coroner will spot the hole in the head right off and shit will hit the fan! Unless, the powers that be decide not to reveal it. At least it broke up the protestors and their rally; I think most of them, at least the peaceful ones, decided to go home."

I said, "I imagine the governor and some of the others of his ilk will probably want it known, to make a point. If all of these so-called peaceful protestors get the idea they might get shot, there's a good chance they would stay home and let the paid idiots to the protesting."

Dawn asked, "What do we do next Chip? Do you have a mission already scheduled or what? I have to go back to my regular job tomorrow morning; after this weekend I'm sure it's going to be the most boring day ever."

"Yeah, added Sam, "I better be on the job tomorrow also, or I won't have a job. By the way Chip, you never told us about pay, other than the job in Columbia was a gratuity and the Richmond hit was paid. Does that mean you're the only one who gets paid?"

"Well," I replied, "If you two will give me the name of your bank, the bank's routing number and your account number, you'll find a deposit there next week. That's the way we will be working, no more paperwork unless absolutely necessary; everything is to be digital; we have to make it hard, if not impossible, in case anyone ever tries to trace anything involving either of us or the Sweet Daddy Creek Club. Understood?"

"Agreed," they both responded!

"Okay; I have been contacted by an old friend who is representing a group of businessmen," "Their businesses are in deep trouble with all this protesting crap going on; they are being pretty much destroyed, robbed and their businesses set on fire; it's ruining them. They are asking us for help since the police have been told to stand down and not to respond to their calls. They are planning to take the matter in their own hands, and try to resolve it themselves," I said. "I have been considering a specific strategy, which if it works, may eliminate much of the problem across the country. I figured we would kick it around and see what you two thought of it.

"It would require the three of us working alone, in different states at the same time, to be effective and have the impact that's needed to quell this chaos that is gripping the entire nation. We, as the SDCT, "Sweet Daddy Creek Team", would be acting in the capacity of consulting agents; we would not be pulling the trigger on these assignments."

Sam spoke up and said, "Well, that sounds less dangerous at least; and intriguing, how do we go about that?"

"Consulting, that sounds as if we will be meeting with groups of people, speaking and advising them," Dawn said.

"Basically, yes! That's what we would be doing. We would be explaining to them how to protect their businesses without getting themselves shot or hurt. Here's how we will hopefully accomplish that little task. Our first step will be to make contact with the "F.O.P.", Fraternal Order of Police chapter, in the city we're going to be working, their cooperation is essential. As y'all know the members of the "F.O.P." are really ticked off at the mayors and city leaders for cutting back on the police department's budgets, even to the point of laying off members and not letting them make arrests.

"The patrolmen who are laid off draw no salary while they are off, and they are pissed about that. Most are looking for some type of temporary job in order to support their families. That's where we come in. The folks who are asking for our help are the large Chamber of Commerce organizations in some of these affected cities.

"The idea or plan, that I want to throw out to you is, provided the Chamber groups and the "F.O.P." are in agreement, we hire those officers that have been laid off as "Security Guards" and assign a couple to each of the participating businesses. They would be on duty inside the business during the most prevalent times, armed with shotguns and strict instructions not to open fire unless, and until, somebody breaks in, enters and begins looting. Then it's "Katie bar the door! Comments?"

Sam began slowly, "On the surface, I like the idea; I'm kind of like you Chip, if we could pull this off effectively, it could have a very positive effect across the whole country. I would need to think about it some more and look for any possibilities where it might not fly and cause problems or something; first thought off the top of my head – I'm for it!"

"Me to," exclaimed Dawn rather excitedly! "About the first time one of those so called peaceful protestors got his butt shot off, the others just may think twice before robbing a store or breaking out the windows; I like the idea! However, I'm like Sam; let's consider all of the possible down sides to the plan. We need to work out possible flaws now and have the solution ready."

"Good thinking," I said; "That's task number one for us right now. Sam, you have been a cop for many years and served in many places, do you have any contacts in places like Portland or Seattle; those are the two who have contacted me asking for assistance?"

"I know the Chief in Portland," Sam replied. "In fact I saw her on the news just recently and she seemed very unhappy about the situation there; she remarked to the reporter that she had been ordered to 'stand down'; she was not allowed to make any arrests or charge any protestor with anything. I believe that was about the same time the hostiles were trying to take over the precinct headquarters there. I did know the executive director of the "F.O.P." there, we served overseas together; he retired from the police force and became the director of the Order. I've lost contact with him over the years, but I'll make a couple of calls and see if I can reach him and renew our old time contact."

Dawn asked, "What can I be doing?"

"For starters," I began, "We need to get a run down on the laws in the state; both federal and state. We need to know the prerequisites for being a security guard, the responsibilities, duties, etc. We need to know how much authority they have and what actions they can take in carrying out their duties as a security person. In other words, research, a lot of research; we must be certain that our people are covered.

"That's your initial responsibility, Dawn; cover our butts! And that's before we go anywhere or do anything. Then, when we have that taken care of, we can set our schedule. You and Sam will need to be able to re-arrange your regular daytime work schedules and get the necessary time off for us to take on this mission. Let me know if you have a problem.

CHAPTER TWENTY TWO

IN THE MEANTIME I called Ed Winters, the SAC –Special Agent in Charge--and a good friend, at the FBI Field Office in Atlanta. I figured it was about time to take a serious look into the activities of the local police and actions of a certain judge. Ed and I had known each other for a number of years; he had pulled a tour in the Air Force then went on to be a talk show host on a local radio station. While in broadcasting he volunteered his off hours with law enforcement. The local police chief was so impressed that he convinced Ed to go to the FBI Academy where, like Dawn, he was on the FBI SWAT team and graduated at the top of his class. He moved on up the ranks and now headed up the Atlanta Field Office.

Ed answered his own phone when I called, "Ed Winters, FBI Field Office."

I said, "Hey Ed, this is Chip Storrington, what are you doing answering your own phone, doesn't Uncle Sam provide you with a secretary?"

"Hi Chip, yeah but even secretaries have to eat lunch sometime. Where are you? What have you been up to lately? I don't think I have heard from you in a year or so; what's going on?" he asked.

"Well Ed," I began, "I need some advice and some answers about a situation up here in South Carolina and I don't want to talk about it with anyone local. I was thinking about driving down your way and buy you lunch, sometime soon when your schedule allows. You tell me when would be a good time for you."

"Hmm, sounds like a bribe in the making; are you going to offer me a payoff Chip? If so you may have come to the right office," Ed laughed.

"How much are bribes going for these days?" I replied.

Ed laughed and said, "Come on down Chip, before somebody over-hears this conversation and gets their panties in a wad. Give me a day's notice and I will make the time; it will be good to see you again. How about Wednesday, my calendars open; make it a late lunch, that way we can have the whole afternoon to talk and catch up on our lives. Let me know where you will be staying; drive safe.

I pulled into the Ritz Carlton entrance shortly after eight o'clock Tuesday evening, after a long day's drive and fighting the nightmarish traffic on I-85. I grabbed my one overnight bag, turned the car over to the valet and let him worry about the parking. I checked in, went to my room, dropped my bag off and went back down to the restaurant just off the lobby; it had been a long day.

I slept in Wednesday morning and went down for breakfast at eight; nothing like the Cut Rate, I couldn't find country fried ham and grits and eggs anywhere on the menu, nothing good and greasy; so I just had eggs benedict and toast. I sat back and glanced through the Atlanta Journal about the weekend shootings and rioting in various parts of town and decided, "nothing new under the sun!"

I called Ed to let him know where he could find me and where we would meet for lunch. He does have a secretary and she answered, "Mr. Winters' office."

She put me on through to Ed and he picked up, "Good morning Chip, welcome to "Hotlanta", I hope you stayed out of trouble last night and got a good night's sleep."

"I did," I said, "and had a very relaxing evening of doing nothing; even slept late this morning and just had a leisurely breakfast here in the restaurant. I don't remember when I've had it so easy."

"What would you like for lunch?" Ed asked.

"It's your town, you pick the place," I replied.

"Well, I'll tell you what; let's just meet at Ted's Montana Grill, just around the corner, about three or four blocks from you on Luckie Street. It will be easy to get to and they serve good old American food; burgers, steaks, ribs, you name it; it's a good lunch place and we can talk," Ed said; "How about one-thirty?"

"That's fine with me," I answered, "I'll see you at Ted's Montana Grill at one-thirty."

I decided to walk to the restaurant, I needed the exercise, and walked into Ted's Grill at one forty-five; it was either a long 'three or four blocks' or Ed couldn't count. He had a booth and was waiting; it was a nice, busy place, even for late lunchers. It had a long wrap around counter at the bar for those who wanted a little mid-day 'toddy' with their lunch before going back to work; the booths were large with a mahogany finish, and high backs that offered a little privacy.

Ed stood to greet me as I approached, we shook hands and I slid into the booth across from him; it had been over a year since we had been in touch. The waiter arrived to take drink orders; Ed said that since he was 'on duty' he would just have sweet tea, the true southern beverage; however, since I was not on duty I ordered a gin and tonic, to help revive me from my long trek from the hotel.

After the waiter left we began just chit-chatting about our past escapades and bringing each other up to date on our most recent adventures.

Then Ed asked, "Well Chip, what's on your mind that you needed to drive all the way to Atlanta to talk about? Must be pretty important or illegal; or on second thought, something that might get me in trouble with my bosses."

"No, I don't think so," I replied. "However, it is something illegal, but not on my part and it is pretty important. And, I believe instead of getting you in trouble with your bosses, it could make you the hero."

"Now you really have my curiosity up." Ed said.

"Well, as if you didn't know, we have a small drug problem up north—in South Carolina that is; and I don't mean just the using and dealing; you have plenty of that right here."

"You bet your ass we do Chip; there is so much traveling through here we can't keep track of even the ones we know about. This is like an interstate drug through-way, from Florida, Mexico and other Central American countries; they don't even slow down. In fact some of our agents say the haulers and mules just smile and wave at us when they go through. The guys are really pissed! They feel their hands are tied; anybody they arrest is back on the road the next day," Ed said.

I listened while Ed blew off some steam. The waiter came back to take our order, both Ed and I ordered the 'special of the day', bar-b-que ribs with fries and a good helping of coleslaw; we both laughed and said that should hold us for the rest of the day.

Ed laughed again and said, "You know what, Chip, I'm taking the rest of the day off; we don't have to rush, nothing special on my plate for the week, so let's have a couple of beers with these ribs when they come; I could use a good cold one right about now – besides, makes the ribs better!"

"Now you're talking," I said just as the waiter arrived with the largest platter of ribs, fries and coleslaw you've ever seen. We both dug-in without saying another word.

Ed did say to the waiter, "Bring us a couple of Buds to wash this down with!"

Finally we looked up, glanced down at the platters; only a few fries and a spoonful of slaw left.

I opened the serious part of conversation, and the purpose of my visit, "Ed what I wanted to discuss with you, I wanted to do in person, face-to-face; it involves some people in serious positions. It has to deal with drugs, contraband, money, police and a judge."

"Any particular reason you are coming to me rather than South Carolina law enforcement, like SLED for instance; they are pretty sharp and do a good job from what I hear." Ed said. "Or, do you think it might involve someone at SLED also?" he added.

"No, I don't think, or have any reason to believe it involves SLED," I said, "But the judge is a friend as are some of the police officers."

Ed asked, "What exactly do you suspect them of, Chip?"

"Well," I began, "It seems that when a bust is made and the evidence, drugs and cash, is confiscated it all doesn't make it to the evidence room and is never disclosed. For example: last weekend on I-95 there was a big haul stopped; drugs and more than a quarter million in cash picked up. Since it was a weekend night, all of the evidence was taken to the judge to hold until Monday morning. Monday morning the judge and two of his patrolmen, local police officers or deputies, carried the haul to the Clerk of Court's office where it is counted, logged in and placed in the evidence room while waiting for the trial to come up.

"It was 'big' news on the street on Monday, as well as headlines in the local newspaper and other media; *'Big Drug Bust on I-95 Saturday – Drugs and $50,000 Cash Confiscated!'* Fifty thousand my ass, the street people say it was more than three hundred thousand! Only fifty thousand made it into evidence. No telling how much drugs were involved and how much was turned in," I finished and left it open for Ed's reaction and comments.

"I know what you're talking about Chip, we have the same problem all across Georgia; you will probably find it in cities other than Alcolu too; I'm sure it is from one end of South Carolina to the other also, just like here. The problem is, what in hell can we do about it?" Ed said.

After thinking quietly for a few minutes, Ed said, "Here's what I can do Chip; I can call my counterpart in South Carolina and put a 'bug' in his ear; tell him that I have heard about a situation in South Carolina involving a certain judge and police officers skimming money and drugs from the various busts. I can suggest he check into the lifestyles and income of those involved, and then let him handle it. That way you were never mentioned and won't be drawn in in any way."

"That sounds great Ed; let's do it. Maybe we can at least slow down some of the crap that's going on," I said.

Ed showed me the latest sights around downtown Atlanta and invited me to dinner with him and his wife Marie and their twin boys, at their Stone Mountain Golf Course home, a thirty minute drive from downtown. After a relaxing evening, a delicious dinner and sitting around talking about different events and telling tall tales to the boys, Ed drove me back to my hotel, I wanted to get an earlier start back to Alcolu in the morning. I knew that Sam and Dawn would be chomping at the bit to get moving on our new escapades across the country. Dawn should have her research completed and we would be ready to move on it.

Sam would have made his contacts with the law enforcement agencies where he had friends or contacts and briefed them on the plans and to get their cooperation and support. Barring any slip ups or misgivings, we were ready to go.

CHAPTER TWENTY THREE

I ARRIVED BACK IN Alcolu around noon and decided to have a quick lunch at the Cut Rate, perhaps see Dawn and Sam there also. Right on target! Twelve fifteen and in walks Sam smiling like he had just eaten the last cookie in the box.

"Hey Chip, how was 'Hotlanta'? That place has more jukin' and jivin' than any other place in the world – I love it!" he declared.

"It's still there alright, but it is a lot different than when I first started going there. Back in the 'old days' I liked it because it was big; it was big city for me. Now, it's about three or four times bigger than it was back then, it's too big for me," I said.

I had sat facing the door so I could see who was coming in, and then – there she was, Dawn -- slowly floating towards me with a smile on her face!

Sam must have seen the look on my face, he turned to see Dawn approaching, he broke out in laughter so loud that it brought everybody's attention to our booth.

Still laughing he said, "It's only been a day Chip, since you saw her! Ease up man."

I stood to let Dawn slide into the booth beside me; she was smiling!

"Welcome back," she said, "did you find out anything new?" she asked.

I briefed them both on my meeting with Ed Winters and that I was leaving that in his and the FBI's hands; they could resolve it however they thought best.

Sam said, "That's a good move Chip, takes us out of it, we're too close to the situation and no telling what would, or could, happen around here. If, and when it blows up, some innocent people could get hurt or ruined."

"Yeah," said Dawn, "It could even be us! Let's keep our distance; some folks in the Clerk's office are pretty close to the judge, and to the law enforcement guys. Most of them are pretty straight and wouldn't get involved in anything like this."

"By the way," Sam began, "I picked up the arrest sheet yesterday morning and saw Jeff's name where he had been picked up for a really minor thing; I actually think he was trying to help an elderly couple; any-way I figured he had news for us so I did the interview with him. He told me that he was talking with a couple of his contacts, one of whom works for the sheriff as an undercover narc agent; anyway, he told me about a dealer's house over in your neighborhood Chip.

"It seems Denny, the sheriff, was using the house over on Carrol Circle, as a focal point to draw out users and other dealers. An older couple who has lived on the Circle for fifty years or more, talked with Denny and told him they thought it was a 'drug house'; they said there was way too much traffic on the street at all hours of the day and night," Sam laughed and continued, "Jeff got a big kick out of it; he said the sheriff thought he was so smart, but an elderly couple called him out on it! Jeff said the sheriff had to close it, but he opened another at the other end of the Circle. I also heard that he had complaints from another older couple on the street, then two nights later shots were fired into the house."

"There's nothing like living in the hood!" I replied. I also thought *it may be time for another late night stroll through my hood.*

Sam continued, "I checked into the report of shots fired, but I didn't find a record of anything; if it was one of Denny's units, he isn't saying anything about it, not yet anyhow. Jeff laughed and told me he hoped the sheriff would have to close that house down also."

I asked Dawn for an update on her research concerning the laws in Oregon and Washington State, specifically Portland and Seattle, the cities where we had contacts.

"The laws are pretty much like any other state or municipality," She began; "It's kind of like if someone breaks into your house and you shoot them, you need to make sure they are inside your house; or as most old time cops would say, *'If you shoot them and they fall backwards out of the house, drag the body back in'!* The same holds true for a privately owned business, too. Since a guard is hired to protect the property he is guarding, it is his or her responsibility for protecting it by whatever means or force that is necessary." She added, "That's paraphrasing the law; as written it goes into a lot more legalese talk.

"If our clients hire guards, especially off duty or laid off cops, to protect their businesses, I don't think there will be any challenge, officially, if and when they shoot or kill a looter who broke through a large plate glass store window and is caught inside the business with an arm full of merchandise!" She finished her statement.

"Very good, thanks Dawn," I said. "I will give our contacts a call back and let them know; we'll give them some time to think about what they want to do. Although, I believe they will want to go ahead with this; they were extremely pissed at what was going on and the loss they were incurring; their insurance was beginning to double."

Sam, who had been sitting quietly spoke up and said, "If they don't take this action, and take it now, there won't be any turning back pretty soon. This Antifa and BLM groups will actually be pulling off a coup of a city. I don't believe I have ever heard of a city, or a state for that matter, being the subject of a damn coup! What is it called, officially that is – a coup de tat – or something like that? You guys have seen the news or heard about one of those groups taking over a police precinct, I think it was in Portland; I can't imagine a precinct of cops letting a bunch of asshole renegades run them out of their precinct! They sure as hell wouldn't if I had been there; they would have taken it only over my dead body!"

"What's the next step?" Dawn asked.

"Well," I replied, "I think I will spend tonight here in town, in my hood, and make a few phone calls to Seattle and Portland. I'll go back out to the Club tomorrow afternoon and begin getting things together and ready to travel. I'll probably see y'all in the morning for breakfast though, probably around seven-thirty if you make it here."

I turned to Dawn, "I know it's only Thursday, but the best I remember you and I had a dinner date for a Friday, but it got interrupted and had to be postponed; tomorrow is Friday again, do you think we could do a make-up date and have dinner tomorrow evening? Somewhere that's nice and quiet, with the lights down low – you know so we can talk. You never have told me all about your adventures at the FBI Academy."

Sam laughed and said, "Chip you are so full of shit! Go for it Dawn!"

Dawn laughed also and asked, "What's so funny Sam, you don't think we can have a nice quiet dinner date?"

Turning to me she said, "I would love to have dinner with you Chip! How about around eightish; you can pick me up at my house, we'll have a drink and go to dinner; you pick the place, anywhere is fine with me."

I looked over at Sam, smiled and said, "See smart-ass, I told you we would get it together when we had another chance." The three of us sat and laughed, causing those round us to look and wonder what we were up to; if they only knew.

Sam asked, "Chip, if we turn this drug and judge stuff over to the FBI, what becomes of Jeff? You know he has his neck out and has been helping us, not only you and I but the department as well; he has made a number of friends over there and those that know his situation support him and want to help him get straight and settled with his family into a quiet, legal lifestyle. I feel like we kind of owe him the opportunity, and, I would like to help him also. But he has to have a job so he can support his family."

"I agree Sam, we can't just hang Jeff out to dry," I replied. "Let me work on it and see what we can come up with. Right off the top of my head, a couple possibilities arise, pretty farfetched, but a possibility anyway. I'll make a few calls and see what I can find out and let you and Jeff know."

Dawn got up and said she had to get back to work before she got fired; she headed for the door but stopped and turned and asked if we were having breakfast in the morning as usual; we assured her that we were and would see her bright and early.

Sam and I sat nursing a last cup of coffee and just thinking; we had a lot of details to work out before the next op.

CHAPTER TWENTY FOUR

I WAS SITTING IN my old recliner in my hood watching TV; it was getting late, eleven thirty; if I was going to make a turn through the hood I better get started. There had been the shooting in my circle, six shots fired into one of the houses. I can't let that happen, not again anyway. Since I have been out of touch for a few days, maybe the old druggies and dealers thought it was all clear; we'll see about that.

I dressed in my night patrolling clothing, got my MK9 and took a stroll through the areas of the hood where the 'night people' hung out. It didn't take long before running into a couple of groups of four or five young guys, probably two different gangs, arguing and getting ready to fight over a drug deal. I spotted a duffel bag on the ground between two older men, in their thirties or so, who evidently were the leaders and main dealers. They were leading the argument, both had a handgun pointed at each other; the duffel bag was open and there were bundles of cash lying on the ground, scattered as if thrown there.

These were the type men who recruit young school kids to run drugs for them with promises of big money and free drugs; it never works out. I raised my MK9 with the suppressor and leveled it at the one who looked as if he was going to fire; I squeezed off a round that caught him in the middle of his forehead. The other one turned and raised his weapon and was ready to fire into the other group of young guys; I squeezed off another round and caught him between the eyes. When my shot hit them, each had his finger on the trigger of his weapon and instinctively pulled the trigger when he got hit, causing each of the weapons to fire.

Both groups started screaming and running as hard as they could to get the hell out of there. When they cleared, I pulled one of my posters from a telephone pole and then walked over to the bodies and laid the poster on the duffel bag full of cash and drugs. Then, like those young folks, I got the hell out of there. I knew someone in the neighborhood had already dialed 9-1-1 after hearing the two shots that had been fired. Cops would be arriving shortly and I didn't need to be anywhere in the vicinity.

At seven Friday morning I was in my usual booth at The Cut Rate having coffee when I heard my named called, I looked across the counter area at the counter-eaters, the folks who like eating at the counter on the red covered spinning seats. I saw Jeff with a cup in his hand. I told him to come on over. He sat down and said that he only had a few minutes because his wife had a doctor's appointment and he was taking her; besides I don't need to get too close to you guys yet, he smiled as he said it.

"Sam mentioned that you had something in the works that might make my life and my family's life a little easier. I'm real interested in hearing about that, Chip," Jeff said. "But in the meantime there was a thing that went down in your neighborhood last night, Chip, did you hear anything about what was going on."

"No, I didn't hear anything," I lied; "I went to bed early last night, I didn't even hear any news. Was it bad? "I asked.

Jeff replied, "Police say, and some of the street talk, says two gang leaders who are heavy into recruiting school kids to deliver deals for them, got into a little shoot-out; according to the cops they shot each other! Don't you think that's a little weird, Chip? How the hell can two people stand in front of each other and shoot each other at the same time. Cops say that's what happened and that's what they're accepting. They are trying to locate some of the kids who were with the two, at the time of the shooting. Oh yeah, talk on the street leans toward somebody trying to clean-up that area of town. You remember a few weeks back when those posters starting appearing on trees and telephone poles; well the street says one of those posters was found on top of a duffel bag that was full of cash and drugs, just like before. Street talk also telling everybody to stay away from that part of town or they might find themselves with one of those posters stuck up their rear end!"

"Now that would be funny," I said. "It would be deserved also, funnier still if it was set on fire."

Jeff laughed and said, "I think you know more than most folks; including the police, about what's going down, Chip. That's good, just be sure to cover your ass and watch your back." He stood and turned to leave.

"Jeff," I said, "I haven't forgotten and I should have some information for you in a couple of days, you going to be around here about Wednesday, say lunch time or so?"

He replied, "Make it a real late lunch, near closing time for the grill, around three-thirty or four; not many folks around here then; less likely to be seen by the wrong people."

"I'll see you then," I said as Jeff walked away.

As he got to the door Sam came in, they stopped, shook hands and talked for just a moment then Sam came on over to the booth and sat down. "Well Chip, old boy, it's just going to be the two of us for lunch today," he said. "I stopped by the courthouse later this morning and Dawn said she would not be able to make lunch today; they have several cases being tried and she needs to be there all day. She told me to remind you of your date tonight." Sam grinned, "I told her not a chance of you forgetting."

After lunch Sam went to work and I decided to go to my little brick house in the hood and make some phone calls.

First on the list was to Ed Winters in Atlanta to get his support and advice concerning Jeff; I had to find him a new occupation. Ed listened empathetically and said he would talk with his South Carolina counterpart and see if they could work something out, maybe find a spot for Jeff, in Columbia, the state Capital. He said he would get back to me.

A couple of hours later, sitting in my recliner, in front of the TV with Matt Dillion racing across the screen in a Gunsmoke re-run, the phone woke me. "Chip," I said while turning the sound down.

"Sounds like I woke you from a deep sleep," the laughing voice of Ed came through. "I think we have something worked out for your friend and contact, Jeff. You have some friends in Columbia at SLED (State Law Enforcement Division) who are interested in talking with Jeff; it seems they have been looking for someone in the Alcolu area. It won't be as a narc agent or anything like that, it sounds like more of a legitimate job or position; something like a nine-to-five type.

"I started by trying to tell them what a nice guy you are, but they said I must have the wrong number; said they knew a guy named Chip Storrington and I wasn't describing the same Chip they knew. As much as told me I was full of crap," Ed said laughing. "Anyway you can expect a call from a Rusty Stevens, a SLED agent who does interviews for the Columbia area; sounds like a nice guy; said he had known you for a long time. He also sounded pleased at the possibility of finding the type person they had been looking for to fill a new position. Let me know how it works out for Jeff."

"I will, and thanks Ed; this will mean a lot for Jeff and his family. Talk with you later."

CHAPTER TWENTY FIVE

SEVEN-THIRTY AND I'M ALL dressed in coat, tie, shoes shined and ready to head out to pick-up my beautiful date for a great evening; a quiet romantic dinner in downtown Alcolu. Dawn's house was located on the west side of town, completely opposite from my side of town; I pulled into her drive a few minutes before eight, got out and went to the door and rang the bell.

The door opened and the glow from the backlight illuminated a dream standing in the doorway! Being very cool, I calmly asked, "Ready?"

"Ready if you are," she replied. "I didn't think about you wearing a coat and tie," she said as she stood there with her long, flowing, blonde hair cascading down over the shoulders of her black and red checkered shirt and blue jeans with the 'worn-thru-looking' holes in the legs. Only one word could describe her -- gorgeous!

"That's not a problem," I declared as I almost ripped the tie from my neck and pulled the coat from my shoulders.

"Is this okay?" She asked. "I should have dressed in something else."

"You are fantastic and beautiful!" I replied. "That's perfect; we'll be comfortable, relaxed and enjoy dinner more." I had not told her where I was taking her for dinner, let that be a surprise.

The *"Mercantile Store and Restaurant"* used to be just that; an old, kind of run-down, general store located on Main Street in the middle of downtown Alcolu. The kind of General Store that supplied the lumber workers, farmers and their families with everything they would need to survive: groceries, clothing, gasoline, oil, feed for the animals, and butcher shop. If the 'Company Store', as it was called, didn't have what you wanted, you didn't need it! It even had the large oversize, pot-belly heater in the middle of the floor, surrounded by a couple of small barrels with a checker board in the middle. The old company store also served as city hall, local lock-up if you got in trouble; and on a Saturday night you could watch movies upstairs from an old 16mm projector flickering scenes of cowboys racing across a ripply, white sheet that had been pinned to the wall. I think this is what some people call "the good old days!"

I pulled into the pretty full parking lot and Dawn said, "Wow! I've never even been to the Mercantile Store and Restaurant before; the prices are above my pay grade."

Dawn started wandering through the restaurant just looking. The walls were designed to look like clothing racks or tables, and they had clothing – overalls, jeans, old timey dresses, children's clothes – mounted behind glass shadow type cabinets. There was even a picture of Miss Alcolu of 1949 being crowned and I told Dawn that I had met her in person. She was impressed.

The hostess came and led us to a booth toward the back center of the dining area, a quiet area she said as we were seated. Shortly the waiter came, lit the candle in the center of the table, and took our drink orders; white zinfandel for me and a chardonnay for Dawn. We sat and looked around the room at the old antique design of the restaurant and chatted and tried to guess how old some of the items might be. The conversation finally came around to her adventures of being selected and attending the FBI Academy in Quantico, Virginia. How she loved the excitement of the lifestyle of some of the operations the agents might become involved in; dangerous she said, but exciting also. She told how she signed up for the SWAT team, was selected and finished with honors that included the firing of different weapons.

Then Dawn said, "That's why I want to be part of the Sweet Daddy Creek Club! From what little I know so far, you and Sam have had some pretty exciting experiences, and I want to also. That little adventure in Columbia just whetted my appetite; I'm looking forward to the one coming up on the west coast. My job at the courthouse, in the Clerk of Court's office is now more boring than ever!"

I looked at her and said, "Dawn, I really did, and do, want to know all about your experiences at the Academy and stuff, and we will talk a lot about Sweet Daddy Creek Club business and operations and all that kind of stuff, but right now you are too beautiful sitting there, for me to talk about anything else except something romantic; I've just got to figure out how to begin! Now, I've said it and got that out of the way, let's order dinner."

She laughed out loud and said, "This should be very interesting, Chip; I want to know how you begin your romantic 'speak'; just how you talk with all the girls you meet," she was still grinning.

"Well Dawn, I'll just tell you!" I said as I took her hand. "When I see you I don't have to talk, my voice won't let me say the things in my head that I would like to say to you; I think it comes through my eyes, they seem to do all the talking. You're like a line from one of John Denver's songs, *"You fill up my senses"*, and I can't talk."

She looked into my eyes and said, "That is so sweet, Chip; but I believe Sam may be right, you're so full of it!" she grinned. "But I love it; I feel as if I have always known you and that we have always been together. I'm so glad that Sam introduced us, brought us together."

"So am I," I replied grinning from ear to ear.

We spent the next two hours or so dining on filet and lobster tail, couple more glasses of wine, talking and looking into each other eyes just like any other 'young teen age' couple. The Mercantile Store and Restaurant didn't ask us to leave, but were probably on the verge of asking, we were the last customers in the place. We got back to Dawn's house shortly after midnight, I walked her to the door, we chatted for a moment and I leaned forward and kissed her; she returned my kiss and we cuddled for several moments.

She said, "I think I better go in, it's late and I have several errands to get done in the morning."

"Yeah, me too," I said. "I have several things that I have to do before next week. I'll call you tomorrow if that's okay."

"Sure," she said "I'll be in most of the day except for a couple of stops I have to make. If I'm not here leave a message and I'll call you back."

She leaned over and kissed me as we said goodnight. I floated on a cloud back to my car and left.

CHAPTER TWENTY SIX

LATE BREAKFAST ON SATURDAY morning, I'm sitting at the counter when Sam sits down beside me and says, "Good morning. I figured you would be here and I couldn't wait to hear about the big date last night. Did she throw you out?" He asked.

"Are you kidding me?" I asked. "No, she didn't and I didn't want to leave; but you know – first date and all – I was the perfect gentleman, I walked her to the door, I left and went home. But you what Sam, I really like this girl and I'm going to try to see more of her, other than business that is."

Sam looked at me smiling and said, "You're like some high school, love-struck kid, Chip! Dawn is quite the girl; not only beautiful but a very nice person as well. I've known her for several years, since she first started working at the courthouse. She likes you too Chip, she told me so."

"We had a really nice dinner," I said, "I took her to the Mercantile Store and Restaurant and she seemed to like it; it was her first time there; we dined on filet and lobster," I added.

"Damn," Sam exclaimed, "I bet she was impressed, I'm sure she loved it; nice going Chip! What's up for the rest of the weekend?"

"Well, for starters, I am going to the Club and begin getting things in order in case I hear back from Portland and Seattle, if they are ready to take some action. I feel that they are pretty fed up with the mayor, the governor and the rest of that liberal bunch and they are ready to be done with it and get their businesses re-opened," I told him.

Sam said, "I'm free for the weekend, so I may just ride out later this afternoon, if that's okay; maybe I can be of some help."

"Come on," I said, "We don't have that much to do since we won't actually be doing the work; we can shoot the breeze and watch the Carolina game.

"By the way, Sam," I said, "I heard back from Atlanta and they have worked something out for Jeff, something with SLED, he would be working in Columbia, if I understood correctly. It seems they have been looking for someone with Jeff's talents; I haven't told Jeff yet, I'm supposed to meet him here Wednesday afternoon."

"That's great news Chip," Sam said, "I know he will be happy about that. I'll see you sometime later this afternoon," he said as he left.

A little after three o'clock the Club's outer alarm sounded and I looked at the screen to see Sam coming through; he parked around back by the garage and came on in. He stopped in the kitchen at the fridge and got a beer then sat to watch the game while we talked strategy on the west coast assignment. Afterwards we decided to double check the weapons room to be certain we had enough supplies on hand for any quick reaction that may pop-up.

Sam left about six-thirty and I decided to give Dawn a call. She picked up on the second ring and knew it was me. "I was just thinking that you had decided not to call me," she said.

"Not a chance," I replied. "Sam came out to the Club, we watched the Carolina, LSU game checked the weapons room and just talked; he left a few minutes ago. Have you had dinner yet?"

"No, and I can't decide if and what I want to eat. I ate so much last night I probably need to go on a diet," she said.

"You want to go somewhere and grab a sandwich?" I asked. "I'm not really hungry either, just something light."

"Sure," she responded; "That sounds good."

"I'm at the Club right now, I'll pick you up in about thirty minutes, you decide what kind of sandwich you would like and where," I said.

As soon as I pulled into the drive Dawn came on out and got in and said, "Since neither of us are really hungry, let's just go to Chic-Fil-A, have a sandwich and just visit."

"Sounds like a winner to me," I replied and off we went.

We pulled into the always busy parking area of Chic-Fil-A, went inside to the always busy dining area; Dawn found us a table while I got into the always long, busy line to place our order, which the cashier said would be brought to our table; he gave me a marker to sit on the table so they could find me again.

I sat down across from Dawn and saw her smiling, "What?" I asked. "Why are you smiling like that?"

She laughed, "You just looked a little uncomfortable standing in the line and having to wait."

"Well, I could have been spending that time sitting here looking at you," I said.

She laughed again and said, "Chip you really are full of it; Sam had you pegged right; you are full of crap," she added still laughing. Then said, "But I love it!"

I told her, "This isn't the most romantic place I have ever taken a date, but I guess it'll just have to do for now."

We just sat for a couple of hours talking about a little of everything that came to mind. I told her about Jeff and finding a position for him; she hadn't met Jeff but knew of his situation from hearing me and Sam talk about it. We talked about how, since we took some serious action, there had not been any more statues pulled down; neither of us had even heard it mentioned on the news any more. Maybe they learned a lesson; there are still patriots left in this country.

As we got up to leave, Dawn invited me to attend church with her the next morning; I could hardly refuse, so we had another date lined up. I drove her home and walked her to the door; she said she would meet me at the church in the morning.

I turned to leave when she called me, "Chip, thanks for dinner, I really enjoyed getting together, I look forward to seeing you in the morning."

She leaned over and kissed me.

CHAPTER TWENTY SEVEN

MONDAY MORNING SITTING IN the usual booth with my coffee thinking *"what a really nice weekend I had"* when Sam walked in and sat across from me and ordered coffee.

"How did the rest of your weekend go?" he asked. "Do anything special yesterday?"

"Not really," I said; "it was just a nice quiet weekend . . ." I was interrupted by a voice coming from behind me.

"He went to church yesterday, that's what he did," said the voice of Dawn as she came around and sat down. The waitress came up at the same time to take our order and in less than five minutes was back with it.

My phone went off as I was taking my first bite, "Chip," I answered. I got up and stepped outside; it was the Portland Chamber contact that I had been waiting on. We did all the polite salutations and he said that they were ready to move on our discussion and get the job done and set the date; the protesters were still doing their thing and destroying even more property. He also told me that he had talked with a friend of his in Seattle who said they were looking into doing the same. The more they talked, he said, they figured they were talking about the same group, the SDCC Team!

He even mentioned that they had heard stories that it was the same team that stopped all those statues from being pulled off their pedestals. He said they would like to see the same type of operation; some of the protest leaders taken out at the same time in two different locations. It shouldn't be too difficult since both cities were under attack all the time now, anyway.

I went back in to finish my breakfast and tell Sam and Dawn the latest. They both got excited and said that they were ready.

"What about your day jobs?" I asked. "Will you be able to get away for a couple of days or so, without losing your job?"

"Not a problem for me," said Sam.

"Nor me," replied Dawn. "I'm ready to get things moving. I've got plenty of vacation days I can take."

"OK," I told them, "Let's move and kick some ass! I will start lining everything up this afternoon and double check with our clients, and maybe we will take a long weekend trip and spend it on the west coast.

"If you need me I'll be at the 'Club' the rest of the day; y'all have my number, although there really isn't much of anything to get ready. We will just get together with the local 'powers that be' to brief them and be sure they understand what we are trying to accomplish," I added.

"I'll come out as soon as I get off this afternoon," Dawn said; adding "I don't have much going on right now; it seems the drug flow has either slowed down or the judge and his crew are keeping it quiet or to themselves."

"That's good, come on out Dawn," I told her, "That way we will have a double check on everything."

Sam said, "Actually, things are pretty quiet at the moment, even in your neighborhood Chip. Some of the guys down at the station were talking about it yesterday; some were saying it was most likely because someone decided to take the law—and the enforcement--upon themselves and do a little punishing. 'They' even advertised that 'they' were going to do so, 'they' gave the dealers thirty days to move out; some paid no attention; we had to clean up several dead bodies! It looks as if most of the others decided it was good advice and moved on.

"Most of those killed, needed killing anyway, they were the big-time dealers and they were taking over the whole trade, running the little folks out. They are the type that ruins small children's lives by getting them started on drugs in the beginning. I would have probably shot them myself if I came up on them doing a deal. No one seems to care about trying to find out who is, or was," Sam added.

Sam took a sip of his coffee, got up to leave, stopped and said, "I've got to get back to work, y'all keep me posted, and yell if you need anything—behave yourselves—also!

Dawn laughed and said, "I guess I better get back to work too." She gathered up her purse and got up to leave and said, "I'll see you later this afternoon, probably be around six before I get out there."

I was running later than I had planned on; I had gone by 'my house in the hood' to pick up a few items I needed, dropped by the post office for my mail, where I ran into several friends and people I haven't seen for a while, stood around and B-S'ed for about an hour; time flies 'when you're having fun'! Before I realized it—I looked at my watch and it was one-forty-five already, so I figured I may as while grab lunch before heading to the 'Club".

I was sitting in my usual booth at the Cut-Rate reading some papers, when I felt, more than saw, a person slide into the booth in front of me. I looked up and there sat Jeff, my friend, and friendly drug dealer, grinning from ear to ear.

I smiled at him and asked, "What—did you just hit the lottery or something? You're grinning like you hit the big jackpot!"

Through his smile he said, "I pretty much did just that, Chip; thanks to you! Wait 'til you hear the news."

"Tell me," I said grinning also, adding, "I know we were going to get together on Wednesday afternoon, but you're a couple of days early; what's going on?"

Jeff looked around to see if anyone was watching, or listening, and told me, "I received a phone call this morning from SLED!"

"What?" I asked, "Are they chasing you?" I laughed.

"Hell no," Jeff said so excited he couldn't contain himself. "They want me to come to work with them!"

"That's great Jeff; you, working for SLED, the State Law Enforcement Division! How in the world did you manage that?" I asked.

He rolled his eyes and said, "As if you didn't already know. But it seems I have this *'FRIEND'*, who has some connections with the FBI and SLED, he put in a good word for me; and I, and my family, are really grateful Chip! You can't imagine how much we appreciate it."

"I'm happy it worked out for you Jeff; I also know you will be a huge success and you will enjoy working for those folks," I told him.

"Who knows, I may need your help on a case someday," I added.

"You just yell, Chip," Jeff said; "After what you've done for me, 'you call and I'll haul!'"

CHAPTER TWENTY EIGHT

WORD TRAVELS FAST, NOT considering the internet, text messaging and all the other social media networks--word of mouth still qualifies as one of the quickest! I had spent most of the afternoon on the phone with contacts in different areas of the country; all asking the same question: "How can I keep my property safe from these butthole gangs that are roaming the streets, under the pretense of 'peaceful protesting', destroying my property and stealing everything? They're bankrupting me!"

I'm deep in thought, actually dozing a little, when the outer alarm sounded; I looked at the big screen and saw Dawn coming, it was beginning to get a little dark, so the lights came on lighting her travel up the path; I glanced at the time on the screen, seven o'clock; she was running a little later than she had said.

I met her at the door, when I opened it I saw she had her hands full, looks as if she had stopped and picked up dinner for us; what a girl, I thought!

"I thought you may be getting hungry," she said; "so I stopped off at the Lucky Corner Chinese Restaurant, I hope you like Chinese."

"I do and that sounds great, I am getting a little hungry and ready to eat," I replied.

Dawn carried the food into the kitchen area, placed it on the counter then looked in the cabinets for dishes to put the food in. She turned and looked at me and asked, "Is this the only dishes you have, paper plates?" She laughed.

"That's all I need," I replied, "I don't do dishes."

"Then why do you have a brand new dish washer sitting here? Has it ever been used?" she asked.

"Not yet; don't plan on it either," I answered, laughing.

Dawn set the table with our 'fine paper china' then opened a drawer and pulled out a couple settings of my 'fine plastic silver service' and placed it on the table as we sat down to eat. The food was delicious and the company much better; we learned a lot about each other, told some tales and funny stories in our lives; had a couple glasses of wine and just relaxed.

After a while Dawn said, "I thought you came to do some work on our new project and get everything set-up. Did you get it all done?" she asked.

"Almost," I replied; "But there is one thing that keeps bothering me."

"What is that?" She asked.

"Well, we'll be traveling to the West Coast to direct these store owners and operators on how to protect their property – safely – and legally. We're talking about you, Sam and I being in three different locations: San Francisco, Portland and Seattle; we will be running interference between the property folks, the local police officers who have been laid off, and the so-called 'peaceful' protestors who break into the businesses to loot and destroy.

"We will be putting property owner and police together so the owners can hire the off-duty police guys as guards to actually protect the property; that is where our basic responsibility ends; we do not do any of the shooting, if it comes to that. We will not be on the scene of any of the activity, although I would like to see a couple of those Antifa bastards shot! They have caused too damn much trouble and are still running free as a bird."

Dawn had been listening to me spout off, finally she asked, "So what's the problem that keeps bothering you?"

I said, "We have the same problem right here in South Carolina; in Columbia, Greenville, and just up the road in Charlotte. I was thinking of contacting some of the law enforcement guys who I know, and already work as guards at some of the larger plants when they are off duty. If we can get several businesses from coast-to-coast to do the same, we could probably pretty much eliminate a lot of the damage being done, or at least have an impact or influence on some of the 'actual' peaceful protestors."

"And?" she asked.

"It's like we discussed originally, when this came up, if several of those bastards were shot in the process of breaking and looting, I believe the 'real' peaceful protestors would have second thoughts before doing it again; at least the ones who are not hired by Antifa and other liberal groups," I replied.

"I agree, I think it would have an immediate impact across the entire country," Dawn said. Then looking at her watch she said, "Oh, I didn't realize it was so late, it's ten-thirty and I've got to go! I don't like being on the road this late."

"Are you working tomorrow?" I asked.

"No, I took tomorrow off; things are slow in the courts right now," she said.

"Dawn, don't take this wrong, but you know there is plenty of room here, if you would like to stay the night; you have your own bedroom and privacy and sleep as late as you would like; or if you would rather, and be more comfortable, I can follow you safely home," I told her.

"I can't do that," she replied, "I don't have any pajamas, no make-up or anything; I know I would be perfectly safe here with you – that is no concern of mine! But I'm sure I will be okay driving home, even as late as it is."

I said, "If you don't mind wearing a pair of my pajamas – there is a drawer full in my bedroom; however, I'm a little short on make-up.

Seriously, I would be more comfortable following you home, or you staying here tonight; more so if you stay here," I added.

She thought for a few moments then said grinning, "If you're sure, and no I wouldn't mind wearing your pajamas and I guess I could go a morning without any make-up," she laughed.

Dawn awoke and looked at the clock, six o'clock, her normal getting up time; she had slept well and comfortably – all night – for a change. She went to the door and cracked it open slightly; she thought she could smell the delicious aroma of coffee brewing and hear the crackling of bacon cooking. She whispered to herself, "Chip is cooking breakfast? I didn't know he had any food here!"

She turned quickly toward the bathroom, stopped by the bed, stripped her clothes off, glanced at herself in the full length mirror, tussled up her hair a bit then got in the shower for a 'quick turn-around'; she hurriedly dressed. Twenty minutes max, she thought, as she came down the stairs and into the kitchen where she found a grinning, from ear-to-ear, Chip. 'DANG', she thought, he looks good, even in the morning!

"Boy that smells good," she said as a turning Chip grinned and looked at her.

'DANG', he thought, 'she sure looks great, even in the morning'; as he said, "I hope you're hungry and ready for a home cooked breakfast for a change."

"I am both—hungry and ready for a good, old fashioned, home cooked breakfast!" she replied. "I don't do much cooking at home just for myself; it's not worth the effort."

"Me either," said Chip; "Did you rest well and get a good night's sleep?"

"I did, best night's sleep in a long time; that is a very comfortable bed; I think I'll just move it to my house," she quipped.

I grinned and responded with, "Well now, just keep in mind that you can sleep in it anytime you like."

Smiling, Dawn walked passed and kissed me on the cheek and said, "Let's eat!"

She stopped at the large window across the back and clicked the button that opened the huge drapes; "Chip, come over here, quick," she said excitedly.

I looked out and there stood a really big buck with wide antlers, looking majestically and protectively over his 'harem' of three deer. Dawn leaned into me kind of cuddly like and said, "That is so great Chip; he looks as if he is protecting his family." She nuzzled even closer then moved toward the kitchen.

CHAPTER TWENTY NINE

AFTER EATING WE SAT and talked, watched a little television, mostly old shows like Andy Griffith, Bonanza and such, then we started watching the news channel. The reporter was telling of more protesting, break-ins, and looting, not only on the West coast, but across the entire nation. We both decided we had had enough and decided to meet Sam for lunch.

Dawn and I walked into the Cut-Rate together and saw a grinning, smiling Sam watching us. He said, "I don' want to hear anything; just don't start any excuses, I don't want to hear; but I missed y'all for breakfast this morning," he began laughing.

Dawn looked at me; her cheeks were almost a bright red as she blushed with a big smile on her face at the same time. "Don't go jumping to conclusions, Sam," she said as she began chuckling. "It was late and Chip insisted that I either stay at the Club or he would follow me home; I decided to stay in one of the other bedrooms; nothing happened. Chip is a perfect gentleman!"

"I didn't say he wasn't," Sam laughed. "I never said that I thought anything happened; I don't even know what you're talking about, Dawn," he said almost spitting out his coffee from laughing so hard. "What's she talking about, Chip?"

I laughed also, "Beats the heck out of me, Sam. All I know is that I spent the night at the Club—in my bedroom—and this beautiful blonde spent the night in one of the other bedrooms; come to think of it—I believe she nailed the door shut when she went to bed!"

"No such thing!" said Dawn with one of her biggest grins —"I left the door partially open just in case — just in case some poor, lonely, lost soul happened to pass and needed consoling!"

We all three cracked up at that; laughing until people around us turned to see what we were up to.

Still laughing Sam said, "I told you Chip, you have to get up mighty early to get the drop on Dawn. Anyway, did y'all get any work done or plans made, or did you just sit and talk?"

"We mostly sat and visited," Dawn answered. But we talked about plans for the upcoming mission also. The news was on the TV and they were espousing about the 'peaceful' protests still going on across the country, and Chip mentioned that he thought it was much bigger than just protesting. I think we all have discussed that before also."

"Yeah," said Sam. "I believe it is a lot bigger than any of us, or the average public, even begins to think. In fact, from what we have discussed recently, I don't believe the average public, the everyday citizen, could comprehend what all it entails."

"I think you're right Sam," I said. "It's a whole lot bigger than all of us; it has been growing by leaps and bounds over the past few decades. The past several administrations, in what they thought was in the best interest of the United States, have cuddled and courted China and given them 'Most Favored Nation' status, to the extinct that China owns much of our country now. Look at how many major plants --- jobs --- have gone to China! Automakers! Pharmaceutical; and many others, too! Hell, they even control our medications!

"The past two or three administrations have considered China as an ally, never as a possible enemy with whom we may have to go to war one day. China has been continually beefing up and building their military into a world power while we, on the other hand, have been letting our military go downhill. Those dumbass politicians in Washington think that China would be our back-up if we ever went to war and had to fight Russia!"

Dawn asked with irritation in her voice, "Why do we keep electing stupid people to run the country? I get so upset sometimes when I hear about some of the crap that is going on in Congress; I think most of them have been there way too long anyway."

"That's for certain!" Sam replied; "Most of them have never really held a job, not a real job anyway; they've been there so long that they have lost contact with the ordinary folks back home. But you know what? I also believe it's the people's fault --- those folks 'back home' don't pay any attention to what's going on in Washington, don't listen to or watch the news --- so come election day they punch in a familiar name, the ones who bought the most ads. I guess that sort of makes us stupid, too! They tell us to push the button --- we push the button!"

Dawn said thoughtfully, "I believe one of our earlier presidents said something to the effect that *'The people are responsible for the character of their Congress. If that body be ignorant, reckless, and corrupt, it is because the people tolerate ignorance, recklessness and corruption'*; I don't recall which one said it, but it's true."

I said, "You know that China has almost two billion people, that's with a "B"; and they are controlled by the Chinese Communist Party (CCP); I understand it's a combination of Karl Marx, Lenin and MaoTseTung, and the CCP has control of all or most of the businesses in China. Like all other nations they have a network of consulates in countries worldwide, and like other countries, it provides them a network of intelligence — worldwide! This network of thieves has stolen trillions of dollars of our research and knowledge. If we just stop and think for a few moments we can easily see some of it; read the labels on items you purchase, not only clothing, but check the label on some of our medications. The ingredients used in our pharmaceuticals; or at least 80 percent or more of it, are controlled by the CCP; and that's according to Chinese news media! When confronted about the origin of the coronavirus, they stated that China could drown the US in a sea of viruses.

"Officials in Washington know for sure that late in 2019, when the COVID19 virus first began to spread, the CCP shut down flights from the city where the virus originated, to other destinations throughout China. But, they continued letting flights go to the U.S. and to European nations. I feel sure those sorry bastards knew that the virus would spread. I also strongly believe that was their purpose, part of their strategy in the 'Peoples War' against us."

I continued, "I have heard pretty well-founded rumors that a Chinese Consulate in the Midwest provided funding to Antifa and BLM protestors to stir up the riots and destruction in that area. I also believe that same is true throughout the entire country; these assholes are getting money from somewhere."

Dawn said thoughtfully, "That's what you meant when you told us that this mission to get property owners to defend their stores themselves, by hiring law enforcement officers who have been laid off, or maybe I should say *'defunded'*, to provide their security, could change the course of this nationwide."

"You've got the picture," I replied.

CHAPTER THIRTY

IMMEDIATELY UPON ARRIVING IN Seattle I went directly to the Chamber of Commerce office for a pre-arranged meeting with a group of the business owners and operators to explain our strategy and to be certain that all were on board for the events about to occur. It was one hundred percent approval to proceed. The size of the business would dictate the number of guards to be assigned to each business.

Next I went to the Fraternal Order of Police (FOP) headquarters for another pre-arranged meeting; this one with the director and fifty 'defunded' police officers who were to be our security guards at the various businesses. After a rather lengthy discussion and passing out assignments to the guards, I returned to the Chamber office.

I was sitting in the plush conference room of the Chamber, after returning from the briefing with the guards. I updated the property owners and store operators and explained, somewhat, the procedures and action that would be taking place. I made clear, in no uncertain language, that once the break-ins and looting began, "Shit would hit the fan!"

They seemed somewhat surprised but very excited about the prospects of protecting their businesses; they especially liked the idea of hiring 'defunded' or 'laid off' police officers as their security guards. Several even suggested that they would like to do the shooting themselves. One said. "Just let one of those SOBs break through my window or door, he won't do it a second time!"

Just after the group left my phone beeped on a special line, I picked up and it was Dawn, as I answered my phone beeped again, I knew it was

Sam; I punched in both lines and coverted to a conference call, "Okay you guys how are you making out, have y'all completed your briefings?" I asked. Both had conducted the same procedural briefings and meetings as I had.

"All done here," said Dawn.

"Me to," replied Sam. "What do we do next Chip, do we stick around or do we head back home," he asked?

"Do either of you see any reason to hang around any longer? If you do that's your decision. I gave some thought about staying another day, but now see no reason to, so I will be heading back tonight; maybe catch a red-eye flight to Columbia." I said

Both Sam and Dawn said they were ready to head back home; they had nothing else to do, and they would probably catch a red-eye also.

"Okay, I'll see you back at the Sweet Daddy Club sometime tomorrow. Since tomorrow is Friday, we may see some results of our briefings tomorrow night and over the weekend," I told them. "Stay safe!"

My flight landed at Atlanta's Hartfield Airport at 12:30a.m.; as I walked into the main concourse, I spotted Sam coming in from his flight looking sleepy, like from a not so refreshing, interrupted nap. We went to the nearby coffee bar and ordered coffee when we saw Dawn coming toward the coffee bar also---sleep in her eyes. It took her a couple of minutes to see us ---that woke her up --- she smiled real big and came in our direction; we had her fresh, hot coffee ready when she got to us.

Still smiling she said, "Now this is service, and really appreciated; I need the caffeine boost right now!"

"Rough flight," Sam asked?

"Not really, a little bumpy at times but I did manage a few winks," she replied.

"It looks as if we're on the same one-thirty flight back to Columbia," I said; "and I believe we're in three different vehicles. I think I'm going straight to the Sweet Daddy Club and to bed --- you guys can also if you would like --- unless you need to get home."

Sam said, "I'm all clear tomorrow and the weekend; I think I'll take you up on that---and sleep late for a change."

"Me too, I'm whipped and ready for a long weekend," Dawn said.

We heard the boarding call for 'Delta flight 3102 to Columbia, South Carolina', so we headed for the doorway. About forty minutes later we were in the approach pattern to descend and land at the beautiful Columbia Municipal Airport.

We convoyed back to the Sweet Daddy Club, drove in the back drive, parked and went inside with no one actually speaking; it was one tired and whipped team! I went to the fridge and got a cold beer and sat down in front of the TV and flipped on the news channel. A few minutes later Sam came down grabbed a beer and sat also. About thirty minutes later Dawn came down wearing a loose fitting jogging outfit and a towel wrapped around her wet hair.

"Boy," she exclaimed, "That shower sure makes a difference; I feel so much better, much more relaxed!" She got a beer and sat with us.

We discussed the day's events and briefings and how the proposals to protect property was accepted, and comments from the different groups. Each of us felt that our individual group was not only acceptable to the plan, but were excited about it. As we talked the news commentator was saying that *'they had received reports of 'peaceful protestors' making plans to protest on Saturday afternoon and evening'*.

Sam said, "Well, I guess we will find out soon enough if our friendly property owners are serious enough to take serious action."

One by one we drifted off to our rooms and to bed; we had had enough for one day --- and night.

I awoke at seven-thirty which is a little late for me, stretched and decided I may as well get up, couldn't go back to sleep anyway. I did my morning workout, limiting push-ups to thirty; my joints and bones felt a little older than usual this morning. I got my shower, got dressed in 'Saturday clothes', jeans and red flannel 'woodsy' shirt and went down to the kitchen.

Looking in the fridge I found a supply of sausage, eggs, bacon, a couple cans of biscuits --- the ones with the little fat guy that gets poked in the belly --- even found a box of five minute grits; this is going to be the breakfast of champions! I got the pot of grits started; put the biscuits in the oven, put the bacon and sausage on --- both --- in the same frying pan; shortly the aroma was too wonderful for anyone to sleep.

I looked up at a grumbling, sleepy-eyed Sam who said, "Do you have to rattle so many pots and pans in the middle of the night? It sounds like you're trying to wake the dead!"

"Good morning," I said as he stumbled toward the coffee pot.

"Bah-hum bug," Sam replied, smiling as he poured his coffee. He pulled up a chair and added, "I've gotta watch the 'master chef' at work here; have to be sure it's edible before I try it."

Dawn came bouncing in dressed in her jogging outfit, looking bright eyed and bushy tail; "That sure smells good," she said. "How long before breakfast is served?"

"About thirty minutes," I answered.

"Good, that's enough time for me to get in my morning run. I'm going to run around the front perimeter a couple of times," Dawn said, "then a quick shower and I'll really be ready for a big home cooked break-fast---don't burn it!"

Breakfast over; Sam said that he would hang out for a while and check the supplies in the garage rooms; Dawn decided she needed to go to her house and check it out and go shopping and I decided I needed to catch up on paperwork and other miscellaneous stuff. Dawn said she would be back late afternoon; we could watch the news and see if our visit had any effect.

Sam and I completed the small tasks that we had going, and then just hung-out watching a couple of old movies and football games the rest of the afternoon. About five-thirty Dawn called and said she was getting hungry and suggested I and Sam come into town and we would go to dinner, and may even have a somewhat balanced meal for a change. We thought that was a good idea we jumped up changed into more suitable clothing and headed in to Alcolu.

We met Dawn at Big Jim's Restaurant, in the upscale dining room, where she already had a booth and was sipping on a glass of white Zinfandel. As we came into the dining room Dawn held her glass up for us to see; we slid into the booth as the waiter came up to take our drink orders --- we both ordered beer.

Dawn said, "I was getting famished so I figured you two must be hungry also; neither of us have had a good solid meal for days."

"Yes 'mother'," Sam said laughing; "We were waiting for you to cook!"

"You couldn't wait that long," she countered ; "I told you I don't cook, not big time anyway."

The waiter returned with our beer and ready to take our meal orders. I ordered a large Filet steak wrapped with bacon and a side of Jim's famous garlic mashed potatoes and a salad. Sam thought for a moment and decided on the steak and potatoes also. Dawn ordered a specialty of the house, the Southwest, barbequed chicken on a bed of wild rice with sides of broccoli and baked sweet potato.

Big Jim stopped by the booth to speak and visit for a moment --- we have known Jim for several years --- "You guys must be hungry, you usually don't order that much food; I'm happy you are eating well tonight, I need the money," he said with a grin as he walked away!

We finished our meal without rushing, just relaxing and chatting; saw a few others we knew, visited and chatted with them for a while before finally leaving and heading back to the Sweet Daddy Creek Club.

CHAPTER THIRTY ONE

WE GOT BACK TO the club about nine o'clock and the three of us went straight to the den to catch the evening news; there it was, all over most of the news channels --- 'spontaneous, peaceful protests have begun in major cities on the west coast', the announcer was saying; *"spontaneous my ass"*, I thought, *"there are several hundred people carrying professionally prepared signs on the streets; they had been prepared and provided weeks prior, they didn't just run out and hand paint signs!"*

Dawn exclaimed, "That's a bunch of garbage, that is real 'fake news'!

"It's a pile of liberal crap," Sam said!

The city was Seattle. The TV camera crews closed in on a group of protestors at the front of a large electronics store filled with expensive 'goodies'; the camera focused on one of the leaders, obviously a paid protestor who fit the image of Antifa. He was yelling into his megaphone about white privilege and justice --- justice for a name I didn't recall ever hearing before; but then it really didn't matter --- like the old saying, 'if you need an excuse, any excuse will do'. Besides, the one yelling was a white, twenty-something, young man who had no idea what he was talking about; he was just earning his paycheck! But, give him credit the guy was getting the crowd stirred up, big time! The cameras began zooming in for close-ups, he was brandishing one of those small, short handle sledge hammers; several others, who evidently were his paid associates, were carrying large rocks and bricks; several of the group started banging on the show windows with their hands and fists screaming all kinds of vulgarities and swears; it was mostly a performance for the cameras.

One of the leaders threw a large rock at the largest window cracking it. Then all hell broke loose and the others joined in, throwing anything they could get their hands on.

"Oh shit," said Dawn, out loud! She looked around at Sam and me, embarrassed and turning a little red in the face. "Sorry," she said.

I said, "That's alright, Dawn, you're right, shit is about to hit the fan!"

The leader with the small sledge hammer went to the door and started banging on the glass; while he was accomplishing his task, a couple of the other leaders kept urging the crowd on, yelling for them to break the windows --- the crowd did just that!

The glass in the door finally gave way and fell onto the sidewalk and inside the store; the large windows shattered with glass flying in all directions; the leaders screaming to the crowd, "Come on, we're going to take this damn place, it belongs to us now!"

He and several others pushed their way into the store climbing over broken glass shards; they began picking up large screen televisions, iPhones and other expensive items; suddenly there was the ear splitting sound of gunfire --- the sound of shotguns being fired filled the night air – the crowd stopped momentarily then dropped their loot, turned and ran like hell, jumping back through the windows and doors from which they had just entered.

When the smoke cleared three bodies lay sprawled on the floor still clutching the stolen items they were trying to get away with. Three smiling, *'defunded'* law enforcement, security guards looked around at the chaos. One of them said, 'I don't guess they will try that little stunt again'!

The sound of sirens kept coming closer; the crowd had dispersed and scattered to who knows where; they just wanted to get out of there and they ran like hell in all directions. The three security guards kept their weapons up and on ready while they waited on the *'still funded'* officers to arrive.

Sam spoke up, "I wonder if the other cities, the ones that Dawn and I had charge of, have experienced their calling yet?"

"Yeah," said Dawn; "This has to have an impact on anyone else who is thinking of joining the Antifa protestors; surely they will have second thoughts now; at least when the word spreads."

The announcer on the screen was saying, "We'll take you to San Francisco where John is covering an even larger crowd of marchers and protestors; it looks as if the majority are peaceful, but some in the crowd are urging them on and it's beginning to get others stirred up as they approach the main downtown area. Hundreds of homeless people live on the sidewalks in the business districts; this area has become their 'homes'. They obviously don't like the idea of protestors coming into their 'private' area knocking over their tents and large boxes that to them, is 'home'. Now it looks as though some of the protestors are planning to start fires." The camera zoomed in on several protestors who had bottles with rags hanging out; the bottles were filled with a liquid --- probably gas!

The camera got in even closer and showed a close-up of one of the hands holding a bottle; you could see a lighter in the other hand; as the camera backed off you could see that it was a young girl probably in her early to mid-twenties. She also had a professional look about her, obviously one of the paid crew, perhaps an Antifa leader or recruiter.

There must have been at least a hundred police standing on the sidelines watching; knowing what was about to happen, but making no effort to break it up before it got started; they had been ordered to 'stand down'! The scene on the TV switched to Portland; we saw the same thing taking place as in San Francisco. The announcer was saying, "It is difficult to tell the difference between San Francisco, Seattle and Portland this evening. Protestors are filling the streets in the downtown business districts in all three cities. The people leading the protests look and sound as if they mean business; several have fired up their Molotov cocktails in the San Francisco area and are looking toward an upscale men and ladies clothing store; others have moved on to an electronics business. A white van has just pulled onto the street and opened its doors. Some of the leaders are reaching inside; oh my God! They are pulling out large rocks, bricks and large hammers, and passing them to the protestors; now they are unloading what looks to be a steel beam that's about four or five feet long; they're planning to break down doors and knock out display windows! Folks, this is going to get nasty before this night is over!"

I looked over at Dawn and Sam; Dawn was getting red in the face and shaking her fist at the television. "I would be happy to shoot those bastards myself," she said almost yelling!

Sam and I looked at each other then back to Dawn, "Calm down we have done all we can, we will be finding out soon enough if it is sufficient to make a difference," I told her.

Sam said, "We feel the same as you Dawn, and we would love to take those assholes down ourselves. Right now I'm fighting to keep from throwing something at the TV!"

The cameras caught one of the large display windows crashing and the doors to the clothing store, torn from the hinges; the camera also caught the flaming trail of a Molotov cocktail as it flew through the air and landed inside the store with its thousands of dollars of stock. Several from the crowd of protestors along with the leaders, rushed into the store swinging hammers and knives. Suddenly three or four security guards stepped forward, leveled their twelve gauge pump shotguns at the leaders who stopped in their tracks; one raised his hand --- it had a gun in it --- that was the last mistake he would ever make! Four twelve gauge shotguns went off nearly the same time; four of the Antifa leaders fell where they stood.

The cameras never showed the security guards faces, only from the shotgun levels down; the cameras also showed the falling protestors and the screaming crowd, as they shoved and stomped and stumbled over each other trying to get out of the store. There was mayhem throughout the store and on the street, as the crowd panicked and fled the scene as fast as they could run, stepping on each other, some trying to jump over those who were moving too slow.

Meanwhile, the announcers at the studio and on the scene were silent, too stunned to say a word. After a full minute of dead air, the camera crew and on scene announcer, running in the opposite direction of the shooting, stopped running and the 'jogging', jumping scenes on the television settled down.

With fear in his eyes the on scene announcer, out of breath said, "Damn folks, that was scary as hell!" The studio immediately pulled the camera from live feed, back to the studio where the host announcer said, "This is a dangerous situation and we are attempting to keep our crews safe; we have instructed them to pull back from the active scene. We will be back in a moment." The commercials began; the commercials were used to cover the confusion of the reporters and give them time to recuperate. It was obvious they were frightened; they thought they were running for their life.

The network was switching back and forth between the three major cities, the scenes were pretty much identical; property and store owners were protecting their property! Scene after scene, from a half dozen different businesses in each city, cameras were catching 'live' footage of people being shot by shotguns held by 'legal, authorized' security guards.

In one city the news lady was reporting that three were killed by shotgun blasts and four wounded in an electronics store; in the upscale ladies' clothing boutique, on the screen, two female looters were dead and three males wounded; in another city the reporter announced two dead and two wounded from apparent shotgun blasts! In the largest of the three cities covered, San Francisco, there was panic on the streets! Panic, mayhem, screaming, yelling; hell it was hard to tell what was going on in that place. The reporters – on the scene and in the studio, sounded as if they were in panic mode also; they didn't know what they should do next.

The television network had four-way, split screens showing four different businesses with the windows and doors broken out; there must have been at least two hundred protestors pushing and shoving; anybody who got in their way were knocked to the floor and stepped over or stomped on, as they grabbed merchandise by the arm full; suddenly the lower portion of each screen was filled with the images of uniformed persons, each holding a shotgun. In one of the stores a loud voice boomed over the cacophony of the crowd of looters, "Stop where you are; put all of the merchandise on the floor, turn around and get the hell out of here --- before somebody gets hurt!"

There were several responses of, "You go to hell, this is ours now; we own this place!" Several of the looters made a move toward the guards holding the shotguns; There must have been five shotguns going off at virtually the same time; five of the front row robbers leading the group, dropped where they stood --- probably dead before they hit the floor!

What followed next was unbelievable! A massive mob turning almost as one, screaming and howling in fear as they ran as fast as they could toward the door; fifty --- a hundred who could tell at this point --- all trying to get through the same door and window at one time. The metal framed door was quickly ripped from the floor and ceiling; people were falling in and out of the store, some caught half way through and knocked down were laying across the bottom frame of the window bleeding and screaming in pain as others used the body to step over the broken window.

If this had been a western movie, it would be called . . . **STAMPEDE!**

There was more blood flowing from those who had fallen on the shattered glass than from the shotgun blasts; they had been stomped on, walked on and kicked as the frenzied mob tried to escape. Adding to the confusion was the shrill sound of approaching sirens. It sounded as if the 'funded' law enforcement, the 'cavalry was on the way to save the day'!

Within an hour the streets of all three cities were empty, deserted except for a few police officers who looked confused, not knowing what to expect next. An open microphone caught one officer's comment, "Holy shit! I'm sure glad I wasn't here; I'm glad those security guards did our job for us."

"Hell yes," said his partner; "If we had 'cleaned house' like they did, we would all be on trial tomorrow and sent to prison! But I'll tell you something else, if I had been here I think I would have joined with the guards and blown a couple of these assholes to hell; jail or no jail! Somebody has got to stop this shit!"

Sitting here in the Sweet Daddy Creek Club, other than the television, there was complete silence; I think the three of us were stunned. Our little visit had done the job! Success!

Dawn, obviously disturbed and fraught said in a quivering voice. "Damn guys, did we cause all of this? There are a dozen or more dead bodies lying in those stores and on the street!" What will happen to them?" She added.

"They will send them to the morgue for ID and processing; as for the ones they arrest, I hope they will lock them away for a long stretch," Sam added.

We echoed in agreement.

The camera switched back to the on scene reporter who was interviewing the Chief of Police;

"What is your assessment of the situation?" the reporter asked.

The Chief answered, "The security guards did their jobs, they did exactly what they were hired to do, and that is to protect the property of the owners; not only that --- I feel certain that in protecting the property --- they saved their own lives! The cameras couldn't show the weapons that some of the protestors carried: handguns, knives, brass knuckles; and anything else that could be used for a weapon. It is pretty obvious that these so called 'looters' meant business. When we check their backgrounds we're going to find that they are not from around here; they were hired elsewhere and transported here to create chaos. Thanks to the owners and security guards, it backfired. God bless America!"

CHAPTER THIRTY TWO

MONDAY MORNING SITTING IN the Cut Rate about our usual time Sam, Dawn and I were rehashing the weekend events and news when my phone beeped. I clicked it open and it was old Jimbo whom I hadn't heard from since we closed the deal on the Sweet Daddy Creek Club property.

"Hey Jimbo," I said, "How the heck are you? I haven't seen you or heard from you and Uncle Sam in a long time; how are y'all doing?"

"Oh---I am so sorry to hear Jimbo; your uncle was a fine gentleman; I'm glad you called to let me know. Do you know the funeral arrangements yet? If not, please let me know when you find out."

Jimbo answered and told me, "Chip I'm pretty sure it's going to be Saturday morning at the Mt Pisgah Baptist Church just up the road a ways from your place. It will be good to see you again, Chip."

"Same here Jimbo, I miss us getting together over a beer and a plate of bar-b-que, is that place still open?"

"It sure is," Jimbo said, "In fact I ate there a couple of weeks ago, it's still good as ever!"

"I tell you what Jimbo, I have a couple of friends and cohorts I would like you to meet, how about I bring them with me, if they are available, and after the funeral we all go get bar-b-que for lunch?" I asked.

"That sounds great, Chip," I will surely look forward to doing just that," he said.

"Me too," I replied, "We'll see you Saturday."

Sam said looking at Dawn, "I think we just got invited to a funeral."

"Sounds that way," she replied. "Who died and why are we going to the funeral?" She asked.

I explained it all to them about Jimbo and his Uncle Samson and myself getting together and me buying the property.

There were a lot of people at the funeral on Saturday, standing room only; that really pleased Jimbo and his family. I saw a familiar face across the church, Jeff; I had not seen or talked with him since he went with SLED and was working in Columbia. I poked Sam, who was sitting next to me and nodded in Jeff's direction. Sam was as surprised as I.

After the services were over, Jeff came over to greet us and was surprised that we knew his Uncle Jimbo and great Uncle Sam. We invited Jeff to join us for the bar-b-que lunch but his family was with him and they were headed back to Columbia. We got to meet his wife and two kids; a nice family who seemed to be very happy. Seeing how happy they were sent chills up my spine.

We got in our cars, Sam, Dawn and me in mine and Jimbo in his car and we followed Jimbo to the old BBQ restaurant. When we drove into the parking lot the two looked at me with questioning eyes.

"Is this where we're eating?" Sam asked.

"Y'all will love it," I told them.

The place was about half full as we entered; Dawn spotted a couple of lawyers she knew; Sam saw familiar faces also.

"Must be pretty good eating," said Dawn; "I feel a little better about eating it," she said smiling.

Jimbo laughed and said, "Y'all are going to love it, if you like bar-b-que that is."

"Bring it on," chuckled Sam.

After eating, most everyone else had left; we just kept sitting and talking mostly about old times in each of our lives; when Jimbo spoke up; "You know Chip we are going to have to sell that other piece of land that Uncle Sam owned, that's where my house is and I have lived on it for almost all of my life. I really don't want to move but I can't keep it up and pay the taxes, the only income I have is Social Security, and that ain't very much.

"You saw my nephew, Jeff, at the funeral today, he wants to buy it but he can't afford to right now. He just got started on a new job in Columbia and this would be a little closer for him to drive every day."

I thought for a few minutes and then told Jimbo that I would buy the remainder of the property in his name, he would own it outright; and when Jeff was able, he could sell it to him, provided Jimbo could live on it at no cost as long as he lived. It was large enough for Jeff to build him and his family a nice house and do a little gardening or farming on the side, or whatever he would like.

Tears came up in Jimbo's eyes and he said, "Chip you can't do that; I can't let you do that."

"Like hell you can't! Jimbo we have been friends for a long time, good friends; and Uncle Sam was my friend too; if wasn't for the two of you I would never have found this place. I'll pay you the same price per acre that I paid Uncle Sam for the front piece. Besides, Jeff will make a good neighbor."

"Chip, are you sure?" Jimbo asked.

"Jimbo, you know what, I ain't going to give you a choice; I'll go down to the clerk of court's office first thing Monday and make the transfer. I know somebody who works there and she will make it happen," I said as I looked over at a smiling Dawn.

She smiled at Jimbo and said, "You don't worry about it, Jimbo, I've got you covered; if you need anything else you just give me a call."

We all then just sat back with a belly full of bar-b-que, ordered another beer, propped our feet up and continued telling tales and laughing at some of the things we did when we were much younger.

CHAPTER THIRTY THREE

MONDAY MORNING WE'RE SITTING at the Cut Rate having breakfast --- Sam, Dawn and myself --- when who shows up but Jeff, surprising us. He slid into the booth beside Sam and asked, "You buying breakfast Chip?"

"What is this," I said, "A highly paid state government employee trying to bum a meal off hard working, under paid day laborers," I replied.

Sam almost gagged on his of coffee. "I was trying to figure out what kind of work I did," he said, still laughing, "Now I know --- I'm, a day laborer; but I don't think I get paid that much."

When everyone settled down, Jeff got serious and told me, "I know what you did for my Uncle Jimbo and my great granddaddy Chip, and I want you to know how much I appreciate it. Uncle Jimbo wants me to go ahead and build a place for the family, there is plenty of room on the acreage; as soon as I get a little more cash saved up, I'm going to take him up on it."

"That will be great Jeff; I know your family will like that," I replied.

Sam said, "I am really proud of you Jeff, I know you're going to do well in your new job; in fact I have already heard some good things about you from some of my contacts at SLED."

"Well, don't you guys start thinking that you have gotten rid of me, at least not yet anyway," he said.

"What do you mean by that?" I asked.

Jeff responded, "Well, my boss has put me on a little assignment right here in Alcolu; he thought I might have the right contacts to run down some information that the agency has been checking into for the past year or so."

He grinned and continued, "It is something you guys are already familiar with; fact is that's what you came to me looking for information about and needing my help. Come to find out the folks in Columbia have been trying to get an inside track for a couple of years. It has to do with some crooked cops and a judge who have been skimming off confiscated cash and 'merchandise'; does that sound familiar?"

"Oh shit!" said Sam.

Dawn said, "You can say that again, I believe it's about to hit the fan!"

"What are the plans," I asked; "When is something going down; and what approach are they taking? Do you have any idea of what's going to happen?"

Jeff replied, "It should be pretty soon now; they have been working for some time on this and I believe it's about to come to a head --- in fact some heads may roll over this! I don't know any of the details yet but I will try to keep you posted about what's going on and when. By the way, I have talked with my boss about keeping you guys informed and he agrees; so I won't be talking out of school."

"That's good Jeff, don't take any chances — with your safety or your new job," I told him.

With that said, I added, "Let's have a good old fashioned, greasy breakfast; it's on me Jeff."

Sam and Dawn looked at each other and Sam said, "This is our lucky day Dawn; the boss is buying breakfast for all of us!"

Dawn laughed and Jeff said, "You guys better enjoy it while you can, Chip doesn't pay very often. I think I'll order steak and eggs."

"Jeff," I countered, "Can you let me hold a couple of twenties, just until payday that is?" The four of us sat for another thirty minutes or so chatting about things in the past – no mention of what the immediate future may hold. None of us wanted to think about it, much less talk openly about it.

Jeff got up and said he had to leave; Dawn needed to get to work and Sam had errands to run for his family. I decided I may as well leave also; I could go check my 'little house in the hood' or to the Sweet Daddy Creek Club and spend some 'lone' time just thinking; I decided on both and left along with the others.

Everything checked out fine in the 'hood' so I headed out into the countryside to my retreat. I was just puttering around the Club going from one thing to another without accomplishing anything. However, I did manage to double check on supplies and items in the weapons room; best to always be prepared; you never knew what the next step might bring.

My phone beeped and I punched in, "Chip Storrington," I answered.

"Hey Chip, Ed Winters in Atlanta."

"Ed, it's good to hear from you so soon," I said. "We go several years with no contact and then, 'bam' we talk twice within a month. What's going on with the FBI Chief in Atlanta?" I asked.

Ed replied, "I just wanted to give you a heads up; I'm coming your way next week; your friends over at SLED in Columbia, asked if we could spare a couple of agents to help with a case they were getting ready to bust. I decided since it was in your neck of the woods I would be one of the agents to go."

"Ed, is this one of those situations that we discussed when I came down?" I asked.

"That's the one," he said. "The guys at SLED are too well known in the area and would be picked up on immediately. They wanted an outsider, an unknown to be the primary instigator and contact person."

"I do believe crap is about to hit the proverbial fan!" I said. Then I remembered and asked. "Ed, do you remember the young fellow I spoke with you about, and you set him up with SLED? His name is Jeff."

"I remember," Ed said, "In fact he is my contact in Alcolu, we have spoken on the phone and will be getting together when I get there. He sounds like a nice, ambitious young man and should make a good partner."

"I believe he will; you'll like him I'm sure. Give me a call and let me know when you will be arriving, we'll have a beer or two," I said.

"Sounds good to me Chip; I look forward to seeing you in about a week," Ed said as he punched off.

I thought it might be a good idea to let Sam and Dawn know what's coming down and that the crap is about to hit the fan they were talking about. I punched in Sam's number.

"Sam Dillinger, how may I help you?" the voice said.

"How may I help you? --- cut the crap Sam; you knew it was me. I've got some news for you old buddy; I just received a call from my friend, the bureau chief in Atlanta, you remember, the FBI!"

"So what's the news, Chip, I know a lot of FBI folks?" Sam asked.

"Well, Mr. Smart-ass, I'm talking about Ed Winters, and he is coming to town next week. He will be helping SLED bust a certain judge and his cronies. Not only that, but you will never guess who his working partner will be," I added.

"Oh shit," said Sam; "Don't tell me it's going to be Jeff, that's getting a little close, if you ask me."

"My thoughts exactly," I said; "I better give Dawn a call and let her know too."

Sam, kind of thinking out loud mumbled, "This sort of puts Dawn in a tight spot, since she works in the Clerk of Court's office and has to deal with the judge, almost on a daily basis. Chip, we best keep an eye on her, be sure we have her back and see that nothing happens to her!"

I replied, "Don't worry Sam, I keep my eye on her all the time anyway; I'll shoot anybody who messes with her or tries anything. I know she is capable, as she says, of taking care of herself. But, it won't hurt to have a couple of other eyes watching also."

CHAPTER THIRTY FOUR

I HAD JUST FINISHED checking the supplies to see what was short and may be needed and making a list; everything from ammo to groceries. Who knows, I thought, I may be cooking breakfast, or even dinner for Dawn some evening—real soon. I want to be prepared.

My phone beeped and I saw that it was Ed, "Are you in town?" I asked when I clicked him on.

"I just arrived and got checked in; being Monday I decided I better get an early start" he said.

"Where are you staying while in our fair city?" I asked.

"I am in room 210 looking out over Main Street and facing the old town clock tower, at the Hyatt Hotel," Ed said.

"Great, get settled in, relax and let me know when you start feeling hunger pains and we'll go to dinner," I said; then added, "Since you're on an expense account, I'll even let you pay."

"Well, that's down right nice of you, Chip; by the way, do you pay taxes---?"

"Ahh, touche`," I laughed. "I guess I'll be paying after all, one way or another."

"The perfect host," he replied.

I said, "Since I will paying; would you mind if I bring a friend, one of my associates; she is up on all the crap that's going on around here?"

"Are you speaking of the gorgeous, blonde, 'dream' you were telling me about?" Ed asked. "I would like to meet her."

I called Dawn as soon as we hung up the phone. She answered on the first ring, "Hey Chip, I was just thinking about you, wondering what you were doing," she said.

"Well, I was just thinking about trying to line up a date for tonight and I thought I would give you a call and see if you might have any suggestions of someone I could ask," I said.

Without hesitation she replied, "Wow; now that is a pretty tough situation to be in Chip; not too many girls I know would go on a date with you; they have to consider their reputations, you know."

"Ouch!" I said. "You really know how to hurt a guy, Dawn. I have a friend in town and we're meeting for dinner and I told him I would invite a beautiful girl to have dinner with us; incidentally, he is with the FBI and is the chief of the Atlanta Bureau office."

"I hate to see anyone embarrassed with his friends," she said. "I guess I could put my reputation on hold for the evening --- to help you out of a jam --- and go with you." She laughed out loud!

"Sam is right!" I said; "forget trying to get 'one-up' on you!"

Still laughing, she asked, "What time and do I need to dress up?"

"How about I pick you up about seven thirty; and dress, just business casual, nothing fancy," I stated.

I called Ed back and told him we would meet him at Big Jim's Restaurant at eight, and then called for reservations.

Dawn and I arrived about fifteen minutes early; the hostess had our table ready and seated us while we waited for Ed. The waiter came and we both ordered wine and engaged in small talk while I gazed into her beautiful blue eyes --- while glancing at my watch and waiting for Ed to show.

Straight-up eight o'clock the door opens and Ed walks in, spots us and heads to our table. I stood and greeted him and introduced Dawn. They shook hands and he sat down saying as he did, "Chip has told me all about you Dawn, in fact I couldn't get him to slow down or stop talking about you when he was in Atlanta a few weeks ago. I must say, he didn't exaggerate either; you are as lovely and charming as he said."

Dawn was turning a deep shade of red; she looked over at me saw that I was smiling; she looked back at Ed for a few moments then she said, "Excuse me Ed, but you men are so full of crap; you sound just like Chip, now. But thank you for the compliment anyway."

Ed and I cracked up while people at tables around us turned to look.

Ed spoke up, "I'm serious, Dawn, I've known this guy for years and never have I heard him talk about a girl like you before. I didn't think he even knew the words."

We laughed and Dawn looked at me and said, "Well I hope he means it; it could get him into a lot of trouble."

I just stared at her!

Grinning Ed said, "I think I will change the subject."

"When Chip told me about you attending the FBI Academy," he said to Dawn, "I pulled out a couple of my books and saw where we were a couple of years apart. I also saw where you were on the Academy SWAT team and in the top of your class; that's pretty impressive Dawn."

"Thanks," she replied, "I was just lucky, very fortunate to have good instructors."

The waiter came to take our dinner orders; Dawn ordered Big Jim's Pecan encrusted chicken with two sides while Ed and I both ordered the bacon wrapped filet with fattening sides like garlic mashed potatoes and butter drenched bread, along with more wine for the three of us.

Dawn asked Ed what the first steps that he and SLED, the FBI and local law enforcement would be taking and what was the timeline they would be working toward. She also asked if either of us, or Sam, would be involved in the operation. And, just how were they going to make the arrests; would it be quiet or a raid somewhere. She was really interested in what all was going to occur.

Ed explained to her that his office, the South Carolina FBI office and SLED had been working undercover on the case for more than a year. He told her that they had done interviews and had affidavits from several individual law enforcement officers who were in on some of the stops and figured something was going on, although they had not personally counted or inventoried the merchandise. They didn't like it and felt certain that they had confiscated a lot more than was being reported and turned in. Ed also explained that they had agents planted among the patrol units that made stops in the heaviest drug trafficking areas of I-95, around mile markers 134 plus or minus, along the Interstate.

After about thirty minutes and a couple more glasses of wine, our dinner arrived; we dined pretty much in silence with just small talk about life in the big city and in small towns like Alcolu. Ed told us about his wife Marie and their twin boys, and some of the hijinks the boys would pull; just plain, old fashioned family talk.

Dawn remarked kind of soulfully, "That sounds like the perfect life; I hope to have a family and a couple of kids someday, when the time is right."

Ed smiled at that remark, looked over at me, then picked up where he left off when dinner had arrived. "These agents have some pretty interesting tales to tell; it's hard to believe what goes on out there on the roads in the dark of night and especially on weekends."

"I can well imagine," I said. "I'm just glad that it's not me out there making the stops and busts; that could get pretty 'hairy'!

"That's for sure!" Ed replied.

"That's why we are having more troopers shot or killed now than ever before," Dawn said. "These drug runners have no hesitation about pulling the trigger on anybody, including deputies or troopers; it makes no difference to them."

"Unfortunately that's true," said Ed. "It isn't just troopers or deputies, but it's the same with our FBI agents and officials in other agencies such as CIA and Secret Service too. There seems to be no respect for law and order anymore."

It was eleven o'clock when Big Jim himself came over to the table and I introduced him to Ed; Jim turned to me and said, "Me and the crew are going home now, you can lock up when you leave; oh by the way Chip, just leave the bill with the cash on the counter by the register, I'll get it in the morning;" he laughed as he walked away.

I remarked, "Is this a hint Jim, that we have over stayed our welcome?"

CHAPTER THIRTY FIVE

AT SEVEN IN THE morning I pulled into a parking space near the entrance of the Hyatt, parked got my phone and punched in Ed's number. He answered right away and said that he was in the lobby and saw me pull in; I had told him last night I would pick him up for breakfast. I got out of my car and met him coming out.

"Let's just walk to our breakfast place," I said, "It's only a block down Main Street; Dawn will probably be there, and I want you to meet Sam Dillinger, a good friend from the old days and a good partner now; we've been in a lot of close scrapes together, especially in Vietnam. He saved my butt several times."

As we walked Ed remarked, "This is a really nice downtown, Chip; it is so neat and clean, how do they manage to keep it that way?"

"Well," I replied, "We've got a very knowledgeable and hardworking city manager; he is very sharp and knows how to keep the mayor and council in check so they don't run away with their ideas and pet projects."

As I turned into the entrance of the Cut Rate Ed said, "A drug store? You're taking me to breakfast at a drug store?" Ed laughed and followed me in. I spotted Sam and Dawn in our usual booth, they already had their coffee.

I introduced Sam to Ed while Ed grinned at Dawn and said, "Good morning, Dawn; I see you got home safely last evening, although I was a little concerned about you riding with that escort who accompanied you."

Smiling Sam said, "If you know him like I do, you have every right to be concerned."

Dawn spoke in my defense, "What is this, pick on Chip day? I'll have you know he is the perfect gentleman when he is with me; always!"

Then she added, "But it isn't my fault!"

That was enough to 'crack up' everybody; even at nearby tables who had overheard; Sam laughed so hard he had tears in his eyes.

After things got settled and somewhat back to normal, Ed said to Sam, "Chip has told me all about you Sam and how close y'all have worked over the years, not only that but I have some friends over at SLED who speak very highly of you. Why don't you become FBI and join me in Atlanta?"

"Nah," Sam replied, "I've done my share with the feds and I'm happier right here at home. Besides Chip, Dawn and I pull off an operation from time to time to keep our interest up.

"Speaking of operations, when is this local thing going down?" Sam added.

Lowering his voice Ed said, "Within the next four to five days I believe. We have a number of agents on site ready to play back-up for the SLED SWAT teams that will be going in; right now we're trying to figure out exactly where the best 'going-in' spot is."

"They must have had another profitable weekend," Dawn said; "A couple of the judge's cronies, his 'personal errand' boys, brought in the weekend's receipts; about twenty-five thousand good old American dollars; neatly tied and wrapped in bundles."

Ed responded with, "Yeah, we're waiting for them to turn-in the other twenty-five grand."

Dawn asked, "The other twenty-five? That's about what we at the office figured; but how did you know how much?"

Sam looked at Ed and said, "You must have some agents inside somewhere, and they must be trusted. Otherwise, the judge would never let information like that leak out."

"You're right Sam," Ed said; "I don't even know who the agents are, and that is good, we don't need someone to slip up and say too much, accidentally or not; could be dangerous. We don't have an accurate count of how much the take was, of course, but the guys on the scene got a pretty good estimate; they are certain it had to be more than fifty to seventy five thousand; plus I'm sure there was probably some contraband --- drugs in the stop also."

Just then Maxine, our usual waitress, came up and in her usual 'smart-ass' way said, "Well Dawn, I'm glad you finally got smart and got a second chaperone to help Sam keep an eye on Chip. If you could see the look in his eyes when you walk in, you would turn tail and run . . . ha . . . ha. . .," she laughed; it was one of those, genuine, 'I don't know where it came from' laughs! Maxine laughed so hard she spilled a little coffee from the carafe onto the table. Still laughing she said, "Would some of y'all like to order breakfast or are yall just going to sit here watching Chip drool looking at Dawn?"

"Damn, you're such a smart-ass, Maxine! You know full well that the only reason I come in this place every morning is so I can see you; I'm watching you when you're behind the counter, I see you when you bend over to pick something up; did I ever tell you that you have a nice big butt!"

I spoke just loud enough for those at other booths and at the counter could hear. Almost at once the place sounded like the fun house at the county fair; the whole place was laughing.

Maxine looked around, smiled and calmly retorted, "Just for that Chip my darling, I'm going to buy your breakfast this morning," she winked so everyone could see, and walked off.

Ed, still laughing, tears in his eyes, said, "I take it you guys come in here pretty often."

Sam, also still laughing, had tears in his eyes too, said, "I told you Dawn, you've got competition!"

Finally the place calmed down and no one was paying attention to us any longer.

"Welcome to the local watering hole Ed," I said.

Suddenly Dawn nudged me in the rib cage and kicked me under the table at the same time.

"What?" I asked. "I didn't . . ."

"Shhh, quiet," she said. Then in a whisper added, "Don't look now, but see those two deputies at the counter; the ones looking at us; they're the ones who brought in the cash from the latest bust on I-95. They have recognized me from the Clerk's office and nodded when I looked up; I helped count the cash and I gave them the receipt for the judge. They keep glancing over here; I think they are trying to figure out who Ed is; they know you and Sam."

"Yeah," I said, "The one with the lieutenant bars is Gary Rollins; he has been on the force a long time."

Sam said, "I think he is related to the judge in some way. They're nice guys but you don't want to cross them; they seem to pretty much run the show in the 'narc' division."

"They may be part of the group we're looking for," said Ed; "I guess we'll find out soon enough."

We kept sitting and talking for another fifteen minutes before Maxine finally brought our breakfast. Ed looked at his plate, grinned and said, "This looks good; I haven't had a breakfast like this since I left Alcolu, about a hundred years ago it seems. Country fried ham, grits with red-eye gravy, eggs over easy and buttery toast; this looks fabulous, Maxine, thanks."

"Enjoy," she said as she walked away.

Meanwhile, our two friendly deputies at the counter had left without our noticing.

Ed told us that he had to make a quick trip to Columbia for a meeting with the SLED folks but should be back by dark anyway. He got up to leave, I was going to go with him, but he said grinning, "Nah, you stay and flirt with Maxine, I'll just stroll back by myself."

Sam said, "Bring some news back, Ed. We're tired of waiting for something to happen."

"Yeah," Dawn added, "Let's get this thing over with."

About thirty minutes after Ed left, my phone beeped, it was Ed; "What's up Ed that was awfully quick?"

"Tell Sam he doesn't have to wait any longer Chip. I got back to the hotel, stopped by my room for a moment then went to the parking garage; I always park on the top deck, never much traffic there. Anyway, my car has been broken into and ransacked! It kind of looks like somebody was looking for something."

"Damn Ed! What could just anybody be looking for in your car?" I asked.

"What happened?" Dawn asked.

"Somebody has broken into Ed's car," I replied.

"Shit!" Sam said out loud. "That must mean the word is out and somebody is on the lookout, trying to find out who, what, when and where!"

I told Ed, "Hang tight Ed, I'll be right there; did you call the cops?"

The three of us; me, Sam, and Dawn were already out of our seats and headed for the door; Ed said he had not called the police yet; he would wait 'til I got there.

"Good," I said, "We're on the way." We didn't run but we probably walked faster than any of us had in years. We took the elevator to the top deck of the hotel parking garage; Ed stood beside his car, the only one on the entire top deck. It was an easy target for anyone who wanted to break in unnoticed.

The front windows were completely broken out; the doors were open, and the trunk had been forced open with everything that had been in it, now strewn around the floor of the deck. Being the typical FBI agent, Ed was checking everything, looking for clues that would give an indication of who might be responsible. Even so, he made it a point not to disturb anything, he would leave that to the local police; they could dust for prints and whatever else they wanted to check.

"Are you missing anything Ed?" I asked.

"I didn't leave anything of importance in here," Ed replied. "I did have my FBI issue .38 revolver in the glove box, that is gone; biggest thing is they made a damn mess! Besides, they aren't very smart."

"How is that?" I asked.

Dawn spoke up and said, "Whether they realize it or not they committed a federal crime; this is an official car of the Federal Bureau of Investigation – and so is the .38 they stole; right Ed!"

Sam said, "You're right Dawn, and I've got a hunch who did this."

"So do I," replied Dawn; "And I believe we just saw them about half an hour ago."

"You don't mean . . ." Ed said as his voice trailed off knowingly. "I'll be damned!" he exclaimed.

CHAPTER THIRTY SIX

ED CALLED ME ON his way back from Columbia, he said he was somewhere in the middle of the swamp on highway 378, he had a rental car and would be back in town in roughly thirty minutes. He suggested I give Sam and Dawn a call and have them meet us for dinner around 'sevenish' maybe at Big Jim's again.

"Sounds like a plan Ed, I'm sure they both will be happy with that; especially if you're buying again," I said.

"Well Chip, you know how it is with official business --- expense account --- and all that," Ed laughed as he clicked off.

I picked up Dawn and we drove into Big Jim's parking lot at seven-thirty; Ed and Sam were already inside sitting at the bar with a beer in their hand and waiting for a table. We joined them at the bar, standing where we could carry on a conversation.

Ed said, "I invited another to join us, but he thought it could be dangerous with him and the four of us; he is a friend of y'all."

"If you're talking about Jeff," I said, "He is right, he is too well known among the crowd that our group runs with. We don't want to stir the pot too early."

"You're right Chip," Ed said; "We don't want to tip our hand just yet, we don't have to do a rush job on this. We have to be certain that we have everything covered; we don't need any slip ups."

We took our time eating and just chatting about a little of everything, until Big Jim came by that is.

Always the smart-ass with a wisecrack ready, Jim said, "Well Chip, I see you and Sam have decided to lock up for me again, we closed half an hour ago and the last customers left about an hour ago; all the other employees have gone home, except your waiter --- I told him that he was on your payroll now, not mine, but that you pay well . . . Ha . . . ha . . . ha!"

"You're a real smart-ass Jim, you know that!" I said. Jim kept laughing as he walked into the kitchen.

Dawn said, "I believe Jim was hinting that it is time for us to leave."

Ed and Sam, grinning, nodded in agreement, so we got up and headed out into the parking lot and home.

Ed Winters awoke from a deep sleep and looked at the clock by the hotel bedside --- two a.m. in the morning --- he was certain that he had heard a noise, at the door, like someone was attempting to 'jimmy' the lock on his room door. The break-in on his car in the parking deck flashed through his mind; he reached under the pillow and withdrew his .38 pistol; rather than getting up, Ed just slid out of the bed and eased himself to the floor beside the bed then he 'scooted' further toward the wing-back chair near the window putting the chair between him and the door.

He heard the lock click open, *'damn, he thought, they must have a key'!* The door eased open quietly and he saw two men enter the room just a few steps, they stopped and raised their arms, *'shit, thought Ed, they've got guns'!* There were several sudden puffs from each gun with the shots hitting the empty bed. When they first entered Ed had raised his gun and was waiting; as soon as he saw the guns fire, he pulled the trigger on his .38 . . . twice . . . and both men fell where they stood.

My phone woke me with its loud, maddening, chirping sound; it was the frantic voice of Ed that greeted me with, "What kind of shithouse city are you involved with here, Chip?"

"Ed, calm down, it's two o'clock in the morning for Christ's sake, you must be having a bad dream," I replied.

"Bad dream my ass! I've got two dead bodies lying here at the foot of my bed," He said.

That's when Ed calmed enough to tell me what had happened; he had already called 9-1-1 and the police were on the way. I told Ed I would be there in a few minutes, I was close by; I had decided to spend the night in my 'little house in the hood'.

When I pulled up onto the block where the Opera House was situated, directly across the street from the Hyatt Hotel, I was stopped; it was blocked off by a black and white police car, blue lights flashing, with the officer standing beside it watching the activity going on a half block from where he was located. I got out of my car to speak with him and it was a cop that I had known for several years. He told me that Liberty Street was also blocked off as were the streets behind the hotel.

I parked in a space where we were standing and he let me on through; I had explained my connection with Ed. The same happened when I approached the lobby of the hotel, I spotted Police Chief Russell Roberts talking with Ed and went over to them; I had also known Russ for many years, as well as most of the other uniformed cops.

As I walked up Russ said, "I might have known you were involved in some way, Chip. Now you've even got the FBI in town, although I guess it may be you they're looking for; no telling what you've been up to." He turned to Ed, "Ed do you need to borrow my cuffs, it may take a couple pair to hold him, he's slippery as hell?" he added.

"Very funny Russ; what's going on Ed, did you have a bad dream or something?"

"You bet your ass it was a bad dream, only this one came to life, in my room, right in front of me! If the noise of them trying to unlock the door had not awakened me, I would be toast now; that would be me in one of those body bags the coroner's folks are carrying out."

Russ said, "You were damn lucky Ed; and a good thing you had your weapon handy when that door opened."

"When I heard the noise at the door," Ed said, "It took me a few seconds to comprehend what was happening. I grabbed my .38 from underneath my pillow – that's an old time habit of mine – I slid out of the bed and scooted behind the chair by the window. Those bastards had noise suppressors – silencers on their guns."

I remarked, "That was very thoughtful of them Ed, they didn't want to wake you."

"Thanks," he said, then asked, "Chip has anyone briefed Russ on all the activity that's being set up?" Then turning to Russ he asked him, "Russ, has anyone from SLED or the Columbia FBI Office called you to discuss what is about to take place in your little town of Alcolu?"

Russ answered, "No, why would anyone; I'm always the last person to know what's going on around here. Want to know something, it pisses me off too!"

Ed and I laughed at the look on Russ's face, a real look of frustration and disgust.

"Seriously though," Ed said, "Russ, we need to get together today and bring you up to date on something. This is a case that has been in the works for some time now, and it's beginning to come to a head; probably later this week."

Russ answered, "You just say where and when; only right now I've got to see this mess is cleaned up before I leave; I think things are calming down and the investigating team will wrap it up shortly. I'm sure they will be working on this one for a long while to find all the answers."

I alerted the two of them to the fact that it was now four o'clock in the morning and none of us had had much sleep. I said, "I am going to my 'little house in the hood', lay my head on my pillow for about an hour; then I will arise get my shower and meet both of you for breakfast, just down the block at the Cut Rate. Goodnight or morning!"

CHAPTER THIRTY SEVEN

SEVEN O'CLOCK CAME REALLY early, especially after only about an hour's sleep; normally I'm up showered and dressed by six-thirty; I must be getting old, I thought, or at least 'older', I feel like it too. I walked into the Cut Rate a little before eight and saw Dawn sitting alone sipping her coffee.

"Well it is about time someone else showed up," she said as I sat down beside her in the booth. "Is something going on that is keeping everybody away from here?" Then she looked up and said, "Oh, here comes Ed now and Sam is close behind."

They came on, sat down and immediately ordered coffee; make it black and strong they told the waitress. I asked Ed, "Where did you wind up spending the night, did you stay in your room?"

"Not hardly," he answered, "The lab guys were still there and the hotel offered me another room; they even had my stuff moved while I was answering questions and checking with the detective crew, they were still there when I left a few minutes ago; they said they would probably be there most of the day also; said since it's Thursday they wanted to finish it up before the weekend."

"What the heck is going on?" Dawn asked

Ed explained to Dawn the events of the evening, after our dinner; like, being shot at by two guys who came into his room around two in the morning and fired several shots into his bed.

"You're kidding me," she exclaimed. "Someone tried to kill you last night? In the middle of the night? In your room? In your bed?" She asked. "If you were not in the bed, where were you?"

Ed explained about hearing the noise and getting over behind the chair with his .38 ready. He looked at Dawn and calmly told her, "When I saw them raise their weapons, that was it --- I just blew their heads off; I wasn't going to wait and ask them any questions --- that was the end of it!"

"Damn!" exclaimed Dawn; "Right here in the middle of downtown Alcolu. Who would ever have thought you could get your butt shot off in the middle of the night, in the middle of the business district! My God --- even while you're in your bed sound asleep."

Maxine, our waitress came to take our order and in her usual smart 'alecky' manner said, "I aint messing with y'all this morning; y'all looking too serious, like you want to hurt somebody."

After she had the order and left, Sam spoke up saying, "Seems to me that someone – who we probably know – is aware of your presence and your purpose, Ed. You better keep a close eye on your backside or that 'someone' will blow it off."

"I believe you just may be right, Sam; especially after that 'someone' broke into my car and made a mess of it, almost before I got checked in yesterday, and then tried to kill me while I slept, all in the same day; hell that's just day one," Ed remarked. "I wonder what day two will produce."

I said, "Damn Ed, I didn't realize I was getting you into a shit-load of trouble, and almost get your head blown off. I hope this whole situation will be settled real soon, before somebody gets seriously hurt."

"It is going to be taken care of shortly," Ed pointed out. "In fact I was going to give you a call today and see if you can make a meeting with me, the leader of the SLED SWAT team, and a few other agents tomorrow in Columbia at the SLED office. They don't want to take a chance of it leaking and the wrong people finding out what's going down and when; they don't know for sure who they can trust in the department here, other than Chief Russell, he will be meeting with us also."

"Sure, I'll be there," I answered, "What time?"

"The meeting is scheduled for one o'clock," Ed replied. "I'm going over earlier in the morning so I can talk with some of the guys I know, and find out what the plans are and when they intend to shut this operation down; I'd like to have a little advance information."

I looked at Dawn and Sam and asked them, "What if we have dinner tomorrow evening, say around eight; I can brief you on what I know and what's going on and just how much we're involved, if we are involved in any way at all."

"Oh, I'm sure all of you will be," Ed said; "I've already recommended that we get all the help we can from you guys here who know the situation better than anybody else, as well as the people we're looking at. I told them about you, Dawn and Sam, and your inside connections and knowledge of all the crap that's been going on for a long time now."

After breakfast we all got up to leave: Dawn back to her job at the Clerk of Court's office, Sam said he had some investigating to do and was heading over to headquarters. He also said that he would keep his eyes and ears open just in case. Ed was going back to the hotel to check on his stuff and the investigators to see how they were getting along, and when they would be finished with him.

I decided I would check my little house in the hood and then head over to the Sweet Daddy Creek Club for the rest of the day.

CHAPTER THIRTY EIGHT

I HAD FINISHED CHECKING over everything and was just taking it easy when my phone chirped; I saw it was Jeff. "Hey stranger, what have you been up to lately?" I asked him.

"We've been right busy, Chip," Jeff replied. "I wanted to touch base with you and see if you've heard the news that our little project is about to come to a head – real soon? Besides, I thought if you aren't too busy or tied up with something, we might get together for a cup of coffee."

"I'm never too busy to get together with friends, Jeff. Where are you?"

"I'm over at my Uncle Jimbo's house, you remember, it's just off behind your property," Jeff said, and asked; "Where are you right now, are you in town, we can stop in the Cut Rate?"

"No Jeff, I'm just out back; I'm at the Sweet Daddy Creek Club; why don't you cut across the field and come on over," I said.

"Are you sure Chip? I know that you were keeping the location kind of quiet and personal." He said.

"Jeff, if anyone knows about the Club, it's you, and Jimbo. By the way are you with Jimbo now?" I asked.

"Yeah, he's right here," Jeff replied.

"Then why don't you tell Jimbo I said to put on his 'glad rags' and come with you; tell him I've got a couple of cold ones in the fridge just waiting on him." I said.

Jeff laughed out loud and came back with, "He heard you Chip and he is grinning from ear to ear and shaking his head yes; so I guess me and Uncle Jimbo will be right over," he said still laughing.

"Oh, by the way," Jeff said suddenly, "Be sure to turn off all those high-tech alarms you keep on; I don't want some secret, hidden, thirty caliber something popping up and taking a shot at us," he chuckled as he hung up.

I met Jeff and Uncle Jimbo at the front door when they arrived; they came on in and Jimbo stopped suddenly, looked around and sort of 'blurted' out, "Damn Chip, this looks just like it did when I used to come here on Saturday nights in the good old days!" Jimbo laughed so hard at what he said we thought he would have a coronary right on the spot.

I went right along with him and answered, "Well Jimbo, I tried to keep everything looking the same as we talked about and what I remembered you telling me. But there is one thing I haven't worked out yet though."

Jimbo said, "What's that Chip, maybe I can help."

"I'm sure you could make it right, or come up with the right answer. What I can't make, and can't find anywhere is some good 'ole' shine, you know, like you and Uncle Sam used to make and haul."

Jeff and Jimbo almost busted a gut laughing so hard. "Come on in y'all, I can't offer you any 'shine' but I do have a couple of cold ones in the fridge; come on and help yourself."

Jimbo was full of questions while Jeff sort of looked the place over. I had to explain, in detail, to Jimbo how I had managed to fix the old place up and why I wanted it to still look like an old barn that's about to fall down.

After hearing my description about needing a place to operate from, plus it was to be my private, relaxing, 'happy place', they understood and nodded in agreement.

Jimbo looking a little soulfully, said in a soft voice, "Now that's truly in keeping with the spirit of what the old time Sweet Daddy Creek Club used to be; it was the 'happy place' for a lot of folks. Aint no telling how many folks met here, got married here, and had families because of this Sweet Daddy Creek Club.

"I was just a 'young'un', a teenager, at the time," Jimbo began reminiscing, chuckling as he talked, "I would meet my daddy and grandpa here sometimes, just about dark, and grandpa would have the trunk of his car loaded with 'shine' that he had just made; we would take off and make deliveries to a lot of the small country stores throughout three counties; hell, sometimes we would even drop some off at those fancy clubs or restaurants in those same counties. Most everybody knew my grandpa, and they knew he had the best 'shine' anywhere; they trusted him."

Jeff grinned and said, "Uncle Jimbo, are you telling me that you used to run moonshine around the countryside? I guess I'll have to 'bust' you; you know I'm a lawman now."

After all the kidding and joking died away, Jeff asked if I was going to be at the meeting in Columbia the next day. He told me that plans were pretty much finalized and that he thought the teams would hit the judge's farm in a couple of days probably at dusk when the judge would be home and settled in for the evening, without a crew of 'personal' bodyguards; his personal staff, or guards, would be handled separately.

Jimbo spoke up and told us, "Not much has changed, there were crooked cops back in the old days and there are crooked cops now. Wanna know something else, it aint gonna change now either."

We both knew he was right --- good and evil, right and wrong --- always was, always will be.

I kind of felt sorry for Jimbo; I've been busy for a while and haven't called him or talked with him lately. So I asked, "Jimbo, tomorrow is Friday, you got any plans for late afternoon?"

"Shit Chip, you know better than that," he answered; "What kind of plans would I have, and to do what?"

I said, "Well now Jimbo, we haven't gone for bar-b-que in a long time, so why don't we just mosey on over the 'pit' tomorrow afternoon or early evening and have us a big plate with rice and hash, potato salad, a dozen corn dodgers, and wash it down with a couple of cool ones."

"Now that sounds mighty fine to me Chip. You want me to meet you there?" he asked.

"Nah, I'll swing by and pick you up, probably around five thirty or six, if that's okay," I said

Jeff said, "Wait just a darn minute, y'all; if anybody is going for bar-b-que, I'm going with you; you ain't leaving me out, I'll take Uncle Jimbo with me since I'm right here anyhow."

Then he added, "What about Sam and Dawn; they'll want to go too."

"Yeah," I replied, "You're right Jeff; I'll ask them, I'm sure Ed would like to go too."

Jeff looked at me quizzically and said, "Ed, Ed who?"

"Ed Winters, he is here from Atlanta, I think he would enjoy some good South Carolina bar-b-que," I replied.

Jeff said, "I'm supposed to see him tomorrow, we're partners on this sting and will be working together; he called me earlier and told me about somebody trying to take him out, right in his hotel room, before we even get started."

Jimbo who had been listening spoke up, "Y'all know what that means, this secret operation y'all are planning ain't no secret no more. Somebody has already let the cat out of the bag; if y'all gonna do something, better do it real soon or it will be too late."

"You are absolutely right, Jimbo," I said. "Jeff we better make a couple of calls, now, even before our meeting tomorrow and let the right people know what's going on; someone could get seriously hurt if we don't."

"Somebody could get their ass shot off; that's what could happen," Jimbo said, then added, "Jeff boy, you be careful where you stick your head."

CHAPTER THIRTY NINE

SEVEN O'CLOCK SATURDAY MORNING we're having breakfast, Dawn, Sam, Ed and I; Ed says, "That was good last night, the bar-b-que, the fellowship with friends and just kicking-back talking about nothing in particular. Chip, I like my temporary partner Jeff, he is nice; I believe he is one you can count on in a tight spot. I really enjoyed meeting his Uncle Jimbo too; they're good folks. Listening to Jimbo tell some of his tales from the old days was great. You could feel what he was thinking, you could feel it within yourself; at least I could. I would like to come back up sometime soon and bring my wife and all of us get together again; she would really like that."

"Anytime Ed, you just say when and we'll do it," I said.

Breakfast done Ed said, "Well guys, this is nice but I have to get to Columbia and find out how we're going to handle this 'wild' thing we've got going." Ed got up to leave, turned to me and said, "I guess I'll see you in a couple of hours."

"Be careful and keep your eyes open, too many people are out looking for you," I said, adding, "I'll be heading that way about eleven, maybe we can grab a quick lunch before the meeting."

"Sounds good," he said as he walked off.

Dawn asked, "Chip does SLED or the FBI have any idea of just what they are up against? Do they have a timeframe for acting or is that something y'all will work out in your meeting today?"

"Well, to tell you the truth, I really don't have a clue, not yet anyway; I'm not running this show, but I would think they have some sort of plan already worked out; they've been working behind the scenes for some time now. I sure as hell hope they have," I replied.

Sam had been sitting quietly taking in all this chatter, "Y'all know something?" he asked. "I understand the fact that they have been looking around for a while and trying to get their act together, but they better think twice about some things."

"Such as," I asked.

Sam continued, "Well, SLED and the FBI usually work big time cases, most of them in the big cities; they may get the impression that since Alcolu is just a small time, hick town, it will be easy to pull this operation off. I don't know if they understand that this shit has been going on around here for a damn long time, they don't know, and neither do we, by the way, just how many cohorts the judge has on his 'payroll', deputies and cops that he recruited back when he was a 'narc' agent on the force. The numbers could be pretty large. Just look around at their lifestyle and then tell me how those guys live like that on such a small salary. Please tell me, I need to up my lifestyle!"

"Another thing that bothers me," I said, "is the fact that somewhere on the backside of his farm or 'ranch' as he calls it he has a firing range, his own private shooting range. I have no idea what he may have out there; probably has a fortified bunker where he stores 'certain' types of items that he doesn't want people to know about."

"Y'all make this sound like 'Crime Central' or something," Dawn said. "Do you really think that this is big time stuff we're dealing with, like those old time mob bosses we see movies about?"

"Never can tell Dawn; we don't know exactly what we are dealing with, and neither does SLED or the FBI; not even our local law guys," Sam said.

I got up to leave and told them I had a couple of stops to make before I headed to Columbia.

Dawn asked, "What time do you think you'll be back?"

"I don't know, but I would imagine around six thirty or seven at the latest," I answered.

"Wanna do dinner when you do?" she asked.

"Are you asking me for a date?" I replied.

"Did you hear anything about a date? I merely asked if you wanted to have dinner. It doesn't take a rocket scientist to come up with an answer; if you would like to have dinner with me when you return, you just say 'yes'; if you would rather not have dinner with me, and suffer the consequences, you can just say, 'no'; it's that simple," she proclaimed.

Sam could hardly control himself he was laughing so hard.

"Well, since you put it that way, I would love to have dinner with you; shall I pick you up about eight?" I asked.

Sam still laughing said, "You may as well forget it Chip, you lost, and you will continue to lose, Dawn has your number."

I got up and started for the door, "I'm going to Columbia where I might be treated with a little respect; I'll pick you up at eight," I grinned at Dawn as I walked off.

I left both still laughing and grinning as I went out the back door to my car. Through many years of training to be aware of my surroundings, I picked up on a couple of county deputies across the lot looking in my direction; nothing unusual about that; they each were standing by their own car; nothing unusual about that; as I glanced in their direction they nodded at each other and reached for their radio; now that is unusual. As I pulled out of the parking lot I watched in my rear view mirror and saw both cars, moving very slowly, pull out of the lot, staying a good half block behind me.

As I drove west toward Broad Street and Highway 378, I purposely made a couple of unnecessary turns; they did too. As we drove out Broad toward Shaw Air Force Base and the open highway to Columbia, I reached for the special built-in, hidden compartment underneath the dashboard and unlocked it, it's a small space, but large enough to hold two of my favorite weapons --- my MK9 and my .357 'Dirty Harry' magnum revolver. I withdrew the MK9 and placed it in a special pocket between the seat and my door.

Everything was going along very well until we were approaching the area of Wateree Swamp where a couple of small dirt roads lead off into two seldom used hunt clubs. Keeping a close eye on my two 'tails', who followed at a distance, one speeded up drawing closer to my car, it stayed there for several minutes then flipped his blue light on, I pulled over to the side of the road, keeping my eyes on the deputy. The second deputy's car pulled up behind the first; the deputy got out of his car and went to the first one and leaned inside where they had a short conversation; must have been about me --- they probably shouldn't have done that – mistake number two; number one was pulling me over.

The deputy rose up, looked at me then went back to his car and sat there. The first deputy got out and walked toward me, I'm keeping my eye on this guy I thought. He approached my open window and spoke, "Let me see your driver's license and insurance," he said.

As I reached for my wallet I asked, "What's the problem officer, I don't believe I was speeding, I watch that pretty closely."

"Just hand me your license and insurance," he said arrogantly.

"Sure," I answered.

"Where are you going?" He asked.

"I'm headed to Columbia," I told him; then I added, "But I don't believe that's why you pulled me over; care to tell me why you stopped me?"

"Well, Mr. Chip Storrington, I don't need to."

"I think you better explain why you stopped me, write me a ticket or arrest me or something," I told him. In the meantime I had placed my left hand down to my side by the door where my weapon was sitting.

Suddenly there was a tapping on the right window, I looked and the second deputy was standing there motioning for me to unlock the door, I shook my head no and told him to come to the other side. The first deputy touched my shoulder and told me to open the damn door; he had his hand on his sidearm, a police .38 caliber revolver --- I opened the door and the other deputy got in and sat down beside me.

The first deputy looked at me and said, "Follow me," and walked to his car. He got into his car and moved forward to the small dirt road leading off the highway down into the swampy, old hunting club grounds.

The deputy beside me told me to follow; I noticed he kept his hand on his weapon also, but didn't unsnap the safety strap. I kept my left hand on my MK9 that was already locked and loaded and only needed a slight pull on the trigger to send my new 'shotgun' rider straight to hell; but let's see what they are up to.

After driving out of sight of the highway the first deputy stopped his vehicle and got out, walked back to mine. My rider got out and went around the car to his partner. I thought good, stand close together, makes a better target.

The first deputy was obviously in charge; a leader, and who knows what other positions he held in this underground criminal nightmare. It was fast becoming obvious he had been appointed as executioner for this job. He stood at my open window and began to ask about the meeting I was heading to; what was it about, was it a law enforcement meeting, did it concern any particular law enforcement individuals, what was my part in the meeting?

Then, just because I asked him if he was a 'shit-brain', he got pissed; he withdrew his weapon, pointed it at me, and said something to the effect that he could blow my brains out. I think he was about to say something else but he never got around to it.

When he hit the ground the reflexes in his trigger finger restricted, firing a round into the dirt.

The second deputy grabbed for his weapon forgetting he had not unsnapped it; with a wild look in his eye he froze for a couple of seconds then panicked, unsnapped it and drew his .38; that's as far as he got.

I got out of my car, went to the newly fallen deputy and pulled the trigger on his weapon.

I returned to my car, turned around and drove back up onto the highway and continued on to my meeting in Columbia. I don't think I'll be late.

I called Ed, "Ed how would you like a really good, greasy, chili dog for lunch, before our meeting? You know, with all the good stuff on it, mustard, ketchup, onions, the works."

Ed replied, "Yeah Chip I know, you're trying to give me a coronary; but hell yeah, that sounds good, where is it?

"Speedo's Fast Food it is; I know where it is, I passed it on the way in; I'll meet you there in twenty minutes," Ed said.

Ed was sitting in his car when I pulled in beside him; he got out and we went inside and ordered at the counter. We got our hot dogs and each got a thick, chocolate milkshake, healthy all the way. Ed said, "We've got about an hour before the meeting Chip; you look a little exhausted . . . no sleep last night, rough ride over, what's going on?"

I responded calmly, "No, plenty of sleep; normal ride over, got stopped by two of our upstanding Alcolu deputies, took me off into the woods, shot at me before I shot them both; left them beside their patrol cars. I guess when they don't check in somebody will be out looking for them. Pretty normal day if you ask me."

Ed, almost choking with a mouthful of hotdog and eyes getting bigger said frantically, "What? Are you kidding me Chip? That's not even funny!"

"No shit 'Charlie'! That's exactly what happened. I was followed out of town by two sheriff deputies' cars, and when I was in the swamp the one directly behind me hit his blue light so I pulled over and stopped, the other pulled in behind him. Only the first cop got out and came to my window, he asked for my license and insurance and then began asking me about our meeting in Columbia. While I was talking with him the other deputy opened the passenger side door and sat down in my car. Then told me to follow the first officer, that's when he drove off the road down a path that leads to an old, pretty much deserted hunt club; they both kept their hands on their weapons.

"When we got out of sight of the highway they stopped, the first officer came to my window with his weapon cocked and pointed at me, when he raised his arm as if to fire, I beat him to it. The other officer drew his weapon so I took him out too. Ed I think we are going to be facing a shit-load of trouble when the teams hit the judge's place. They know something is going on and they are preparing," I said.

Hyperventilating Ed asked, "By any chance did you happen to know the two cops or get any ID?"

I gave Ed the names and badge numbers; he pulled a note pad from his coat pocket and thumbed through it, "Damn Chip those two are some of the people we are looking for, they may be Alcolu deputies but they have been part of a large drug operation for years' they have ties to the drug cartel out of Mexico. Their names keep popping up in connection with the cartel frequently.

"We need to move on to our meeting and see if we can get the right people together before the meeting begins. Damn Chip, this may be a lot bigger than any of us thought. Dawn was right, 'stuff' is about to hit the fan – big time!"

CHAPTER FORTY

AFTER THE MEETING ED told me that he had called the 'big' director's office in DC, he decided that since the two deputies had known ties to the cartel, that the boss would want to know. He said he expected to hear back in a couple of days. The SLED operation had been put on hold until they heard.

Ed said, "I imagine they will send a couple of special agents down, guys who specialize in this area; you know they have been watching and trying to get anything they can on these drug cartels; we're talking big time, Chip. I'm sure you know that these M-13 gangs, made up mostly of Hispanics from Mexico and other South American countries, have spread throughout our entire country. They pretty much control the government of Mexico already, if we don't watch it they will be taking over this country as well. You know like the old time crime boss type operations that flourished here in our country for so long. We don't need them, we have enough problems already."

"Speaking of problems," I said, "I talked myself into one before I left Alcolu, with Dawn. Actually," I smiled, "it is a nice problem to have."

Ed saw that I was grinning and said, "It doesn't look like you think it is much of a problem; you look more like you're looking forward to it."

"I really am" Ed; "She asked if I wanted to have dinner tonight when I got back into town; I implied that she was asking me for a date. She insisted that she wasn't, but I would suffer dire consequences if I didn't show up."

"Sounds like you better move towards home," Ed laughed.

"I'm on my way," I replied.

The ride back to Alcolu was uneventful, just a quick stop by the florist for a dozen roses, and another at the candy shop for a box of chocolates and then heading for home; however, since I was passing the 'beverage' store, I thought a nice bottle of Copper Ridge Zinfindel would be a little 'topping on the cake'.

I pulled into her drive a little before eight, gathered up my 'I'm sorry, treaty-gifts' and got out of the car where I caught the whiff of steaks grilling outside, smelling really good, I might add. I rang the doorbell and in a few moments it was opened by this gorgeous lady holding a long handle grill fork in her hand and a large beautiful smile on her face.

"You're just in time," she said; "The steaks are almost done, baked potatoes about ready in the oven, salad on the table, and, ooh, I see you brought the wine, how thoughtful; it will make the meal so much better.

"Roses, chocolates; now you make me feel even more guilty, Chip. Since I gave you a hard time when you left this morning, I figured I should make it up to you and cook dinner for you. Come on in and get settled, I'm sure you have had a tough day, beside I want to hear about our meeting," she said.

"Nah," I replied, "You won't believe the boring day I've had," I said jokingly.

"Well are the plans all set, the date, and who is doing what?" she asked

I answered, "No, right now they have put the operation on hold for a while."

"On hold; I thought they pretty much had everything lined up, had their ducks in a row," she said, sounding a little disappointed.

I guess I was kind of leading her on by dragging out what had happened, so I explained about the two deputies, the shootout, what Ed had found out, the connection with the Mexican drug cartel and his contacting the 'big' FBI boss in Washington who put the operation on hold temporarily. I thought Dawn was going into hysterics when I finished; especially about the shootout.

She sat the wine, the roses and the box of chocolates down and came over to me and threw her arms around me, "My God Chip, you could have been killed; you take too many chances; you can't do that," she said with her voice sounding a little shaky and cracking.

She had her face against mine and felt so warm and soft; I felt something wet against my face, I pulled back slightly and looked at her, she had tears in her eyes. I hugged her tighter and pulled her closer. We stayed that way for several moments; she pulled back and looked me straight in the face but didn't speak; she just looked at me, then she leaned her head in and pressed her lips on mine and we kissed for the first time for real. It was one of those slow, long kisses that said more than just a kiss; my heart was in my throat!

Finally we pulled apart, looking a little embarrassed, she stuttered, "Oh, Chip I'm . . ."

"Stop right there," I muttered. "Don't say anything, especially don't try to say something like 'sorry'; please don't spoil this moment. I want to remember this exact moment the rest of my life." I leaned over and kissed her again and we held on to each other for a long while . . .,

Until Dawn suddenly pulled back, laughed, and said, "The steaks are going to burn; help me get them off the grill or we will be eating peanut butter sandwiches for dinner," she said still laughing. Then, "Chip you go check the steaks and I'll take care of the inside stuff."

The steaks, baked potatoes, peas with carrots and hot yeast bread, and the wine, was fantastic; but then peanut butter sandwiches with Dawn would have been just as fantastic. Suddenly, I felt a slight tremor pass through my body --- strange --- I had felt it a couple of times before, always it seems, when I'm talking with Dawn.

After sitting and just talking for at least an hour, I began gathering our plates and silverware together when she asked, "What are you doing Chip?"

I answered, "After you cooked such a delicious dinner, the least I can do is the 'KP', I used to be quite good at it; I guess I must have been, my old army drill sergeant kept sending me there."

She laughed and said, "Well you're not in the army now and I'm no drill sergeant; however, the orders for the evening are to leave the dishes, go into the den and relax after eating like that. I'll put the dishes in the dishwasher later."

We took our glass of wine with us into the den; it was nice and warm and cozy; made me feel good all over.

Dawn turned the television on with the sound low, it was an old movie with Jimmy Stewart, a western with a romantic twist to it, Jimmy got the girl, of course. We just lay back on the sofa, Dawn in my arms; so this is what heaven is like, I wondered.

I was dreaming I was walking around in my socks when I awoke and discovered Dawn had taken my shoes off and was gently rubbing my feet. I started to jump up but she said, "Shhh, just be still and relax; you went to sleep and I didn't want to wake you, I like sitting here watching you sleep. You have had a long and strenuous day and you're tired, so go back to sleep if you want."

I looked at my watch, "It's after twelve," I exclaimed, shocked; "I'm keeping you up; it's way past your bed time."

"I'll determine when it's my bed time," she said softly, smiling. "Now I'll tell you like you told me a couple of weeks ago, I have a guest room and you are welcome to sleep over rather than drive all the way to the Sweet Daddy Creek Club this time of night."

I looked her in the eye and told her, "Dawn, you don't know what you are saying, and you don't. . ."

She snuggled up loser to me, kissed me long and tenderly, then said very softly but firmly, "Chip, I know full well what I'm doing, and you do too; we've just never talked openly about it."

I grinned like a kid, kissed her again and said jokingly, "But I don't have any pajamas or my shaving gear."

She laughed out loud and said, "Chip, I don't think you wear pajamas --- anytime, and I don't believe you will need them here either." She pulled me up and we headed toward her bedroom.

CHAPTER FORTY ONE

I WALKED INTO THE Cut Rate for breakfast at seven o'clock sharp; Dawn had decided to take the morning off; I saw Sam and Ed already eating and having their coffee, Sam asked, "Where is Dawn?"

"We had dinner last night and she said that she was taking today off and she would see me later today," I said. Sam and Ed looked at each other and smiled.

Sam said, "Ed was just telling me about your day yesterday. I think those buttheads are not only getting brave, but reckless also. Ed tells me that they were in patrol cars and in uniform; that's pretty stupid."

Ed added, "Yeah, but to have Chip drive his own car and follow, while he drove the patrol car down into that swampy mud-hole, and then take a shot at him, was more than stupid, those guys were crazy."

"You can say that again," I remarked, "I even have my doubts about them actually being legitimate deputies, even though they wore the uniform and drove the vehicles. I have known a lot of cops in my years, local, county, federal and even some cops in other countries; they just don't act or operate like these two did; they did too many stupid things to be real and trained law enforcement officers. In fact, you were going to check into their background, Ed, were you able to find out anything that we didn't already know?"

Ed replied, "I haven't heard back yet; I sent their information and pictures back to the bureau so they could run them through the system. If they're in there anywhere, it will pick them out; we should know in a couple of days at the most."

"What are you thinking, Chip?" Sam asked

Just then Jeff walked in and sat down with us. "I hear you had a tough day yesterday, Chip. The whole SLED department was full of chatter last night and earlier this morning. I don't know if you have seen the news this morning, but the newspaper had a headline that said that two Alcolu County sheriff's deputies had a shootout among themselves and both were killed. TV said the same thing."

"What?" I asked somewhat louder than usual. Folks around us turned to look in our direction. I toned it down a little and repeated myself.

"What did you say Jeff; do they really think the two shot each other?" I asked.

Jeff replied, "That's what the word is around SLED and the local FBI office. I stopped by the sheriff's office on the way here; they had received a fax of the photos and Dennis said they were not Alcolu deputies, he didn't know who they were, where they got the uniforms or the vehicles. The patrol cars were not part of his fleet, he said.

"You know something," Jeff said, looking in my direction with a slight smile on his face, "This kind of reminds me of some of the shootings that occurred near where you live, Chip. Remember, it seems like somebody was trying to clean up the 'hood.'"

"Well, Jeff," I answered, "I sure hope they got it cleaned up; I don't get back over there much anymore. I haven't heard of anything going down in that area for quite some time now, either."

Jeff answered, "Nah, I think mostly everything is pretty quiet, just some of the small mom and pop stuff; the only thing I've heard mentioned is concerning the Hispanics over on Robney Street. The word is that some new Hispanics have moved in and taken over the area; some think they are elements of the M-13 gang that is spreading across the country; that's the group that is controlled and operated by the drug cartel out of Mexico."

Sam said, "It's hard to believe they would try to infiltrate a small town like Alcolu; I can't see that much money floating around here."

"It's smart marketing, Sam," Ed responded, "Location, location, location; and we're in a great location for the smugglers and runners. I-95 is like a drug freeway between upstate New York and Florida. You guys remember why we started talking about this in the first place? It's too tempting to the local, underpaid patrols that make the stops and have to confiscate --- and count --- the hundreds of thousands of dollars that these asshole drug running gangs bring through here. I often think I can't blame them for skimming off a few thousand. These are the guys and gals who put their lives on the line every day for the rest of us and they barely make enough to keep groceries on the table for their kids. Well, you guys will have to excuse me for getting on my soapbox, but it burns my ass to watch some of the crap that goes on."

Sam, Jeff and I gave Ed a silent round of applause, he had expressed our feelings also.

"Well spoken, Ed, you speak for all of us," I said.

Sam said, "I don't suppose we'll know anymore until Columbia hears back from the 'big' boss in DC."

"Probably not, but we need to stay in close contact with each other on a daily basis," Ed replied.

"We never know," Jeff said, "Things could change overnight, or in the next hour. And, they just may start changing real soon; sooner than any of us could possibly suspect."

"What are you talking about Jeff?" I asked.

"Well Chip, since you got me a new job working with SLED with some cross-over with the FBI, it has opened some doors that I never knew existed before. I have been doing a lot of research; research into the activities of our friendly, favorite judge and some of his contacts."

Sam asked, "What the hell are you talking about Jeff, what kind of research, and what did your research show you?"

"Yeah," said Ed, "I haven't been able to find out anything about this 'judge' or anything about his activities or close associates; normally with the bureau's information center I would be able to tell you when he takes a leak or crap. But this one must have some connections somewhere that keeps him clear from any of the authorities, legal authorities that is."

Jeff began speaking softly and lowly, "Those two guys who targeted you in Wateree Swamp are not even the tip of the iceberg, they are so far down the line that the organization probably will never miss them, or even acknowledge that they heard about the event."

"How do you know this Jeff?" I asked.

"I told you I'm doing a bunch of research, that's how I'm finding out stuff; stuff that surprises the hell out of me," Jeff retorted.

"Go on," Sam said anxiously.

"I don't have any details yet, and certainly nothing I can prove, but it seems a certain local judge, or supposed to be 'judge', has himself a bank account, or two, maybe more in a couple of other countries," Jeff responded. "Like I said, I don't know any details or where all he has accounts or how much he has stashed away for 'a rainy day'; or maybe just for a prolonged vacation somewhere.

"Hell, in fact I don't even know for sure if I'm correct or not; I may not know what I'm talking about; I told you that '*I'm*' doing the research; I'm no researcher, or whatever you call it, I was just trying to get a little information on the judge, then one thing kind of led to another and I was off and running like I knew what I was doing." Jeff looked slightly confused as he stopped talking.

Ed, who had been jotting down notes, asked Jeff, "Jeff, do you recall how you ran across the stuff that you did find; you know the website or page or whatever?"

"You're the FBI wizard," Jeff replied, "I'll get with you and go over the few notes I made at the time, maybe you can press it further, at the big info center in Washington. They have all the necessary technology and smart 'techies' to find out most anything."

I asked Jeff, "Tell us some of the stuff you did find out that made you suspicious in the first place."

"In the first place I started by trying to check into his finances, his bank account and so on; his account doesn't have a powerful lot of money in it, more than I'm used to though. Anyway I noticed a lot of activity over a long period of time and it seems like periodically he would transfer money to a bank in another country."

I interrupted, "What country, Jeff?"

"You mean what countries, there were several but I couldn't tie them all together," he said. "I couldn't follow the trail but I feel sure that Ed's partners could pull it together and get a trace. I had never even heard of a couple of the places; like Maldives, Vanuatu, Montenegro; then there was a bank in the Cayman Islands and one in Switzerland. He must be moving a lot of money around to get to all of those places."

Ed said, "That's how he hides his 'loot', he moves it from one country to another; and I think, if we can get a trace, we will find that those particular countries do not honor extradition agreements with the U.S. either.

Then Ed announced he was going back to his hotel room, "If my room hasn't been blown up or ransacked or something worse, I'm going to try and run down what you're talking about Jeff; in fact, if you don't have any commitments right away, you may want to come with me. I'm going to call my office in Atlanta and the Columbia Bureau's office and get the ball rolling, see if we can't get something done.

"I'm free until I hear back from Columbia; I would love to see what you or we, can come up with; this is getting pretty interesting," Jeff answered.

CHAPTER FORTY TWO

AS I LEFT THE Cut Rate I phoned Dawn to see if she wanted to meet me for lunch at Big Jim's around one, she agreed and asked what I was doing the rest of the day. I told her that I was going out to the Sweet Daddy Creek Club; I needed to play catch-up on paper work, I had not thought much about paper work for several weeks, actually much longer.

"Is there something I can help with?" Dawn asked.

"Not that I can think of right now," I replied, "But if you would like to, we can go there from lunch, we can drop your car off at your house and just take mine."

"That sounds great," she said.

I took the rest of the morning to run various errands, check my back-log of mail at the post office and then to visit the sheriff and police chief offices. Just wanted to keep up to date on what was happening in our city. I also needed to go and check on my 'little house in the hood'; be sure it hadn't been fire bombed or the victim of some other drastic calamity.

I also wanted to do some thinking about just how much Dawn should know; I'm pretty hesitant about letting her get involved any further in this latest escapade. An attempt had already been made to take me out. Anyone close to me would be in danger also. I don't want anything to happen to her --- I would take it personal, real personal! Something very special was happening between Dawn and me and I was not letting anybody spoil it.

I had just gotten seated when Dawn came in, as she got to the booth she leaned in and kissed me lightly and sat down across from me. "What was that for?" I asked.

"What?" she asked.

"The kiss," I answered

"Because . . . because," she blushed, "I enjoyed last night, the dinner, everything; it was the best evening I've had in a long time, and I . . . I just . . . wanted to kiss you. Is that a big deal," she said, still blushing.

"Not at all," I kind of stammered, "Only it doesn't happen often enough."

Dawn grinned and said, "Well, we will just have to work on that. Let's order, I'm hungry."

We ordered and took our time eating, we were in no hurry; we talked about little things and would reach across the table every now and then and touch hands which would send shocks through my entire body. I asked about her job; I knew she had missed several days.

"I'm taking a two week vacation; with all that's going on I thought it best that I step out of the picture for a while," she told me.

"Good; I'm glad to hear that. It will ease my mind a little, I have been concerned about your safety, but we can talk about that after we get to the Club," I said.

Leaving Big Jim's we dropped her car off at her house and headed to the Club for the rest of the day. After getting out of town and into the open farmland country, I noticed in the rear view mirror a car had unexpectedly appeared, from out of nowhere it seemed. I didn't mention it to Dawn, but I realized it was an unmarked car like the deputies' drive. I reached down to the special pocket where I keep a weapon, but I didn't take it out; didn't want to alarm Dawn. However, shortly I had to let her know, since I drove past our turn-in path without slowing.

"Chip, are you asleep?" she asked; "You just missed our turn."

"I know; don't get upset, but I think we're being followed; don't look around," I said; we don't want whoever it is to realize that we know. We will just see how long they will stay on our tail. We're coming up on the county line; let's see if they back off."

The car followed us several miles into Kershaw County before turning around and heading back to where they came from. "I believe they are trying to find our hang-out," I told Dawn.

Dawn asked, "Could you tell who it was?"

"Not really, but it looked similar to the unmarked cars that the sheriff's department uses," I said. After a few more miles I thought it safe so I turned around and we headed to the Club. We both kept a sharp eye out for anything that hinted at suspicious.

Dawn said, "I noticed you have been driving with one hand on the wheel and the other down by your side, I assume you have a weapon conveniently handy."

"I wouldn't leave home without one," I replied.

"Well, after this little episode, I think I will start keeping my little, snub nose .38 with me from now on," she countered.

Arriving at the Club, we passed through all of the alarms and parked in the back by the garage; not that anyone could see through all the trees; and if they tried to come onto the property we would know and that would be the last place they would ever go --- except maybe to hell.

I was busy in my office paying a few bills online, going through mail I had picked up at the post office; it had kind of stacked up on me. There was nothing real important except maybe the statement from the Philippine National Bank in New York letting me know that another large deposit had been made into my account; thanks Vince. Sam and Dawn would be happy about that also; I sent them online checks while I was paying the other bills.

I kept hearing noises from the kitchen, like pots and pans rattling. I called to Dawn, "What's going on in there, you're making a lot of noise."

"Just getting things in order to cook dinner," she responded.

"Dinner," I exclaimed, "Now that sounds worth the noise. Where did you get the groceries," I asked?

"Out of that large bag you carried in for me," she said; "How does spaghetti and meatballs with cheese and sauce, sound?"

"Making me hungry already," I answered.

My phone beeped and I looked at the screen, 'Jimbo, I thought, what on earth would he be calling me for; hope he is alright'.

"Hey Jimbo, what's going on, are you okay," I asked?

"Oh yeah Chip, I'm alright, but I thought you ought to know a couple of sheriff's men come by here earlier today; they was looking for Jeff. I asked them what for and they said he might be in a lot of trouble. I let them talk; I didn't tell them that Jeff worked for SLED and the FBI; they acted like they didn't know. They were trying to 'bull-crap' me."

"I'm glad you didn't tell them anything, Jimbo. I believe they were the 'bad guys'; some of the crooks that Jeff and his bosses are looking to put behind bars," I told him. Then I added, "They didn't threaten you or try anything did they?"

Jimbo answered, "No Chip, I woulda kicked their butt if they had," he laughed.

"Jimbo, now you hear me, if anybody comes around trying to give you a hard time, looking for Jeff, threatening you or even just looking mean towards you, you stop and give me a call right then and I'll come and we both will kick some butt."

Jimbo cracked up at that and said, "You got a deal Chip; I ain't had the opportunity to let loose in a long time; I think it would do me good," he said still laughing.

"Me too Jimbo, you take care and I'll talk with you later, call me anytime," I said.

Dawn came into the office asking "What's going on, is somebody after Jimbo, or Jeff?"

"Somebody's been around looking for Jeff; I need to get hold of him right away and let him know they are on his trail; he's gotta be extra careful now that they have him connected with whatever they think is going on," I told Dawn.

"And, that means you are going to have watch every step you take also, Dawn. If they have connected Jeff, it's most likely been through me; and if that's the case they probably have you connected too," I said.

Dawn asked me, kind of 'smart-alecky' like, "Well, what about you? I think they have your number too, so you are going to have to be even more careful; don't you think" she added still grinning?

"I can take care of myself; I am probably the last person they want to come into contact with – and that's a fact," I said!

"You don't think I can take care of myself," she asked?

I replied, "Of course I do, but not like I will; they will get the word that if something happens to you, no matter how small; no matter if it was an accident or not; no matter if they were anywhere near or not; no matter what the cause; they better get on their knees and give their heart and soul to God, because their ass is mine!"

I have never heard Dawn laugh as hard as she did then.

"You laugh, but it's a fact," I stated.

She finally calmed down somewhat and came to me, wrapped her arms around me and hugged me close and whispered, "I know you would, Chip, and I love you for it;" she kissed me and kept her head on my shoulder.

After a long while she whispered in my ear again, "Chip, if we don't move we will be eating burned spaghetti for dinner;" she laughed and broke away and went into the kitchen. It wasn't long before the delicious aroma of hot marinara sauce and spaghetti filled the entire Club, along with the smell of freshly heated Italian garlic bread as it lifted and floated through the inside air.

It was a slow, delicious but relaxed meal and we spent a long, leisurely evening, Dawn snuggled close in my arms, head on my chest and we just talked; neither of us would be able to tell what we talked about.

Around midnight Dawn looked at the clock, then at me and said, "I may need to borrow another pair of your pajamas tonight," smiling.

"You don't need pajamas," I said as I got up, took her hand and moved toward the bedroom.

CHAPTER FORTY THREE

AS WE GOT OUT of the large shower and began dressing, Dawn asked, "What's for breakfast? Do you have plans for today?"

As I stood there watching her, I said, "Originally I was planning to see if I could find out more about who followed us yesterday; but, the longer I stand here, I realize those plans are subject to revision very quickly."

She laughed and responded with, "Those were your plans, not mine; I might have planned differently," she kept on laughing.

After a lunch of cold sandwiches I left, telling her that I was going into town and see what I could find out. I left her standing at the door grinning like a possum that made it to the other side of the road. She blew me a kiss as I drove off.

I stopped in at the Clerk of Court's office to check on latest rumors floating around town, the Clerk's office was a good place to hear the latest gossip; they had good coffee and many of the local attorneys hung out when they were not too busy. Word was that there had been a couple more I-95 stops with merchandise and cash confiscated; nothing new anymore, just routine. I went on by the county sheriff's office and the local law enforcement, I wanted to check in with Chief Russell and get the word from his viewpoint; he was closer to the operation than any other local folks. He still had not heard about any updates or changes to the original plans, other than it had been put on old temporarily; I think they were trying to find out who it was taking shots at me; probably wanted to know why they missed.

I stopped by the Cut Rate for an afternoon coffee; Ed and Jeff were there having coffee also. As I sat in the booth Ed asked, "Any more pot shots or people trying to kidnap you?"

"Not even funny Ed," I answered kind of 'smart-alecky'.

Jeff interjected, "Must be because you're privileged, so they decided to transfer their attention to me."

"What're you talking about," I asked? "Someone take a shot at you too?"

"Not exactly," Jeff replied; "They were going to; you remember Uncle Jimbo telling you that somebody had been out looking for me?"

"Yeah, he told me just the other day," I said.

"Well, I've been keeping a close eye on everything ever since, at my house, at Uncle Jimbo's, and about every move I make," Jeff said, "Late yesterday afternoon as I left town and headed home to Columbia, I noticed a car on my tail; it would keep dropping back several car lengths, then move back up closer. I think they did that thinking I wouldn't notice I was being followed.

After we got on the highway, probably not too far from where they hit on you, the car pulled up beside me in the left lane; by this time we're doing about seventy-five; anyway, the guy in the passenger seat kind of grinned and raised a pistol --- I was waiting for that --- I jerked my wheel to the left and rammed the car full blast, at seventy-five miles an hour. The last I saw of that car it was heading through the trees in the swamp. I figured that if the crash didn't kill them, some gator would have a free supper.

"By the time I got home I heard on the radio that there had been an accident on highway 378, and that two bodies had been recovered. Neither had been wearing a seat belt and had been thrown from the vehicle; one man was dead at the scene while the second died on the way to the hospital."

"Damn Jeff!" I responded to his details; "These assholes are beginning to get nasty and on my last nerve. If we don't get something moving pretty damn quick, officially, then I'm going to see what I can do myself."

Jeff laughed, "You going to clean up the county like you cleaned up your hood; hell, I'll help you."

Ed finally spoke up and said, "I guess you two know what you're talking about, but if it's along the track I think you mean, count me in, I'll be glad to help also."

I chuckled and told them, "You don't know what you're saying; you guys may not like the manner in which I operate if I get pressed to tight."

"Hell, Chip, we've all been there, especially in this business; you don't know me as well as you may think," Ed said.

"You know me Chip; not too much difference between the way the two of us think and do things," Jeff responded.

I invited both Ed and Jeff to take a ride with me on Friday evening, told them I would buy their supper.

"Where to and what for," Ed asked?

I replied, "Just a little ride, maybe to nowhere and nothing." Ed and Jeff looked dubiously at each other but didn't say anything.

Friday evening I picked them up around eight o'clock and headed out highway 378 towards Florence; they still didn't asked where we were going; we just made small talk as we drove. Finally Jeff couldn't take it any longer, "You buying us dinner in Florence Chip? Looks like it's going to be a late supper. I hope you're not hungry Ed."

I took the exit off I-95 and pulled into the Texas Steak House and said, "Let's eat, it's late enough, and I know you both have worked up a good appetite trying to figure out what the hell I'm doing. To tell you the truth, I'm not too sure myself; we'll find out later."

After a good steak dinner we're back in my car and heading down the ramp getting back on I-95 South toward Alcolu. About half way to the

Alcolu exit, between exits number one thirty four and one forty, we saw it --- flashing blue lights --- exactly what I figured we would find somewhere along this route. I slowed and counted four county deputy vehicles; they had pulled over a large SUV and I could make out two men with their hands cuffed behind their backs.

Ed and Jeff were sitting on the edge of their seats; Jeff said, "Looks like a traffic stop, I-95 is the Daytona of this state."

"Let's take a look," I said as I pulled off to the side of the road. "Do you guys have your badges with you; if so you better get them out, here comes one of the deputies and he has a hand on his sidearm."

As the deputy came to the window Ed had his FBI credentials with his badge and was holding it out of the window so the deputy could easily see it. Jeff was holding out his SLED badge also.

I asked the deputy, "Everything all right; this just a traffic stop, any problems?"

The deputy was obviously shaken and in an even shakier voice replied to Ed, "Oh no sir, we've got everything under control. It's just the usual small time drug runner."

We opened our doors and climbed out of our vehicle, Jeff said, "They do a lot of running on weekend nights on this stretch; let's see if we can help."

As we approached the group of deputies and prisoners, one deputy stepped out toward us and asked in a very loud voice, "Stop right there; who the hell are you, and what the hell do you think you're doing, " I noticed he had his hand on his weapon also?

Ed and Jeff were holding their badges out where the lieutenant could see them; he looked shocked and asked, "What are you guys doing out on the highway this time of night?"

I glanced at his name tag, Lt. Rollins; I looked up at him, I knew him, not well but from the force and around town. I smiled and said, "Hey Gary, they have you out doing the dirty work now days?"

"Nah," he responded; "Just when we're short-handed I fill in so somebody can take a weekend off. This is the usual weekend drug bust, you know, the I-95 drug freeway."

In the meantime, Ed had gone over to where the drugs and cash money was lying on the ground behind the deputies' car. Ed picked up several bundles of money and thumbed through it; then looked at the stacks. Jeff came up to Ed and also looked at all of the cash lying on the ground. He asked Ed, "How much do you think is there?"

Ed remarked, "There must be at least seventy-five thousand; plus there is a big haul of drugs too."

I'm kind of standing back; I didn't want to create any unnecessary suspicion, but I couldn't resist the temptation to ask, "What the world do you do with all this stuff, drugs and cash; that you find on the weekend especially?"

Lieutenant Gary said, "We carry it back to headquarters and put it in the safe until Monday morning, then it's taken to the judge and the Clerk of Court's office and counted." Then he gave a little laugh and added, "They get to keep it; until the trial comes up that is; I wish they would send some of it my way."

We politely laughed at his humor.

We stood around chatting with the officers while they wrapped up their business and were ready to leave the scene. I offered to buy coffee and doughnuts at the next exit, about three miles further on I-95.

Lt. Gary said, "It's getting pretty late, we need to get back so we can turn all of this in to headquarters; maybe another time."

"Another time," I replied; "You guys stay safe out here, we'll see you later." Me, Jeff and Ed got back into my car and drove off leaving the deputies to complete their duty. I dropped them at the hotel where Ed was staying and where Jeff had left his car in the hotel parking lot.

Ed asked, "Do you think they will actually turn in all of the 'loot'?"

"I wouldn't be surprised if they did," Jeff answered; "They know that we know about how much cash was there, even though it had not been counted; they're not too smart, but not that stupid either – I don't think."

"I'm like you Jeff, I believe they will turn all of this haul in Monday morning; they don't want to take any chances of getting caught with their hands in the cookie jar," I responded. "I'll call Dawn and get her to check it out just to be sure."

CHAPTER FORTY FOUR

IT WAS AFTER MIDNIGHT when I got back to the Club, I waited until morning to call Dawn, before she left for work. I briefed her on the previous night's happenings and she said she would watch to see what was brought in and who brought it. We agreed to meet for lunch at one o'clock.

I walked into the Cut Rate a few minutes before one, Dawn was already there; so were Ed and Jeff; they had left the seat next to Dawn for me. Wonder why?

As I sat Jeff said, "You're gonna love this Chip, wait 'til Dawn tells you what's happened."

"Unbelievable," Ed added.

Now they really had my curiosity up. "Well, don't keep me in suspense any longer," I said.

"You're not going to believe this Chip," Dawn began, "But the judge didn't show up this morning. Two of the deputies brought the material in this morning and waited while we verified the count and contents."

"Where was the judge," I asked? "We don't know," she replied. "We not only don't know where he 'was', we still don't know where he 'is'," she added with emphasis.

"What do you mean by that; 'don't know where he is'," I asked?

Jeff spoke up, "Just what Dawn said, nobody seems to know where he is right now; he's not at his ranch or farm, and wasn't planning to be out of town, not that anyone was aware of anyway."

Dawn said, "We've been trying to locate him all morning, we have left messages everywhere we thought he might be. I spoke with Mona, his wife, this morning around ten and she told me that he had left home early Sunday afternoon, said that an emergency had come up. Three or four sheriff's deputies had come by the house mid-morning and they met for about an hour; he left shortly after that. She said she had not heard from him yet, but that he would probably call when he had a chance."

"That is strange," I said.

Ed said, "You don't think that he has skipped town, do you?"

"Hard to say," I answered. "If he thought that you and SLED were getting close, no telling what he may do."

Then I asked Dawn, "How much confiscated material and cash did the deputies bring in this morning?"

"They had seventy-six thousand dollars and change, plus a small pile of drugs. Not all that big of a deal as far as the drugs go, but seventy-six thousand is a pretty good haul, if you ask me," she said. "They would normally skim a little off that amount."

Sam came in and pulled up a chair; "Where have you been keeping yourself for the past couple of weeks, Sam; I haven't seen you around here" I asked?

"I have been busting my butt, that's where I have been. 'Somebody' shot and killed two dudes in the swamp, dudes who were dressed like deputy sheriffs; at least that's what I 'think'; the official word is that the two shot and killed each other. But you and me Chip, we know that's bullshit. And, another thing, there was a mysterious accident in the swamp, the same swamp where the shooting occurred; two other 'dudes' were killed in that. Somebody been messing around in your 'hood' again Chip," Sam responded?

I didn't reply to that, best to let it be. "Dawn was just telling us that the judge is missing and didn't show up at the office this morning," I said.

"That's another damn thing," Sam said, "The sheriff heard about it and now wants me to look into it; I'm trying to stay as far away from that little scenario as I can."

Ed added, "You guys realize it's only been one day; not even a full day yet. Hell, maybe he went fishing or something, decided at the last minute that he wanted to take the day off."

"Yeah, you may be right Ed," Jeff said; "But if you really believe that, I need to talk with you; you see, I've got this large, beautiful bridge that I can't use anymore and I'm trying to sell it . . ."

Everybody laughed, even Ed who responded, looking kind of thoughtful, when all had calmed down; "You could be right Jeff, so what we can do is set up a road block on your bridge --- you know --- your bridge to 'nowhere', and when the judge comes off at the other end we can nab him."

Dawn, looking a little perplexed and thoughtful, said slowly, "If I'm reading you right Ed, you're implying that "Jeff's bridge to nowhere" could be his ticket out of town; like maybe in an airplane – his 'bridge'."

Sam added, with a smile, "And the 'nowhere' is our 'we don't know where', or even have a clue."

At this point all of us were in a joking, yet a somewhat serious mood. So I added my two cents worth, "Then the roadblock on the other side of the bridge could be an airport somewhere --- maybe on the other side of the world."

"Damn, I didn't know y'all were so smart," Ed retorted, laughing even more. "You have sat here and repeated everything I was thinking, or was going to think later."

This created quite a buzz among all of us. We agreed, that what began in jest and expanded on was actually a pretty good possibility of a carefully thought out plan. Ed's phone buzzed and he got up and stepped away from the booth to answer it.

Maxine, our regular 'smart-ass' waitress came over with the coffee pot and started pouring for everybody as she said, "With all of the giggling and laughing and 'grab-assing' going on at this booth, I assume you're still getting paid with my tax dollars; y'all taking the day off or something," she laughed as she went back behind the counter, still grinning.

Ed came back and in somewhat of a whisper told us, "Okay guys, it's on again for tomorrow, late afternoon around five thirty or six at the latest. Three teams of eight each are going to hit the ranch at the same time from different directions. Perhaps we'll find him trying to clear out or hide anything that could possibly be used as evidence. I guess we'll know more then.

"Jeff, you and I will be on separate teams; because you are from this area and easily recognizable, you will be on one of the FBI teams, I'll be on a SLED team since these folks don't know me." Ed reported.

Dawn asked the question that was on my mind, "What about Chip and me; what will we be doing; will we be on one of the teams?"

Ed answered, "No, you two can watch from a distance, since y'all aren't officially law enforcement guys. The Bureau Chief and the team leaders realize that y'all played a critical role in putting all of this together, but decided it best if the teams did the dirty work. You guys live here, the team members don't. We don't want you to suffer any repercussions over this operation."

Dawn summed up our feelings, "Well crap!"

CHAPTER FORTY FIVE

DAWN AND I AWOKE about five thirty, she rolled over and kissed me and said sleepily, "I think we better get moving; a lot is supposed to happen today."

After she had gotten off work at the Clerk of Court's office yesterday, we dropped her car off at her house and went to Big Jim's for a leisurely dinner, then out to the Club around eleven.

I watched her as she rolled over me to get up, that's as far as she got.

Freshly showered and dressed we slowly ate a lunch of sandwiches and chips. We went down to the weapons room where I opened the vault and pulled out a drawer that contained a number of handguns. I picked up a .357 magnum, a rifle and a couple boxes of shells for both and began loading them; Dawn picked up a .38 caliber revolver like the police use; she got a box of shells also. Neither of us had said anything about taking weapons with us we just knew that if we were going to be watching the action, even at a distance, we wanted to be covered.

"I like the smaller, light weight feel of this better," she said lifting the thirty-eight so I could see it clearly. Then she added, "I guess you're going bear hunting with that .357."

"No, just want to be sure if we get jumped, we jump back a little harder, that's all," I replied.

When we had everything we thought we may need we climbed into my big Ford F-150; you never know when you might need the extra power. We had selected a spot about a quarter of a mile from the judge's property, in an off the road area that could contain some pretty tough terrain. We had also dressed for the occasion, again, just in case.

As we backed out of the garage I looked over at Dawn who was grinning at me. "What?" I asked.

"Nothing," she replied grinning even more.

"Well you're sure grinning about something; want to tell me about it?" I asked.

She chuckled and said, "To look at us, anyone would think that we were the ones pulling off this operation, not the FBI or SLED. Fact is they wouldn't even let us go with them to watch. So we're going to go to the 'bleachers' to keep an eye on everything, just in case they happen to need our input," she chuckled more.

I laughed and responded, "You never can tell when opportunity knocks."

About thirty minutes later, roughly fifteen miles south of town, I slowed down and turned off the main highway into some partially cleared land,that still had water standing from the last hard rain; it was muddy and the chance of getting bogged down kept increasing each yard we went.

"Pocotaligo Swamp," I said; "The wild garden of South Carolina. Keep your eyes open Dawn, you're apt to see most any kind of wild creature in here."

"What kind of wild creature?" she asked.

"Mostly deer and wild boar," I said, "Some have said bear has been spotted in this area; I'm not too sure about that however; it's possible though."

We're moving at a snail's pace to stay out of the mud holes when Dawn asked, "Are you sure you know where we're going; is this part of the judge's property?"

"No," I replied, "We're on the outer edge of Pocotaligo Swamp where it borders his property on the south. The primary SWAT team will be going in from the north with other teams coming in from the east and west." We drove about another half mile through trees and more mud holes; I didn't let Dawn know, but I was beginning to get a little concerned about getting bogged down out here in the middle of nowhere and having to call for help to pull us out, even with the winch on the front.

After driving and feeling like we were going in circles, we came to a small, mostly clear area. I was somewhat familiar with the area because I had been in here hunting a number of times. I pulled in between a couple of large pine trees, where we would have a pretty good view over into the judge's property, and parked. I reached behind my seat and raised the rear seat to retrieve a pair of high power binoculars from the storage bin, I handed one to Dawn.

"Do you think we will be able to see anything going on over there? About how far is it?" she asked.

I replied, "It's at least a couple hundred yards, maybe more; we may be able to get a glimpse of some of the action; depends on what the teams run into." I reached down and turned on my police scanner and tuned it to the frequency I thought the team leaders would be using to stay in contact and coordinate movements.

I raised my glasses up and began scanning the horizon in and around the judge's property; I could make out figures on the ranch, near the large dirt berm where the judge had his shooting range. I assumed these figures were probably hired hands --- 'unofficial' deputies; they were all dressed alike, in uniforms. As I kept scanning, far off in the distance from where Dawn and I were situated, I passed several objects that caught my eye; they looked out of place for this area. I turned my scan back to the left until I relocated the 'objects'.

"Hell," I muttered, "Those aren't strange 'objects', there's a couple of jeeps or ATVs out there."

Dawn asked, "What are you talking about, you said this is so deserted and swampy nobody would venture on this side? What jeeps are you talking about?"

"Keep your glasses handy and off to your right, there are a couple of vehicles in the distance, they look like either jeeps or ATVs," I replied. "As deep as they are in that part of the swamp they better have some large mud tires or they might not get out. This is about the only way in or out; they will have to come by us to get out of here, unless they try to dodge their way through the trees. Keep an eye on them and let me know if you see anything or anybody moving around."

I cranked the engine and began moving the truck, "What are you doing?" Dawn asked.

"I'm just going to turn cross-wise on this little path so we can block it, in case they decide to leave, and try to come out this way," I answered.

"Are you crazy Chip? You just told me they are probably armed with some type of assault weapons; we're just sitting here with a couple of side arms," she said, adding, "Yeah I know, you've got a big one, but a .357 mag is no match for an AK-47 or AR-15 or something like that."

I got my truck in place where I wanted it, blocking the trail; it would also provide us a shield if they attempted to take a few shots at us. I checked my .357 to assure that it was locked and loaded and stuck it into my belt. Dawn watched me and got her .38 revolver and stuck it into the waistband of her jeans muttering while she did, "Okay buttheads, come on."

I turned my attention back to the shooting range and berm where I had seen figures moving about. It looks as though they were behind the berm; concentrating on the berm, I saw what looked like a door swing open; I watched as several of the figures went inside. I thought, 'that sure as hell isn't just a berm and shooting range, it's some kind of hidden storage bunker'. I watched as the 'unofficial' deputies came out, each carrying a box, they loaded the boxes in the back of a large pick-up then covered it with a tarp and tied it down.

I pointed it out to Dawn and she said, "That could be some of the weekly merchandise they confiscate and forgot to turn in."

"Most likely," I responded; "But I can assure you one thing, they won't find any cash in with it."

"What do you think they did with all the cash they grabbed?" Dawn asked. "Do you remember Ed telling us that they had discovered several accounts with banks in other countries?," I asked.

"Yeah; he said the Bureau is trying to run down the accounts and get access to them; they were looking for any information concerning whether or not he had funds in any of them, hidden or not," She answered.

"Well they've already found a couple with his name, or at least so similar that they are certain the accounts are his. An account he had in Switzerland was closed and the funds were transferred to a bank in the Maldives. That account keeps a fairly large sum in it, but nothing to arouse suspicion, however, the FBI was able to determine that large amounts had passed through that account on several occasions; it's getting real interesting, " I said.

All of a sudden we heard gunfire coming from the judge's ranch. The teams must have moved in. Dawn and I both raised our glasses and could see what we figured were a couple of the SWAT teams returning fire as they moved in. There must have been a couple dozen of those 'unofficial' deputies scattered in the immediate vicinity, some behind the berm with what looked to be AR-15 assault rifles, firing blasts at the teams as they moved forward.

The gunfire was getting heavier. I raised my glasses and swung them to my left, I could spot several men climbing into the Jeeps or ATV; they had weapons. The vehicles started moving in toward the property line, all but one of the vehicles, and it moved in our direction for a few yards and stopped. It looked as if they were keeping their eyes on where the gunfire was coming from; evidently they were not aware of our presence; that was a good thing, for us that is. I felt certain that they were well armed with assault type weapons while me and Dawn just had our small arms with which to return fire if necessary.

I took out my cell phone and punched in Ed's number; "Damn Chip, you picked a fine time to call, we're up to our ass in smugglers right now," he shouted.

"Well so are we, me and Dawn," I retorted. I could hear the shooting going on, loud and clear.

More calmly he said, "What are you talking about Chip; where are you, are you some place close?" he asked.

"Me and Dawn are about two hundred yards south from where you are, and if you will calm down a bit I'll tell you something you may want to know," I said.

"Why do you have Dawn out here with all the shit that's going on; do you hear all the gunfire, she could get hurt or killed out here; this shooting is aimed at us, it's not a bunch of happy hunters," he said still shouting above the noise.

I replied, "You know she is one of our special agents, so she is authorized to be here; besides I wouldn't have let her come if I didn't think I could take care of her. Now listen Ed, There are at least three vehicles over here, on the real swampy backside of the judge's property; they're not actually on the property, but just off in the tree area, that's where we are located also. Two or three of the vehicles, I think they are jeep or ATV types, have started moving closer to the property line, there are several men in each vehicle and they are well armed; they're probably going to catch your teams from the rear and in a crossfire. There is another vehicle that stayed in place and if they try to leave, they will be coming right into where Dawn and I are sitting."

Ed yelled, "Damn Chip you two better get the hell out of there as fast as you can."

"We can't move too fast Ed, too much mud and too many holes; if they come this way I think we can take them out," I replied.

"Y'all just sit tight," he responded; "I'll take care of it as quickly as I get a break from here. These assholes are coming out of the woodwork, no idea how many there actually are. I'll get back to you."

Ed turned his attention back to the problem at hand; he suddenly realized this was no loosely organized bunch of drug dealers and corrupt cops. There was too much organization behind this scenario. He opened his shoulder mike to speak to the SLED team leader and heard what sounded like pretty heavy gunfire, "Bud, this thing is looking bigger than we thought; there are more of these assholes out here than we expected. I can see them coming out of the woods, they must have a camp back in there somewhere. I've noticed they are well armed, too; I'm pretty sure they have a few AK-47s and no telling what else. What are you running into on the west side?"

Bud Crawley was a former Marine from back in the hills of South Carolina and had more combat experience than most, he was, as they say, 'battle hardened'. Bud said, "Ed, this is what I cut my teeth on, only it was back in Vietnam not in this country. Who would have 'thunk' it. But I'll tell you what, this aint no little bunch of crooks like everybody thought. These 'sum-bitches' have been trained a little and they are standing their ground.

"I have called in for air support from headquarters and they have two choppers on the way with about twenty guys on board. I think some of them are your type troops – FBI - that they recruited from Columbia and Atlanta. When they set down and crawl out of the choppers, we're gonna unload on these assholes and show them what a fight really looks like.

"As soon as the choppers land, Ed, you start your team in and I'll do the same on this side and we will close the gap on these bastards and squeeze the breath right out of them; be careful though, it may take some damn hard squeezing."

Ed heard the approaching choppers and told his crew to get ready to move in and keep their heads down if they didn't want it blown off. He watched as the two choppers set down blowing dust and spray from the swamp water over them; the reinforcements began jumping from the choppers almost before they completed their touchdown.

Ed yelled to his crew, "Move out and watch your ass; we've got a mess to clean up out here, let's get it done."

As they moved in closer it seemed as if all hell had broken loose; heavy automatic gunfire broke out and Ed felt like it was coming from all directions. This gang was firing AK-47s, AR-15s, they were well equipped he thought. Suddenly one of the choppers exploded sending up a ball of flame and smoke hundreds of feet high. "What the hell . . ." he started to ask when his mike headset blasted in his ear.

"That was a damn RPG, Ed," Bud yelled into his mike; "Get ready for some more incoming heavy fire. We've got a few tricks of our own; let's take these little shitheads out, we're moving on in, let's close the gap and pinch these 'sum-bitches' together, real tight."

The next thing Ed saw was a couple of RPGs launched from Bud's area and landing in the middle of the berm causing another explosion and flames shooting skyward. Must have been ammo stored in there. Not any longer. Ed yelled to his men, "Let's move on in and clean up this pile of shit; they have already thrown down their weapons and want to quit." He opened his mike and said, "Bud, you there?"

"Right here Ed, we're just mopping up the wet spots. We've got it under control. They didn't like the idea of us having the big guns also. That took the fight out of them."

CHAPTER FORTY SIX

I HAD NO SOONER closed my phone when the vehicles on our side of the property began moving in our direction, but then another came up behind the first; looking through my field glasses I counted four men in each. I got Dawn's attention and pointed out the vehicles approaching, moving slowly, we could also see that every person was armed with some tough looking weapons.

Dawn asked a little excitedly, "What are we going to do Chip?"

"I don't think they have spotted us yet," I replied, "But they will any minute now. Stay low behind the rear of the truck, I'll stay here at the front, it spreads us out a little bit anyway. Hold your fire until they're in our range; their weapons will cover more yardage than ours."

The first vehicle must have seen us it stopped, the second pulled around to the side of it and into a real mud hole and got bogged down tight. The driver must have hit the gas pedal because he had the wheels spinning and mud flying. The people in both vehicles jumped out with their weapons at the ready level. The guys in the bogged down vehicle got stuck in the mud up to their ankles; two of them fell face first into the mud when they tried to take a step, the others started slowly moving in our direction.

Dawn looked over at me and I motioned for her to keep quiet and stay down until I gave the signal; I whispered, "Train your weapon on one of the men to our right and I will take the left. Have your extra cartridge handy so you can change it quickly, when you hear me fire open up, make each shot count."

As they approached one of the men fired a quick burst, I guess to see if anyone was there; possibly thinking the truck belonged to some hunters who were in the wooded area. But I heard one of the shots ping off my truck just above the door on the opposite side from where me and Dawn were crouched. Dawn looked at me and I motioned to hold on a while longer, until they got closer. As they got within about fifteen yards one of those assholes raised his weapon and fired a burst right into my truck, blowing out the windows and putting holes in that side. I already had his ass in my sights --- I pulled the trigger and he dropped right where he stood. Immediately I heard Dawn fire and saw another shithead drop. The others started to spread out, except the three who had jumped into the mud, Dawn and I both fired almost simultaneously and all three of those bastards went down face first. The driver of the stuck vehicle never made it out of his seat, I caught him in the middle of his forehead with a .357 round; there were two more hiding behind some trees in the mud, we couldn't see them.

In less than five minutes we heard a vehicle coming our way through the mud and the mud holes, without slowing. It pulled up alongside my truck and Ed jumped out of this military type vehicle, it looked like one of those that carried troops into a battle area. The back of the vehicle popped open and five uniformed agents with bullet proof vests that had FBI imprinted on the front and back, jumped out with weapons ready. Ed raised his field glasses to survey the area and saw the 'scum troops' hiding, he motioned his guys to get them. Meanwhile he saw a couple vehicles getting closer to our side of the judge's property; about the same time two more of the military vehicles pulled up and fifteen more agents jumped out with weapons at the ready. Ed spoke with a lieutenant and pointed out the vehicles further in the swampy area; the lieutenant nodded and motioned for his men to follow, and spread out, as he moved forward.

Dawn and I had stayed behind my truck, keeping a low profile, trying not to get hit by flying bullets. I walked around to the other side of the truck; I stopped and told Ed, "Look at all those damn holes in my truck Ed, who is going to pay for this, you or the Bureau?"

He responded with, "Shit Chip, I believe it was you who started all this crap and called in the cavalry, we came running in and saved the day for you. What do you expect?" He grinned as he walked off in the direction of his team leader.

Dawn came up and put her arm through mine, smiled and said, "I guess we showed them didn't we."

I leaned over and gave her a quick peck on the cheek and replied, "That was some good shooting lady, remind me not to get on your bad side."

Ed, who had been watching, came up smiling and said, "If you two want to make out, why don't you go on home; we pretty much have this situation under control out here."

Dawn blushed and I told Ed, "I don't even know if my truck will run after this; at least they didn't kill my tires." I got in the truck turned the switch, and it cranked right up. Dawn climbed in and we told Ed we would see him later and asked him to give us a call when he found out anything; like who were all these assholes doing the shooting and cleaning out that underground merchandise hole, and what kind of merchandise was it – drugs?

CHAPTER FORTY SEVEN

DAYLIGHT WAS SLOWLY FADING away as Dawn and I got back to the Sweet Daddy Creek Club. I suggested we take a quick shower, get dressed and go into town and have a quiet, leisurely dinner. We were both pretty tired, partly from the stress of the shootout and needed a break. She readily agreed. We deserved it.

About an hour later when we got out of the shower, we dressed casually and headed in town for dinner at Big Jim's arriving around nine o'clock; so we would have a late evening dinner I thought, who would care but us. We were having a glass of wine before ordering dinner when Jim came to our booth and sat down beside Dawn.

"Did you hear about the big shootout at the judge's place this afternoon," he asked me?

I answered, "We heard something was going on but haven't heard any details. Have you heard anything about what's happening?"

Jim must have read my face because he looked me in the eye and said, "Don't shit me Chip, if it's something big, you're in on it in some way."

"I really wouldn't know what you're talking about Jim," I responded.

He turned and looked at Dawn and said, "I don't know why you don't just leave this guy and run away with me;" he got up laughing as he walked away to bother other friends at another table. Dawn snickered as Jim left.

After our quiet, slowly eaten, late night dinner Dawn suggested we go by her house so she could pick up some different clothes to take back with us to the Club. On the way she said, "I tell you what Chip, let's just spend the night at my place. In the morning we can have breakfast with Sam and Ed and find out what all went on today, especially after we left."

"Well that's a right tolerable idea," I remarked. "But I don't have any pajamas with me."

"What kind of remark is that," she retorted? "You don't wear pajamas, in fact you don't wear anything at all, you just let it all hang out," she giggled.

"Me? I don't recall you wearing anything either," it was my turn to laugh.

We looked at each other and both laughed. "But isn't it fun and nice and we do enjoy ourselves," she remarked.

"I love it," I declared!

We pulled into her drive and she leaned forward looking out of the windshield, "Wait a second," she said; "Something doesn't look right; I always leave a small light on in the entrance and hall," she was looking a little quizzically.

"Maybe the bulbs burned out and need to be changed," I countered.

"I just changed them recently," she said.

I reached down by my left side and withdrew my .9mm, pulled the slide back to insert a cartridge; "Give me your key and wait here, let me go check it out," I told her.

She pulled her .38 revolver from her purse and said, "I'm going with you."

She sounded so firm that I wasn't about to tell her no. We got out of the car slowly and quietly and walked up on the porch, being careful not to let the boards creak under our feet. She handed me the keys and I carefully inserted it into the lock and turned it, slowly, so it wouldn't make a sound when it clicked open. I had brought a small flashlight with me and held it in front of me without turning it on while I slowly pushed the door open. I had my weapon raised in front of me also, just in case.

It was very quiet, and very dark inside; I took a couple of steps in and to the side before turning the flashlight on, I could feel Dawn's breath on the back of my neck and her hands on my back as we eased further in. I swung the light around the room in an arc; unbelievable, the room was a wreck.

I whispered to Dawn, "Stay here and stay still while I look around; stay down low also."

I slowly walked through the different rooms – they were in the same condition – trashed; somebody had been looking for something. But there was nobody in the house; they must have done the damage and got the hell out. I flipped on the light and went back to the living room where Dawn was and flipped on that light also.

I saw tears building up in her eyes so I put my arms around her to comfort her and told her that it was okay, everything was going to be alright, I would take care of her.

She pulled back from me, looked me straight in the eye with her tear filled eyes and said, "I don't think so Chip; not by a long shot. I'm going to make it 'not alright'!"

I was somewhat shocked at her reaction, "What're you talking Dawn?

"This pisses me off, that's what I'm talking about! Some asshole breaks into my house and wrecks the place; no, it's not going to be alright."

I didn't say anything for several minutes; besides, she was still holding her .38 caliber, police revolver in front of her. We walked through the entire house and it was pretty much a shambles, furniture turned over, drawers pulled from the dresser with the contents strewn across the floor. It looked as if they had fun with her panties and underwear; probably danced around the house in her underwear before ripping it into shreds.Closets were emptied with her clothing on the floor, shoes scattered everywhere.

She turned back to me and I pulled her close in my arms and said lightly, "You sure have pissed off somebody; you may have even made them mad."

She grinned at that and squeezed me closer; I could feel her relax some. She remarked, "Well it looks as if we have some work to do."

"Right now," I replied, "We better call the police; they will check for prints and any other possible evidence. Get yourself prepared for a long night while they do their job.

Three black and whites and two plain, unmarked vehicles arrived about the same time; Chief Russell came in one of the unmarked units. When saw me he said, "I should have known I would find you here too, Chip. What's going on?" He looked at Dawn as he asked.

Dawn replied, "When we got home this is what we found; some butt-face had wrecked my house."

Russell told her that his people would check it out thoroughly and they would find whoever did it and try to put them away.

Dawn looked back and told him, "Not if I find them first, Russ."

Russ said, "You be careful Dawn, that judge and some of his cronies would love to get your pretty head on their chopping block. You let us handle it; that goes for you too Chip, I don't want to find any dead bodies lying around the city.

"You two can go ahead and leave anytime you're ready, we've got everything covered here and some of the crew will probably be here most of the night looking for prints and anything else they can find that might help," Russ told her. "You can gather up any clothing or stuff you need, too; give us a key and we will lock up. Give me a call sometime tomorrow and we'll set a time for you to come down to the station and look over the report and see if anything is missing."

One thirty a.m. we walk into the Club, tired and ready to hit the sack. Not a whole lot of talking going on just more chit chat small conversation;

we stripped and got in the shower; probably the quickest shower we ever had, dried with plush towels and climbed in the bed. Dawn snuggled up really close to me and I could feel her entire body close around mine as she drifted off to sleep; tired, stressed, but finally relaxed.

CHAPTER FORTY EIGHT

I GOT UP EARLY, about five-thirty, brewed me a cup of coffee then went out on the deck above the garage and sat back relaxing. I was watching two doe drinking from the swampy water while a fairly large gator kept his eye on them. He waited for a few moments then slowly slid quietly into the water aiming toward the deer; about that time a rather large buck bounced out of the trees running to the water's edge where he stopped; he was making some weird kind of noise, 'buck warning noise' I guess, as he watched the gator approaching. The two doe jerked their heads up turned and bounded out of sight into the woods. The buck stood for a little longer with his head held high, looking majestically at the now stopped gator. 'Big Buck' slowly turned back to the woods and strolled royally toward his 'harem'. Protecting those whom he loved; I could understand that.

I put nothing on when I went out, not even my underwear. I was sitting out in nature 'naked as a jay-bird'. I heard the door behind me open. I turned and Dawn was standing there looking a little shocked, but never the less grinning from ear to ear; she was wearing a short, loose fitting, silky robe.

She walked around in front of me and said, "Now this is a refreshing sight to see so early in the morning."

I was almost embarrassed but managed to say, "It is refreshing, you should try it."

She smiled and said, "Thanks; I believe I will."

With that she pulled the tie that held her robe and let it fall where she stood – she was as naked as I was. She stood for a moment then said, "Just sit right there while I get my coffee, would you like a refill," and reached for my cup? I watched as she walked naked back into the house; unmatched beauty, I thought, I must be in heaven.

A couple of hours later Dawn said sleepily, "I'm hungry let's go in and fix some breakfast." We went into the kitchen, still naked, and scrambled half a dozen eggs, fried sausage patties, cooked some five minute grits, made toast, then we sat and ate – still naked.

I looked at Dawn and said, "I could get used to this 'no-clothes' thing." She laughed.

After a light lunch of soup and sandwiches we decided to put clothes on and go into Alcolu and see what the latest gossip was, concerning the raid at the judge's ranch, and find out if they had located the judge yet. Monday afternoons are slow at the Cut Rate with very little counter or booth traffic; Dawn and I sat at the counter so we could overhear any scuttlebutt that the cooks and serving staff might offer. Pretty slim pickings, just rumors like 'I heard the judge has run off with a lot of the county's money'; to 'someone said today that they heard the judge was found dead out on his ranch'.

We were finishing our coffee and ready to leave when Sam, Ed and Jeff came in. They pointed to a booth and ask us to come on back with them, which we did. As we got to the booth I remarked, "Well what has the 'three horsemen of the Apocalypse' been up to?'

Ed was the first to speak, "You sure as hell have started something big this time Chip. I had no idea when you came to Atlanta and talked to me, that you were getting ready to stir up a 'shit-storm' of trouble. But it's a good thing you did; something needed to be done and done right away. You guys won't believe all the crap we ran into."

"Ed almost got his head blown off with one of those AK-47s when one of those drug heads blasted off several rounds at him," Sam said. "It's a good thing he is young and fast, he heard the first shot and hit the ground before they could get a second burst off. He did manage to pick up a few splinters from one of the wooden beams that held up the storage berm."

I saw a couple of bandages on his left cheek. "Anybody else get hurt," I asked?

"Just a few dozen illegal aliens; members of the drug cartel, I believe," Jeff responded.

Ed said, "I'm pretty sure that what the judge had begun, probably as a small, get some extra cash type operation, maybe got out of hand and grew out of his control. But I will tell you, those assholes were well trained and knew how to fight a skirmish, hell, a battle. Well, you and Dawn heard the shooting over in the 'bleacher' area; in fact you even ran into some of the cartel guys on your side when they were heading out to come to the rescue of their friends that we had tied down. You were in a firefight too; I'm glad neither of you were hit."

Dawn replied, "You couldn't be more glad than we are; when those vehicles started in our direction I didn't know if we would make it out of there or not. You brought the cavalry in and saved the day; and our butts."

"Well Dawn, I'm sure happy that we could be of service, 'we aim to please,'" Ed remarked.

That was a well-timed remark, it kind of 'broke the ice' and loosened the atmosphere a bit.

Ed, looking more serious said, "There is something you guys don't know yet. In fact, I just found out myself, on the way here. They found the judge."

That shocked all of us. We sat in stunned silence for several minutes. Finally Jeff gained his voice and asked, "Where did they locate him? In one of those 'far away places' he used to talk about?"

"Probably on some beach in that Maldives country where he had a bank account," Sam said.

"Nothing like that," Ed responded, "He was still on his ranch."

Somewhat startled, I retorted, "Now you're shitting us Ed. This is no joking matter; if he was on the ranch he would be screaming and he would be in custody by now."

"Oh he is in custody alright; they found him a shallow grave with several bullet holes in his skull. Yeah, he is in custody alright, in the county morgue," Ed spoke solemnly.

That stunned, shocked silence came back over the entire group. No one said anything for a long time. Dawn broke the quietness and thoughts of all of us and stated what we all were thinking, "Then all this time we thought he had skipped town, he was actually lying in a grave, buried in the dirt of his own farm . . . or ranch, as he liked to call it.

"I didn't like the SOB, but to be shot and buried like that; he may not have even been dead when they threw his body in the grave and threw dirt on him . . . damn," her voice faded away.

Ed and I looked at each other, as did Sam and Jeff; we all turned toward Dawn, it was Sam who spoke up, "Dawn, you can't fret and get too concerned about this. We all know and agree he deserved punishment, but none of us think he deserved what he got."

Jeff commented, "I agree with Sam, he didn't deserve to go out like that; but, he knew the risk he was taking; a dangerous risk at that, when he first got involved with that group. They're mean sons of bitches; other people's lives don't mean crap to them. They wouldn't hesitate a nanosecond to blast a hole in somebody's head --- man or woman," he added looking at Dawn.

In the meantime, I had been sitting there listening, but thinking to myself, *'the judge was no fool, he was very smart; he had a very good operation going and he was raking in a lot of money, more than he needed, or would ever need for all that matter. He was too wise about the law, crooked cops and crooked people in general. I just don't think he would endanger himself or his operation by getting involved with any Mexican cartel'.*

Sam said, "You're mighty quiet Chip, what's going on in that thick head of yours?"

Dawn added, "Yeah, you've been awfully quiet; you're never quiet for that long."

I looked at the group and told them, "Maybe we've been looking at this from the wrong angle." I explained what I had been sitting there thinking.

"Well, we do know that he is, or was, one smart cookie; and that he had a good thing going," Jeff said.

"I don't think I like where this is going Chip; maybe you better tell us a little more about those thoughts running around in that head of yours," Ed said. "We all have agreed that the judge was a bad guy – 'the' bad guy; we don't need a bunch of bad guys running around here. You wanna tell us more about what you're thinking?"

Dawn suddenly asked, "What about all those foreign bank accounts and all the money he had stashed in at least three different countries? What happens to those accounts; to all the money?"

"That's kind of what got me thinking," I replied. "What if he isn't the one who opened the accounts; or maybe he opened them as joint accounts?"

That stunned looked returned to all the faces. Ed asked, "What in Sam-hill are you talking about; I think I need a little more explaining before I can grasp the picture you're painting, Chip; keep going."

I continued, "Well stop and think for a minute; the situation was getting tight, 'they', whoever 'they' are either knew or figured that law enforcement was on their trail, even getting real close, too close for comfort and they thought they better wrap it up and get the hell out of there, or here. They were beginning to feel the squeeze. But much of their merchandise, cash, drugs or whatever, was located on the judge's ranch. The judge wasn't aware of any cartel connection. Maybe the judge started hearing rumors about his operation and his crooked cops; maybe he started asking too many questions. Then 'somebody' --- 'somebody' thought the judge was beginning to figure things out, maybe even asking questions about the cartel and the 'somebody' decided the judge needed to go. It's just a theory, that's all; but what if?"

"What if? What if what," Dawn asked?

"Yeah," said Ed. "What's kicking around in that brain now Chip? What if you just come right out and tell us this theory you're giving birth to. You've got our interest roused up so let us in on it and we will help you think it through."

Sam laughed and, "I bet this is going to be one hell of a doozy. When Chip gets talking while he is thinking, there's no telling what may come out."

I answered, "Well if you folks will give me a few minutes of quiet time I'll tell you some of my thoughts and what some of the possibilities may be. Like Dawn said a few minutes ago, all that money is sitting in several banks in different countries; we don't know all the facts yet or which countries and banks, but somebody's name or names are on the accounts. I believe we can rightly assume one of the names is the judge's, and if there is a second name, whose name can it be?"

Ed slowly began to speak; you could tell he was deep in thought as he spoke, "Let's take this idea one by one: first, we know that the judge was involved in a money scam, skimming confiscated cash from drug busts on the interstate; secondly, he was also taking part of the drug haul, or at least we think he was. Maybe he had nothing to do with the drugs, he was just interested in the money – the cash; another person was keeping the drugs; that was actually being run by the cartel, hence the cartel connection.

"When we started getting too close and questions began flying, that 'somebody' we mentioned a while ago decided it was time to pull the trigger; disappear and let the cartel work out their own details. That's why, when we hit the ranch, we ran into virtually an army of tough looking, ready to fight Hispanics. They had taken over the entire ranch and they were in the process of trying to move everything out of there when we kicked the door in."

I responded to Ed, "That's a pretty farfetched scenario you've outlined Ed, and I can go along with part of it; but this is the judge's ranch, his little empire, surely he must have been aware there were strange goings on here, he ran a tight ship, from everything I've heard about him."

"I agree," Ed replied. "But someone, or our 'somebody', may very well be someone very close to the judge; someone, like a relative or close friend."

Dawn, looking a little disconcerted, said. "Surely you don't think one of his relatives would kill him, throw him a ditch and shovel dirt in on him for a grave; that would be inhumane and cruel."

Sam said, "Dawn honey, you have no idea how these types can behave, you would never believe what cruel is until you saw some of the results of what people are capable of. Get Chip to tell you sometime about some of the stuff we saw when we were in Vietnam. The American people would never believe it; could never grasp what another human being is capable of."

Ed said, "Sam is right Dawn, this can be a nasty business. In fact you have witnessed some of it with all the local 'peaceful' protests around the country. But back to the issue at hand; we know now that the judge will not be collecting any of his hidden stash, so the question is, 'who will try to collect'?"

Jeff said, "Probably one or more of his close contacts, you know, the ones that helped bring in the loot."

"I don't know about the 'more than one' concept; I don't think we will find it to be more than one," I said. "Too many involved waters down the pot, so to speak. I believe our next step is to find out if anyone is missing. We need to know if 'somebody', especially 'somebody' close to the judge has quietly disappeared recently."

Ed announced that he had a conference call in an hour so he got up to leave.

Sam looked at his watch and moved to get up saying, "I've got to get back to work; I have been out more than I've been in lately and if I don't at least show up I can kiss my job and my retirement goodbye. I'll see you guys later; call me if you find out anything new," with that he was gone.

CHAPTER FORTY NINE

AS DAWN AND I were getting in my car, Ed and Jeff were getting into Ed's rental car. Before I cranked the engine Dawn blurted, "Chip look."

I glanced over at Ed's car; Dawn said, "No, not at Ed's car, look at those two guys in the car behind Ed's, on the next row over. They're watching Ed and Jeff awfully close. I don't think Ed knows they're being watched."

I took my hand off the key and didn't start my engine, keeping my eyes on the other car and the two occupants. From where we were sitting, they sure looked a lot like Hispanics, kind of what cartel bastards would look like; why are they so interested in Ed and Jeff, I wondered. Hell, I knew why they were interested. I reached down beside my seat and pulled out my .357 magnum and laid it on the seat. Dawn saw me but never said a word, she simply reached into her purse and took out her .38 police revolver; she knew.

As Ed's car pulled from the parking lot, the other vehicle moved out also, slowly following. I punched Ed's number into my phone, he answered immediately.

"Ed, you have some company on your tail; they must have been waiting for you and Jeff to come out of the Cut Rate. Dawn noticed they were keeping a close eye on you, what do you want to do? You want me to take them out – permanently," I asked jokingly --- kind of.

Ed laughed, sounding slightly nervous, he thought for a couple of minutes then responded, "Maybe they just want to play games; let's play with them Chip. Here's what we will do; let's head out of town on 521 South toward Manning, about ten miles out there is a State Road that leads off to the right toward Paxville, it's a pretty narrow paved road, but dark, no street lights around, just the 'old man in the moon'. It's getting pretty dark now, so when we get to where I think it's far enough away from anything else, I'll stop, I'm sure they will stop too, wondering what I'm up to. You stay far enough behind them so won't be noticed.

When I stop, you pull in a little closer and put your lights on them also. Be extra careful when you get close, no telling what these assholes will try. Do you have your weapon with you?"

"I wouldn't leave home without it," I replied. "Besides, I've got back-up; Dawn already has her .38 revolver out, locked and loaded."

Ed came back with, "You be extra careful and take care of her, I plan on coming to your wedding," he laughed.

We were several miles out of town when I saw Ed's car turn right off 521 and head west toward the small town of Paxville; the car following turned there also, albeit keeping a distance, I guess they never considered they had been spotted and were being followed also. We must have gone two or three miles when all of a sudden Ed's car accelerated, pulled to the side and even more quickly spun around facing the vehicle following him and stopped dead still in the middle of the narrow road, with his headlights lighting up the other car. Both doors of Ed's car flew open and I could see both Ed and Jeff crouch behind the open doors.

The other vehicle stopped just as quickly and their front doors popped open, I could see two men jump out and kneel behind the doors. I drove within about thirty to forty yards of the vehicle and slammed on my brakes; Dawn was ready and we both jumped out behind our open doors and crouched, with our weapons raised and ready. The two guys quickly jerked around and looked in our direction with a startled, 'what the hell', look on their face. They were blocked in. The driver suddenly turned back toward Ed's car and fired a quick burst from an automatic weapon. That was to be his last. Ed's shot went through the car's open driver's side window and took the top of the guy's head off. My .357 magnum shell caught the other in the face.

What we didn't know was there were two more in the back seat of the vehicle; they jumped out on each side and went running for the open field. Before they could jump the small ditch on each side of the road I saw both of them fall, into the ditch. I turned quickly at the noise from Dawn's .38 revolver; she had nailed the cartel asshole on her side of the car before he could make it to the field. I saw Ed and Jeff crouching and slowly moving toward us, they stopped at the vehicle, looked inside then Ed waved us on.

Jeff said, "Who took those other two out? While Ed was busy with that automatic fire, I nailed one on the passenger side; but then I saw two more jump out and start running to the field and before I could get a shot off, they both fell into the ditch."

He looked questioningly at Dawn, "Dawn, you . . .?"

"I just got one shot off," she said. "The man with the big cannon got the other."

"Damn," Jeff stated, "Remind me not to get on your bad side."

Ed looked through the vehicle shuffling all kinds of crap out of his way, "This is a damn rat's nest, it's filthy; hamburger wrappers, moldy fries on the floor; we probably did them a favor by shooting their sorry asses, otherwise they likely would have died from 'towmain' poison or something."

"So, what do you want to do with them and the car," I asked?

Ed was already on his phone calling his team leader; he motioned to the phone to let me know that was what he was arranging. I looked round at Jeff and saw him searching the bodies for identification.

Ed closed his phone and said, "We will have a crew out here in about thirty to forty-five minutes, they will bag the bodies and clean up the mess and tow the vehicle in to the local compound." He looked over at Jeff and asked, "Find anything Jeff?"

"So far driver's licenses and green cards and some cash but not much; these guys are just some of the low-life laborers; they're not paid very much for their dirty work. Get the keys and pop the trunk, let's see what they carry back there," Jeff answered then added, "Did y'all notice all the tattoos covering their head and necks; gang members."Ed opened the trunk to another messy introduction; beer cans, soft drink bottles and cans fast food wrappers and other nasty looking stuff. Jeff reached in and pulled back a small blanket from underneath all the crap, uncovering several weapons; the automatic firing kind; like flip the little switch and it suddenly became a machine gun type.

Dawn looked in and remarked, "It's a good thing they were in the trunk. If they had them inside with them, it might not have been as easy to take them out; they may have taken us out first."

About thirty minutes later we saw headlights approaching from the direction of highway 521, help was arriving. As the convoy of three Sheriff's Department vehicles and one tow truck pulled up, I saw Sam getting out of the lead sheriff's car.

"Well Chip, what in hell have you done this time?" a typical Sam opening statement for me. "I was just getting settled in for a nice quiet evening when I got the call. As soon as they mentioned your name I knew it meant trouble. What happened, did you screw things up at the judge's place?"

Jeff laughed and told Sam, "Don't give him such a hard time Sam, he and Dawn saved me and Ed from getting our heads blown off."

"Well now, I'm happy to see that he has some redeeming value; I'm also glad that 'Old Chip' is on our side, he comes in handy at times; like saving somebody's ass – mostly mine when trouble hits," Sam kept on picking on me.

I responded, "Where the hell does this 'old stuff' come from? If I'm not mistaken . . . 'old' buddy you and I are the same age, maybe a month or two apart. In fact I think you are the older one."

Ed spoke up and said, "If you two kids will stop arguing for a few minutes and get our stuff together we can get the hell out of here.

I spoke to Sam and told him, "Well 'old' friend, if you finish up your end of this little fiasco, call me when you have a moment and let's get together at the Club and see if the three of us can put some sense to all of this. There's a missing link; maybe we can find it.

CHAPTER FIFTY

TWO DAYS LATER SAM, Dawn and I were eating grilled cheese sandwiches and baked French fries at the counter in the kitchen; Dawn had done the cooking. Sam took a bite of his grill cheese, then a bite of a French fry, made a screwed up face and said, "Dawn, you make a great grill cheese, but where on earth did you find these make believe French fries, they taste like . . ."

"They are pre-fried French fries, you're 'supposed' to just pop them into the oven and they are 'supposed' to come out bright brown and crispy. Why, don't you like them," she laughed. "Never mind," Sam retorted, "If I suddenly drop dead I'm sure the coroner will call it 'death by poison'. Anyway, what did you have in mind Chip, about the missing link?"

I answered, "Well to tell you the truth, I've had this thing on my mind for the past several days or more, ever since we talked about it at the Cut Rate awhile back. I haven't been able to shake it either. There's something there that I can't put my finger on, can't quite figure out."

Like what." Dawn asked?

I replied, "I don't know right off; if I did it wouldn't bother me so much. That's why I asked y'all to come out to see if together we could get a handle on it."

"Where do we start," Sam asked? "What do we know for sure?"

"That's the key," I answered. "What do we already know?"

We sat there slowly eating our grill cheese sandwiches, leaving the fries, no one talking; just silence at the table. Dawn got up went to the fridge and got a beer without saying anything. She sat down, then suddenly said, "Oh guys, I'm sorry, I didn't ask if you wanted another beer," she started to get back up.

Sam said, "Well since you're already up, I will have another, Dawn, thank you."

"So will I," I said.

Dawn brought two more cans to me and Sam. "You know what I'm running around in my head?" she asked. "Chip, you said something was missing; that there is a missing link. What if that missing 'link' is a person? You know, we thought the judge was missing for several days; he was a 'missing link', until they found his body."

"I think you are right Dawn," Sam said. "I can't figure what 'thing' or anything else that could be missing that would explain this scenario."

I chimed in, "It must be something big enough or important enough to bring the large number of cartel people in, like what we have been running into. It sort of has to be some big money missing, and whoever the caretaker is, or was, is missing also, or something. Dawn, do you know if any of the people who usually bring in the confiscated merchandise hasn't been around lately? And Sam, how about the deputies; are there any that hasn't shown up for duty recently?"

"I think we have found our starting point," Sam declared. "A word of caution, especially you Dawn, since you're right there in the courthouse; be extremely careful and keep a sharp eye and ear out for whoever is near. We have no idea who or how many may be involved in this shindig."

"Sam is right, Dawn; I don't want anything to happen to you," I said with special emphasis. "In fact . . . nothing better happen to you; I won't just 'hurt' somebody; they won't know what 'hurt' is until I get through with them."

"Damn Chip, I believe you really mean that," Sam said.

"Trust me," I replied.

Dawn blushed and smiled, laid her hand on mine, "I can still take care of myself, you know."

Sam grinned and said, "I believe Ed is right. It won't be too long before we're all heading to a big wedding."

Dawn blushed even more.

All I said was, "We best get busy and try to find out who is missing from around here and just where they are right now."

Dawn got up and told us that she was leaving; "My boss, Jimmy, you know the Clerk of Court for the county, he has been asking about me lately. Cases are running slow and there's not a whole lot of work we can do right now. I guess he wonders why I'm out of the office so much; I think I should make an appearance, or I won't have a place to make an appearance at," she smiled.

"Are you coming back here?" I asked.

"I don't know, I haven't been asked," she replied. "I may have to stay in the hotel since my house was wrecked."

"Dawn you're full of crap too; you must have been around Chip too long," Sam stated. "You will be back; besides, Chip isn't about to let you check into a hotel, not as long as he is around," Sam kind of let out a chuckle at that.

"You're really funny Sam, you know that." Dawn responded.

"But he is right," I said as I watched them both leave; Sam was going back to work also.

Dawn returned about seven-thirty with Chinese for dinner; we sat on the floor around a large square table in front of the television to eat. As we ate she told me that she and her boss, Jimmy, had a pretty long discussion about what was going on in the county. He told her that he suspected she had been working with me and others since the judge went missing. Jimmy and I had known each other for a number of years as friends, not close friends but the speaking and having coffee together kind. He also had met Ed and of course already knew Jeff from official business; like the many times Jeff had been arrested and gone to court.

Dawn said, "I asked Jimmy about people going missing recently; if he had heard of anyone, or noticed if any of the regulars had not shown up as usual to turn in confiscated items and merchandise – like cash from some interstate stop."

"And?" I asked.

"Well, he told me some things had changed but not a whole lot; that Gary, the team leader, was no longer with them, he didn't know why the change, Gary had been there a long time and was talking retirement. Other than that, everything was pretty much the same, a couple of new faces on the interstate task force, that's all," Dawn concluded.

"Maybe we should begin by finding out why Gary is no longer part of the group and who some of the new faces are," I remarked.

"Sam is checking on that as we speak," Dawn said. "I called him as soon as I left the courthouse and briefed him; he told me that he would check on it right away."

I looked at the clock, "Eleven-thirty, I think I'm going to jump in the shower and then to bed," I said; "would you care to join me?"

"I thought you would never ask," she replied.

We got up and dropped clothing, piece by piece as we headed into the bedroom; by the time we got to the shower we were already naked. We stood for several minutes just letting the warm water cascade down and over our bodies. We soaped each other up and stood hugging for a while before rinsing off the soap and slowly drying each other. Dried and warm we climbed into the bed and snuggled.

CHAPTER FIFTY ONE

DAYBREAK COMES EARLY THESE days, five-thirty in fact; I'm having my first cup of coffee out on the deck, sitting buck naked as usual, looking out over the swampy waters. A rather large buck with a wide spread slowly strolls from the woods and goes to the water's edge; he looks around the periphery taking his own time doing so, his head held high as if surveying his kingdom; this S.O.B. buck has an ego, pride; he finally lowered his head and took a drink then raised his head and looked out over the water. I think he is watching for his 'friend' the big gator that seems to rule over the water. The buck turns and looks into the woods and snorts. Immediately three doe came prancing out and up to the water's edge and began to drink. I thought this is the same big 'guy' I saw last week with his harem; he's got it made, he is living a life of luxury. I laughed to myself.

The smell and sound of country ham frying in an iron frying pan brought me back to reality. I turned in my seat and looked into the kitchen at the most beautiful sight I could ever imagine . . . Dawn, dressed like me, buck naked, standing in front of the stove cooking breakfast. I realized that I was hungry; the country fried ham, grits and eggs would be good too.

Dawn came out bringing my phone which was beeping; I watched every ripple of her body as she walked toward me and handed me the phone. She had the biggest grin on her face than I had ever seen.

I looked at the time on the screen as I took the phone, seven o'clock, who in hell would be calling this early; I punched in to answer saying, "Chip here."

"Good morning Chip, this is Ed, did I wake you?"

"Are you kidding, I've been up for hours," I replied. "I've been sitting on the deck watching the deer play. Why are you up so early?"

"Sam and I are at the Cut Rate waiting and we were wondering if you and Dawn were coming in for breakfast," Ed said. Then he added, "We have been looking into our 'who may be missing' theory."

I responded, "Give me about half an hour, I'll check with Dawn and see if she can make it also."

"What?" she asked; "Check with me about what?"

I explained to her while we went inside; "I need to jump in for a quick shower," she said.

"Let's do it," I replied smiling.

"A quick shower I said," she declared still grinning.

"Okay, okay, I agree; we do have to move quickly if we're going to catch them before they leave," I responded.

A quick rinse off and dressed, we headed out the door.

Thirty-five minutes later Dawn and I sat down in the booth with Ed and Sam. "Where's Jeff," I asked?

"Not here," Ed replied, "He said that he was spending the day with his uncle and would catch up with us later. Anyway, I received a call late last night from a friend at the Bureau's headquarters in DC; I had asked him to try and run down some of those bank accounts we had talked about. He said that it was almost a 'wild goose' chase; the first account, the one with the earliest opening date was in a Swiss bank; that one had stayed there for a number of years with fairly frequent deposits. About three years ago the account holder transferred the funds to a bank in Montenegro. We're talking several million dollars by this point, with all the deposits and transfers that were being made. We thought we had hit pay dirt, but it turns out who ever this guy, or people are, closed that account two years ago."

"Why would large banks like those open and close accounts so often and evidently so easily," Sam asked?

"Money," Ed declared. "All of those off-shore, non-traceable, type accounts bring in big time money for the bank. Right now we are in the Maldives, no idea what we may come up with from there. I'll tell you folks one thing however, whoever is behind this is going to extreme limits to keep it and himself hidden and out of sight."

Sam said, "I have been doing a little checking myself, since we talked yesterday, Ed; and those little countries you just mentioned do not have extradition agreements with the U.S."

"Then they will get away Scott free and clean," Dawn said.

Ed responded with, "Not necessarily, Dawn. Sometimes we have been able to work a deal with some of those governments, for a fee of course, and they will let us go in and pick them up."

"Hell, I don't even know where Montenegro or that 'Dives' places are. I'm not sure I ever even heard of them," Sam stated.

We kept talking and discussing the possibilities for another half hour; drank more coffee and were eating a couple of doughnuts when my phone beeped. It was Jeff.

"How do you rate a day off," I asked jokingly, then, "Yeah I know, Ed told us you were spending the day with Jimbo; that's good Jeff, he needs some company now and then, he's getting older and too much time by himself is not good. You take care of him and tell him we said hello."

Ed said, "Tell Jeff to hold on a minute;" he turned and asked the group, "Why don't we all get together this evening, say, at Big Jim's for dinner about seven or eight, depending on when Jeff can make it?"

"I heard that," Jeff responded, "Make it seven thirty and I'll be there."

"Seven thirty at Big Jim's it is," I told him. "Take care of Jimbo and tell him we'll go for bar-b-que real soon."

Sam said, "Well folks, I'm still working for a living so I guess I better show up for work or I won't have a place to show up at. I'll see y'all tonight."

We finished our coffee and went off in separation directions.

CHAPTER FIFTY TWO

"WHERE THE HELL ARE you? We thought you would be here an hour ago; we're at Big Jim's," I said.

Jeff's voice sounded a little uptight. "Some of your 'asshole' friends have me boxed in, that's where I am."

"What the hell is going on Jeff, are you alright?" I asked.

"Hell no I'm not alright Chip. I was leaving Uncle Jimbo's place earlier when I noticed this car sitting off to the side and down the road a ways; when I pulled out they got in behind me and followed for a little bit, I decided to lead them out of the area, I didn't want them to go looking at Uncle Jimbo's house. After five or six miles a shell went through my back windshield, at the same time a car was approaching from in front of me. I saw some shithead lean out of the window with what looked like a weapon in his hand. I wasn't going to let that bastard shoot me so I whipped the wheel and turned sideways on the road like Ed did the other night; by that time I already had my .9mm Smith and Wesson out. I took a couple of shots at the car in front and I think I nailed the one with the gun."

Jeff continued, still sounding nervous, "Right now there are two in the car that followed me and one in the other. I've got three more magazines with twelve rounds each, I called 9-1-1 when I realized they were trying to take me out, but I thought you might be closer. I don't know who to trust from the sheriff's department"

"Shit Jeff, you hang tough, the cavalry is on the way; I'll put in a call to the state patrol on the way."

I punched my phone off and told the group, "Let's go, Jeff is in trouble." I explained as we rushed to our vehicles. Ed and Sam got into my vehicle with me and Dawn and we all headed North catching Highway 521 outside of town and speeded through the small town of Rembert, so small there are no traffic signals. After about four miles out we cut off on a backroad that wasn't paved but leads to the back side of Jimbo's and Jeff's property; it was a shortcut that I knew Jeff took at times.

It was only a few minutes when we saw several sets of headlights in front of us; one was on our rim while another was boxed in between the other two; we could see flashes of light from the vehicle directly in front of us, looked as if from an automatic weapon. The boxed in car must be Jeff; the third vehicle was firing in two directions, one at Jeff and the other at the back set of headlights, which was returning fire.

I punched in Jeff's cell number; he answered immediately, "Jeff, you okay? We can see your vehicle and that you're taking fire from both sides as well as returning fire. Who does the last vehicle belong to?"

Jeff responded and sounded as if he was gasping for breath, "I think that must be the cavalry you called in – the state troopers."

"Jeff you sure you're okay, have you been hit? There's a lot of gunfire down there," I said.

"Yeah Chip; I caught one in the right shoulder or chest and I think I'm losing blood pretty quickly; I thought I was about to pass out a few minutes ago but I had a root beer in my hand when they jumped me, I guess I must have held on to it because I took a couple of swallows and it kept me awake."

"You hold on Jeff, I'm coming in and we'll take these bastards out – permanently – you just hang on." I punched off and told the others that Jeff had been hit and I was going in after him.

"Not without me," Sam stated.

"Nor me," Ed declared.

"And you're sure as hell not leaving me," Dawn declared.

I had driven my shot-up Ford F-150, with the holes in the passenger side door from the little skirmish at the judge's ranch. "If you're going with me you better hang on," I told them. "Dawn you stay in the passenger seat; Ed, you and Sam jump in the back and hold on but keep your weapons pointed at those assholes, I'm going in wide open, you guys take them out as we pass through; I'll stop at Jeff's car; Dawn you jump out and see if you can help Jeff, call 9-1-1 for an ambulance. I'll aim this truck for that other bunch that has the trooper pinned down; they'll scatter like a covey of quail. You two on back can take them out also, unless I beat you to it," I was holding my .357 mag.

I floor boarded my F-150 and rushed toward that first bunch who kept shooting, blowing out my windshield; sorry bastards. They must have thought I was going to run them down – I was – they scattered to each side of the road where Ed and Sam picked them off; they didn't move. I kept the pedal to the metal heading straight toward Jeff's car. Dawn already had her hand on the door handle, I stopped and she jumped out, I headed for the other vehicle. They must have gotten confused, they turned from one direction to the other and back again; we could see fear in their eyes. That was the last thing those eyes would ever see.

I stopped the truck and flashed my lights at the trooper's vehicle, after a moment he flashed back and began moving toward us. When he got out of his vehicle Sam came over, surprised, and said to him, "Jim, what are you doing in a trooper's outfit? Chip, let me introduce James Claymore, an old time troop from my Vietnam days; Jim this is Chip Storrington, also from my old Vietnam days. We're going to have to get together and swap tales over coffee or a drink somewhere."

Jim responded, "You just say where and when Sam; it would be good to get together again."

Ed said, "I see headlights; must be the ambulance Dawn called for."

"We will be seeing several more state trooper vehicles coming shortly," Jim said; "I put in a call when the gunfire started. I wasn't sure just what kind of a rat's nest I had run into."

"Let's get back up to Jeff's car and Dawn and see what kind of trouble he's in; he told me that he had been hit," I said.

The EMS guys were getting ready to load Jeff into the ambulance when we arrived back on the scene. Jeff was lying on the gurney and the EMS were putting last minute tape on a bandage on Jeff's right shoulder as we walked up; he looked a little weak but he smiled at us and remarked, "You and Dawn scared the shit out of them Chip, they thought you were going to run them down. Hell so did I," he said in a sleepy voice as he drifted off to never-never-land.

One of the ambulance guys grinned and said, "You'll have to talk to him later; he was in a lot of pain and going into shock, so we gave him a shot to relieve it; he probably won't even know when we get him to the ER and in a room at the hospital. He'll rest comfortably the rest of the night.

"That young lady there pretty much saved his life; when we got here she had ripped his shirt open and was using it, applying pressure to the wound to slow the bleeding. He was bleeding profusely and may have bled out by the time we got the call and got out here; it's pretty dark and we're not familiar with this area. She did a good job," he remarked.

Ed took it kind of hard; Jeff was his partner for this operation and though they had only known each other a short time, they had become close friends. As the ambulance pulled off Ed came back over where we were standing and remarked, "Jeff is a good man; a good partner, I should have had his back."

Ed was so mad he was shaking; I've seen him upset before, but not like this.

"I'm going to do some real ass kicking before we get through with this," Ed said through clinched teeth. Looking at me he said, "Did you guys see all the tattoos on the bodies? They're gang members – MS-13 gang members. The tattoos covered their neck, head and probably most of their body. Next time I may not shoot their sorry ass, I'll just remove the tattoos, I'll skin their ass while they are still breathing."

"MS-13?" Dawn asked. You mean those Mexican gangs from Mexico?"

"They're taking over big time in our country right now; hundreds are pouring across the Southern border without being detected. They are committing heinous crimes and seem to be getting away with it. But not anymore; if those in power won't do something, I will," Ed voiced in hard, firm words; he was still shaking from anger.

I told him, "You had no way of knowing somebody was gunning for Jeff. You guys were off for the evening and supposed to be home relaxing. Which reminds me; I need to run by Jimbo's house and let him know what has happened and that Jeff will be alright. Is that okay with you guys," I said looking at the trio that came with me: Ed, Sam and Dawn.

We wrapped up all the loose ends and provided Jim with the information he needed for his reports and watched the ambulance drive off heading to the hospital with Jeff; then we left for Jimbo's house. I didn't want Jimbo to panic if he looked out and saw all of us approaching so I called him and told him to put the coffee on, he had visitors on the way. The outside lights were on when we arrived; we all got out and as I was about to knock on the door, it opened and Jimbo said, "Y'all come on in, the coffee's fresh and hot and I've got some fresh home baked Southern Pound Cake to go with it."

Jimbo poured each of us and him a cup of coffee and pointed to a dish of sliced pound cake; which by the way was the best I've ever eaten. We were just talking about different things when Jimbo looked at me and said, "Chip you ain't crapin' me; I think you folks have come to tell me that Jeff has been shot. Well I already know, when the late news said a little while ago that a SLED agent had been injured in a gun battle with unknown subjects, I figured it was Jeff; then when you called and told me you were coming by, I knew for certain. The reporter said the agent was injured, not killed, so I figured he was alright."

"We just didn't want you to be worried and hear rumors," I replied.

"I appreciate y'all thinking about me folks; Jeff had just left here a short while before the early news came on. I will say though, I was right concerned. How about some more coffee," Jimbo asked?

"Thanks," Ed said, "Not for me, I'm ready to call it a night."

We all agreed so we bid Jimbo goodnight and headed home.

CHAPTER FIFTY THREE

DAWN AND I WERE sitting on the deck, naked as usual, watching two rather large gators watching a rather large buck standing near the water's edge, head held high but you could tell he had one eye on those two gators. I could just about imagine the conversation going on between the gators: the first gator, which was larger, and looked a little older, says to the younger one, 'I'll stand watch while you go grab that buck and drag him into the water and we'll have a feast'. The smaller and younger looking gator looks across at the big buck, then over to his right at his bigger partner and says, 'Isn't that the same big ass buck you started after last week; the one that looked at you, snorted and stomped his feet and you turned and went out to the middle of this pond? Huh? Isn't that the same one and you want me to go after him; by myself? I may be younger than you, but I ain't no fool'.

Dawn suddenly asked, "What are you grinning at? You've seen those gators and that buck before; what's so funny about them?"

I laughed out loud and told her about the conversation between the two gators. She burst into laughter until she had tears running down her face. When she could get her breath and stop cackling so hard she said, "Chip I don't know about you; talking to gators and reading their minds . . ." she started her laughter all over again; it was infectious; watching her got to my 'funny bone' too so we both sat there laughing at virtually nothing.

As we got up to go inside we glanced over to the water's edge, the rather large buck was looking up at us, I told Dawn, "The king is smiling at us."

Still grinning she answered, "I believe you're right Chip."

After a quick forty-five minute shower we decided to go into town and visit Jeff in the hospital then catch a bite of lunch with Sam at the Cut Rate.

Jeff was in good spirits and feeling great for having just been shot in the chest a couple of days earlier. However, he was ready to get out of 'this' place, he told us; not complaining he insisted, but enough is enough; said he had been down too long and was ready to go. The nurse came in while he was talking and told him 'tomorrow'. The doctor was going to release him the next day.

Me and Dawn got up to leave and she asked Jeff, "Can we bring you anything?"

"Yeah," he said emphatically, "You can bring me a hamburger and fries and a cold beer. This hospital food is for the buzzards."

The nurse laughed and said, "No, no, no; not today, maybe tomorrow after you get out." The hospital is just a couple of blocks from the Cut Rate so we decided to walk and came up on Sam as he was headed there also. Sam had visited with Jeff earlier in the morning.

"Sure glad to see Jeff doing so good and healing fast," Sam stated. "When we saw all that blood the other night, I wasn't too sure how bad he had been hit; from what I understand, a few inches lower and he might not have survived."

"He was very lucky," I said; "Have you seen or talked with Ed the past couple of days?"

"He had a meeting at SLED in Columbia yesterday, said that he would be back here today," Sam said.

"Any idea what the meeting was about?" I asked.

Sam replied, "One thing was to review the raid on the judge's place and about the attack on Jeff. Since he is a SLED agent they want to get to the bottom of who in hell would chase down one of their agents. They don't like the idea of one of their own being the target. I also believe they were providing an update concerning the foreign accounts and money transfers; don't know for sure but I would think so; they have had teams of investigators in and out of the judge's office and ranch for days now. I don't know if they have come up with anything or not."

We went into the Cut Rate and sat in our usual booth. Maxine, 'our' smart ass waitress came up with the coffee pot and three cups; she just stood there looking down at the three of us with a kind of smiling, glad to see you, smirk on her face. "It's about time you guys got back in here; the boss says with y'all gone for a few days business picked up and he started making a profit since y'all stayed out so long." She laughed loudly as she walked back behind the counter; we also heard her mutter, "I'm real glad to see y'all."

We had been talking for about a half hour, discussing all the different events and happenings during the past few days and weeks when Ed comes in and joins us. We were anxious to hear what the latest was.

Ed had just begun telling us about the meeting when Maxine came up with a cup and poured coffee for Ed. She said, "If you guys are not too hungry, we've got some of our famous, fresh homemade chicken salad; you can have it on a plate or a sandwich toasted, it's really good. Not only that, but to celebrate y'all staying out of trouble, I've saved each of you a slice of fresh, homemade apple pie; how does that sound?"

We all answered, "You've sold me, bring it on."

Ed picked up where he left off when Maxine interrupted him, "SLED and the Columbia Bureau office has closed out the judge's ranch; they've done all they can there and sifted through all of the information they could find. They turned it over to local authorities who are locating the judge's family members. They will probably have a battle on their hands trying to divide whatever assets he had. Or maybe I should say 'whatever' the IRS leaves for them.

"The attack on Jeff has me really pissed off. From everything SLED could come up with it was more or less trying to get even. Somehow the local cartel enterprise thought it was Jeff who upset their little apple cart and was trying to take over their business. Evidently they don't know, or didn't, that Jeff was a SLED agent now; they were familiar with his drug dealings in the past and I guess they thought they would take out the competition."

"This 'cartel' thing scares the hell out of me," I said. "They're getting too powerful and too brave; it seems they have a complete operation located right here in the county. Fact is, I believe they have an army here, seems to be a lot of them and they're well-armed too. That's probably how the judge and his cronies got involved; probably painted a beautiful picture of wealth and life on a tropical island beach somewhere."

"Perhaps that's how they started sending money to those countries that I never heard of, to those foreign banks," Sam stated.

"You're probably right on that Sam," Ed responded. "I think I mentioned to you guys before, that the accounts in Montenegro and the Swiss account were closed and the funds moved again; they are trying to find a pattern in the movement so they can determine the next resting place; something was said about an island country called the Maldives, I'm not sure just where that is; I'll have to look it up on a map."

Dawn added, "I'm not sure, but I think it's somewhere in the South Pacific. I've heard of it, it's one of those sunny tropical paradises I suppose."

"So what's the next step Ed?" I asked.

"Not sure Chip; it's all pretty much up to Bureau Headquarters in DC. The Columbia Bureau and my office in Atlanta are coordinating everything right now. They may take days or weeks before making a decision, you know how the government operates. But I'll tell you something --- I haven't seen my wife and kids for over two weeks now --- I'm leaving tomorrow morning and going home for a long weekend; I don't want the boys to forget who their daddy is."

"Don't blame you," I said.

"You deserve a break, besides the kids will be excited to see you," Dawn added.

Sam told Ed to 'go for it' and not to worry about this situation; it'll all come out in the wash.

CHAPTER FIFTY FOUR

IT WAS THURSDAY MORNING, me, Dawn and Sam are sitting in our usual place at the Cut Rate when Dawn exclaimed "Here comes Ed . . . and he's not alone; there's a lady and two boys with him, must be his family."

"I wondered when he was getting back," Sam said. "When he said a long weekend, he meant it."

"He needed a break, he's had a strenuous time since he first got here," I added.

Sam and I stood and pulled a table to the end of our booth so there would be enough room and seats for all.

Grinning Ed said, "If you guys will behave yourselves and mind your manners, I'll introduce you to my family. This beautiful lady is my wife, Marie, and, these two rabble-rousers are our twin boys, Eddie and Skipper."

Dawn and Marie hit it off right away; they were about the same age and from what I could tell, by catching a little of their conversation, had a lot of interests in common. The twins were thirteen and had their iPhones and were playing games and paying no attention to the rest of us.

Ed began telling Sam and I that even though he was taking the weekend off, he spent a lot of time on the phone with DC Headquarters, even with the 'big dog' himself, the FBI Director. They discussed the events in Alcolu, the cartel, gangs, missing money, foreign bank accounts, and a dozen other things involving smuggling and drugs.

"He was especially interested in how all of this came about and who was involved," Ed stated; "I explained your interests and mentioned the

Sweet Daddy Creek Club and told him y'all were an independent, investigative and mission oriented team. I told him that you worked mainly in the U.S., but if the mission called for it, you would go to outside the states also. I hope I didn't tell him anything I shouldn't have.

"He said that he had heard the name, Sweet Daddy Creek Club somewhere before; helping police units resolve situations during riots or something; said y'all sound kind of like a mercenary group."

"Did you tell him 'we go where the money is?' Sam asked.

Ed replied chuckling, "No, but I think he got the picture."

Skipper came around to the back of the booth and asked, "Dad, when are we going to eat, I'm hungry?"

"Me too," said Eddie.

"Just as soon as the waitress gets here to take our order," Ed replied. "Meantime y'all look at the menu and decide what you want, ask your mother too."

Our favorite waitress, Maxine, came to the booth and looked us over, just standing there for several moments then said, "Mr. Ed, that's a mighty fine looking family you have there; those boys are so well behaved, I don't know if you should let them associate with this bunch."

"You know Maxine, I hadn't thought about that; they'll probably have to go to counseling after this," Ed told her.

Maxine laughed until she could hardly take our order. "What y'all going to have this morning?" she asked, still grinning.

Everyone placed their order, Maxine wrote it down and as she turned to go back to the counter she muttered, "I guess we'll call this, one 'greasy side up'".

"I didn't realize Marie was coming back with you," I remarked to Ed.

"Actually, I didn't either; we were just sitting in the living room talking when she asked, 'why don't me and the boys go back with you for a few days; you can bring us back home when you get the chance?' Neither of us could think of a good enough reason not to, so they packed their travel bags and here we are.

"I think what did it was, I told her about eating bar-b-que and meeting Jimbo and just kicking back relaxing and shooting the breeze about old time days. What are the chances we can get together again with Jimbo and kinda hang-out at the bar-b-que place?"

"I'm quite sure old Jimbo would love to; Jeff may be recuperated enough that he could join us," I said. "However, Eddie and Skipper may get bored listening to a bunch of 'old folks' talking."

Ed said, "Don't worry, the boys will be fine, they love bar-b-que and everything that goes with it; rice and hash, coleslaw, corn dodgers, and especially the banana pudding that goes with good old fashioned bar-b-que. Besides they brought their iPhones and iPads; they won't know we're anywhere around anyway, once they get into those gadgets."

"Good," I said, "I'll give Jimbo and Jeff a call and see if they can make it; how does Friday night sound, will that suit y'all?"

'That's good with us," he replied.

Maxine arrived with our food and everybody dived in like they hadn't eaten for several days. As we were finishing our meal Ed's phone beeped. After his call he looked at Marie and said, "It looks as if you and the boys will be on your own for most of the day, I have to be in Columbia for a meeting at ten o'clock."

Dawn spoke up and said, "Not to worry Ed, that's not a problem. Marie and the boys and I have some sights to see here in our fair city. The boys will love seeing the swans at Swan Lake; you take care of your business and we'll have this under control."

Marie said, "This sounds great, I'm looking forward to it. You do what you need to do Ed, we'll be fine, and Dawn will be a great tour guide."

"Don't eat too much today while you're touring, I was thinking that we would celebrate Marie and the boys being here by having dinner at the

Mercantile Store and Restaurant," I announced. "I think y'all will find that interesting, as well as eating some great food."

Dawn said, "Oh Chip that will really be great, they'll enjoy that."

"It's a done deal then; give me a call when you get back from Columbia Ed and we'll set a time. Dawn and I will pick y'all up at the hotel. I'll call this afternoon and make reservations," I said.

Third cup of coffee, breakfast finished, Ed got up and stated, "Well, it's off to Columbia for me; Marie you and the boys can walk back to the hotel and take a look at the downtown, you'll like some of the architecture, especially the Opera House. Alcolu is a pretty unique city; the powers that be have done an excellent job keeping the city growing while updating things.

"I'll give you a call as soon as I know what time I'll be back Chip, it shouldn't be too late though. You can let the others know; but don't forget, tomorrow night is 'bar-b-que night'; I want Marie to see the bar-b-que hut and meet Jimbo and Jeff if they can make it." He kissed Marie on the top of her head, mussed up the hair on the boys' head and told them, "You two behave and take care of your mother; I'll be back this afternoon."

Sam stood and said, "Well folks, this is mighty nice but some of us still work for a living; I've got to get back on the 'beat' or I might not be working, or living."

Dawn told Marie that she would walk back to the hotel with them, her car was there. I had several errands to run so we split and headed in different directions. Since I hadn't been to my 'little house in the hood' in several days, I figured I best check it out in case somebody had decided to wreck it like they did Dawn's house. I had already moved anything of value or interest to anyone, to the Club so there was nothing for anyone to take. Maybe I mean, 'no incriminating evidence' that is. I smiled at the thought.

I pulled into the drive of my 'hood house' got out and went inside, everything was quiet and orderly as I had left it; empty fridge except for a six-pack of beer, I popped the top on one and sat down in the living room and turned on the news. Nothing much had been happening in the hood lately; a few low level drug busts; three shootings up on Robney between the Hispanics and the 'no-accounts' across the street. I guess the Mexicans were getting tired of making pay-offs even if they were afraid of deportation. The country's immigration system was so screwed up that the police weren't paying a lot of attention to them, illegal or not.

Dawn had mentioned that since I spent most of my time at the Club, I should sell the 'house in the hood' and just move everything to the Club; said that I didn't need the house any longer anyway; it was a thought. Since all seems well in the 'hood' I left to go to the Club to change clothes for the evening dinner at the *Mercantile Store and Restaurant* with the group. On the way out I drove through the tough part of the 'hood' where a lot of the action usually happens; I smiled to myself as I spotted a couple of my warning posters still on telephone poles; maybe they'll stay there as a reminder, I thought.

CHAPTER FIFTY FIVE

I WAS JUST 'PIDDLING' with different things at the Club; checking, and re-checking, our supplies, ammo, groceries, really just killing time when Dawn called. "Where are you," I asked?

"I'm at my house, she said, "Since the contractors completed their work a couple of weeks ago and everything was back in order, I brought Marie and the boys here after we toured the sights downtown and Swan Lake. They're good people Chip, I like them," she stated. "I'm looking forward to dinner tonight."

"So am I; I came back to the Club after I left the 'hood' and I discovered something," I told her.

"What? Is everything alright? Are you okay? Did somebody break in?" She was full of questions.

"No, no, nothing like that."

"Then what did you suddenly discover?"

"Well, I discovered that this is a right lonely place if you're not here with me," I said.

All she said was, "Chip . . ." I think I heard a tear in her eyes.

About four-thirty Ed called and said that he was just across from Shaw Air Force Base and would be back at the hotel in about twenty minutes and wanted to know what the plans were for the evening. I explained that Dawn and I would pick him, Marie and the boys up around seven and go for a quiet dinner at a really quaint restaurant that I would like for him and Marie to see and experience.

"That's great Chip, sounds good and the food has to be good if you eat there. Oh, by the way, don't make any plans for next week; I'll explain tonight over dinner," he closed his phone before I could respond --- strange.

Seven forty-five Dawn and I sitting in the front with Ed, Marie and the boys in the back two rows of my GMC Denali SUV, we pulled into the parking lot of the restaurant. The two boys were the first ones out and running for the door, they had already let it be known they were hungry and ready to eat; all-American growing boys, full of energy. As we got out of the SUV, we saw Sam pull in and park; he and his wife, Renay got out and joined us as we went inside.

Ed and Marie were really impressed with the old Mercantile Store and Restaurant. Ed, Sam and I, and the boys, sat at a large table while Dawn and Renay took Marie on a tour of the restaurant. Marie really liked the old décor; some of the original fixtures were still there: a large, pot-belly coal stove in the center of what had been the main shopping area, next to the stove was the traditional checker board, sitting on a small barrel with two upside down boxes for players to sit on. Further down were a couple of old time counters on which old time merchandise was displayed, although not for sale, old denim overalls, plaid shirts and such on top.

While the ladies toured the place and the boys were busy with their iPhones, I asked, "What did you mean when you ask me not to make any plans for next week? What's up?"

"You and I will be in Washington for a couple of days," Ed replied.

"Washington, as in DC?" I asked.

"That's the one," he responded.

"Would you care to tell me what we will be doing in the 'hot-seat' of the country?"

Ed said smiling, "Well, if J. Edger were still alive, we would be meeting with him; instead we will meet with the current director, the 'big' boss."

Sam glanced at the boys and said softly, "Dang Ed, that's big time when 'the' big boss calls you in, you sure you two aren't in some kind of trouble?" He grinned as he said it.

A little startled and surprised, I asked, "I'm not FBI, why would he want to see me?"

Ed said, "I guess we'll find out on Tuesday, that's our meeting date; until then you know as much about it as I do. We'll fly out of Columbia on Monday; reservations have already been made for us at the Marriott across from the White House; FBI Headquarters is just down the street."

The touring ladies returned to our table; Marie marveled at the restaurant and raved about the old stuff. Dawn and Renay had given her a brief history of how it used to be the center of the town's social life and activity. Ed told them about our scheduled trip to DC and that we would be gone for probably two days. He asked Marie if she and the boys would rather go home to Atlanta or stay in Alcolu in the hotel.

Dawn interrupted, "Why don't they stay here, they can stay at my house, I have plenty of room and the boys will have space to run around in; it will be much more comfortable than being cooped up in a hotel room. What do you say Marie, I would love for y'all to stay?"

Marie looked at Ed and asked, "How long do you think you'll be gone? I don't want to put Dawn out, we can catch a flight back to Atlanta; we were planning on going back later this weekend anyway. I love it here but that's a lot on you Dawn."

"Please," Dawn said looking at Marie; "you won't be putting me out at all, I would really love to have you and the boys stay with me."

"If you're sure," she told Dawn.

"I'm positive Marie; we can relax and visit while they're gone."

"It looks like it's a done deal, Ed; I believe they have it all worked out and you won't have to worry about it, besides, I don't believe you're going to have much of a say in it," I told him.

"That's good with me; I don't like leaving them in Atlanta alone, there's so much crap going . ."

"Ed," Marie interrupted, "the boys . . ."

"They've heard it before and they'll hear a lot worse before they grow up."

The waiter came to take our drink orders; the boys ordered Pepsi and the rest of us ordered a glass of wine.

While waiting for the drinks we just chit-chatted about the uniqueness of the Mercantile Store and Restaurant and a few other things until the subject of going to DC came back around. We all were more than a little apprehensive about what the FBI Director himself would want to talk with a couple a local folks about; even though one was his own agent while the other was not even connected with the Agency. We all agreed it was kind of strange.

Sam spoke up and said, "You two go ahead and do your job and meet with the big boss in DC; y'all seem a bit anxious about Marie and the boys being left here. But, you don't have to worry about them; I'll keep watch and take good care of them.

"Hey, Eddie, Skipper, do you guys like to fish?"

"Yeah," they both chimed in!

"Alright then, while your dad and Chip are gone, we'll get in some fishing time. I know a good spot; bream, catfish and a few bass. If we catch a mess of 'em, we'll bring them back to Dawn's and maybe cook some on her grill. What do you think of that?"

"That sounds great," Skipper said,

"That will be super," Eddie exclaimed, "We haven't been fishing in a long time."

Dawn said excitedly, "Y'all catch 'em and I'll cook 'em."

"You've got a deal," Sam declared as everybody laughed; laughter that broke the more serious DC mood that had set in.

CHAPTER FIFTY SIX

SEVEN THIRTY ON TUESDAY morning, Ed and I were sitting in the outer office of the 'big' man himself, the Director of the FBI. The secretary had brought us coffee when we first arrived; I guess waiting for the Director to give the signal to bring us in. Instead, the door opened and there stood an actual big man; must be about six-four and two hundred pounds, maybe a little more; basketball or even NFL type. FBI Director Tim Walker walked over to us, coffee in one hand, the other stretched out to shake hands.

"You must be Chip Storrington," he said as he looked at me; "I'm glad to meet you. I've heard a few tales of some of your exploits, and of your team, too; I believe you call it 'The Sweet Daddy Creek Club' team, I would like to hear more about that sometime," he smiled.

Looking at Ed he said, "Ed Winters, I recall meeting you a number of years ago, when you first came on board I believe; maybe even another time when I visited Atlanta."

"Yes sir, we have met a couple of times in the course of business," Ed replied.

"You're right, sometimes it's a right nasty business," Tim said.

We sat and talked just passing time, getting acquainted when Tim suddenly changed the subject. "Chip I know you're wondering just what the hell you're doing here, and I don't blame you. Ed and I talked about this on the phone; you're the one who kicked this operation off by bringing information concerning drugs, money disappearing, the drug cartel and that rather large operation down in South Carolina. We've been doing some checking and somehow the cartel built up a huge operation; that judge's ranch had become the headquarters for one of their southeast operations; I-95 was their main supply line; still is for several other of their operations too; the main ones are the MS-13 gangs and human trafficking.

"As you are aware, thanks to you and your team, we have broken up the ranch headquarters and taken it apart. The raid on the ranch paid off pretty well for us, it gave us some clues where and what to look for; not only in tracking down cartel locations, but where to begin looking for the missing funds; no telling just how much is out of the country; that's where you and Ed come in," he took a breather.

I asked, "If all of that money got out of the country, how can my team be of assistance, you have the experts at finding people on the run and missing money; I'm not quite sure how we can help."

Tim began slowly, "As officials of the United States government, we cannot go into another country, without their permission of course, locate someone, make an arrest and bring them back here. Even if we got permission, too much red tape involved, would take forever."

"I still don't see . . ." I interrupted.

"Hear me out on this Chip," he said. "Have you ever heard of the country 'The Maldives'?"

I responded, "Well, for some reason that country came up in a discussion I was having with someone just recently."

Tim continued, "Ed and I have already discussed all of this earlier on the phone, that's why I asked you to come in person. The Maldives is a non-extradition country; even if we were to locate the person or persons who ran off with all the funds, we couldn't get them out of the country, not legally anyway. We could probably get the Maldives bank to cooperate, by bribery of course, to locate the account holding the missing funds. And, if the funds are no longer there, but have been moved somewhere else, they might let us know where they were sent. This is all pure speculating of course; we have no way of knowing for sure."

I looked over at Ed, then back at Tim, "I still don't see how my team and I fit in with all of this," I remarked. I also thought, *'This shit is getting deeper and more serious by the minute'*.

"It's pretty simple," Tim continued, "The United States government agency, the FBI wants to hire you and your team, as an outside contractor to run some errands, unofficially of course, and without the knowledge of the government or any of its agencies," he grinned.

I looked back over at Ed, who grinned too, but still didn't say anything.

"So you want someone to run a covert operation, out of the country, and bring somebody back so they can be arrested and tried in court," I questioned?

"I knew you would understand Chip," he stated still smiling.

Suddenly we were on a friendly, first name basis; very quickly we had become close, old time friends.

"You and your team will be on your own, if anything goes wrong, the United States government knows nothing about it and will deny any knowledge or connection with you, the Sweet Daddy Creek Club, or anybody connected to you. We will provide transportation for the team to a point; after that you make your own arrangements for everything. The agency will provide you with advance funding, identification if needed, or you can do your own IDs, passports, and whatever else you think you may need. Ed will be part of your team during this operation. He has run some covert ops on occasion in the past; he's good and knows what he is doing. He will be placed on a 'leave of absence'; he will carry no identification or anything linking him with this agency or the government in any fashion," he looked at Ed, who nodded in agreement.

Tim punched a button on his phone and a few minutes later the secretary came in carrying a tray with coffee and Danish breakfast treats. Coffee poured, Danishes being consumed, talk about the nasty weather predicted for the DC area; that's it, I'm thinking? "Tim, let me get this straight ---you want the SDCC Team to go 'invade' some country that most people have never heard of; you don't want anybody to know anything about it; you want us to find some damn body that the entire FBI can't locate; kidnap him, her, or they --- whoever in hell they may be --- smuggle them out of the country and deliver them to you,"

Tim took another sip of his coffee and a bite of his Danish and said, "That's about the size of it."

"Tim you must be crazy as hell. When do we start?"

He handed me a packet of material, smiled and stated, "You've already started. All the information that we know and that you will need is in this package; your 'unwritten' contractor's agreement, travel vouchers, contact numbers for emergencies, and so forth. Your guys will need to commit the numbers to memory. Ed has all of the information and instructions also including your starting point, that country you said most have never heard of --- The Maldives. That's the last place we could place the missing funds; we don't have a clue yet as to who the suspect is, or where he, or her or they, may be; that's your job, to fill in the blanks."

"Great," I stated. "Incidentally who is paying the up-front costs and the final mission accomplished bill?" I asked.

"You'll find a voucher for some of the up-front expenses; as for the final bill, when the job is completed and when, if, you return you can submit your statement to me and I'll see that it is cleared immediately," he grinned like a Cheshire cat --- 'if'; he didn't know if I caught the remark or not.

The rest of the morning, until the middle of the afternoon, we spent touring and getting acquainted with some of the many departments at the FBI Bureau headquarters on Pennsylvania Avenue, in the middle of the nation's Capital. We headed back to Reagan International Airport for our return flight about three o'clock.

CHAPTER FIFTY SEVEN

ON THE FLIGHT BACK to Columbia Ed and I discussed our meeting with Tim Walker, the top 'dog' at the FBI; a man with an awful lot of power in our country. Ed said that Tim was rough and tough on his workers, especially agents in field offices, but that he was fair and easy to get along with and you could trust him. That was good enough for me.

"Well Chip, it looks as if you're working for the FBI now," Ed said. "Actually, not only you, but the entire Sweet Daddy Creek Club team; this will be some of the mercenary work you spoke about when you came to Atlanta and started all this mess."

"As a matter of information, I believe this makes you a part of the Sweet Daddy team too," I stated . The captain came on the intercom and informed us that we were in the final approach to Columbia Metropolitan Airport. I asked Ed, "How do you think Marie and the boys will take it when you tell them that you're going out of country and will be gone for an extended period of time; right now we don't have a clue how long this little venture will take.

"I've been thinking about that," Ed said thoughtfully; "They're not going to be real happy, but I've had to be gone for long periods before, it's just part of the job. Besides, I guess we'll find out soon enough."

When we got to our car I mentioned to Ed, "It's six-thirty, why don't I call the girls and tell them we're going to Big Jim's for dinner; that way they'll have time to get ready and get the boys ready also."

"Sounds good to me," Ed replied.

I rang Dawn's number, she answered on the first ring, "We were waiting for you to call; we figured it was about time for y'all to be getting to Columbia."

"Just got in the car and leaving the airport, we'll be there in about an hour or a little better; we will swing by your house and pick you and Marie and the boys up and go to Big Jim's for dinner. That'll give y'all time to get ready by the time we get there," I told her.

Dawn said, "Chip since it's running a little late and he boys are starving, why don't we just meet y'all at Big Jim's; we'll go ahead and get a table, you and Ed just come straight there, that way it won't be such a late night for the boys."

"That's good with us, we'll meet you there in about an hour," I said.

Meanwhile, Ed had been looking through some of the paperwork Tim had given us; "It looks as if our first stop on this adventure is going to be that group of islands in the South Pacific, the Maldives. How much do you know about the Maldives, Chip?"

"What? You think I don't know about the Maldives? Hell, I know a lot; I know it isn't in the Unites States, 'ain't' that enough?" I joked.Ed laughed and said, "That's about all I know too. I guess we better get out maps and encyclopedias and learn a lot more about that country before we get there. I wonder what the people are like, what are their customs, do they manufacture products, or is it an agriculture economy and stuff like that.

"By the way Chip, I've been meaning to ask you if you have briefed Dawn and Sam on all of this. Do they know they are going travelling half way around the world?"

"I haven't told them anything yet, since I didn't know anything before our little meeting with your boss this morning, I said. We pulled into Big Jim's parking lot at seven forty-five, went in and found Dawn already had the table; she and Marie were having a glass of wine and the boys with a Pepsi.

Ed gave the boys a hug and mussed up their hair, just to hear them kick-up a false fuss, then he kissed Marie. I sat beside Dawn and leaned over and hugged her and gave her a quick kiss. The boys grinned, shrugged their shoulders and said, "Uuggh; there's too much smooching going on in here."

Ed and I both ordered a 'Goose Island' beer and the girls another glass of white Zinfandel. Ed asked Marie, "Well how did the visit go, did Dawn throw you and the rambunctious ones out?"

Hardly," Dawn said emphatically. "What a pleasure it is to have y'all here and the boys were perfect; well behaved, mannerly, perfect little gentlemen; I love them."

Marie said, "That's so kind of you Dawn to let us stay with you; we enjoyed every minute. We talked, laughed, Sam and the Boys went fishing and caught enough for a good old time fish fry, Sam is a good cook, especially on the grill; I don't know what he added, but that was some of the best fish I've ever eaten."

"I asked Sam and Renay to join us tonight," Dawn said, "But he had to pull a shift at the department and Renay was babysitting for a friend. I wish they could have made it. By the way, Sam said that Jeff has been released from the doctors and went back to work in Columbia today; said that he is doing fine."

Our waiter came up, followed by Big Jim, who told the waiter, "Treat these folks real nice and be sure to give Chip the bill, he might leave a tip on it, never can tell," off Jim went laughing as usual."

I called after him, "A jolly old soul Jim, that's what you are --- jolly and old."

After the laughter settled down Dawn asked, "Okay you two, you know we are dying to hear how your meeting went and what happened."

Ed looked questioningly at me; I looked back and we just kind of went into a stalemate for a few moments, without either saying anything. I finally decided Ed wasn't going to begin explaining, so I started.

"Well, you see it's like this; Ed's boss thinks he has been working too hard and I have been helping, so he wants us to go on vacation for a few weeks, with pay of course."

It was Marie's turn to speak up, "Chip, I believe Dawn is right, you are full of crap," she laughed, but it was a serious laugh. She turned to Ed, "You are full of it too, if y'all think we are going to believe something like that. Now what's the real story?"

Ed, looking sorta sheepishly answered, "Chip is now working for the FBI on a special mission that will take us out of the country for a period, we don't know for how long though."

"Out of the country," Dawn asked?

"Yeah, out of the country; not just me and Ed, but you and Sam too," I replied.

"Me and Sam too," Dawn exclaimed? "What's this all about Chip; I think you and Ed better do a lot more explaining."

"Well, you've been saying all along that you wanted to be part of a special operations team, now you are; the Sweet Daddy Creek Club Team has been contracted by the FBI for a special, undercover mission; which we can't talk about right now and here. I'll give Sam a call and we'll get together at the Club to discuss it more in detail."

Ed said to Marie, "We'll stay here the rest of this week and go home Sunday afternoon. I'll have to get things in order in the office and be sure all bases are covered while I'm gone; I'll come back here afterwards so we can work out the details and make arrangements."

Dawn suggested that they go ahead and stay in Alcolu and they could discuss the plans and make all the arrangements while they are here;

Ed could call his office and let them know the situation, since he was going to be gone anyway.

Dawn said, "Marie and the boys are settled in and just getting used to everything around here; they'll be more comfortable with you here, Ed."

"I don't want to wear out our welcome Dawn, we've really enjoyed being with you and Chip and the others, but this is a lot on you, to have four strange people wandering around your house all hours of the night."

"Well, first of all, you're not strangers, we're friends, and I really enjoy y'all being here; I wish you would stay. You and the boys don't need to go traipsing off to Atlanta and be by yourselves right now; please stay," Dawn pleaded.

Marie looked at Ed, then said to Dawn, "If you're sure . . ."

"I'm sure," Dawn replied before Marie could complete her response. "It's a done deal."

Dawn continued, "Okay you two, now that that's settled we want to hear the rest of the story. And, what's this 'not just you', but me and Sam too? Where are we supposed to be going?"

"It's nothing out of the ordinary, just a simple short run out of the country, do the job and come back home," I lied while grinning. "You've always said that you like the beach, we're going to one of the best in the world, I think. Have you ever heard of The Maldives?"

"Yes, just recently when you and Ed were talking and Sam said that he had researched several countries that had no ties to the United States; that's where I heard about it. I have no idea where it is located or anything about it," Dawn stated.

"Neither do I," Marie said.

Ed spoke up, "That's why we have got to get our act together and find out not only where it is, but more about the place and its people."

The waiter arrived with our food, "Let's have a nice, relaxing dinner tonight; I'll call Sam later and have him meet us tomorrow and we'll locate this Maldives country on a map and try to determine what we'll be doing," I said. "What about one o'clock, we'll meet at the Cut Rate and go from there to the Club to see what we can do."

CHAPTER FIFTY EIGHT

A quick chicken salad sandwich for lunch in our usual booth, the newest foursome of the Sweet Daddy Creek Club Team: Ed, Sam, Dawn and me. During lunch Ed asked, "Tell me what this club is you guys keep talking about." The three of us started at once to explain it when he stopped us and said, "How about one at a time? I can't understand all of you talking at the same time."

After explaining the Club and how it came to be I said, "Well, you'll find out for yourself in a little while, because that's where we're going to meet, and we better get started if we're going to get anything accomplished. I guess the first step is finding The Maldives on the large map I have in the conference room; we can decide from there what the next step will be."

Ed and Dawn rode with me and Sam drove his car; we needed the backup so we wouldn't be stranded if an emergency arose. As we left the highway, turning onto the very small path leading into the woods I looked at Ed and smiled, he was looking a little anxious.

Dawn noticed the look on Ed's face and laughed, "Don't be too concerned Ed, Sam and I were both frantic the first time we came here, we about lost it and we gave Chip a hard time. You'll be surprised and will like what you see."

We pulled up to the first security point and I stopped next to the old, dead tree; I punched the code into my key fob and the little door swung open revealing the key pad and I entered the code and we drove on. I glanced at Ed he looked a little flabbergasted but didn't say anything. I thought it would be a shocker if we entered through the front of the Club this time, just so Ed could get the full effect. When we broke out into the open area, Ed couldn't take it any longer.

"Where in hell are you taking us Chip? Here we are in the middle of some damn woods somewhere, I don't have a clue where, and all I see is a rotted out, falling down old barn. Don't tell me that is where we are meeting; no telling what kind of varmints are running around inside, snakes and stuff."

I didn't say anything, I just pulled up to the front and opened my door and got out; Dawn was laughing as she got out of the car and said, "Come on Ed, I'll protect you."

Ed began laughing and said, "I don't know what, but you guys are pulling some crap on me."

He had a hard time believing all the security steps we went through to get inside; once we stepped into the large room he couldn't believe his eyes, all he could say was, "Amazing; absolutely amazing, I don't believe this falling down, old barn could offer anything so amazing."

Sam came in while we were standing there, he saw the look on Ed's face, laughed and asked, "What do you think Ed? Isn't this just the most eccentric place you've ever seen?"

"Eccentric may be an understatement, just plain crazy may be more like it." Ed replied.

"Okay you guys, let's get down to business; there's cold beer and drinks in the fridge, grab what you would like and we'll go into the conference room where we'll have room to spread out and take a look at the map," I told them. As we went into the conference room I opened the doors to a large cabinet on the wall where inside was a very large white board. Then I opened the laptop that I kept on the conference table pulled up Google and searched for a map of the Maldives; I placed a red sticker on the location of the Maldives Islands; I turned and looked at the group and asked, "Are you ready to travel half way around the world?"

Dawn excitedly asked, "Are we actually going to that place, in the middle of the ocean, near India and Somalia and no telling what else?"

Ed spoke up and stated, "It's also close to China and Vietnam, but, it does have redeeming values," Ed smiled at Dawn, "It's a popular beach resort; people from all over the world go there to vacation," he paused, then added, "And to escape from the law. It is officially the Republic of Maldives and their government doesn't have an extradition agreement with the U.S.; makes it a good place to hide and live in comfort and luxury."

I then informed Sam and Dawn that the Sweet Daddy Creek Club team was now working for the FBI on a covert operation in a foreign country undercover and must remain unidentifiable at all times. "Ed is now part of our team; he is our direct connection to headquarters, although he has to remain anonymous also," I instructed. "Another really important function of Ed's job, he is going to set the schedules, make arrangements and, most important – pay the bills."

"Not I," Ed stated, "I'm just a poor bucker like you guys, Uncle Sam will be paying the expenses and we'll have to account for it. I suppose so we need to keep track of what we spend; you know an estimate of some sort. I'm sure when we get back we'll have to complete expense vouchers, at least Chip and I will."

Sam, who had been listening quietly asked, "Do we know where to begin when we get there; do we have contacts there?"

"The answer to that is, no and no," Ed said. "We'll have to make our own contacts; according to my folks we should begin by getting acquainted with and get to know some of the officials at the Bank of the Maldives; that's the biggest and is the center of all banking activity in the Maldives. However, we will have to be extremely careful in talking with these people, if we ask too many questions, it will arouse their curiosity and they may start asking questions themselves."

Dawn suddenly asked, "Wait a minute, why are we going to The Maldives, what are we looking for anyway? I know we're trying to locate missing money and who ran away with it. We don't even know who we are looking for, do we?"

"Sam has been working on that," I said. "Sam, give us an update on what you've found out."

"Well it got right interesting," Sam began; "I had lunch a couple of times with the sheriff, we've been friends for many years; I mentioned that I hadn't seen several of his deputies for a while and asked if he was cutting back on the numbers. He said that he wasn't cutting anything; in fact he needed several more deputies. I think I must have got him to thinking because a couple of days later we had lunch again and he brought it up. He told me that he had to tighten up on discipline and keep a closer rein on the troops; said he checked and found that four of his deputies were on leave at the same time, from the same shift. He let them know that better not happen again.

"But then Denny got serious and said that one of his lieutenants was missing. He had put in for a two week vacation, which he had coming, but didn't return. He went checking on him and couldn't find him; he went to the lieutenant's house, he lived alone, he and his wife had separated several months before and were getting a divorce. So he contacted her and she had not heard anything from him either. Now here's the really interesting part, the lieutenant is none other than the first cousin of the dead judge!"

"You mean Gary Rollins," Dawn asked? "Gary and the judge were very close they hung out together even when they were off duty. Surely you don't think Gary killed . . ."

"The one and only," Sam interrupted .

"What else did you find?" I asked.

Sam said, "He has skipped, not just town but the country as well. After talking with Denny I did some deeper investigating and found out that he purchased a one-way ticket on Delta to Amsterdam in Europe. I don't think he is planning on coming back."

"Doesn't look like it," I remarked.

"But why Amsterdam," Sam asked?

"It doesn't make any sense," Dawn said. "I'm sure that would be easily traced and I feel certain that most European countries have extradition agreements with us, I don't understand that at all."

Ed stated, "We know he purchased a one way ticket so it's safe to assume that his plans don't include coming back to the U.S. We also know that his first off shore bank account was in Switzerland, but that's now closed. We discovered that from there those funds were transferred to the Bank of the Maldives; that's why we're headed there. We're not just trying to locate the missing millions; we have to find the person or persons who took the funds, figure out a way to get them out of the Maldives, stay alive while doing so, then bring them back to the U.S. so we can arrest them and they can stand trial. We can't arrest anybody until we have them back on U.S. soil."

I asked Ed, "What did your boss, Tim, say if we can't find the individuals who pulled this off and skipped the country, what then?"

"Simple – don't come back without them," Ed responded. "He's not concerned that much about the killing of the judge or the missing funds; what he is extremely concerned about is the cartel connections in this country, especially since it is showing up in small, country settings. He thinks the cartel is getting a foothold on the very threshold of our nation. He told me that if we don't put a stop to their expansion, our government will be as helpless as the Mexican government is now."

"When do we make arrangements?" I asked.

"We already have them; DC made all of the arrangements: travel, hotel, rental cars and everything is already paid for," Ed informed us. Headquarters is overnighting additional information and individual credit cards for each of us plus checks payable to each of us in the amount of five thousand dollars each. Tim also said to tell y'all not to get too carried away, you'll have to account for it somewhat when you get back; he laughed when he said it, but there will be some accounting, I'm sure."

CHAPTER FIFTY NINE

THREE DAYS LATER THE Sweet Daddy Creek Club Team is sitting in Business Class on a Delta flight that will take us to Manila via San Francisco where we will have a two hour forty-five minute layover; we'll change planes and airlines for the next leg of our flight on Quantas that will take us on to Singapore where we'll face a three hour layover before boarding Male` Air to the Maldives, Male` International Airport. I suppose Male` is a much smaller airlines or 'puddle jumper', according to the schedule.

A meal in the Manila International Airport is another experience. Sam said, "I don't know if I'm eating breakfast, lunch or a midnight snack; hell, I don't even know where I am, what time it is or anything else right now. I'll have to make an effort to catch-up and get my body clock adjusted."

Dawn laughed and said, "I decided I would wait until we get to wherever it is we're going, then I'll try to readjust myself."

"I'll just be happy to get there, this Maldives place, get the job done and get back home without any problems," Ed remarked.

"From what I've seen in brochures and on the internet Ed, you'll be on the phone calling Marie and telling her to catch the next flight. The Maldives has some of the most beautiful beaches in the world," I said. "It's a real tourist resort area."

Ed responded, "I don't believe Tim would foot the bill for Marie and the boys. It's costing a little over three grand for each of us, round-trip, that's just the airfare."

I didn't mention it to the others, but I had flown out of Manila Airport several years before and the runway had potholes from one end to the other. I just prayed we wouldn't hit one before lifting off into the 'wild blue yonder'. Singapore International Airport was much nicer than the Manila airport so I assumed the runways were kept up better also.

After a meal, a short nap and tour through the Singapore airport we boarded the Male` Air flight to the Republic of the Maldives where we touched down about three hours later. The Male` International Airport is located on Huhule` Island; we had lost all track of time; about all we knew at this point was we had been on an airplane or in an airport for the past twenty-seven hours, including lay-overs. We were tired and ready to stay in one place for a while. I spotted a sign that said, 'Huhule Island Hotel'.

I told the group, "Let's go the concierge desk and find out where our hotel is."

The young lady at the desk smiled as I showed her our reservations, she looked it over and said, "Sir, your reservations are for the Male` Hotel."

"Fine I replied, where is that and how do we get there?"

"The hotel is on Male` Atoll, you may take one of the ferry boats tonight or wait until morning and take one of the local sea plane flights, they depart every fifteen minutes," she responded.

Dawn said, "Oh no, I don't need another flight or a boat ride."

Ed and Sam agreed and asked, "Can we stay here in your hotel for tonight and go to the other tomorrow?"

"Yes; we would be happy to accommodate you for the evening," the lovely, smiling young lady replied. How many rooms will you need," she asked looking at Ed?

Ed looked at Sam and asked, "You want a separate room or do you want to get a room with two beds? Chip and Dawn can bunk together."

"Wait a minute," I said, a little startled, "That's assuming a lot of ... "

"Assuming a lot of what," Dawn asked? We stay together at home; does that mean we can't when we're traveling?"

Sam laughed out loud, "There you go again Chip; you better give it up, she out smarts you every time. Hell, you must be the only one who doesn't know you're as good as married." Still laughing, he looked at the concierge lady and said, "We just need two rooms for tonight."

"Would you like me to cancel your reservations on Male`," she asked?

I answered, "No thank you, we have some business on Male` before we leave.

A fascinating, leisurely dinner in the Huhule Island Hotel dining room set the stage for four hungry and tired travelers to settle in for the evening. We agreed there would be no 'early risers', we would sleep in and meet for breakfast around ten o'clock in the coffee shop in the hotel lobby.

I was at the concierge desk at nine-thirty making arrangements for a local seaplane flight to Male` when the others showed up. After a quick breakfast we went back to the airport for the short flight to Male`; one look at the seaplane and we weren't too sure about flying, maybe we should just take one of the boats instead. However, forty minutes later we landed, or docked at the Male` Airport no less anxious than before boarding.

Ed asked, "Where's our first stop, and what do you have in mind, Chip?"

"Well, a couple of things that I didn't mention before; it kind of found its way to the back of my mind, I guess. When we stopped over in Manila I called an old friend and banker, actually he is Chairman of the Philippine National Bank; I told him what we were doing and asked his advice."

Sam said, "I remember you talking about him in other conversations, Chip; he handles a lot of business for you doesn't he?"

"That's the one, Vince Barredo, he looks after some of my affairs in this area of the world. Anyway we discussed the Bank of The Maldives, they are part of The World Bank; Vince knows the president and has done business with the bank before; he said he would give him a call and let him know we were coming. I hope that will grease some wheels for us."

When we walked into the bank's lobby and looked around we saw luxury; we also saw Americans, Europeans, Chinese, Japanese, and most every other nation represented among the customers transacting business in this Island paradise bank. Hell, we may even run into Gary Rollins too; I told the group to be on the lookout just in case. I approached the desk of a young man sitting near a group of offices; I gave him my card and asked to see Mr. Similei, the name Vince had given me.

He looked up at me and said, in perfect English, the most desired language in the Maldives, "Please wait here a moment, I'll let Mr. Similei know you're here."

Shortly this Maldivian native came out with his hand outstretched, "Good morning Mr. Storrington, I've been expecting you; our mutual friend, Vince, contacted me a few days ago and told me you would be stopping in." He looked at my cohorts, "Please, all of you come into my office." He said something to the person at the desk as we went into his office.

We exchanged greetings and made small talk for several minutes; the young man from the desk came in carrying a tray with bottled water, and American soft drinks. Mr. Similei said, "If you prefer coffee it will only take a few moments." We all declined and opted for soft drinks and water.

"Mr. Similei," I began, but he interrupted me.

"Please, my American friends call me Jimmy," he smiled and said, "I guess it's because 'Similei' and 'Jimmy' sound very much alike."

I explained our mission, at least the part of trying to locate our missing person and the funds he absconded with. I didn't tell about bringing that person back to the U.S., one way or another.

Jimmy said, "Vince told me about the missing funds and that you would be looking for information concerning the suspect and any accounts he had with the Bank of the Maldives. Also, a representative from your

Consulate came to see me a little over a week ago, looking for the same information. After Vince told me that you would be stopping by, I had my people look into all of the recent transfer accounts, both transferring in and out.

"I did not meet with this person whom you are looking, a Mr. Rollins; none of my people remember ever personally seeing or meeting him. He had opened two separate accounts, in two different names, but the accounts were opened electronically. Accounts opened in this manner may be done without anyone physically being present. Banking laws in The Maldives are pretty liberal; we have account holders from many countries throughout the world. I suspect that many of them are like your Mr. Rollins, as you say, 'on the run' from law enforcement. My employees who were auditing the accounts discovered both accounts had been closed two weeks prior and the funds transferred to the National Bank of Vanuatu."

"What was the balance in his accounts?" I asked 'Jimmy'.

"It was very sizable, slightly more than eleven million U.S. dollars; I recall my accounts supervisor informing me of a large account closing, but the name did not mean anything to me at the time," he said. "Not until Vince called me."

After another half hour of chit-chat, mostly about the islands of The Maldives and of our new destination, Vanuatu, where ever in hell that is. We thanked 'Jimmy' for the information and hospitality and left the bank.

"Okay Coach, what's our next move," I asked Ed.

"The boss said 'don't come back without him', so I guess we travel on," Ed replied.

Dawn said, "We checked out of the other hotel and all of our belongings are here on this island, and we have reservations at the Male` Hotel here, why don't we stay on Male` tonight, get our schedule changed and make arrangements for our next stop."

"I agree " Ed replied, "Let's find the hotel, check in, make our flight arrangements and accommodations and then tour this plush island. Then we can look for this 'van-oo-ah-too' place on a map back at the hotel tonight."

"That sounds like a winner," Sam responded.

Back at the hotel we went to the concierge desk where sat another beautiful Maldivian young lady. "May I help you?" she asked.

Ed spoke up and told her, "We will be leaving tomorrow and need to make flight arrangements and reservations to Vanuatu; we'll need accommodations there also."

"I'll be happy to make all of the arrangements for your party, sir," she cooed at Ed.

Dawn grinned and nudged Ed, "Better be careful Ed, I'll tell Marie when we get home."

"You won't have anything to tell her, except how good I have been," Ed informed her while grinning from ear to ear.

The lovely concierge lady got all of the information she needed from Ed and told him she would have everything sent to his room within an hour or so.

We had a couple of hours to kill before dinner so we ventured to the beach area behind the main hotel building where we saw some of the most beautiful bungalows sitting above the bluest, clear water I have ever seen. The four of us stood in awe of the gorgeous sight.

Dawn, obviously amazed, marveled, "I would love to come back to this place on a long vacation someday."

I merely said, "Maybe we can in the near future." All heads turned toward me.

CHAPTER SIXTY

OUR MALE` INTERNATIONAL AIRLINES flight out of The Maldives took us to Sydney, Australia where we changed to Air Vanuatu for a direct, eleven hundred mile flight into Port Vila International Airport located on the island of Efate`; Port Vila is the Capitol and the largest city in Vanautu. After gathering our luggage and loading it into our rental SUV we went directly to our hotel, The Grand Hotel and Casino which was only about ten minutes from the airport. After check in we had dinner in the hotel restaurant and went to our rooms. We had agreed on a brief rest and then would meet in the lounge for a cold beer or glass of wine.

Before leaving Male` I had placed a call to Vince in Manila to recruit his assistance again, this time with the folks at the National Bank of Vanuatu located within walking distance of the hotel. There is a one hour time difference between Vanuatu and Manila so I waited until ten o'clock local time before calling Vince to ask if he had made contact with the bank. After jokingly giving me a hard time, asking if I was trying to spend all the money in my accounts at one time, he added, 'Not to worry though Chip I recently sent another rather large deposit to your account; and of course deducted my fee,' he laughed. You're all clear, he said I have spoken with a Mr. Jean` Pierre, he is French but has lived on Vanuatu all of his life and is highly respected; he will be expecting your call. I thanked Vince and told him to keep my deposits large and the fees small.

Dawn and I met Sam and Ed in the restaurant for breakfast; we discussed our next step and tried to come up with some kind of plan; this was the last step in the series of transfers Gary had made in moving the funds around the world so they couldn't be traced; he was smart, but not smart enough, we were here. We decided against informing the U.S. Consulate we were here, as we would under normal circumstances, as a courtesy. We also decided not to inform the local police. This was to be a top secret, undercover, special ops assignment that most likely would involve some 'back alley' contacts that could get nasty. The fewer people who knew we were here and the less they knew about what we were doing the better. We didn't need or want any slip-ups; just get the job done and get the hell out of the country.

After calling Mr. Jean` Pierre and setting a three o'clock appointment, we also decided to walk the downtown area of the beautiful city of Port Vila, just to familiarize ourselves with the city and the people, and get our bearings. We walked back to the hotel.

Dawn was marveling at the sights, "Why don't we walk the 'board walk' and have lunch at the restaurant on the water, we have plenty of time." What she called the 'board walk' was an above the water wooden walkway that led to several over the water bungalows and a small restaurant; all sitting on flooring over the beautiful blue waters that was filled with colorful fish of all kinds. Everything looked so fresh and clean. The luxury bungalows were arranged in a circle about fifty yards out over the water.

"I still want to come back here someday just for a vacation," Dawn said.

Sam laughed, "You mean your honeymoon, don't you?"

She laughed and replied, "That would be okay with me too," she looked at me, I didn't respond.

Three o'clock sharp we're standing in the lobby of the National Bank of Vanuatu looking at the surroundings of the beautiful building; you could easily see the French influence in the architecture. A security guard approached and asked if he could help us; maybe he thought the 'gang of four' had come to rob the bank. Not too far off actually. He escorted us to a desk down a short hallway where an attractive young lady sat; we introduced ourselves and she told us that Mr. Pierre was expecting us.

She took her phone and spoke to someone, then told us that Mr. Pierre would see us now and showed us into a large office befitting a large bank, with luxury displayed throughout. Jean Pierre verified that a Mr. Gary Rollins did have an account with the National Bank of Vanuatu; a very sizable account at that, he wouldn't disclose the amount in the account. He became quite interested, and inquisitive, as to why we were investigating one of his customers.

Ed then explained to Jean`, who had asked us to call him by his first name, that he was an agent with the American FBI and we were investigating a double murder, Mr. Rollins had become a suspect and taken large sums of money from other people, including the local government that he worked for.

Ed told Jean`, "We are hoping to speak with Mr. Rollins and talk with him about returning to the United States, return the portion of money he may still have and stand trial; with his cooperation our courts will go very easy on sentencing him; probably no more than a slap on the wrist."

Jean` replied, "Only because we are mutual friends with Vince in Manila do I provide the information I give you; otherwise, it would have to go through both your government and mine and would take years of red tape, even to receive a negative reply."

Ed asked, "Is there a possibility that you could place a hold, or lockdown on Mr. Rollins account, in case he were to get nervous and try to transfer the funds elsewhere."

"I'm sorry, but I'm afraid not," Jean` replied; "It would present too much risk for me personally and for the bank also. It would endanger our status as a trustworthy financial partner to independent financiers and money handlers everywhere."

Another thirty minutes of worthless small talk we left Mr. Jean` Pierre's office; as we came out I noticed the security guard standing against the wall just outside Jean's office. I wondered if he had listened in on our conversation. I wasn't the only one; Ed, Sam and Dawn had picked up on the guard's close presence also. We left the bank and stepped into the bright sunlight of this tropical island paradise and decided to stroll through the downtown business district where many small shops were hawking their merchandise trying to make a decent living.

We had gone about three blocks when Ed said, "Let's cut down this side street, it looks interesting."

Sam responded with, "Good idea Ed, four's company, five could be a crowd."

"He picked us up as soon as we stepped out of the bank," Ed said.

Dawn asked, "What four and what crowd, do y'all know what you're talking about?"

Ed told her, "You didn't see a stranger pick up on us and has been following for the past several blocks. Don't turn around; let him think we don't know."

We zig-zagged for a few more blocks and then went into the direction of our hotel, as we got close our friend turned off and left us. He must have figured we were not looking for anything in particular. Little did he know; he had told us a lot; first that we were and would be watched and followed during our visit to this paradise. And, two, that we are in potential danger from somebody we don't know and strange looking folks who may be getting paid to take care of us.

I told the group, "Our friend was not the security guard from the bank, which means the guard contacted somebody else who set in motion the following act. I believe the person following us was a law enforcement type; there's something similar about all law people, must be in their training, they seem to have similar traits and certain characteristics. You have them too, Ed.

"This is our alert call guys, we know someone is wondering why we are here asking questions; they also know we are Americans, are there other Americans here, even we know there is at least one other --- Rollins."

"With eleven million U.S. dollars in the bank, I don't think he needs a part time job as a cop," Sam declared.

"I don't mean as a cop," I said, "But maybe as pay-offs to protect his identity and location. We've got a lot more checking to do if we're going to find out just where he lives and hangs out. We will have to be on our guard and very careful; we know that Rollins has already killed a couple of people, so he won't hesitate to kill again. And another thing, finding him can be extremely difficult, too; a few of these islands are uninhabited, with his money he may even own one of the islands by now."

Back at the hotel I went to the concierge desk while the others went into the lounge for an afternoon cool drink. I ask to see the manager of the hotel and was directed to a small complex of executive offices on the opposite side of the lobby. Concierge had already called ahead and a thirtyish aged lady met me as I stepped into the office.

"How may I help you Mr. Storrington," she asked with a slight Southern U.S. drawl?

Caught off guard, I remarked, "You don't sound native or French; you sound more like where I'm from, the south, in the United States."

She laughed and smiled, "I'm originally from Atlanta, Georgia but I majored in the hospitality business and this is my best assignment yet, I can't imagine a better place to work. Please call me Susan."

After more 'home town talk' about Atlanta, and how she had landed such a wonderful position with fantastic working conditions and a great boss, I got down to why I was here in her office. I asked, "How would I go about finding other Americans who are living here in Vanuatu or on a long term visit? I heard that an old friend from South Carolina had pretty much moved to one of the islands."

Susan went to her computer and opened a file and scrolled for two or three minutes, stopped and turned to me and said, "This is my file of foreign visitors; I try to find out from various sources when Americans show up on any of the islands, it's unofficial of course, actually more of a hobby of mine and may not be completely accurate. The latest entry I have is a Mr. Rollinberg; his entry says he came by way of Virginia; it doesn't have a home address. However, since foreigners cannot own property in their own name, he entered into a long term agreement for very large acreage on the island of Nguna, a beautiful place but not too many tourist go there and it's rather a quiet place. You can only get there by seaplane or water taxi unless you have your own boat. The port and terminal are very nice, although heavy type shipping of cargo and supplies comes through Port Vila."

I thanked Susan and joined my group in the lounge, who was surprised at the information I had received in such a short time. I had also checked with the concierge lady about the water taxi service and learned it was an hour trip with taxis leaving every thirty minutes in either direction. A seaplane is only fifteen minutes. I opted for and booked a water taxi for a ten o'clock run to Nguna which was located north of Efate` the island on which we were staying. I had looked at a couple of seaplanes sitting in the Harbour, didn't like the looks of them, not sure they could even fly.

CHAPTER SIXTY ONE

ON BOARD AND BACKING out of the dock at ten sharp; dressed like other tourists, shorts, flowered shirts that hung to our knees, sunglasses, and wide brimmed hats; we certainly looked the part, real authentic I'm sure.

Sam chuckled, "We're damn lucky the captain doesn't have a mirror on board; one look at ourselves and we'd all jump overboard." Then added, "All but Dawn she looks very beautiful."

"I was getting ready to slam you Sam, if you included my outfit in same category as the rest of you," Dawn come back laughing. Our captain for the Nguna trip was, "Just call me Jim," he told us. "All of you look fantastic and your clothing very nice," laughingly he said.

Ed had already gotten himself settled in for a nap on a large tarp at the stern; he lay there grinning at the rest of us. "You guys may as well sit down and relax for the next hour; we don't know what we may run into once we hit land."

Captain Jim kept busy manning the boat while telling us about Nguna Island, "A beautiful place," he said. "Mostly agriculture, they grow much corn, cocoa beans, coffee and coconuts. A few of the large farms, or as you say in American – ranches, have many cattle. They ride horses to take care of the cattle, you know like in America Gunsmoke."

Captain Jim laughed loud and hard as did the rest of his passengers. He talked almost all the way to Nguna; friendly, outgoing middle aged native with a great personality. Ed asked Captain Jim if he would be available for our return trip; he readily agreed.

We were maybe a half mile out when Captain Jim pointed towards land and said, "Nguna, we are soon here." Almost immediately he jerked his head to the right and yelled, "What is going on? That boat is not looking, he is not slowing, it may hit us if he does not . . ."

The larger boat looked like someone's huge luxury yacht, it began turning at the very last moment, but not quite soon enough and its tail caught us just enough to knock a hole in the side of Captain Jim's boat and capsize us. Before we went over Ed yelled, "Look at that son of a bitch grinning, they did that on purpose." Before Ed finished several shots hit our boat as we went over the side, "That son of a bitch is shooting at us," he screamed again.

As I topped the water I saw the yacht turning to make a second round; Sam, Ed and Dawn had seen it too. I already had my .357 magnum out of the back of my waistband, I looked at Dawn and she was pointing her .38 police revolver at the returning yacht, I glanced at Ed and Sam, they had their weapons leveled at the big boat also; I thought, that shithead just took his last shot at anybody.

The yacht slowed and drew in closer and as it did four shots must have hit him at the same time, we could see his head explode as if a stick of dynamite had gone off in his mouth. Another head popped up to look over the side, but won't pop up again, four more shots rang out and he fell over the side. I looked for Captain Jim, his eyes were about to pop out of his head, he was clinging to the wrecked side of his boat, obviously in shock, tears streaming down his face. The yacht surged forth and opened its throttle, I carefully and slowly aimed my .357 at the back where the gas tank is located and squeezed the trigger. Bingo! The yacht exploded into a thousand pieces flying across the clear blue waters; pieces of the yacht hit the side of our wrecked boat.

Ed had 'hand walked' holding to the side of our upside down boat to try and comfort Captain Jim who was crying and saying over and over, "My boat, my boat, how can I feed my family, my business is lost, my children, my boat is gone."

Ed told him, "Don't worry about your boat or feeding your family, we will see to it, you can get another boat."

"I can't, I do not have money to buy another boat," Captain Jim protested.

I told Captain Jim not to worry, "Right now we have to get to shore."

Dawn said, "A boat is coming, I think it's a fishing boat."

A trawler pulls up beside us and throws a line that Sam caught; we pulled ourselves to the trawler and crawled up the rope ladder hanging over the side. It was a tuna trawler on its way back into port. It had a four man crew, all smelling like fresh fish; under the circumstances it was a very pleasant smell, we were all safe aboard.

The captain and crew were all questions concerning what had caused the explosions; they thought they had seen two boats; was anyone hurt or killed? We assured them that we were all safe, thanks to them. I didn't want them to know what actually happened and that at least two were killed in the explosion; the last thing we needed was the local cops after us. Ed looked at me and nodded in agreement. We certainly did not need or want the local police, French gendarmes, or whatever they called the national law enforcement, to start asking questions. Hell we don't want them to even know we're here.

Dawn remarked, "Well guys, it's a good thing we didn't bring all our possessions with us even though we are going to need a change of clothes when we get ashore. I wonder if there are some ladies' stores where I can go shopping."

Ed smiled and told me, "Better get your wet billfold and money out Chip, she may need a lot of it; she'll be starting from scratch and will need an entire new wardrobe."

Sam inserted his thoughts, "This is going to be an expensive swim for you Chip."

"Madame, there are many ladies' shopping places on Nguna; I should know, my wife visits all of them often," the trawler captain remarked laughing. He was of French descent. Then he added, "They also have a few men's shops that serve us," as he looked at Ed, Sam and me, still grinning.

We turned Dawn loose in an area of lades' shops while the four of us found a men's shop. Captain Jim was hesitant at first but we convinced him that he could not shop for a new boat in wet clothing. He was bewildered at the thought of a new boat and kept saying no, he could not accept. It didn't take us too long to convince him that it was okay and we were buying him a boat; we had to have some way to return to Port Vila. I told Ed, it would not be a problem; I would include it on my expense report.

"Yeah; right," was all he said.

Dawn entered a ladies' shop as we agreed to meet in an hour, more or less, back in front of the same dress shop; we found a men's store close by and within thirty minutes we were all re-outfitted with new clothing for the day. We returned to the dress shop that Dawn had entered, found a coffee shop across the street and got a table on the sidewalk where we could watch for Dawn. Two cups of coffee and two beers later Dawn returned from the opposite direction, wearing beautiful flowery, knee length shorts, matching blouse, sunglasses and a wide brim hat; 'Miss Tourist of the day'; we kidded her relentlessly for the next hour before telling her how gorgeous she really was.

She had been the only one of us who paid attention to our mission and tried to remain incognito – she said, "You told me to dress as a tourist, so here I am." She looked at us men and said, "In the company of the captain of a yacht and three of his crewmembers."

By now Captain Jim had gotten in the spirit of our American joking attitude, "I think if I hire a crew, I think I find experienced hands to work on my boat," he laughed and tipped his new captain's hat. When we purchased new clothing, we got Captain Jim dressed in a true captain's outfit, complete with the hat; he loved it and his pride showed. He said, "Wait until my wife and kids see me, they will be very happy also. I thank you very much, this you did not have to do; the sinking of my boat was not of your doing." Then Captain Jim muttered kind of softly but very firmly, "If I find who was responsible I will castrate them and hang them over the bow," he looked at Dawn, blushed and said to her, "Miss Dawn, I am so sorry, I should not speak of such in your company, please forgive me."

Dawn blushed and told him, "Not to worry, I feel the same as you; I might do worse than you."

Three hours later at the marina dock workers were busy unloading Captain Jim's new boat and launching it; the new well-dressed skipper had a smile that reached from horizon to horizon. It was a very nice and comfortable boat and it would be easier for our skipper to book many trips in his beautiful new 'taxi'; it was twenty-five thousand U.S. dollars' worth of beauty and comfort. At home the price would be minimum seventy-five grand plus.

Ed looking a little skittish remarked, "It's a good thing that you have an unlimited American Express Card. My limit would only cover the fuel for one fill up."

We went to where they were launching the boat; maybe I should call it a ship, it was twice the size of Captain Jim's original boat. Not only that, this fellow had twin 8-valve, single overhead cam Mercury engines with computer controlled fuel induction system; it was 60 horse-power rated and set up for law enforcement activity; strange that.

The engines were purring when we went on board, Captain Jim was already at the controls checking everything out, talking with the marina sales people and running the engines through their paces. The grin had never once left Captain Jim's face. He turned to us and asked us, "Are you folks ready for a trial run?"

"Let's go for it," Sam called out, "Run this ship down around the sound and let's see what it will do." Everybody was excited.

A quick trip around Nguna Atoll and back to port was a great test. I told the group and Captain Jim, "It's getting late in the day and that afternoon sun will quickly fade, I think we should head back to Efate` and our hotel and start over tomorrow morning; I don't believe we will accomplish anything else today. Captain Jim, will you be available for us tomorrow?"

Looking surprised and slightly insulted that I should ask such a question, he replied, "Mr. Chip, Miss Dawn, all of you; I will be with you every day you are here, and longer if you would like. I do not understand your question; of course I will be available anytime you say, you just purchased a boat and I will drive it for you."

"It is your boat Captain Jim, not ours; the papers are in your name, you own the boat. By the way, all of the boats have names, your old one had a name; what will you name this one?"

"I do not know, I haven't given thought to naming it; I know, I will name it 'Chip and His Team' boat."

We laughed and told him, "No, no, you name it what you like."

Dawn and Sam had been in a huddle talking among themselves, Dawn suddenly spoke up and said, "You could name it the 'Sweet Daddy Creek Boat.'"

Captain Jim jumped at it, "That is it," he exclaimed. "I overheard you talking and you said you had a 'happy place' called Sweet Club or something. That is the name of the new boat. It is done."

Dawn came to me and ran a finger over my eyes and hugged me.

CHAPTER SIXTY TWO

NINE O'CLOCK WE MET Captain Jim at the marina in Port Vila, a short walk from the Grand Hotel and Casino; we boarded the 'Sweet Daddy Creek Boat' and stowed the small satchel each of us carried in a closed bin on the inside. Captain Jim called me off to the side and said to me, "Mr. Chip, in your conversations I cannot but hear some of the things you speak of; I know you are looking for an American man who has come here to live, that he ran away from police in America. This man owns a big farm on Nguna and has many of our people working for him, I have several cousins who work there; they do not like him. After I arrived home last evening I phoned one of them to inquire on him. My cousin tells me that he is cruel to his workers; he threatens to kill them. He has a lot of friends who have power on Vanuatu; it is said that he has very much money.

"My cousins tell me that he is a much dangerous man; he carries his pistol on his side everywhere he goes, without fear. He is friends with all of the police officers, he tells them, and some of his workers that he was a policeman in the U.S., he shows his badge and his pistol and tells that he is authorized to use it."

I told him, "Thanks Captain Jim, we know he is dangerous that is why we are here to take him away from your country. Do you know where on Nguna he is located, where his farm is; is it guarded and how many guards does he have?"

"I will phone my cousin before we pull anchor and I will ask him all these things," He said.

While Captain Jim made ready to depart and while he was calling his cousin, I briefed the others about the conversation with Captain Jim. I also asked, "Did y'all bring your weapons; I don't know if we will need them or not, but I never would have expected to need them yesterday when we were run down and shot at." I pulled my .357 magnum from my back waistband and checked it.

Dawn opened her small, over the shoulder bag and took out her .38 police revolver, she checked it while Sam and Ed were checking their weapons.

Ed remarked, "I'm gonna have to get me a cannon like yours Chip, if we keep getting into scraps like we have so far."

"Me to," echoed Sam grinning. "The more we're around Chip the more we're getting shot at."

Captain Jim came to where we were standing and stated, "I spoke with my cousin, he is at home today and will guide us to the farm when you are ready. He also told me that some of our other cousins will be happy to help us if we get into trouble and need help. They had heard, and I told them about the attack on us yesterday, they told me to bring my weapon and to advise you to bring weapons also. He has his paid guards and the local police will help him, he pays them and does many things for them. My cousin thinks the police will fight for him if necessary. Mr. Chip, we have to be very careful, this is dangerous."

I placed a hand on Captain Jim's shoulder and told him, "This is not your fight, you do not have to go with us; you stay at the marina and keep the boat safe and ready for when we return."

"I will not leave you," Captain Jim said tartly, "I do not leave my friends when trouble comes, I stay with them until it is finished. I came prepared to fight if we have to; I show you. Captain Jim opened a large, locked bin and inside was an AR-15, an AK-47, two rifles that looked to be .30caliber and three 9mm pistols with several magazines for each. He smiled at us and said, "I am ready my friends; some of my cousins are also ready to help us."

He would not listen to our protests but said very clearly but grinning broadly, "Me and my cousins we will be part of your 'Sweet Daddy Team', we will show them."

Dawn and Sam laughed and told him welcome aboard to the Sweet Daddy Creek Team. Grinning like a possum chasing a chicken, Captain Jim poured power to the throttle and we were on our way back to Nguna; and what else we didn't have the foggiest idea, we would know soon enough, I thought. Uneventful trip from Port Vila to Nguna and we pulled smoothly into the docking space; Captain Jim knew this place very well. We saw two men standing on the dock looking in our direction; I nudged Ed and Sam and told them to keep an eye on them. The two men raised their hands waving at us, Captain Jim waved back, two of my cousins he told us; that was a relief.

We told the captain of the 'new' boat that we were going into the nearby hotel restaurant for breakfast and coffee, he said he was staying with his boat and visit with his cousins; I don't think Captain Jim had stopped smiling since he first saw the boat, probably slept with a smile on his face. As the four of us walked off the dock toward the hotel we could hear the Captain telling his cousins in a mix of native dialect and English about his new boat as he was showing them around.

The hotel was definitely an upscale, luxury resort destination, for tourists from all over the world; and many were here already. We were seated and ordered and the waiter brought coffee. A young man of about twenty to twenty-five; as he poured our coffee, in a whispered tone he said, "My name is Coolsby, my Uncle Jim said you would be coming sometime today; he just called and told me that you were on the way; anything that you may need I will be happy to bring to you. Thank you for saving my uncle yesterday."

Later when Coolsby brought our food and leaned over the table to place the plates in front of us, in his low voice he said, "I believe you may have company already. The two gentlemen sitting near the entrance have been watching you since you have arrived. I believe they are, as you say, undercover police people; I do not like them, be careful." He then went about his business of serving other customers.

Ed, still eating, glanced at the two men and said, "Evidently they, or Rollins, have been expecting us."

Sam said, "Yeah after their little fiasco on the water yesterday maybe they figure it isn't going to be so easy to get rid of us."

"Well as far as I'm concerned," said Dawn, "After the little fiasco that dunked me in the ocean, I'm certainly ready to kick-butt."

That lightened the mood; we teased Dawn light heartedly – but serious about getting dunked. Our late breakfast over, we paid the check and decided to take a leisurely walk back to the docks, which was only a couple of blocks. When we turned the corner out of sight of the hotel our two 'friends' from breakfast appeared by our side.

"Wait up a moment," the first one said as the second person moved to a position slightly behind us. "You are American, yes?"

Ed said very clearly, "We are American, yes; who are you?"

Sam had turned and was facing the person behind us. The first one pulled out his wallet and showed us his badge, "We are with the police department here on Nguna and we had reports of trouble on the waterway yesterday, we are investigating the incident. Do you have identification?"

"We have proper identification and papers we are here legally on vacation; we are not under suspicion for anything, now if you gentlemen will excuse us we will be going," I told them as we started to walk away.

The first man, who said that he was a special agent, said, "I do not think so, you must accompany us to headquarters." When he said this he placed his hand on his sidearm, as did the one behind us.

From around the corner of the building a voice said, "I do not think they will do that; remove your hand from your weapons, very slowly and carefully." The voice then spoke in French to some people we could not see at the moment; they came from inside the building, disarmed the two police who were looking a little scared at this point, they took them into the building; that was the last we saw those two.

The 'voice' came over to us and said, "Welcome to Nguna, I am Dante` a cousin of your boat's captain; we have to be very careful here the police are everywhere and they are up to no good. Your fellow American who hides here has turned the law against those of us who must work to live and feed our families. We are not many people on Nguna; he has become the boss of the police. We would like to give him back to you." He smiled.

Ed told him, "That is our plan; we hope to capture him so we can return him to the United States where he will stand trial for murder. But first, we must find a way to get him out of your country, to a place where we can arrest him and take him prisoner."

Dante` responded, "That will not be a problem, my cousin, the happy Captain with the new boat," he chuckled in midsentence, "will be most happy and pleased to take you in his new boat to a place where you will be safe and can transport the prisoner to America. Also, I wish to thank you and your team for saving my cousin's life and purchasing a new boat. He is very happy; he will be honored to do anything to help you; and so will all of his family. On Vanuatu our families are very close together and depend upon each other to survive."

Captain Jim came up and said that he had seen us talking with two men; when his cousin Dante` appeared he knew there was trouble, so he came. Dante` began explaining to Captain Jim what we had told him about getting the American off the island and out of the country so we could take him back to America.

Dante` speaking to his cousin said, "I told them that it would be no problem, that you would take them to a safe place where they could catch a flight back to their country with the prisoner, that we would help them all the way. You would need to take them with you on your new boat to one of the islands not of Vanuatu, but a neutral country. Is this possible Cousin Jim?"

Captain Jim laughed and remarked, "With my new boat I think I could take them all to America myself."

Everyone laughed at Captain Jim's statement and he got serious and said, "I have been to some other island countries before, I have charts and we will look at them and decide which is the most practical and safest. With my new boat I can reach most all of the nearest ones with no problem and have plenty of fuel."

I interjected at this point, "We have to find Rollins first and sneak him off Nguna; we will have to keep him someplace while we get out of our hotel on Efate`."

"That will not be such a big problem," both Dante` and Captain Jim agreed; "we will keep him company until we meet in the country you choose."

Ed said, "Why don't we find a place where we can discuss a plan of action, and Captain Jim if you can bring the charts you mentioned, we will set the course we will take."

"There is a small restaurant just around the corner, a quiet place, maybe two blocks," Dante` said, "We will go there and go over the charts for travel out of the area."

Captain Jim told us, "I will be back momentarily, I will get my charts of these waters so we can decide upon a destination and the route we will take; I shall return."

The restaurant was pretty much deserted at the time of day, we had plenty of room to lay out the charts; after much discussing and carefully reviewing the charts, currents and possible patrol boats, we decided on a route that would take us around the back side of Nguna to Port Vila where

Dawn, Sam, Ed and I would get off and return to our hotel to close out our business there. Captain Jim, with his new 'crew' consisting of cousins Dante` and one other would accompany him to New Caledonia to the port city of Noumea where we would meet. Captain Jim assured us that he could easily make the trip; it was two hundred ninety nautical miles, across open water, from Port Vila to the Port in Noumea, New Caledonia; he said that he had made the trip one other time in his old boat. "In my new boat, it will be nothing of a trip," he said grinning.

In the meantime the Sweet Daddy Creek Team would fly into Noumea and make our travel arrangements back to the U.S. with our passenger.

I reminded them, "You keep forgetting that we must first find Rollins and get him off his farm and off Nguna; that may not be so easy."

Dante` smiled and said, "You worry too much Chip, my people will handle that. Some of our cousins are already looking for this Rollins; right now he is on his farm. We think after the water attack he may be, as you say, 'laying low'; or staying on his farm for other reasons; no one has seen him in town recently. I also have friends on the police department, and I have sent two to the farm to bring Rollins in to ask him concerning the death of one of his employees whose body was found four days ago. It was badly beaten and left in a ditch beside the road, next to Rollin's farm. I should hear from them anytime."

Dawn said, "Well, if you guys are through with all of your planning, and since we are sitting in a nice restaurant, I suggest we eat lunch."

"That's the best plan I've heard yet, "Sam echoed.

CHAPTER SIXTY THREE

THE SWEET DADDY CREEK Team, along with Captain Jim and two of his cousins were sitting on the new boat; mostly just trading funny stories from our background, but also bringing into the conversation, the serious action we were undertaking. We heard someone approaching and looked up and saw Dante` hurrying down the dock, almost running, toward the boat. He looked mad as hell. Something has gone wrong was my first thought.

"Oh shit, there must be trouble brewing," Sam uttered.

"I think you're right," Ed replied. "Get ready for all hell to break loose."

Dante` came running up out of breath, "Chip, Ed, we have some problems; my two friends who are police are dead. Some of my family found their bodies just outside of the farm, they had been stripped of their clothing and tied to a tree; their stomachs were cut open and the intestines spilled out on the ground. This may be a warning to Vanuatuans – that was the way of the ancient people of our country before they became civilized; they want to frighten us off."

Dawn, looking bewildered asked, "Why would they cut their stomach open?"

"To eat them!" Dante` stated as a matter of fact; then added, "Miss Dawn, pardon me but in ancient Vanuatu, in the early sixteen hundreds the culture of the many island natives was cannibalism. The nation did not begin to become more civilized until Captain Cook arrived in the early seventeen hundreds."

I put my arm around Dawn's trembling shoulder to comfort her, "You don't have to worry about that now days; I agree with Dante` that was just a type of warning to put a scare in us."

"Well they sure succeeded, in me at least," she said.

Dante` proceeded to tell us that he had notified most members of his family and they were getting together friends and some of the farm's former employees who had been mistreated by Rollins and the 'bosses' at the farm. It sounded as if this was the proverbial 'straw that broke the camel's back'; from the way Dante` was describing the feelings, things were going to get real nasty.

I called the Sweet Daddy Creek Team off to the side to discuss the state of affairs we were facing; under no circumstances could we risk an international incident. We could not have any publicity involving an American citizen; it would be disastrous for this to hit the news media anywhere in the world.

Ed reminded us, "We must remember we aren't here, we do not exist; if anything happens to us or news gets out it will be denied by the U.S. Government, they do not know us; we are on our own guys."

Sam said, "I guess we're a team without a country."

"That's about the size of it," I replied.

I motioned for Dante` to join us and explained the predicament we were in. Very firmly he assured us that we were not to be concerned. He, his family and the friends that had already been recruited had all details under control; Dante` himself was appointed to command the operation since he had been an officer in the Vanuatu National Police for many years before he retired. His sense of authority and firm instructions made it obvious who was in charge of the coming assault on Rollins' farm; from the description he gave it would be an assault for sure. He insisted that our team did not have to participate if we did not think it wise. We had already discussed it and decided that it was necessary in order for us to complete the mission we were assigned.

Dante` explained that once they had Rollins in custody, Captain Jim would institute the plan for returning us to Port Vila where we would get a flight to New Caledonia departing the nation of Vanuatu entirely. He explained further that he and Captain Jim would deliver Rollins to us at the port in Noumea alive and without injuries --- if possible.

The assault on the American Rollins Farm was set to happen in two days, on a Saturday morning at five o'clock; 'Commander' Dante` said that most of the guards and on site workers would still be asleep in the bunkhouses provided for the most loyal workers. "We will catch them off guard and cause fewer casualties," Dante` said.

Dante` briefed our team on the schedule and the plan; he had divided his people into two teams, the first would approach the property from the water behind the farm, on the dock, while at the same time team number two would try to take the primary entrance on the mainland without any shots being fired or injuries to anyone; they would attempt to get the cooperation of the local guardsmen.

After the briefing I called the Sweet Daddy Creek Team aside; Ed was already on his secure international cell phone speaking with somebody back at FBI headquarters, I assumed it was the big boss himself, Tim, the director. Twenty minutes later, after being put on hold a couple of times, Ed closed his phone and sat thoughtfully for a few moments.

Ed looked up at the rest of us, "Here's the plan; an undercover, covert operations seaplane will pick us up at the port in Noumea on Monday evening just after dark; provided we stay alive long enough to get there; and fly us to an unofficial port in Brisbane, Australia where we will be met by members from our Australian Embassy, who will escort us to the embassy where we will officially arrest Rollins on a charge of murder and numerous other items. Our team will then escort him back to the United Sstates. Embassy officials are handling those details."

There was quiet among the team as all sat thinking. Finally Sam spoke up, "As we know, especially Chip and I, from experiences in Vietnam and other places, that most anything can happen --- and usually does, when you least expect it. I like this team of ours and I don't want to see anyone get hurt, much less killed; we have to be extremely careful and watch each other's back at all times. I'm telling y'all here and now, we all leave together or we don't leave."

"Damn Sam, now you're talking like the old Vietnam Sam I know; and you are right, we're in total agreement."

"Roger that for me, too," Ed chimed in.

Dawn stood and walked in front of the rest of us and just looked at us, "I have no idea what you three are talking about or may be thinking," she shook her head, tossing her long, blonde hair over her shoulder; "But when I leave here I'm taking all three of you with me, whether you're walking or not; I don't leave anybody behind. As Sam just said, 'we all leave together or we don't leave'; is that clear?"

Me, Ed and Sam turned to look at each other, and then we looked at Dawn and simultaneously sputtered with a laugh, "Yes dear."

I told her then, "That's okay, but you stay real close to me; when we get back to the States you have some answering to do."

"What kind of answering," she asked?

All I said was, "You'll find out."

Ed and Sam just laughed.

Dante` came over to where we were sitting to let us know that everything was in place and ready. Ed and Sam would go in with the group on the front of the farm, Dawn and I would go with him and Captain Jim and five others from the dock. It sounded as if our group would be making an amphibious assault; Dante` had a war plan all figured out. The land assault team would assemble a mile from the front of the entrance to Rollin's farm at four a.m. while our amphibious team of two boats, Captain Jim's and one other smaller boat, would wait off shore a quarter of a mile and then land promptly at five. He explained that there were usually a minimum number of guards at the docks so we shouldn't have any major problems driving inside to link up with the other team.

He further explained that as soon as they captured Rollins they would quickly take him away to an unknown area; Dawn, Sam, Ed and I would hustle straight to Captain Jim's boat so he could get us back to Port Vila to catch our flight to New Caledonia. We would meet back up with Dante` and Captain Jim in Port Noumea and take custody of Rollins. Then we were on our own for getting him back to the U.S.

CHAPTER SIXTY FOUR

AT FOUR A.M. DAWN and I were aboard Captain Jim's boat sitting off shore waiting, watching the clock; we both managed to get in a fifteen minute nap before Captain Jim woke us and told us he had notified the other two boats to move forward. It was beginning to rain and Captain Jim said it was the beginning of monsoon season and the rain would probably last most of the day. As we approached the dock we doubled-checked our weapons and made sure they were locked and loaded.

Five a.m. we're docked and Captain Jim unlocks the large storage bin reaches in and takes out two AR-15 rifles and hands one to Dawn and the other to me and hands us each three magazines fully loaded and tells us, "Be careful, do not take any chances; shoot first, ask questions later." He also passed AR-15s to the four men from the other two boats.

Captain Jim gave some instructions, which I couldn't understand, to the other men who turned back to the dock; one went aboard a rather large yacht while one of the others boarded a smaller boat, similar in size to Captain Jim's first water taxi that got smashed earlier. I noticed they both raised the engine covers, they were disabling both engines; there would be no escaping from this farm, not tonight.

As we moved inland we began hearing gunfire; a short burst at first, then a barrage of rifle fire, probably from AR-15s that are so popular here, seems as though everybody has at least one. The rain kept pouring on us as if being poured from a bucket. We had on lightweight plastic ponchos which kept us dry from the outside, but it cut off any airflow that could cool the body a mite on the inside.

Gunfire of all kinds were echoing off the surrounding waters, rifle fire, handguns, automatic firing that sounded heavier than the rifles or AR-15s; this is getting serious I thought. The closer we got the more intense the gunfire. The rain continued pouring, it was dark and you couldn't see your hand in front of your face. I felt something touching my arm and turned to find Dawn holding on to my sleeve, she had a very nervous look on her face but she smiled when I turned. Sam and I had experienced things like this many times in Vietnam and other wars. Ed was looking a little anxious also, even though he had been on numerous FBI raids equally as dangerous. Hell I thought, I'm anxious too; I'm always a little anxious and up tight on raids, in fact if you aren't, you're a liar.

After slipping and sliding through a grove of trees and bushes we broke out into a large, open, muddy yard that had been a beautiful green garden spot before the rain turned it into a slippery, muddy field behind the big house. Captain Jim crept next to me and whispered to me, "I don't see any guards, they must be near the front trying to defend the house; we must be careful, Rollins will probably think this is his escape route. He will be heading for his yacht with his crew and a couple of guards."

No sooner than Captain Jim had spoken the words the door to the big house, actually a mansion, opened and out ran Rollins and four of his men; they ran right into our open arms. The guards swung around with their weapons raised as Captain Jim and his men fired a blast from their AR-15s, the guards dropped into the mud on the spot and never moved.

Rollins was screaming, "Don't shoot, don't shoot," his hands were high above his head, he fell to his knees still screaming, "Don't kill me, please, don't kill me."

Sam and I stepped out where Gary Rollins, from Alcolu, South Carolina could see us. Rain still pouring down upon us, he was horrified and in shock when he saw us. He stammered and stuttered his words, "Chip, Sam, what are you doing here? No one knows where I am, not even my family, I never told anybody, I . . ." he looked at the others suddenly recognized Dawn; I think he went into total shock as he screamed, "Dawn, here, this can't be happening;" he fell face down into the muddy water. Sam reached down and pulled him up before he drowned.

Sam said, "Get up you son of a bitch, you ain't dying here, you're going to face a jury for murder and a dozen other charges."

"You bastard," said Dawn, "You killed your own family for money."

"And to get away from the cartel that is looking for him," I added. "Maybe we ought to let the cartel take him; they'd know what to do with him; it would sure as hell make it a lot easier on us."

About that time Dante` and his men came around to where we were. "It is finished," he said, "Those who were not killed have surrendered and are being carried off to jail. We will keep him safe until you get him aboard a plane for America."

Rollins suddenly became more alert and shouted at me and the team, "You can't arrest me you bunch of shitheads, you mean nothing in this country; you can't extradite me either, the U.S. doesn't have a treaty with the Vanuatu Government. Ha, ha, the joke's on you shit-for-brains;" he looked at Dante` and told him, "You're nothing here, I own the police force, they are my good friends, I pay them well, so screw you too."

Dante` said nothing, he just looked at Rollins and smiled.

That made Rollins a little nervous and he looked at me and Ed. He recognized Ed as being with the FBI; I don't give a shit if you are FBI, you can't arrest me here," he smiled nervously when he said it.

Ed calmly said, "My friend, I did not come to arrest you; neither did Sam, Dawn or Dante`, you misunderstand, we're kidnapping you and taking your sorry ass back to the U.S. and you will stand trial in Federal Court. How about them little green apples."

As Dante` led him away all he could say was, "But . . . but . . . but . . ."

Dante` looked over his shoulder and said, "We will see you in Noumea day after tomorrow."

CHAPTER SIXTY FIVE

AS WE BOARDED THE plane in Noumea for our flight to an uncharted airport in Brisbane, we bid Dante` and Captain Jim goodbye and thanked them for their assistance in apprehending Gary Rollins; we couldn't have done it without their help.

Captain Jim reached out and pulled Sam, Dawn, me and Ed together, "I do not like to see you leave; you have become like my family, I will miss you until you return." He looked at Dawn and smiled very big and told her, "I think I will see this bride and her husband," looking up at me, "pretty soon. I will put together a wedding cruise around Port Vila and Nguna that you will never forget."

Dante` was right on time as we arrived in Noumea. He met our plane and brought with him a scared, hungry, tied up and groggy Gary Rollins. Dante` had already spoken with the pilot and crew of our plane and I think he told them that the prisoner was dangerous and crazy and would try anything to get off the plane; he asked the crew to keep an eye out and help us keep him on the leash.

We made an uneventful flight to Brisbane; Dante` had given Rollins a shot of something to keep him calm; he slept he entire trip. Dante` had also sent a food basket for the team and Rollins if he ever woke up.

In Brisbane, Australia we were met by embassy personnel and three cars; before getting in a car, Gary Rollins, a U.S. citizen was presented with papers authorizing his arrest and extradition, officially placed under arrest for murder, handcuffed behind his back and placed in one of the cars with an armed guard, a U.S. Marine assigned to duty in the American Embassy.

The Embassy provided sleeping quarters for each of us and then re-arranged our travel schedules for return to the U.S. escorting one prisoner; this made our lives a lot easier and much simpler.

"I will be glad to get back, get my family together and get home," Ed stated.

"Same goes for me," said Sam.

I said, "I'm ready to get back to 'my happy place' and stretch out and do nothing for a while."

"I'll be very glad to get back to your happy place too," Dawn said laughing.

Two days later the Sweet Daddy Creek Team plus one prisoner headed down the walkway for our flight to Sydney where we changed to a direct flight to the U.S.

Direct flights aren't all that 'direct' many times, although the stopover in Sydney wasn't much; we then had stopovers in Singapore, Manila and Tokyo which weren't all that bad, it gave us a chance to stretch our legs and walk around in the terminal for a bit. Then it was non-stop on to San Francisco and connections for our flight to Columbia after stopping briefly at the Dallas-Fort Worth Airport.

The Columbia Municipal Airport was a beautiful, welcoming sight to see as we left the plane and walked into the brightly lit terminal with its several typical airport shops busy as usual. Everyone was happy to be back with the exception of Gary Rollins. I glanced up and saw the smiling face of Jeff and three of his fellow SLED Agents.

"How nice to have a welcome home party meet us," I said.

Ed stepped forward, grinning and said, "I'm certainly happy that my partner came to greet us; he can take this bag of crap off our hands."

"We aim to please, that's what we're here for," Jeff responded, "To protect and to serve," he added with a jokingly grin on his face.

Ed and I officially turned over our prisoner to the South Carolina SLED agents. Ed spoke up and remarked, "Well folks, I don't know about you, but I am heading to the big city of Alcolu where my wife and kids are waiting for me."

"I think I will join you Ed, because your wife and kids are at my house and I'm ready to get home also," Dawn said.

"That goes double for me, I haven't seen my wife in two weeks now," Sam said. "She may have gotten used to me being gone and run-off with somebody else."

I looked them over and said sarcastically, "You poor, lonesome, neglected people, I feel so sorry for you, you don't have to go home to a cold, empty old house in the hood. My heart bleeds for you."

Amid all the laughter, Dawn came to me and put her arms around me, hugged me as tight as she could and said, "You poor, poor, baby, you just come with little Dawn and I will take care of you." Then she kissed me on the cheek, grinning from ear to ear.

"I think I'm going to my happy place deep in to the woods and spend a couple of days doing nothing," I told the group; "I may even turn my phone off."

Dawn glanced at me, looked across at Ed and said, "I know what I'll do," she began; "I'll go with you to your 'happy place' and Ed can go to my house, that way he and Marie can have some privacy."

"Now that's the best solution I've heard all day," I remarked.

Six o'clock Saturday morning, sun just getting over the treetops, it's really nice sitting out on the deck buck naked and soaking up the fresh air and sunshine this time of the day. Looking out over the swamp, my own 'mountain stream', I see the two gators arguing back and forth to see who was going to go to the water's edge and speak to 'Big Bad John', the large buck, as he watched over his harem of three does while they drank from the cool water.

The door behind me opened and Dawn come out dressed the same as me --- naked as a jay-bird, she was carrying two cups of coffee, she handed one to me as she sat on my lap and turned to watch the gators and deer. Someone once said, 'It doesn't get any better than this'.

ACKNOWLEDGEMENTS

I have found that in the writing of a novel it is difficult, at least for me, to set a specific time schedule to sit down and begin writing. I rather like the idea of writing when the inspiration hits, or I come up with a new twist to the story or one of the characters. That makes for a very erratic schedule among family schedules; special thanks and love to my devoted and 'believing in me' wife for putting up with me during these times.

Also, very special thanks go to a dear, and long-time friend, Elaine Fauling, who spent many long hours doing a 'tell me like it is' read and proofing of the manuscript for the Sweet Daddy Creek Club. The reading was tough – the copy I gave her to read was in small print. Thanks for sticking to it Elaine.

Gratitude to Ed Winters an 'old time' radio DJ, newsman and my advisor --- who kept me straight on what I said about people, places and events --- he's also my oldest son, Tom, Jr.; I guess he didn't want his old dad to get into trouble.